ALL THE STARS DIE

JOHN F.D. TAFF

All the Stars Die

Print ISBN: 979-8-9924837-3-4

Cover Art by Samuel Araya
Book Design by Todd Keisling | Dullington Design Co.

First Paperback Edition

"In the Dim Meadows, Desolate" previously appeared as "The Desolated Orchard."

Bad Hand Books
www.badhandbooks.com

ADVANCE PRAISE FOR JOHN F.D. TAFF'S

ALL THE STARS DIE

"With this outstanding story collection, *All the Stars Die*, John Taff tears holes in the firmament of the universe, revealing the terrors of what we cannot see. A wonderfully eerie, haunting, and awe-inspiring read." —Alma Katsu, author of *Fiend*

"In the age-old tradition of the ultimate entertainment, John Taff is a storyteller. It's old school and it's new. It's haunting but has hope. Not because Taff wraps his stories in bows, but because he's so damn good you can't help but feel lifted. The dialogue is off the charts, the voice is as welcoming as a plush couch found in haunted woods. Nobody is doing what Taff does. If you read him at fifteen, he'd be the guy who got you into books. If you read him now, you'll renew your vows."
—Josh Malerman, *New York Times* bestselling author of *Incidents Around the House*

"A powerful and original take on cosmic horror that, despite revealing the dreadful darkness beyond the stars, remains richly and painfully human, bound up in suffering, loss, and regret."
—Brian Evenson, World Fantasy Award-winning author of *Song for the Unraveling of the World*

ALSO BY

JOHN F.D. TAFF

The End in All Beginnings

Dark Stars: New Tales of Darkest Horror

This is for Chris Frisella, one of my best and oldest friends for more than forty years. Here's to forty more, even if it ends with our heads in mason jars sitting on a shelf next to each other.

TABLE OF CONTENTS

BEGIN AND BEGIN AGAIN

Starting Over and Over with John Taff

1

It isn't that ideas are cheap. But they're not particularly rare, either. If you're working in the horror field, there is a wealth of material available to you, from such traditional figures as the vampire and werewolf to creations of H.P. Lovecraft and his circle to the cybernetic nightmares of our present age. Things like plot structure, the role of conflict and complication in a narrative, writing a climax that surprises the reader, the use of dialogue to reveal character and advance the plot, are all subjects most new writers have some sense of. Writing the beginning of a story, though, putting together the words and sentences in such a way that they grab the reader's attention and pull it into the narrative: that's a challenge. So when we talk about starting a story, the more important question is not, where are you going to find an idea? It's how do you write those opening sentences?

John Taff has been writing for a little while, now, and he knows how to begin a horror story. Indeed, the half-dozen long pieces gathered in *All the Stars Die* showcase his ability—his proficiency at crafting the opening of such stories. Rather than reviewing his career or the major themes of his fiction, either of which would make a decent subject for an introduction such as this one, it seems to me more interesting to examine the beginnings of the stories collected here for what they show us about Taff's (considerable) skill as a writer. Such exercises can tip over into the technical and pedantic, not to mention, the repetitive, so I'll try to keep the analysis short but relevant.

2

Here's one way to begin a horror story:

> *"I know exactly what you're goddamn thinking," said Asia, taking a swig from his beer.*
>
> *"You know...?" stammered Dan, caught off guard, a forkful of dripping beans poised midway to his mouth.*

All the way back to Aristotle and the *Poetics*, and probably for as long as people have been telling stories, the advice to anyone writing a narrative in whatever form has been to start in the middle of things (*in media res* is the Latin phrase for it) and catch the reader up as you go. The half-dozen stories here follow that general dictum. But the devil cavorts in the details, which is to say, it's the way John Taff follows that instruction in each of his stories that is of interest.

Take this first example. Taff drops us into the middle of a conversation. There are two men, one of whom is drinking deeply (note that word, "swig") from his beer, the other of whom is eating. It's a social situation, a meal of some kind, which indicates some degree of familiarity between the men, possibly friendship. But the opening statement's pair of adverbs ("exactly" and "goddamn") makes it as much an act of aggression, an invasion of mental privacy, as the next car in the conversation train. Combined with Asia's pull on his beer, it immediately establishes a tense situation between him and Dan, whose reactions reinforce the tension. He can't finish the question Asia's statement provokes; indeed, he stammers his words. For him to be caught off guard indicates not just surprise, but that there's something he should be protecting from discovery, and perhaps Asia's discovery in particular. The almost comical detail of the fork stopped in the midst of its journey to his mouth further illustrates how startled he is by Asia's insistence. Everything about these opening lines highlights the difference between Asia and Dan, from their mannerisms to the fact that one is drinking beer while the other eats beans. In a little over thirty fairly uncomplicated words, Taff establishes a situation in which one character is in clear possession of information, possibly a secret, he does not want the other to know, that he is downright nervous about the other knowing.

And (of course) we want to know it, too.

3

Here's a second way to begin a story:

> *"This weather is an acquired taste, n'est-ce pas?"*
>
> *The grey sea churned under a grey sky as the massive* Carpathia *passed, throwing spumes as it cleaved through the water, leaving a sickly, colorless foam in its wake. The ship was on its way to Cherbourg, on the northern coast of France. From there, it would be just a short jaunt to Lyons-la-Forêt, just east of Rouen.*

I imagine most readers are familiar with the words Charlie Brown's beagle, Snoopy, uses to open his repeated efforts at writing a novel: "It was a dark and stormy night." To the best of my knowledge, the line originates in 1830, at the beginning of the English writer Edward Bulwer-Lytton's *Paul Clifford*. Since then, it's been used by numerous writers in addition to Snoopy, sometimes seriously, sometimes less so. Even if Bulwer-Lytton's sentence has descended to the realm of cliché, it still illustrates a valid point, namely, that describing the weather can be a useful way to start a narrative.

Consider the way Taff begins this story. The adjective, "this," does a lot of heavy lifting, especially in light of the rest of the sentence. There's something about the conditions the speaker and the person they're addressing are experiencing that requires acknowledgment, some way in which they are out of the normal, or at least the usual. Whatever that is, whether excessive cold or heat, rain or sun, might be appreciated with some effort, but in the meantime, is a way for the questioner to establish an immediate rapport with the person they're addressing. The French clause which ends the sentence, which translates "isn't it," is another means by which the speaker might connect with their addressee, but even if the person is ignorant of the language, its use lends the speaker a certain cosmopolitan air. It introduces an element the following paragraph will pick up on, the concern with France, and not Paris, but a small town in Normandy.

The second paragraph also clarifies the matter of the weather, as well as the location of the speaker and the person they're attempting to engage in conversation. It is gray, which implies cold and overcast, and we're on a ship, a big one. The use of a ship as a means of travel suggest that the story is set at some point in the past, before the airplane took over as the preferred way to cross long distances. (Indeed, there's something a little antique, a little Henry James, about the speaker's stitching a bit of French onto the end of their question.) The description of the foam the ship produces as "sickly" and "colorless," as if drained of some necessary, vital element by contact with the vessel, uses the pathetic fallacy to add to the gray color of sea and sky an element of unease. This note picks up and extends the associations introduced by the ship's name. The *Carpathia* was an actual ship, most famous now for rescuing survivors of the *Titanic* disaster. The ship's name comes from a central European mountain range, which runs from Poland down to Serbia, passing through Austria, Ukraine, and Romania on the way. It's the Romanian stretch of the mountains that seems most relevant, here, as it runs through Transylvania. For any reader familiar with Stoker's *Dracula*, the name alludes to the Count's home, while associating it with a sea voyage calls to mind the doomed trip of the *Demeter* which brings the vampire to the shores of England. Here, the destination is France, so the ship's name need not be taken as an indication we're in a retelling of Stoker's novel; all the same, it helps to add to the uneasiness evoked by the diseased foam.

I have to confess, the literary critic in me wants to spend more time on the idea of cleaving the ship's movement introduces, especially as it prefigures and relates to certain elements in the subsequent narrative. But this is an introduction, not a prolonged critical study. I'll let you discover it for yourself.

4

Here's a third way to begin a story:

> *"I shouldn't ask for your help, and you damn sure shouldn't be offering, kid. Leastaways not to me, leastaways not if you know what's good for ya, so...scram," the barker said, fingering the dusty brim of his hat, which slouched on the cold, marble counter beside his plate. "Believe me, you don't want to get involved in this."*
>
> *But I did.*

For a third story, Taff begins with a character speaking. This time, it's what sounds like a command but is in fact something more subtle. Obviously, whoever is speaking has been offered help by whomever he is addressing. Note the number of "not's" full and contracted studding his sentences. Note, too, the rhythms of his speech, the parallel clauses in the first sentence, the repetitive phrasing in the second. Note the colloquialisms, "leastaways," "damn," "kid," and "ya." It's not too much of a surprise to learn the speaker is a barker, a figure employed by a carnival to use his voice to manipulate a crowd. And if we can be swayed by someone telling us what we want to see or hear, how much more susceptible are we to the ploy of reverse-psychology? Consider the barker's use of "should" in the first sentence. The verb is used here in the conditional mood, which is to say, to express something that is possible but not a fact. In other words, although the barker ought not to be asking for assistance, just as the kid ought not to be proffering it, neither of those things is in fact the case. It's as if the barker is acknowledging a moral order in which he is not participating, a salute to whatever remains of his conscience. Calling the object of his address "kid" does more than recognize age difference, it emphasizes the addressee's youth and by implication inexperience and ineffectiveness—again, employing reverse psychology to encourage the kid to prove that they are not. Ironically, there may be some or even a great deal of truth in the barker's description of himself in the second sentence as someone unworthy of help, but the second, longer portion of the sentence once again calls attention to the kid's lack of knowledge in the ways of the world.

The barker's hat with its dusty brim is the sole detail in this opening that seems to indicate the man is in an authentically bad way. The dust on it hints he's been wearing it while walking dry, possibly dirt roads, as the description of it as slouching suggests a covering old and worn enough to be losing its shape. Yet the next line he delivers, once again insisting on steering the person he's speaking to away from him and his troubles, renews the ploy of baiting the kid to do exactly what he's telling him not to. It's a masterful verbal performance.

The response with which the first-person narrator introduces themselves to us is the opposite in every way of the speech we have been reading (possibly a little too quickly). Where the barker is verbose, the narrator is terse. Where the barker employs elaborate sentence construction and attenuated language, this speaker is blunt, declarative. If the barker's language sweeps us into the story, the narrator's forces us to pause.

If I were in that literary-critical mode I've mentioned above, I might talk about different registers of speech competing and conflicting in the story that follows. That's on top of all the other stuff.

5

Here's a fourth way to begin a story:

> *"She's coming," Hough said, plucking the cigarette from his mouth and grinding it against the warped boards of the porch. "She's coming, and I wish she wouldn't. I don't think I can hold out any longer. That's the truth of it."*

There's a bit of Latin in one of M.R. James's most famous stories, "Oh, Whistle and I'll Come to You, My Lad:" it goes, "*Quis est iste qui venit*," which translates, "Who is this who is coming?" It's a great question to ask in a ghost story, and it's equally appropriate to ask here. Who exactly is referred to by the pronoun, "she," and why is her approach something Hough would rather avoid? It appears Hough knows the identity of the woman of whom he's speaking, just as his expression of doubt over his ability to "hold out" invokes desire, albeit of an inadvisable or even forbidden stripe. As Hough sees it, at least, this unnamed woman's arrival is within her control, as evidenced by his use of "wouldn't." It's another verb in the conditional mood, indicative of a state of affairs contrary to fact. It's not hard to imagine this as the opening to a different kind of narrative, one with comic overtones, concerning a life-long bachelor pursued by a woman whose desirability portends the end of his rambling ways. It's the kind of understated comedy Faulkner could have pulled off, or possibly Steinbeck. This story, however, has more in common with Elizabeth Bowen's "The Demon Lover," in which a woman unconsciously anticipates the return of a long-dead, sinister lover. But where Bowen's protagonist remains unaware of the fate closing in on her until it has literally enclosed her, Hough knows what is on its way to him. The cigarette he extinguishes on the porch might as well be the last smoke of the condemned man. One way, perhaps the most common, for a narrative to generate suspense is for the writer to withhold information from us, to make the entirety of the plot a secret we learn by degrees. Yet it's equally possible to tell the reader what's in store for the characters and then show them how this occurs, changing our attention from simple incident to more complex causality. This is what's happening here, as Taff shows us the origins of Hough's connection to the woman who is coming, and how he embraces her return.

In the next paragraph, Taff has another character reading Jonathan Franzen's *The Corrections*, which seems to prefigure his story's concern with memory and with family; though of a different kind than Franzen's. It's a nod to the reader I appreciated.

(And later in the story, there is the apparition of a figure I have yet to forget. You'll see.)

6

Here's a fifth way to begin a story:

Officer Bill Tyson heard the sound three times. Twice in this world, once in another.

The other world was Midnight Land, and it was this world that would, ultimately, claim him.

Members of law enforcement, whether Sheriff's deputies, police officers, or federal agents, feature in a significant amount of horror fiction. If you think about it, this makes a certain amount of sense. An officer of the law has access to resources the average citizen does not, from informational to investigative to weaponry. Their badges give them the authority to look into circumstances from the strange to the violent, and the expectation that the people they speak to in the course of their investigations will answer their questions honestly. They are part of a larger organization they can draw on to assist in their work, whether in terms of research or physical confrontation. If horror stories can be seen as eruptions of the chaotic into the world, then law enforcement serves as a representation of order.

(Needless to say, the officers of the law can easily become the instruments of repression, embodiments of authoritarianism, devoted to maintaining order at the expense of everything else. The very things that give them an advantage in confronting the horrific can become the means of tyranny with just the slightest nudge.)

All of which is to say that by identifying his protagonist as a member of law enforcement, Taff frontloads the story with information about him. At the same time, we learn about the mystery he will confront, the sound that repeats three times. There's no elaboration on the sound, which combined with the definite article, makes it singular. Tyson hearing it three times calls to mind the narrative structures of fairy tales, in which the heroes often require three attempts to complete a task. The association with the fantastical is picked up in the second sentence, with its revelation that Tyson's third experience of the sound occurs in a world distinct from our own, one the third sentence calls "Midnight Land." It's a name that might have originated in a fairy tale, or in the pages of a writer like Ray Bradbury. The link between midnight and the malevolent supernatural are many and well-known. After all, who envisions the activities of witches, vampires, ghosts, etc. with the bright noon sun? At the same time, the middle of the night has additional symbolic dimensions, representing the place, both in the individual psyche and larger community and culture, which remain hidden, occulted. Whatever Midnight Land is, the fact that it is going to claim Tyson is ambiguous. It may foreshadow his death within or because of this other world. But it may foretell his becoming part of the world.

There's a tension in these opening lines between the world in which Bill Tyson is a member of his local law enforcement and the world of midnight. This tension is the story's engine; here, we hear it kicking over.

7

Here's a sixth way to begin a story:

> *The end comes and we aren't any more aware of it than we are of the beginning. Or even the middle. People just aren't that aware of their lives, passing through them like ghosts through a ruined manor.*
>
> *Let's just stick with the end, okay?*

If you've been reading this collection straight through, then you may read these opening lines through a meta-textual lens, and indeed, it's hard not to think Taff was aware of this in placing this story last. If you've skipped around in the book, then it's possible you've come to this story second or fifth—it might even be the first one you read. Whatever the order in which you encounter it, the story starts with the end, with a broad observation about our general failure to recognize its arrival. Beginning with the end is a strategy Taff employed in the two previous stories, but the tone here is different, reflective, rooted in a pair of comparisons it's worth unpacking. The first involves the process of human growth and development. We don't recognize the end of our lives as we didn't recognize the start, or even the broad span between those poles. It's a balanced figure. However, there's a distinction between our final moments and our first. As we approach our last minutes, we presumably do so with some measure of intelligence, self-awareness, which makes our failure to recognize our end a mix of irony and tragedy. Something of the same might be said of our inability to know the middle while we are in it. The start of lives, however, is a different affair. It's possible Taff is referring to birth; it's also possible he means conception. Either way, we can raise the same objection: how conscious of anything can a newborn be? Or a single-celled organism? Our failure to register the beginning of our lives is not a matter of thought processes: it's a matter of fundamental mechanics. Neither a newborn nor a zygote is physically capable of the cognition necessary to conceptualize their origin. To include this in his extended comparison is to suggest that our brains are not built to comprehend any of the major moments in our lives, except in retrospect. It's an evocation of one of the central conceits of the part of the horror field known as cosmic horror, our inability to understand fully the universe of which we are part. Taff's comparison refines this to make it a matter of biology.

From the material, the story's opening moves to the spectral, comparing our lives to the transit of ghosts through a "ruined manor." To call us phantoms is to emphasize our lack of substance, our intangibility, adding a physical dimension to its description of our mental limitations, emphasizing our inability to effect our environments in any meaningful kind of way. The second half of the simile is equally interesting, presenting our lives as great, historic houses which have already been not just damaged, but despoiled. Both ourselves and our surroundings exist in a condition of aftermath, of a catastrophe we (were not aware—could not be aware) were born into.

Small wonder the formal tone of the opening paragraph, with its reduction of human existence to an idiot haunting of a devastated structure, should give way to a more informal address to the reader, an offer to avert our gaze from the existential calamities of our lives to the more approachable details of their ends. There's an echo of Lovecraft's "Call of Cthulhu" in these lines, and in a more general sense, Taff's story is in dialogue with Lovecraft's. In both cases, those sweeping beginnings propel us into the rest of the story, into the narratives that will bear out their assertions.

The end, we think. *Yes, tell us about the end.*

8

Within *All the Stars Die*, you will encounter stories of secret monsters, of legacies of corruption, of Faustian deals, of dispossessed gods, of the hideous legacy of racism, of cosmic horror of the most sublime kind. I've taken you through the beginnings of these stories; now it's time for you to make your way into them.

—John Langan

AFTER THE CUT, THE BLOOD

I.

"I know exactly what you're goddamn thinking," said Asia, taking a swig from his beer.

"You know…?" stammered Dan, a forkful of dripping beans poised midway to his mouth.

Asia nodded, cocked his head back over his shoulder to where he supposed Dan was looking. Asia's son, Hi, played there with the other children on the playground in the city park hosting the family barbecue.

"Yeah, don't think I don't know. But it's okay, man. Everyone has the same question. Where'd that white kid come from, anyway?" Asia laughed, knocking back the rest of his beer, setting the empty can next to the three others lined up there on the picnic table. He smiled at Dan, closed his eyes.

It was good to be here, good to be home. He could smell cigarettes, the meat sizzling over charcoal, the chlorine from the nearby pool. He could hear kids laughing, his many aunts gabbing while playing Hearts. The steel *spoing!* of horseshoes clattering to rest.

He did it often, closed his eyes and just listened, just smelled, just touched. What made it different than in the past was, when he opened his eyes, he could *see* all this, too.

That was necessary to prove it wasn't a dream; he really was here and not crouched in a swampy rice field halfway across the world, duck-walking under a curtain of bullets fired by an army of pajama-wearing boys and old men, and *pretending* he was home.

Asia. That's what they'd called him over there, his platoon. His name was really Asa, his Biblical-minded mother said it had been the name of a King of Judah. It meant *healer* in Hebrew.

The men in his platoon didn't care particularly about his mother or The Holy Bible.

You gonna wade through swamps in 'Nam with that name, it's gonna have to be Asia.

He'd been home for six years now, but he could still hear their voices in his head, as clearly as whispers through darkened jungles. Because of that, he was sometimes afraid it wasn't real, all this, being *here.*

He'd wake up in a cold sweat in his bed, Hen's curves there next to him. He'd gasp a few terrified breaths, his hands *skritching* across the mattress, trying to find his rifle. He'd stop them before they woke Hen and set her to asking if he was okay. If he was having another bad dream about there, being back *there.*

How could he tell her his fear was all this *was* the dream—being home, being with her, in their own house—and the terrifying dreams were what was real?

What was dream, what was real?

Different things at different times.

That answer was as comforting as it was damning.

"Well, it does seem strange and all," Dan said, hesitation in every syllable. "I mean, Hi and I being the only white people at this barbecue."

Asia opened his eyes. "You mean you being the only honky here who ain't family?"

Dan laughed nervously.

"Most people assume I knocked up a white chick," Asia said, cracking open a beer he'd fetched from the nearby cooler. Billy Beer. *It's the best beer I've ever tasted, and I've tasted a lot.* It almost made him laugh. Cold water dripped down its surface as he raised it to his lips.

Here's to President Peanut, he toasted silently. This one he drained in four huge gulps. He wiped his lips and frowned across the table at Dan.

"But that can't be. I mean, look at him," he said, knowing his words were becoming fuzzy at the edges. He should probably eat, with all this food cooking around him. Asia's various aunts and cousins had already noticed. Hen had noticed but hadn't pushed. Yet.

"Hi over there ain't got one drop of black in him. None. And he's most likely seventeen years old, and I'm only twenty-seven. Only ten years apart. I mean, I was precocious and all, but not that kinda precocious. Don't even know if my dick worked at that age. Leastways for anything other than pissing."

He laughed, knowing it was too long and too loud. Several family members turned to look at him, but he smiled and waved.

"You adopt him?" Dan asked.

God bless you, Asia thought. Dan really did treat him as if he were white, too, just like him. Mostly that was fine, but sometimes...? Well, it didn't take into account any degree of reality.

"Shit, man," he laughed, this time more quietly. "What adoption agency in these United States gonna let a black couple waltz out with a blonde-haired, blue-eyed white boy?"

Dan started to fumble for an answer, but Asia cut him short.

"That's the thing about a story, ain't it? They gotta be told at some point," he said, looking over his shoulder at the boy, supervising the younger kids on the playground equipment. "Might as well be you listening."

Asia brought another beer up, plonked it onto the table, pulled back the tab. He slid it down into the beer, took a sip.

"I can play the banjo, can you believe that shit?" he said, closing his eyes. "Not real good, but I can play a lick or two when pressed, which isn't often these days. Black cat playing country music? I'm a regular Charley fuckin' Pride.

"I can play, but Hi? That boy can *really* play. Fiddle, banjo, guitar. He's like…a prodigy or something."

"Who taught you the banjo?"

Asia chuckled. "Hi's brother, a Nashville session player. I met the guy back in '69, right before I went over to 'Nam. He taught me a little hillbilly music, the kind before it cowboyed up and became country and western."

"Wait…I don't understand. Hi's brother?"

Asia took another swig of beer, opening his eyes and staring off into the distance.

"Most people I bother to tell at all, I just say he was Hi's daddy. But only my family knows he was really Hi's brother. What they don't know, though, is it's so much more than that. When I'm finished, you'll know, though. You'll know."

He took one look at Hi, in the playground helping the younger kids on the swing set and the teeter-totter.

The boy's form shimmered, rippled in the heat.

"Someone oughta," Asia said, squinting into the sun. "That's what Lenus said before he told me his story."

II.

Lenus tossed his battered suitcase onto the bed, whose springs creaked miserably under the sudden load.

Christ, he thought. *That doesn't bode well for the ol' back.*

He stood there near the door taking it all in, holding his banjo case by the handle. The sheer curtains stirred in the breeze of the open window, the dense Memphis air rushing into the room like the ghost of the china shop's bull. The faded wallpaper, curling in places, spattered with mysterious stains. The battered radio, the even more battered chifforobe. The threadbare carpet, pocked with cigarette burns. The thin, wrinkled bedspread. The thin, wrinkled pillows.

The place smelled of cigarettes and spilled beer, the ghosts of farts and lovemaking past.

It all seemed like it should have a deeper meaning.

For certain, they'd be the last things he'd see in this life.

Sighing heavily, he leaned the case against the washbasin, doffed his hat, tossed it to the bed to rest cocked atop the suitcase. He drew a yellowed handkerchief from the breast pocket of his suit, wiped his mostly bald head, drew it over his face. He replaced the cloth, turned to stare at his reflection in the scarred mirror hanging next to the chifforobe.

Old, he chuckled. Damn, so old. *How the fuck did this happen anyway?*

Nineteen hundred and sixty-nine. Who knew he'd live so long? And look even older for it. Not him, for damn sure.

He remembered various bandmates and session musicians he'd sat in with over the course of nearly six decades. His group. Old Bill Brown. Squirrelly John Russell. "Britches" McGowan. Stanley Urich. Doc Japhet Reynolds. Persimmon Stu Garrett. He could hear their voices in his head, ghosts of ghosts now, as they were all dead before him.

How'd you get so poorly, Len? Mayhap the liquor, said one. Or the blue sage tea, another laughed. Mighta been the ladies. Yeah, too, too many of 'em. That last one was Squirrelly John. Man, Lenus could still see him squatted over his kit, sticks clutched in one birdlike hand, cigarette hanging from his lips.

How he missed him. How he missed them all.

If anything, that was as much a reason for why he was here in this flophouse as any other. A few years ago, his pockets stuffed with cash, he wouldn't have been caught dead in a place like this.

Now, he was going to be caught dead in a place like this.

That made him chuckle, and he braced his hands on the little washbasin under the mirror, laughed until he couldn't breathe, until his vision swam.

The other voices in his head joined, too.

Underneath them all, he heard his brother's laughter. Not vicious or vindictive at all. Not like he might have been, like Lenus always imagined he should be. No, just the high-pitched, fluty laughter of an eleven-year-old boy.

Lenus stepped back from the mirror, not wanting to look into it and suddenly see his brother's face. Young, unlined, distant, receding like in the rearview mirror of a car.

The edge of the bed bumped his calves, and he fell back onto it, the springs jouncing.

Enough of this shit. Fumbling with the clasps of his case, he rooted inside, his hand brushing the cold handle of the Colt wrapped in an undershirt as yellowed as his handkerchief. He found the bottle of whiskey he'd been saving, uncapped it, and had dinner there on his bed.

Much later, Lenus awoke. The room swam in night. It oozed through the open window, with the thick breeze and the sounds of cars and people on the streets. Wan light, diffused through the sheer curtain, fell into the room, gave everything a jaundiced pallor. The flashing of the hotel's neon sign burst in bright detonations of yellow, then lurid red.

He raised himself in bed, sat up. His open suitcase took much of the space, though he'd scooted it over in his sleep. It now teetered on the edge of the mattress. Yawning, he fumbled it closer to him, grabbing at its contents to ensure they didn't spill onto the floor.

There wasn't much inside, certainly not anything worth saving. No, he'd pawned everything he'd owned before coming here, more to get rid of it all than to make money. Gone was the chunky gold watch Bob Wills had given him what seemed like distant ages ago, the guitar Jimmie Rodgers had used during a recording session Lenus sat in on, a tie Hank Williams loaned him the week before he died, and Lenus had never had the opportunity to return.

All passed over to the pawnbroker for a few bucks Lenus stuffed into a bulging wallet with the rest of his cash. Lenus hadn't looked back when he left the shop, the little bell over the door ringing. Didn't want to see the big, sweaty man rake the stuff off the counter, disappear them into the backroom where they'd be further appraised, tagged for sale.

More than that, he didn't look back because he thought there might be more than just regret, like Lot's wife turning to salt or Orpheus being hauled to the underworld. You never turned back.

Never.

So, now the suitcase held only a few articles of clothing, a couple of loose pictures, a bottle or two of hootch, and the gun.

The gun.

He'd killed his brother with a knife, long ago in a life that seemed like a barely remembered story. It'd been a slow, hard death as his brother leaked red over the grey rocks and green lichen, the ground stained in purple patches.

Not for him.

No, it would be quick for Lenus. A bullet in his mouth, from the barrel of the pearl-handled Colt revolver Lefty Frizzell had given him. He'd kept that back from the pawnbroker. Someone else could hock it after they found his body.

He'd push the gun in and up, as old Jerry Purcell, the best fiddler Lenus'd ever known, had shown him. Jerry had been a gun nut and often talked about killing himself, though everyone knew he didn't have the balls to actually do it. Instead, he drank heavily, and had driven off a cliff in the Great Smokies going to a gig in Gatlinburg in his fresh-off-the-lot '58 Spruce Green DeSoto Firedome. Drunk as a skunk more than likely. It took them three days to haul his car out.

In and up would go the gun, against his upper palette, tasting the metal and the gun oil. Aimed so the bullet sped directly into his brain and ended it all. Not a neat way to go, what with the blood and gore he'd certainly spread all over the room. Lenus did have a pang of guilt about the unlucky hotel staff member who'd have to clean up the mess he left behind.

They'd be the last person who'd have to clean up one of his messes, the last mess he'd ever make.

Lenus hefted the suitcase over, removed the weapon. He thought about unwrapping it, staring at the gun as he'd done so many nights before. But he no longer needed to do that. No longer needed to talk himself into what he planned to do.

Instead, he slipped the parcel under the other pillow, patted it as if tucking it in for the night. He'd get one more good night of sleep, aided by the second bottle he filched from the case before kicking it to the floor.

He took a couple of deep pulls from the bottle, recapped and set it onto the nightstand. Kicking his shoes off, he leaned back onto the thin pillow not covering a gun, closed his eyes.

Outside, the sounds of traffic lulled him quickly to sleep.

Here's where the story would normally tell you he slept fitfully, that he dreamt horrible things. His brother's face as the knife opened his belly, the blood splashed everywhere.

His own face exploding from a bullet that punched up through the top of his head, flecked the tattered wallpaper with blood, brains and bone.

But he dreamt none of this. In fact, he dreamt not at all.

He slept quietly, snoring as the moon outside climbed the sky, descended past the tops of the darkened buildings. He slept through the relative silence of three a.m. that fell over the streets, his fellow hotel guests fast asleep, too.

Only the curtains on his window stirred, flicked by the insistent evening breezes swirling in, caressed away the beads of sweat that formed on his forehead, his upper lip.

Lenus was hungry when he awoke, ravenous. The whiskey he'd downed last night burned in his gut. It filled his bladder, too, but was also probably the reason he hadn't awakened in the night to pee. But he did so now.

Washing up at the sink, he changed his undershirt, threw on a button-down from his suitcase. When he looked at himself in the mirror, he shrugged. It was the best he was likely to look these days.

Drawing on his jacket, he left the room, locking the door on the way out. His stomach rumbling, and with no clear destination in mind, he decided to find a diner, grab himself breakfast.

Breakfast before suicide? He savored the incongruity, but figured why go on an empty stomach?

The sun was harsh, and the sounds of the street were more

discordant than those heard from the window of his room. The air smelled of diesel, the mud of the Mississippi, industrial fumes. A few people bustled past him, already dressed for what promised to be a warmer day. Ties were loosened, shirts were unbuttoned, dress length climbed past calves.

Just down a block or so looked to be a luncheonette. As he approached, he smelled the twin aromas of cigarette smoke and good, black coffee. He pushed inside, gasping a bit at the cold bite of the air conditioner. Lenus was born in the poverty of the deep south, and air conditioning always struck him as nothing short of miraculous. Made him wish he'd plunked down a few more dollars for a room cooled by one, but sleeping at night, in the heavy heat, made him remember his childhood, what he'd done.

What he came here to finally do.

"Seat yourself, sug," came the waitress' voice as she circled by, two tickets in one, a pot of coffee in the other. "Be with ya in a sec."

Lenus doffed his battered hat, took a seat in an empty booth near the door. He looked up at the menu behind the counter, decided on his breakfast.

The waitress appeared, plunked down a china cup, sloshed coffee into it.

"Need cream?" she asked.

He shook his head.

"Didn't think so. What'll you have, sug?"

"Scrambled eggs. Pork chop. I'll have potatoes, too. Throw in a couple of biscuits and keep the coffee warm. Thank you, ma'am."

She darted away, and Lenus saw a folded newspaper left on the seat beside him. He squinted at the print, felt around for his glasses but realized he must have left them in his room. Sighing, he returned the paper, folded, to where its previous owner had left it.

Lenus saw the diners were mostly black, a fact he hadn't noticed when he'd entered. Not that it bothered him. The music business was more integrated than most walks of American life, though not by much.

The waitress swam back into view, carrying his plate of food and the coffee pot. She plunked it before him, swirled more coffee into his cup.

"Everything look good? All right, I'll let ya eat."

She spun away, and Lenus heard her at the table behind him.

"You sure you don't want anything more than coffee?"

"No, ma'am," said a young man. "Got just this much money 'til I report. Trying to stretch it."

Lenus turned in his seat to see a young black man, no more than twenty, seated alone as he was. He wore a cheap, ill-fitting suit, an open-necked, button-down white shirt. His long, thin hands spun a coffee cup in lazy circles.

He caught Lenus' eye, smiled.

'Til I report.

Lenus knew just what the kid meant, and it soured his stomach a little. The year 1969 was not a great year for young men reporting.

"Excuse me, miss" Lenus said. "Put his tab on mine. Can't send him overseas with nothing but coffee on his stomach."

The kid looked at him in surprise, then nodded.

"Thanks, sir. You don't have to do that."

"And you don't have to do what you're doing. So, we're even," Lenus said, then turned back to address his own breakfast.

He heard the kid order a few things, then went back to eating.

As he finished, the waitress came back by to give him his check. He slapped a ten down onto the table, stood and settled his hat onto his head. The kid was eating off two plates, pancakes on one, eggs, bacon and toast on the other.

Lenus tipped his hat to the kid, then to the waitress, went out into the dense Memphis air. He looked up and down the street, with nowhere in particular to go.

He shuffled slowly down one block, then another. He passed an empty appliance store, a closed bar, a dress shop, a record shop. He stopped before the window there, gazed in at the racks of records. Album covers from Tammy Wynette, Loretta Lynn, Glen Campbell, and a cardboard cutout of Johnny Cash were taped to the window.

He felt a pang in his chest, a longing at seeing those faces. Some of them he'd worked with, jammed with, drank with. The lingering memory of those days, knowing they'd never come again, stirred powerfully within him, and he turned away, shaky now, and headed back to the hotel.

He was postponing the inevitable.

As his mother had always said, best be at it and get it done.

It was time to get it done.

Back at the hotel, he sat heavily onto the bed, the springs twanging. It was hot and sweat poured from his skin. Sighing, he produced his handkerchief, drew it over his head.

Looking across the room, he caught sight of his banjo case propped against the wall near the sink. He considered it ruefully, as one might a favorite pet you were forced to take to the pound, abandon.

Lenus felt tears gather at the corner of his eyes. Who would he leave the instrument to?

No one.

He had no family anymore, no sons or daughters. No lovers. His friends were all dead.

He wondered why he hadn't just pawned the damned thing with all the rest of his stuff. But he couldn't have, no more than he could've his arm or his leg.

Clapping his hands against his knees, he rose, crossed the room. He lifted the case gently, carried it back to the bed. The case's clasps were battered, the brass chipped and discolored from use. Inside, the banjo was nestled in well-worn crushed blue velvet.

The Gibson Granada was a masterpiece of a banjo, one of the world's truly artisan instruments. Five-stringed with a flat head and a one-piece flange, this was the banjo Lenus had played since acquiring it from its original owner, an old medicine-show performer, in 1937. Its drum was darkened from use, the resonator battered, its frets worn. The ivory inlays along its neck had flaked away over the years.

He lifted it from its case, respectful of its age and place in his heart. Settling it across his lap, he held it like a lover, his left hand on the neck, his right curled atop the strings. He thumbed the fifth string, tapped at the third. Bum-ditty-bum-ditty-bum-ditty.

There was no way he could do what he came here to do without playing this old girl one last time. But it was blasted hot in the room. So, he settled the instrument gently into its case, shrugged out of his jacket.

First, he went to the window, opened it wide. Then, he opened the door, propped it with his suitcase to keep it open, so a thin breeze carried through the room. Once done, he sat back on the bed, lifted the banjo and nestled it familiarly to his body.

His mind blank for a second, he gently tapped the strings, and the instrument thrummed to life. Just a few random chords, and then his reflexes took over, and soon he was playing something old and simple, "Cotton Eyed Joe."

He closed his eyes, let his crabbed hand knock the strings, felt the music pulse from the drumhead into his belly. Unbidden, the image of his brother Hiram coalesced in his mind. Slightly smaller than Lenus had been, tow-headed, wearing dirty bib overalls, barefoot. He looked sadly at Lenus, opened his mouth to speak.

Lenus screwed his eyes more tightly, as if they could be closed enough to prevent this.

Len, why'd you have to go and…

There was a knock at the door, and Lenus' eyes snapped wide, his splayed hand palmed the drum and strings to still the banjo's sound.

"Hey, just heard you in here. Thought I'd stop in and say…"

For a disconcerting second, Lenus thought it was his brother in the doorway, bare feet slick with blood, red ichor dribbling from the front of his soaked overalls.

But it wasn't. It was the young man from the luncheonette, the one he'd bought breakfast for. Lenus saw they both recognized the other at about the same time.

"…well, first, thanks, I guess, for breakfast and all," the kid said. Lenus thought of him as a kid in the same way he thought of anyone under the age of 30 these days. Seeing him standing now, Lenus thought of him slightly less as a kid.

He was tall and rangy, ropy as his mother used to say. His face was long and lean, his hair closely cropped, his eyes dark and penetrating. But his smile was wide and easy, and he wore it as if it was familiar and comfortable.

"Ahh, it weren't a thing," Lenus said, trying hard to breathe normally, to dispel the twin ghosts of his brother. "Man's gotta eat, 'specially a man in uniform."

"Well, I appreciate it, sir."

"Sir? Come on now, name's Lenus. What's yours?

"Asa Hopkins," he said, stepping into the room, hand outstretched.

Lenus reached out, shook it.

"So, you enlisting?" Lenus asked, releasing his hand.

"Yes, sir. Heard they was gonna enact the draft pretty soon. Thought it might be better in the long run to volunteer before they go and do that."

Lenus nodded. "You're probably right. Still, sorry to hear it. Sorry to hear anyone still has to put on the uniform and go fighting. Thought we might have learned ourselves and important lesson after WWII, but after Korea and now Vietnam, seems the lesson was just we liked fighting too much to give it up."

"I'm still waiting. Every time I go over the enlistment center, they say there are delays, and I'm to come back. Been checking every day this week. Burned through my money day before yesterday, so breakfast today was appreciated."

"Hmmph," Lenus muttered. "You come to enlist free and all, and they put you off?"

"Well, sir, you know...," Asa shrugged.

Lenus did know. He knew exactly, and it angered him, though he couldn't think of much to say about it. It was just the way things were and talking about it did no good.

Asa chuckled softly. "Well, sorry to disturb. Just heard that banjo and it reminded me of my grandma."

"No bother, son, none at all," Lenus said. "So, your grandma played?"

"Oh, yes, sir. She sat on the porch in her rocker most evenings pounding away at it. I learned to love the sound, though I never could get her to teach me. By the time I got to asking seriously, she wasn't too right in the head, if you'll excuse me. Mostly just sat picking the strings or slapping the head until my mother'd take the instrument away. Then she just rocked and hummed."

"Well, you're welcome to pull up a chair and listen for a spell, if you like," Lenus said, warming to the unexpected conversation. "Haven't had an audience in some time."

"You play professionally?"

"Used to. Been scratching at hillbilly music for more than fifty years now."

"When grandma was younger, she had an old radio wired to a car battery in her sitting room. We listened to it all the time, the National Barn Dance on WLS, and course the Opry on WSM. She loved that music. Sure do wish she'd stayed around long enough to teach me."

"I can teach ya, if ya got time to learn before you ship out," Lenus blurted, before even thinking about the words. "Clawhammer's pretty easy to pick up. Hell, I learned when I was…"

He let that thought fade, though.

"You serious?"

"As a heart attack, son," Lenus said, licking his lips, which had gone dry. "Tell ya what, you sit in here with me and listen to my stories, and I'll teach you the banjo. Leastways before you head on over."

Asa smiled, then it faded. "I'd love that, really. But I think I gotta find a job, so's I can eat until they induct me. I ain't even sure how I'm gonna pay for this room tonight."

"Well, you're in luck, Asa Hopkins, because as it just so happens the Lenus Culpepper School of Banjo comes with free room and board. I'll take care of it all, 'til it's your time to leave."

Asa's frown deepened. "Why'd you do that?"

"Honestly, I'm a bit lonely son. Having someone to talk to would pass the time and ease my heart a bit. So, you in?"

Asa's face didn't soften, though he seemed to be considering Lenus' offer.

"Alright. Suppose I gotta eat and sleep until the army sees fit to call me up. And I ain't gonna lie, learning the banjo has always been a thing for me."

"It's settled then," Lenus said, rising and shaking Asa's hand. "Let's head down and pay your room up for a few days. Then, it's back up here for your first lesson."

He clapped the young man on the back, laid the banjo in its case, and the two men left the room, closing the door behind them.

"So, you hold the banjo like this, cross your lap, with the drum here resting between your legs. You'll wanna rest it on your knee here," Lenus said, demonstrating with his instrument. "To get it stable and such, but see how it rocks when I do? Nope, 'tween the legs is best. Then let the drum just fall back against your belly."

He passed the banjo over to Asa.

"You give her a try there."

Asa positioned the banjo as he'd seen Lenus do.

"There, good. When you get her set properly, you'll know because you won't feel the need to support the neck with your left hand at all. See how it sits there just as quiet as a sleepy cat? That's great. Now, on to petting the cat."

The two men passed the next hour or so in the dim, muggy hotel room trading the banjo back and forth. Lenus would demonstrate something a few times, then Asa would try to replicate what he'd seen.

When he finally got to the point where he was showing Asa how to play the clawhammer way Lenus favored, he stopped and shook his head.

"You're picking this up fast, son. Way faster than I ever did," he said. "It took me months just to learn what I just showed you in about an hour."

"Well, I did pay attention when grandma was playing," Asa said, gently rapping the strings, popping the third string and plucking the fifth. Over and over. "I guess I just picked it up, even though I never really knew it."

Lenus sat back in his chair, slumped.

"That weren't me. I guarantee it."

"How'd you learn then?"

Lenus' face fell, his eyes darted to the window. The sky was darkening a bit, and the air pushing in was heavy and wet. Storm coming, probably.

"My little brother had all the musical talent in my family," Lenus sighed. "Yeah, you might say I picked it up from him. Hiram."

Asa continued to strum, waiting for Lenus to continue.

"What say we pack it in for today, go and get us supper? You gotta be hungry, sitting here with me all day learning."

Lenus took the banjo from Asa, laid it back in its case, closed the lid.

They walked in the early evening fog to the luncheonette where they'd eaten breakfast. Lenus ordered a smothered chop and potatoes, Asa had a burger and fries, and more than few Cokes.

When they finished, they walked back to the hotel in silence. Clouds had pushed in over the roofs of the warehouse and plants, black and ominous against the twilight purple of the sky. Flashes of distant lightning illuminated their puffs and swirls, and the air had the ozone tinge of electrical storms.

They climbed the steps to their rooms. Lenus knew Asa held back from tearing up the stairs to hang back with him.

In the hallway between their rooms, Lenus turned to Asa.

"Interested in a nightcap?"

"Nah, gotta head on over the enlistment office tomorrow, see if my number's up yet. Need to be ready to go."

"Breakfast before you head out?"

"Sure thing!" Asa said, smiling.

"Well let's meet down in the lobby at around seven. That work?"

Asa nodded.

"Great. Well, then good night. Looks to be great weather for sleeping with the window open. See ya tomorrow."

They parted ways, and Lenus went to his room feeling curiously lighter, even though his dinner rumbled in his stomach. He locked the door behind him, went to the window and forced it open all the way. Rain had begun to fall, gentle now, but with the promise of strengthening presently.

He stripped down to his skivvies and slid into bed. The sheets felt deliciously cool against his skin. He looked at the shape of the banjo case propped against the wall near the sink, and for a moment, his heart seized.

It looked like a person standing there.

A kid.

But he blinked, and it was gone, lit by a flash of lightning revealing just the shape of the case.

Lenus exhaled heavily, lay his head on the pillow. He reached under the other pillow, brought out the gun. It, too, was just a dark shape in the night, but when the lightning burst like a flashbulb, it looked like the head of a striking snake.

He studied it for a minute, not really considering the use he'd brought it for, finally just sliding it back beneath the pillow.

His dreams came and went, punctuated by lightning and thunder.

But he remembered none of them.

The next day, they started early in Lenus' room.

"So, you was telling me yesterday," Asa said, the banjo set between his legs, his hand crabbed, brushing and popping the strings.

"What's that now?" Lenus asked, lost in thought watching the young man's slim fingers. They'd met for breakfast, and Asa, restless, had left for the enlistment office after. He'd come back in about two hours, just shook his head.

"About you learning banjo playing from your brother."

"Didn't exactly learn it from him, leastways not like you mean," Lenus muttered, before he really thought about what he was saying.

"How'd you mean then?"

Lenus looked up, fixed Asa with a look.

"Tell ya what, you practice today and mayhap I'll tell you that story. What could it hurt?"

Asa looked up, confused. "Hurt?"

Lenus shook off the question.

"It's all hurt, kid," he said. "All hurt."

"Huh?" Asa said, his mouth full of burger and fries, which seemed to be the only thing he ate, outside breakfast.

"I said, you tell me your story over lunch, I'll tell you mine when we get back. My story isn't fit for a place like this," Lenus said, poking at the meatloaf on his plate.

"Why not?"

"Well if I told you right now, might as well tell the whole damn story. You first," Lenus said.

Asa chewed thoughtfully. "Not much to tell, really. Born and raised in Tunica. Mom raised four of us. I got a brother and two sisters. My daddy was killed by the Klan when I was about eight.

Never found his body or exactly who did it. My older brother left home in '66, no one heard from him again. Two sisters are younger, twelve and fourteen. Momma wanted me to get out of Tunica, find someplace safer to live. I went for the Army instead," he shrugged. "If they'll ever take me."

"They'll take you," Lenus snorted.

"How can you be so sure? Ain't no place falling over themselves to take black men."

"They'll take you because they always need ammunition," Lenus said. "And black kills just as good as white."

Asa stopped with the hamburger poised near his lips, measuring what Lenus had said.

"Anyway, after my daddy was killed, we spent a lot of time on my grandad's farm. That's where I learned to love hillbilly music, from my grandma and her playing. What she listened to on the radio. That's about it for me."

They ate in silence for a bit, Asa polishing off the hamburger and starting in earnest on the fries.

"Well if you ain't gonna tell me your story right now, just tell me a little about yourself. You said you was a session player for a lot of country artists."

"That's right. I grew up in southern Missouri. Learned to love the music in just about the same way as you. Radio. Gospel music. Fell into it when I was a teenager and never looked back. Played in medicine shows, then in the radio barn dances popular in the 20s and 30s. After the war, the record business got really big, and I hooked up with some of the artists, played on tours and whatnot. Eventually settled into a role as a session player, recording with the biggies."

"Like who?"

"Oh, too many to name, but people like Hank, Flatt and Scruggs, the Carters, Bill Monroe, Lefty Frizzell, the Louvin Brothers, even Charley Pride and Dolly. Lots. Maybe every act passing through Nashville, I sat in with and played at one time or another. Too many to remember," Lenus laughed.

"So, Mr…"

"No, no 'mister.' Call me Len," he said, pronouncing it as *lean.*

"Okay. So, Len, was the banjo the first instrument you learned?"

"Hell, no. We wasn't rich. Banjos were expensive. But when I was young, guitars could be had cheap. That's what I picked up first. My brother played the fiddle, then the banjo when we earned enough scratch to buy one."

With the mention of his brother, Lenus grew silent, poked at the food on his plate.

Asa changed the subject. "You ever play on stage at the Opry?" he asked

"The Opry?" Lenus said, chuckling. "Sure, kid. Bunch of times."

"What was it like?"

"Hot. Cramped. There are places backstage smell like mothballs in an old jockstrap. But otherwise, I wouldn't trade those experiences for nothing."

Lenus poked around a little on his chop, then set the fork and knife down across the plate.

"I ain't as hungry for this as I thought," he said. "What say we get pie before we head back?"

Asa, who'd finished his fries and drained his third Coke, nodded enthusiastically.

They'd gone up the hotel staircase slowly to their floor. In the hallway, Asa made to come to Lenus' room, hear his story.

"Not tonight, son," Lenus said, still trying to catch his breath. "Don't much feel like talking tonight. But after you visit the enlistment office tomorrow, you head on up, and we'll talk."

Lenus turned, then turned back, fumbled in his pocket. He handed Asa a five-dollar bill.

"What's this for?" Asa asked.

"Breakfast tomorrow on your own. I'm sleeping in."

"Len, you don't have to do that, man."

"We done had that conversation, Asa. I got more money than I know what to do with. Go have breakfast, see the Army tomorrow. If you ain't shipping out, come see me when you're done. I'll teach you some chords."

Lenus shuffled off to his room, feeling the young man's eyes on his back.

Inside, he stripped, climbed into bed.

He closed his eyes against the shadows, slid his hand under the pillow to caress the gun hidden there. Sooner than he expected, he was asleep.

"What'd they say?" asked Lenus, letting Asa in late the next morning. The young man strode into the room, obviously agitated.

"Not today," Asa said, fuming and pacing. "Not today and not today and not today."

"Well, what's the hold up, they say?"

Asa turned on him, looked curiously.

Lenus straightened up, held himself with the exaggerated regality of a drunk.

Asa narrowed his eyes but didn't comment.

"The corporal at the office thinks it's funny to give a negro the runaround, that's what the problem is. Probably thinks the army should have a strict no negros policy."

Lenus considered what he heard, filed it away.

"So, I guess..."

"Yeah, tomorrow and the day after and every damn day until this guy's had his laugh, I guess," Asa said, then looked at the ceiling and sighed. "Sorry for cursing."

"If you think that's the worst thing I ever heard—hell, the worst I said myself this morning—then you ain't been paying attention," Lenus said, laughing to loud, wincing when he realized it. "You feel like learning banjo, because I can understand..."

"No," Asa said, his voice sharp as a knife. "I mean, yes, I want to learn today."

"Okay, well then let's get set up here. Same schedule as yesterday. We study a little, go down and have lunch. Study a little more, then dinner."

"And after dinner, you tell me your story."

Lenus, who had hefted the banjo case over to the bed, paused undoing the clasps.

"You don't want to hear that story, son, I promise."

"I do, Len. I do."

It was Lenus' turn to sigh. He opened the case and lifted the banjo, handed it to Asa.

"Why go and ruin a perfectly good day?" Lenus said, sitting on the bed, jouncing the springs.

Asa sat on the only chair in the room, placed the banjo in his lap as he'd learned.

"You all right?" he asked.

"No."

"You drunk?"

"Yep."

"Want me to come back later?"

"Nope. Expect it's best to just get to it. The learning, that is. The story'll have to wait, but not much longer. I'll need to be drunker before I get to it."

"Look," Asa said. "If it's that bad and you don't want to tell it, there's no need."

"Nah, someone's gotta know, I suppose, to understand."

"Understand what?"

"Everything before. Everything after."

Asa didn't know what to say, so said nothing.

"All right," Lenus said, slapping his thighs and standing. "Let's learn some chords. We'll start with the easiest one, the G. Then we'll do the C and the D7. That covers most country and bluegrass songs. Then lunch."

After lunch, they went back at it, Lenus drilling him on chords, correcting his finger placement, telling him to keep his hand clawed properly, helping him keep time.

Lenus could tell Asa was becoming frustrated, but he kept at it. Lenus suspected the kid knew it was taking his mind off something he didn't want to think about anyway.

As the sun slid below the bottom frame of the window, Lenus called a halt to practice, said dinnertime was here. Asa walked to the bed, put the banjo back in its case as gently as laying a baby down to sleep. He closed the case, snapped it shut.

Lenus nodded appreciatively, clapped him on the shoulder.

"You have a tie to wear with that jacket?" he asked.

"Yeah, one,"

"Go put it on with your cleanest shirt. We're going somewhere special tonight; I think we both earned it."

Asa looked curious, but Lenus pushed him out the door with the admonition to meet him downstairs in twenty minutes.

Lenus waited in the lobby, dressed in his own nicest shirt and tie, hat in hand. Bounding down the steps came Asa.

"Well, don't you look sharper than a tack," Lenus laughed. "Let's go have a nice meal."

Outside, a cab waited, and Asa, surprised, held the door as Lenus got in, then climbed in after him. The cab trundled through the early evening streets of Memphis, maybe a dozen or so blocks, then pulled in front of nondescript building with a green awning and darkened windows.

Lenus stepped out, and the cab sped away.

Marco's was spelled out in florid script across the awning.

Asa flashed Lenus a doubtful look.

"This don't look like no restaurant that's gonna want to see me inside," he said.

"Don't worry, kid. It's a whole new world," Lenus said, then whispered close to his ear. "Besides, I got *a lot* of money."

Eyes were raised the moment they opened the door and stepped in. But Lenus discretely pressed money into a variety of hands, and eventually the two were seated in a private room. It was small and dimly lit, dark green walls with paintings of landscapes.

A small, round table with four chairs dominated the room. The table was covered with an immaculate white cloth, completely set with a bewildering variety of glasses, flatware and plates. A decorative cloth napkin, elaborately folded into a swan, sat on each plate.

The maître d' closed the door once they were in the room, as if hiding them from the rest of the diners. Lenus knew this, but let it go. He'd kill them with kindness tonight, smother their snubs in money.

He took a seat, and Asa sat across from him.

"Never been in a place like this," he said, uncertainty tinging his voice.

"Ain't but a restaurant like the luncheonette down the street. Don't let the fancy carpets and men in tuxedoes fool you. They serve food here, just like anyplace else."

"Then why'd we not just go to the luncheonette?"

"I fancied myself a nice thick steak before...," Lenus said, trailing off. "Figure'd you like one, too."

"They ain't happy about me being here."

Lenus lowered his menu. "Now, you gonna ruin my meal and yours? Don't worry about any of that shit. You know what color places like this are interested in? Green. Green's all they're interested in, and I got that to spare. So, we're going to have a nice dinner here, like two gentlemen of means out on the town. You in or you out?"

Asa considered this, then smiled slowly. "I'm in."

"Great! I recommend as big a steak as your damn fool stomach can eat, cooked rare. Anything else is a damn slap in God's face."

After the finest meal Asa would have for many years, the two left the building. The night was quiet, the air still muggy from the heat of the day. Lenus picked at his teeth, and Asa bent over, clutched his belly and groaned in delight.

"Like it that much, huh?" Lenus asked.

Asa looked up. "Ain't never had steak before, leastways not like that. And those potatoes...what'd they call them?

"Potatoes dauphinoise."

"Oh, man. Even the salad. Never been much for salads, but wow. And dessert."

"And the drinks, don't forget those. Best bourbon I've had in a while."

"Best bourbon I've had ever."

"So?" Lenus asked.

"I could get used to it."

"Better stick a sock in it for a few years, at least. The Army won't be serving you anything like that. You'll get rations and stuff slopped onto tin plates. Strong coffee and shit on a shingle."

Asa stood, frowning.

"Now, don't go and let me spoil the evening for ya. Just forget I said that. Cab should be here any second. We'll find a liquor store, then head back to the hotel."

"Didn't have enough to drink at dinner?" Asa asked, cocking an eye at him

"Son, if I'm gonna tell you my story tonight, and I feel I gotta, I'm gonna need to be a skosh drunker than I am now."

The cab pulled up to the curb at that moment, and they climbed in, went in search of an open liquor store.

III.

The first record album, the first music I heard anyone play besides my family, was Old John Carson. Ever heard of him? No, not the host of that show on television. Old John was the finest fiddle player ever.

My uncle Jeph bought Fiddlin' John's record when it came out, a recording of "Little Old Log Cabin in the Lane," with "The Old Hen Cackled and the Rooster's Going to Crow" on the B side. He had an old Victrola he kept at my granny's house. You know, the antique crank kind.

Well, we burned up that record. Played it so many times, in my granny's parlor, out on her porch, dancing and carrying on, we wore out the grooves. Old Jeph had to go out after a few months and buy another.

My whole family loved to whoop and kick their heels up when that record played. My momma was a quiet sort, but even she kicked it up when the music started. And my pa, well old pa was a sharecropper, always working, always busy. Seemed to me he never slept. But he loved his music. He played a passable fiddle, too, and loved to saw away with his brother Jeph on the banjo most nights, until we got that record.

The record, that damned John Carson fiddling record changed everything.

Everything.

Gotta make you understand, here, because it's important. Music were changing' then. Before, it was just all ordinary folks out in the barn or on the porch of a house in some holler, out in the middle of nowhere. Maybe someone had a banjo or a fiddle, an old guitar, hell even a piano if they was well off.

But the music was live and spontaneous, played by someone's daddy or uncle or momma or granny. It was free and unadulterated, at a time when I guess our country was, too. Innocent. Or at least naïve, I expect.

Then came radio. Meant they had airwaves to fill, and music was one of the first choices. That meant you had to have people who knew what they was doing. People who could play instruments professionally, could sing and hit the notes.

People who made money, for the most part, doing it.

If radio opened the door, record albums kicked the door off its hinges. Especially when cheap record players made their way into houses. Now most people had a radio of some sort. They was cheaper to buy. But we hadn't electricity back then, and no one knew to connect a battery to the thing to get it working. So, we didn't have a radio 'til later, just old Jeph's Victrola.

At any rate, there weren't no hillbilly music, as it was called then, on the radio until '23, when the first barn dance show came outta Fort Worth. But it all kinda came right around the same time. The explosion of hillbilly music, the cheap records.

Suddenly there were people playing our music and getting paid for it.

Now, I don't need to tell you money is a powerful lure, but particularly in the 1920's in this country. Everyone thinks it was all wine and roses and champagne here until the Depression hit in '29. And maybe it was in New York and Chicago and St. Louis. But not in most of the country, especially in the south.

It was a hardscrabble life for most folks. Menial jobs, just eking out a living and nothing more. Support your family with food, a few clothes, a roof over their head. Not much else.

When all this started, my pa got stars in his eyes. If others could make money from this, why not him? Well, he weren't very good, that's why. Passable for a jig on the porch out in the middle of nowhere, not for radio or records. And he, bless him, knew this straightaway.

But if he could teach his sons to play? I was just ten. My brother Hiram was only eight. We'd each already picked up licks on Jeph's banjo, and our family had a guitar and a fiddle. I was passable at the guitar, but the banjo escaped me. Looking back, I think it were my hands, too small to make the chords and such.

But Hiram. Jesus Lord, Hiram was a natural musician. He picked up the fiddle at six years old, and by the time he was eight, he sawed away at it like an old timer. Same with the guitar. Never took to the banjo much, but he could play it if pressed.

And his voice. That sweet, high voice of a young boy, like in those church choirs I'd heard on the radio and such. Just beautiful. When he sang, people wept. I tell you plainly. They wept. Between his angelic voice and his fiddle playing, it was like nothing anyone in our little town heard before.

I couldn't sing at all. Couldn't find the tune nor keep it when I did. Like wrasslin' a gator. Sometimes you're on top, but mostly you're below water getting bit and muddy. But I could back him. I could do that, stand beside him and play my guitar. But mostly I faded behind him, faded away as people listened to him.

I prayed to get better, oh I prayed on that hard. At church on Sundays, in my bed at night, with Hi snoring softly next to me. Prayed God'd help me practice harder, get better so's I could stand up on stage with Hi and not feel some degree of humiliation. To play music with him and not get cuffed by my pa when we was through.

We played a lot in them days, all over the county. My father trotted us out to church picnics and such, where we played. We even had a name. Hiram & Brother. Yeah, that was me. Brother. Couldn't even use my name in the billing.

Sometimes we'd just stand on a corner in town and play. People'd toss us a penny or so. Mayhap a nickel. We'd make a little change, and course, pa'd take it. Had to support the family.

But it was okay. I mean I was only eleven by then. Hiram was nine. And I loved my brother. I want, I *need* you to understand. I was never jealous, leastways early on. I loved him, purely. He was my little brother, and I was fiercely protective of him. I knew he was better'n me, and that was all right.

At least I thought so.

At least I told myself so.

Until that night in the woods.

By '25, Hi and me was playing gigs everywhere, it seemed. Political rallies, union meetings, revival tents, all sorts of places. Making a little scratch for the family. Nice to have a little money coming in. More bacon with the beans, you know?

But money, lord, don't it change things? Even a little bitty bit of it. And for us, it was just that and no more. Just a buck or so here and there. But it set something in my pa on fire, low and banked 'til then.

See he was a drinker, but during Prohibition, you had to be secretive about it. There were bootleggers everywhere and secret places to drink, if you really wanted to. And pa? Well, he done it a little when he had almost no money. But once money started to roll in, he stepped up in a big way.

He went to work drunk and came home drunk. He took us to gigs drunk. And that might have been okay were it not for the fact he was a damn mean 'un. Darkened and sour on hootch. Hit us more. Even momma, until grandma stepped in and stopped it. But she never stopped him from hitting Hi and me.

Kids, right? We was just kids, and we were yoked, making money for the family now like an old brood mare pulling the plow. You gotta whip her to get her going? Right? Well, that's what they thought back then, anyway.

But you think ole Hi got hit? Well, truthfully once or twice. If he whined about being tired or hungry or thirsty instead of doing what pa wanted. But it was me got it most. Even when I didn't really do no wrong. I think he hit me because he wanted to hit Hi. He just couldn't. Not only was he suddenly the family's meal ticket, he looked like an angel.

Wouldn't be right to be whaling on an angel. So, I took his licks and mine, and, again, I was fine with it.

But, well, that weren't true. It preyed on me. I was thirteen then, getting older and all, and I objected fiercely to being hit all the time. No one to defend me the way granny defended momma.

Certainly no help from Hi. Oh, he was sorry when I was hit, particularly if it were for his sins. But he just turned away when it happened.

I felt mostly alone, though it seemed I was always around people. People kicking up their heels to what Hi and I played. Dancing and carrying on, drinking out back when they thought no one noticed.

I felt alone, and that's a horrible thing for a child to feel. Alone within his own family.

Though the only time I could truly be alone was at night. I slept in a small bed in a small room just outside momma and pa's bedroom. Shared the bed with Hi, who had the talent for dropping into sleep anywhere, at any time. Like a toddler still and eleven years old.

I took to getting up, sneaking out of the house. Momma was a sound sleeper, and pa more than often was passed out, snoring like a passing train whose boiler was about to blow. I snuck out and walked in the dark, peaceful woods alone.

Most nights, if the weather cooperated, I was out tramping through the darkness of the hills surrounding our house. It was exhilarating, freeing in a way I had never experienced before. I wouldn't feel that way again until I was out touring with the bands I played with until I settled in Nashville, became a session player.

Back then, with the pale starlight marking my steps, or the moon if I were lucky, breathing the cool, night air, I felt like, well, the only boy in a fairy tale.

If my momma had known—hell, I suspect even if my pa had known—they'd have thrashed me good. First, outta disobeying them.

But second, out of fear. Fear of me being outside, in those woods, after dark, alone.

Maybe not.

Our little farmstead was just south of Corridon, which was a town, but not by much. Lead mines and stuff scattered all over the southern part of Missouri, that's about it. Hell, town got a post office in ought-one, and they was still talking about it when I was a kid.

But I'd heard my parents and granny whispering nights out on the porch, after they thought we'd gone to bed. Well, old Hi had. He'd be breathing softly, hand at his mouth, sucking his thumb. My father'd walloped him, but he still did it in bed at night.

I'd be up, waiting for them to go in and head to bed. And I'd be listening.

On occasion, they'd talk of a rich guy who owned one of the nearby mines, how he'd brought something back from overseas, Germany or France or such place. How he'd taken whatever it was down into the mines and done…well, something. The gossip weren't particularly sure. Just *something*.

I didn't precisely understand it, but they whispered about opening a door, letting something in.

Always something, nothing definitive or known.

Something bad, though.

Whatever it was hadn't gone back through the door, but had stayed here, out in the dark woods. And it was doing bad things.

I couldn't make heads or tails of what they was saying on those nights, but I did know strange things were happening in the area around us.

A girl miles from us, in a little house like ours, was snatched away in the middle of the night. She'd gone out to the family barn for a pail of water, singing as she went. Her family heard the song stop suddenly, and when she didn't return from her chore, they went to find her. The spilled pail of water was there, but she wasn't. No signs of a ruckus, no footprints other than hers. Like she'd been lifted up to heaven, raptured away.

No one ever saw her again.

Other things, too. People seeing weird things in the woods, what my folks called skunk apes. But other stuff. Stuff too strange to describe much less comprehend. All blamed on this mysterious rich guy and the somethings he'd gotten up to with whatever he took down into the earth and switched on.

Since no one could be any more specific, it didn't bother me much. Ghosts and boogums and haints and whatnot. I was thirteen, by god, and I didn't believe in such things anymore. The only spirits were those my pa and his friends drank out in the woods, beyond where Hi and me played our music, beyond where the ladies sipped lemonade and the children danced and carried on.

So, I'd sneak out into the woods and walk and think.

Sometimes I'd pray, pray to be a better musician, pray for my parents to be proud of me.

In the blessed silence, by myself.

Or so I thought.

One night, this'd be around May or so, well before the heat set in and the nights were bathed in sweat, like they are in Memphis here. It was a clear night, stars a-twinkling in the sky. I crept from my bed, Hi's thumb corked in his mouth, and stepped lightly across the creaking floorboards.

Granny was partially deaf by now, so no real need to extra quiet as I opened the front door and slipped out.

I ran down the steps and into the yard. Always felt so exhilarating to be out in my nightshirt, like I was racing through the world naked. Down the lane from the house, I cut across the cow pasture, to where the woods began, black against the foothills. A little crick twisted between the pasture and the trees.

The hills rolled into the night, blotted out the stars like the shoulders of some slumbering giant. And the trees, well they bled together into one dense stain of darkness. Patchy here and there, with only hints as to what lay within.

I'd generally scrabble around the banks of the crick, plunking rocks into its mirrored water, disturbing the coons and possums and what not getting a drink. I'd think about what was going on in my life. Where we'd played, what songs we were working on, when pa'd belt me…and why.

Mostly why. Why he hit me, why I couldn't be better at my instruments. Why I just couldn't seem to learn to play the banjo or the guitar better'n I could. Pa told me many times I was holding Hi back, holding all of us back. I had to learn to play better, keep up, sing harmony.

All seemed to be my fault, least how pa saw it. And he made sure I knew, that I was always thinking about it.

But I was trying. I mean when I weren't out in the fields picking or in school or playing at some event, I was practicing. Hi practiced with me mostly, but everyone knew he really didn't need to. It was more to keep me company.

"You'll get it, Len," he'd say to me. "Just keep at it."

"Damn, Hi, I wish you were just in me, playing this here instrument with my fingers. Be a whole lot easier," I'd say.

"Don't let pa hear you cuss, Len. He'll thrash you for sure. And I don't need to be in you. You can do this."

I'd laugh all sour like, go back to fingering those damn chords.

That night, as I traipsed the riverbanks looking for crawdads, I thought about all that. And at some point, lost in thought, I wandered into the woods.

Ever go to church real early? Like when no one's there, not even the pastor? It's an eerie feeling. I been to a couple of Catholic churches for weddings or funerals and such. You get there early, with the lights off and nothing but the candles lit. All those statue's eyes following ya. It's weird. It's like, even when there ain't no people there save yourself, there's something there. Some presence.

God, I guess.

I stopped there in the night forest and felt it. I was alone and yet…not. Something was in there with me in the darkness of the whispering tree branches.

I thought it weren't nothing but the animals. I mean the deer and the coons and the possums and such, they all are up at night, grubbing around. Probably just them I felt.

But I knew, even as I thought this, it weren't it.

This was something…other.

Bigger.

I kept walking anyway. I loved the cool air under the trees, the way the moonlight fell to the forest floor in little silver patches, as if flakes of the moon had drifted down like leaves.

But as I got deeper into the woods, the air turned dense and gummy. I could feel it greasy on my skin. My bare feet stepped into what I thought were puddles of mud, but it felt sticky and jellied between my toes.

There was a smell, too, a smell I couldn't place. Almost like the catfish or crappie we'd pull from the little pond up the road a piece from the house. That strangely familiar, fishy odor mixed with the rotten pond weeds and scum.

But this smelled meatier, saltier.

I wrinkled my nose, now thinking there must be a dead animal nearby. This smell was close, but not quite.

This smelled dead, true, but somehow alive.

Now, I don't mean like one of them monster movies you see at the picture show. No vampires or whatnot. I mean it smelled like a living thing, with that tang of death there on the end.

I'd never smelled anything like it before, and as I tried to place it, I saw something between the trees up ahead. The ground before me divided to the left and to the right, climbing up the hills, with a holler in between.

Pulsating between the tree trunks and branches, there came a pale purple glow. Misty looking. It kinda oozed through the trees, like mud between toes. But it didn't behave much like light. No, it were more like a fog or a low cloud, billowing, flowing with that strange light.

I stopped, checked myself, as now I felt I must still be asleep back in my bed with Hi, dreaming all this.

As I neared the holler, I slowed. This all felt wrong now, and I don't just mean I was scared, though I was, yes, I was. No, I mean it felt wrong, out of place, as if something had happened that shouldn't oughta happen.

Something in that holler felt aggrieved, as if it were wronged by whatever was happening.

I stepped closer, through the screen of a few trees with massive trunks, and saw…

Well, at first, I didn't know what I saw, you understand?

I was thirteen, pretty unworldly for this day. Never even kissed a girl at that age, much less seen one naked, leastways not *that* part.

What I saw made me feel a lot of things, but the most powerful was squishy down in my guts. No, lower. In my balls, if you'll excuse.

I imagine you been with a girl at this point. Well, I sure hope you have if you're fixing to head over to Viet Nam and fight. You seen the honeypot, then, if you take my meaning plain.

That's what it looked like, a large vertical slit in the air, like a woman's parts or the devil's foot, take your pick. All pulsing and purple and steaming.

I had no conscious idea of this back then, mind you, but something within me took it for that, deep down to my bones, and reacted accordingly.

As my young boy mind tried to make sense of this, something else asserted itself from within that cleft, emerged as if a distant womb were giving birth.

A gush of foul-smelling liquid burst into the holler, splattered the trees and the leaves and the damp, loamy ground. From within that purple split emerged legs...at least that's what I thought they were at first. They grabbed at the sides of the fissure, pulled it wider, and the thing behind them pushed ahead, pushed through.

I backed away, prepared to run, until I struck a tree trunk and froze.

What slid through that fissure was unlike anything I had never seen, my mind had never imagined.

It was a monstrosity. Parts of different animals glued together by a child. Its legs were really tentacles, like on an octopus. But the body was huge, the size of the motor cars I had seen while we were in Corridon. Bloated and misshapen like a spider's, covered in stiff, bristly hairs,.

A ring of glassy black eyes circled the space I'd guessed was its head. And atop were a huge rack of sharp, many-pronged antlers. Now, I'd seen me deer up close. When my pa and his buddies would go hunting and bring in one they needed to butcher, hanging from a tree in the yard.

I ain't never, and I mean never, seen antlers as big and mean-looking as these.

The thing squelched through the gap, which rippled and reformed after it was completely through.

Then it just sat there, dripping goo and filth that ran in a stream toward me.

It didn't move, and those marble eyes in its head didn't move either.

I knew they saw me, were looking right at me.

I knew this thing had come for me.

Or not *for* me, precisely.

Because of me.

Now, I don't know how I knew that right then, I just did. And it terrified me every bit as much as the sight of the damn thing.

I ain't ashamed to tell ya I pissed my drawers then, soaked 'em.

After a spell where there were no sounds in the forest save for the thing's dripping and its many tentacles a-feeling round, it spoke.

It wasn't exactly speaking out loud like you and I do, and it weren't like those television shows where people speak to each other with their minds. It was sort of…in between, like everything else about it.

Hello, Len, it said, with a country drawl like mine. Even pronounced my nickname right.

"Hello," I stammered, feeling my wet drawers stick to my thighs, hoping against hope I hadn't soaked my nightshirt, too. Momma was gonna kill me.

Then, it'd be pa's turn.

Out for a stroll through the woods, I see.

"I guess."

Little late for that, ain't it?

"Who are you?" I asked, really wanting to ask *What are you?,* but thinking twice.

Mostly because I was afraid of what its answer might be.

Oh, names are so unimportant, right? I could tell you mine, but you'd never be able to hear it right, much less pronounce it. It'd seem…wrong on this air.

"Well I really oughta be going home now. So, I'll tell ya goodnight…sir."

The thing rumbled in what I took to be laughter.

I guess as to how you need to get back home and practice, so's you can get at least as good as Hiram. That way your pa'll stop tarring ya for slacking.

I'd turned to run, basically, but then stopped, turned slowly back.

"You know my brother?"

Oh, surely, I do. Surely, I do. That voice of his. So beautiful.

It said beautiful, but the way it said it, I don't think it meant it at all.

"Yeah?"

The thing sighed. *Singing. Playing the fiddle. Picking the banjo. He does it all, right, Len? And does it all soo good. So much better'n you, anyway.*

I bristled. "How'd you know such a thing? You're just a…well, a monster, is all."

That low chuckle again, raising goose flesh on my naked arms.

Oh, I am surely that, child. Surely. Still, stings, though, right? Even coming from such as me. Stings to hear your pa's words about you, doesn't it?

I was still half turned, prepared to bolt at any second.

"Yeah," I muttered.

You could do something about it, you know. It's in your power.

"I practice all the time. All the damn time. And I just can't seem to get it. It ain't fair. I do all that and get whupped anyways."

I felt myself tear up, and it made me angrier still. I wiped my eyes and nose with the sleeve of my nightshirt.

It ain't fair. Not by a long shot.

"And then all Hi does is get up and play. He barely practices at all, but he just gets up afore everyone and does it. Perfect like. Pa never whups him. Only me."

No, not fair at all Hi should have all the gifts and you none.

Well, I gotta say that hurt worse than hearing my pa's words outta whatever that thing was, and then I really burst into tears. Big ones that left me hitching my breath, streams of snot running down my face.

Hi with all the gifts and me with none, I thought? Damn. Just... damn.

You didn't listen. I said you have the power to change all that.

"Yeah, how's that?" I sniffled.

Where I'm from, there are ways. If you want it badly. If you're strong enough.

"I do, I do. I want it so badly. I want to be able to get up there and play like Hi. I want to make my momma and pa just as proud of me as they are Hi," I shouted.

I can help.

"How?"

Bring him to me.

That stopped me. Bring Hi here? For what?

Suddenly, I felt over my head, stuck in something I knew would be hard to pull loose from.

You want his talent, 'dontcha? Want it bad? You have to be strong enough, then.

"I am strong enough," I shouted, my little tough boy ego wounded. "Strong enough for what?"

To take it from him.

My mouth went dry as a stick, and my tongue glued itself to the roof of my mouth.

"Take?" I croaked. "From Hi?"

I accept your offer. Bring him to me.

Now, I'd been to church more than enough to know God don't take offers or make 'em. I prayed more than once for things I wanted—my grandad to live, for a baseball bat, for more records to play on Uncle Jeph's Victrola. Got none of it in return.

Because He don't work that way. He don't make bargains or grant wishes. He does what he does, and you just have to live with it. But I realized, standing there in my pissy britches, the fishy-dead smell of that thing in my nose, there are other gods, darker ones, who do. Who listen for that voice through all the static. Who listen because they're keen to strike a deal.

Who can, like this one, crawl their way in through a hole in our world and take you up on that offer.

So, I did what anyone would have.

"Okay, so what'd you do?" asked Asa, taking a nip from the bottle Lenus handed him.

"Well, what do you think?" Lenus said, slurring his words just a little. "I ran."

Asa laughed, passed the bottle back to Lenus. It held about a third of the amber liquid still, and it sloshed as Lenus took it.

"This is the best story I ever heard," Asa said, a bit too loudly for this late hour of the night in a hotel room whose walls were old and thin. Lenus shushed him, took a drink. "But I think you're drunk."

"No more'n you," Lenus said, sounding slightly wounded. "But that ain't it. What I said is true."

"All right," Asa said, taking the bottle back, and leaning in toward Lenus, slouched on the bed. "What happened next, then?"

I told you. I ran. Ran through the darkened woods, my piss-soaked drawers riding up on me, my piss-soaked nightshirt flapping in the breeze.

Ran, ducking tree limbs, hopping over fallen trunks, sloshing through the little creek, then pell-mell through the cow pasture and back home. Didn't try to be quiet or anything, just pounded up the steps, threw the door open and clomped into the front room.

Weren't probably later than about three a.m. Everyone was sound asleep. So, I stood there breathing heavy, wondering what to do. Wondering what I had seen.

Wondering what I had just agreed to.

I looked back at the open door to my bedroom, saw Hi fast asleep, thumb still corked in his mouth. I knew I couldn't go lie in bed next to him. It weren't just my dirty feet and pissy clothes.

I knew I couldn't go in there and lie next to him because he was an angel, and I'd just made a deal with…what? The devil?

With god.

With some other god.

Still trying to put it all together, I simply laid down onto the floor and fell asleep.

Got woken up with a short, sharp kick to the ribs.

"What in the holy hell are you doing lying here on the floor covered in mud and smelling of piss," my pa asked, giving me another kick to punctuate his question.

I didn't have to pretend to be disoriented or sleepy.

"I dunno...I dunno, pa."

"Honey, don't kick the boy," my momma said, careful to speak softly to my pa so's not to have him turn on her. "Can't you see he sleepwalked during the night? Poor thing likely don't know where he is or what happened."

She offered her hand, drew me up.

"Well, you ain't cleaning any of his stuff. Let him wash out his drawers and nightshirt himself," he said, then turned and stomped from the room.

Momma helped me change outta my clothes. Then she brought a pitcher of water and a cloth, told me to clean myself up. After I did, she told me to go outside and wash my things as pa'd said, hang 'em on the line when I was finished. Then come in and have breakfast.

I gathered my clothes, still caked with mud and smelling awful, and did as she said. She'd already put water and soap in the tub out back, placed the washboard inside.

I'm glad they made me wash my own things. Because as I scrubbed my nightshirt across the board, I saw streaks of livid purple through the suds. They stood out from the spatters of mud and the green stains of grass and leaves.

I scrubbed harder, unwilling to answer any questions.

Inside, my pa cuffed me again, almost as an afterthought, and I sat down to a bowl of cornbread mush and a glass of milk. Hi ogled me from across the table, but said nothing.

Later, we had to dress in our show clothes, so we could head out and play at a quilting social a town over. We all packed our stuff for the five-mile hike it'd take us to get to town. As we walked, my pa bitched and moaned about me, about how I needed to grow up and stop pissing my diddies, about how I needed to learn to play better so as not to make Hi look bad.

Same old chapter and verse.

I said a whole lotta "Yes, sirs," but not a whole lot else the entire way.

When we got there, he'd mostly quieted, though he blew up when we'd come off stage later, saying as how I'd missed a note or two. He clouted me a good one, made my ear ring, then marched off.

Hi watched it all in silence, put his fiddle back in its case and snapped it shut. Then he said something made my blood boil, instantly.

"If you'd stop doing what he doesn't like and start doing what he does, he's apt not to hit you as much. Or at least not as hard."

He picked up his case, walked away.

I stood there, so immediately and violently angry at him I trembled. Some old lady saw me and stepped over to touch my arm.

"Something weighing on you, son?"

I swallowed all that anger, and it went down like a bale of dry hay wrapped in barb wire.

"No, ma'am," I said, smiling sweet as ice cream on a hot day. "Just a little overheated, s'all."

"Well, we can't have that, can we?" she said, putting her arm around my shoulder and leading me away. "Not for the brother of such a fine musician. Let's go get you a nice, cold glass of lemonade, wash that dust right out your throat."

I went with her, and it was good and all, though it did nothing for my anger. Later, I got whacked for that, too. Why hadn't I brought some for everyone?

It was on the long walk home—me straggling at the back, Hi up front between momma and pa—I began to think about what that antlered thing in the woods had offered.

Began to think about how to get Hi to come out there with me.

"Wait a minute. You mean…?" Asa said, sitting up in his chair. "Aww, hell, no."

"Don't jump ahead. Let me finish."

Asa looked doubtful, took the bottle back. Its contents were almost gone, just enough for one more pull.

"But Imma finish this, then."

Did I really think that thing in the woods was real?

I dunno. Still don't, though I guess that sounds silly.

Did I think it could give me some of Hi's talent? Or at least make me play better?

Don't know that either, though I guess as how I do now.

All I knew was I'd been offered a way, an out, if you will. A path to being better than I was.

I aimed to take it, yes, I surely did.

Question was how to get Hi out there with me, to find that monster again.

I lay awake a few nights quiet, pondering on this, trying to come up with how to get both of us out of the house with no one hearing, and into those woods.

And then, how to find that cleft in the holler again.

I also prayed to God. The one I learned about in Bible school, sitting in a cramped room with other kids. Reading those old Bible stories of Samson and Delilah, Noah's Ark, Sodom and Gomorrah.

I prayed to him even though it was plain the God in those stories was a dick. Self-righteous, needy, and not prone to helping anyone, unless it was really helping Himself. I prayed to him, nonetheless.

I prayed to our savior, too, Jesus Christ. He was, to me at least, the silent partner in religion. He never seemed approachable, the kind of guy you brought your problems to. Sounds odd, I know. But Jesus always had a kind of standoffish presence. Sort of a "Listen, don't bother me with your problems. Bring them to my father."

I prayed to him anyway.

Nothing came of it. No answers, no bargains, no wishes granted or miracles bestowed. I was still the same shitty musician when I woke up as I had been going to bed.

Hi? Well, Hi seemed to be pulling away, as if he sensed some hint of the battle going on inside me. He got a little snappier at me for screwing up on stage, taking my pa's side more and more. Seemed to get, as we say in the country above his raising. A touch too full of himself for my taste.

Which was bad since I knew there was a god out there, out in the woods. A god who'd come through that strange purple split, who'd be happy to do what I asked.

A god who didn't only *listen*.

A god who *did*.

The last night before we went out, I prayed to it instead.

"Gotta take a break before I get to the end here," Lenus said, standing woozily and stretching. "Also think I need to fortify myself before I proceed."

He reached below the bed and produced a second bottle.

"Fortification courtesy of the Starlight Liquor Store," he said, twisting the cap on the bottle and taking a swing. "Now, to the restroom. When I return presently, we'll continue this sorry story."

Asa reached out as Lenus passed, put his hand on the man's arm.

"You sure about all this?"

"All what?" Lenus replied, teetering but steadying himself on Asa.

"The second bottle. Finishing your story."

"That's the thing about a story, ain't it? They gotta be finished at some point," he said. "Might as well be you listening."

With that, he left for the bathroom down the hall.

Asa sat, head in hand, until Lenus returned.

It was about a week later I finally screwed up my courage enough to take Hi into the woods.

It was June, and the night was thick and sticky, but the sky was clear as a bell, and an almost-full moon lit everything buttery yellow.

We'd gone to bed with the windows open. It was oppressive in the house, with the heat and the still, heavy air. Pa had suggested sleeping out on the porch, but granny and momma put the kibosh on that. Too many bugs for their taste.

Hi and I went to our bedroom, door and window left open in the hopes of catching a breeze that never came. Stretched out atop the sheets in only our britches, slick with sweat.

Hi had started to drift into sleep, but I couldn't. The heat and my racing mind kept me awake. I knew I needed to get this started before he fell asleep, because rousing him meant rousing the entire house.

"Hi," I said, poking him. "Hi, wake up. Hi!"

He rolled over, groaning.

"Let me sleep, Len," he said. "I'm awful tired."

"Come on, wake up," I said, shaking him. "We got something to do."

"It's night, Len. What's there to do?"

"We're gonna sneak outside and go into the woods."

He lay there silent, and I thought he might have drifted away, so I prodded him again.

"Stop it!" he hissed. "You're gonna wake up pa. You want a thrashing tonight? Besides, why'd we go into the woods now anyways?"

"There's something I want to show you."

He rolled over immediately, and I knew I had him.

"What?" he asked, almost breathless. "What'd you find? Arrowheads?" We was always finding Indian arrowheads in the cow pasture or when pa ploughed up the field. Hi was entranced by them, had a collection of his best finds set up on the windowsill.

"Sure, a whole bunch of 'em," I said, and I immediately felt guilty. Strange because what I was contemplating was much worse than lying to him. After the stretch of all those years since, that's perhaps the biggest regret I have. Lying to my brother about something he dearly loved.

Now he was interested, and he rolled over to me in bed.

"Where? Can you show me?"

"Course, idiot. Why'd you think I woke you?"

"Take me, Len. Let's go! Were there a lot of 'em? Big ones?"

"Sure thing. Lots. And you can have them all, if'n you want." I had no particular liking for the things, seeing as they hadn't served the dead Indians all that well.

"Come on, Len! Let's go," he said, leaping up from bed.

"Shh!" I warned, getting up myself. "We got to be quiet or we'll wake everyone. And then you'll never see all of them. You know how they feel about us going into the woods."

That stopped him, the first little sliver of disbelief crept into his voice.

"Well, then, how'd you find them?"

I considered lying to him again, but no. "I been getting up at night and going into the woods."

I could barely see him in the dark of the room, but I saw his eyes fly open wide.

"At night? Why?"

"To be alone for a while. To talk to god, I guess."

"About what?"

"Stuff," I said, tearing up despite myself. "About being better at playing."

"Oh, Len," he said. "That ain't important."

Made me as instantly angry at him as I was just a few days earlier, when he'd said that thing after the gig at the quilting bee. I took it to mean it wasn't important for me to be better, as then I might be better than him.

Stupid, I know, but there it was.

"If you want to go and see them, shut up and follow me. Quiet as a mouse, Hi. Or we're caught."

We crept from the room. No need to open our squeaky bedroom door. Across the parlor to the front door, out onto the porch. Then, we was off the porch and outside. I wanted to whoop and holler, outside in the bright moonlight in naught but our drawers. But I shushed Hi, seeing he wanted to do the same.

We padded across the yard, then Hi stopped.

"What're you doing?" I whispered. "Come on!"

"I'm thinking if we're going into the woods, we need protection. I'ma getting pa's hog knife from the barn."

"No, wait…," I said, but he'd already trotted off.

Pa's hog knife was a big old thing, long as a machete and kept so sharp it could cut a piece of paper. Pa used it to dispatch chickens mostly, as they's all we was likely to have in the way of meat. It got its name, though, from the one time pa had acquired a hog, and the knife was used to slit its throat.

Hi came back with the knife, swiping it through the air menacingly.

"Now, we can defend ourselves against bears and Indians," he said.

"Ain't neither in these here woods. No bears, and the Indian's long gone. Stop swiping that thing around before you cut yourself," I said. "Now, let's get moving."

We set off across the cow pasture, cross the creek, swollen with summer rain, and into the woods. Hi didn't hesitate at all, just followed quietly behind in my footsteps.

The woods smelled of growth, that green-sap smell of things pushing up from the soil, spreading their fronds and leaves and such, sending roots into the earth. It smelled good, heavy with unseen flowers and the scent of damp.

But there was the fish-dead tang I'd gotten a whiff of before, and I knew he was here.

My entirely pliable god.

We went on through the woods, crossing fallen logs and weaving in out of the trees. I had a fair idea of where that holler was where I'd seen him, and though we curved around and zig-zagged, I always brought us eventually to heel.

As we approached, my heart fell and my determination wavered.

The holler was dark and empty, no fissure, no strange purple light, no mist.

"Where is it?" Hi said, speaking for the first time since we entered the woods, impatience coloring his voice.

"Just up ahead here," I said, wondering what the hell I was gonna tell him if...

There was a pulse of air that nearly knocked us flat. We staggered, held ourselves against the trees.

There, in the holler, about five feet above the ground, the air ripped apart with a sound like tearing fabric...which I suppose it was. The split started at two points, top and bottom, tore its way to the middle.

When they met, there came a loud hissing sound, and a burst of lilac light flashed between the trees.

"Len," Hi said, "What...?"

"Shut up!" I snapped, watching my god pull itself from the cleft into our world. The purple light suffused everything, and the mist poured out onto the ground like blood billowing in water.

I stepped forward, grabbing Hi's hand in mine. He stumbled a few steps, called my name again, but I yanked him behind me.

We came to within just a few feet of the thing's arms. The front two were raised, weaving in the air, mesmerizing. Almost took our attention from the thing's bristly head, its ring of eyes, its crown of antlers, sharp as daggers.

You have come.

Hi jerked in my grip, fell to the ground beside me.

"Yes, sir."

And I see you have brought him. To fulfill the bargain.

"Yes, sir," I repeated, tugging at Hi to stand, but he didn't. Or more likely couldn't.

Only one thing remains for you to realize your desire.

"What?" I asked, and I will tell you, true as the one God above, I had no real idea what this thing meant. Not really, not truly. If I had, there's no way, none, I'd have went ahead with it.

I knew it meant something for Hi. I just had no idea what.

I tell myself that now, and it salves my burns, if you take my meaning. Makes me feel better about what followed.

A sacrifice.

I'd been kind of expecting that, in my childish way. Something given for something given. Even the hoary Old Testament God I was familiar with operated like this.

Nothing granted without payment.

I expected blood. Maybe I'd lose a finger or two.

Not that. Lord, not that.

Stand, Hiram. Stand before me.

Hi whimpered, but I drew him gently to his feet.

Your brother wishes for a drop or two of your true-given talent.

Hi turned to me, shivering.

I think, dear God, I think right then is when he realized there was no secret cache of Indian arrowheads for him out here.

I think he realized there was only bad.

"Len?" he asked again, and the sound of his quavering voice against the hissing mist of that split broke my heart.

Do you understand?

"Len, no," he said, starting to cry.

I almost ran then, ran and left him to the beast. But the sight of him standing in his underdrawers, streaked with mud, holding the knife and crying piteously kept my feet still.

You will have to come with me, Hiram. And your talent stays here with your brother.

Hi turned to me with tears in his eyes.

"Why?"

"Because I can't do the things you can!" I blurted, anger clouding my vision again. "Because it ain't fair. What you got that I don't. It ain't fair pa wails on me and not you. None of it's fair. I want to be able to stand there on stage and not feel invisible, not feel guilt and panic because I can't keep up with you. I'm tired of it, Hi. Sick to death."

"I'm sorry, Len. I am. But I can't help it."

"Yes, right here, right now, you can help it, Hi. You can help me."

"Then, fine," he said, passing the long knife to me. "Fine. Take it. Take all of it and be done. You think I'm not tired, too, Len? Really? I'm just as tired as you. Of people staring at me like I was a freak. Of people comparing you and me. Of pa whipping on you, me not able to do nothing. Of making money but having it all taken by pa to drink it up rather than buy momma or granny something nice.

"I'm tired, too, Len. I guess as you should just take care of both of us now. Put us out of our misery."

I heard his words, but they didn't really make it through the pall of my anger.

I snatched the knife from his hand, hefted it.

Sacrifice, the thing repeated.

I swung the knife, the keenly sharpened blade so thin at its tip I couldn't see it whickering through the air between me and my brother.

He didn't cry out, just looked at his stomach. A thin red line appeared, then widened. A rivulet of blood rushed down his stomach and soaked into his drawers. The line split, like the fissure in the air, and the dark, glistening coils of his intestines bubbled out.

"Len," he said, then fell to his knees, his hands scrabbling at his guts, trying to keep them from spilling out completely.

As Hi knelt there with his guts in his hands, tears streaming down his cheeks, bleeding onto the damp forest floor, the creature hummed to itself, thrummed its strange tune into the already densely packed air.

What'd I feel then?

Kinda strange energy flowing through me? A transfer of talent between me and my brother?

I felt nothing.

Nothing at all.

I'm shamed to say I don't just mean I felt nothing like a completion of my bargain with that creature.

I mean I felt nothing about my own little brother kneeling there, dying right before me.

All I could think at the time was becoming a better musician, a better banjo player or fiddler or whatever kind of player I could bleed out of Hi. I could take part of that into me and be the success I knew I could be, what my pa wanted me to be, tried to beat into me.

The thing's humming continued, and it was like a great chorus of voices—pained, weeping voices—all harmonized on some chord of lamentation that made my teeth jiggle in my head, my eyeballs pulse.

The god's arms slithered out like snakes to clasp Hi, enfold him gently, lift his limp and spent body from the ground. It bore him close, snuggled Hi next to its gross and bloated form like a sleeping infant.

It is done, Len. It is done.

"I don't feel any different," I said, my mouth dry and gummy.

Be that as it may, the bargain is complete.

"What now?"

Go.

"What about Hi? Is he…is he…?"

He is. But my world is different. I will take him there, and he will rise again to play our music. How my brethren will dance and sing.

Then it hit me. Not so much the exact nature of what I done, but close enough for it to smack me right in the face.

"But Hi… What'll I do without him? What'll I tell momma?"

What you will. It is nothing to me.

"No, wait," I said, rushing forward, tripping in the muck of its fluids and those of my brother.

It had already begun to pull itself back, retreating into the fissure. The purple light spat and hissed, and the mists squelched around its bulk as it wriggled away.

As I clawed my way to my feet, the split sealed, the violet light snapped off, and the stinking mist dissipated. It left me standing in my dirty drawers, spattered with mud and purple slime and blood, stunned as a caught fish.

I stumbled away, back through the woods.

I was at the cow pasture before the tears hit.

When I got home, my noisy return woke everyone.

What a sight greeted them, I chuckled, though none of it's funny.

There, a son covered in filth of all kinds, streaked with blood, blubbering so hard it took three blows from my pa's fists to bring me to my senses.

And nowhere to be found…nowhere at all…the other son.

IV.

There was silence in the room when Lenus finished his story.

Asa nearly dropped the half-empty second bottle,

"What happened?"

Len stirred, feeling the alcohol strongly now.

"Oh, there was quite a ruckus. I got a thorough, life-changing beating from my pa. Momma, granny, they all let it happen. And I did, too. I deserved it, didn't I? I mean, they didn't know, all they wanted was to know what had happened, where Hi was. But I couldn't say. I was truly stunned, and my mouth, my brain just wouldn't accept what had happened, couldn't make the words come out to tell anyone.

"I wasn't protecting myself, understand, leastways not right then. Had I been able to speak at that point, I'd ratted myself out to them. Told them what I'd seen…what I'd done. But my brain was taxed. I simply laid there on the floor as that man, that miserable pissant of a man, beat the ever-loving shit out of me."

Asa set the bottle down, and Lenus could see his hands shaking.

"What then? I mean, they go looking for him, for Hi?"

"Oh, sure. In the morning, my pa walked to a few nearby houses, got a group of men together to go out into the woods and find him. But all they found was the blood he'd spilled there in the holler. The purple slime staining my drawers. I reckon—because they never mentioned again what had happened, where Hi had gotten off to—they figured it out, some of it anyway. Became part of the gossip other families whispered about evenings on their own porches.

"After, well, things were never the same. Pa basically left me to my own, never laid a hand on me again. Momma retreated into herself. Granny passed quiet like about six months later."

"And you? Did you get what you wanted? Was it worth it?"

"Me? Well, I ran off after granny died. I was fourteen then, feeling my oats, unwilling to let my pa benefit from what I'd bargained for. Struck out on my own, eventually found a band to hang with. And the rest, as they say, is history.

"Did I get what I wanted? Nope, and that's a hard answer to give, considering what I just told ya. But nope. I practiced hard, gave myself blisters on my fingers and bled onto the strings. Most nights I collapsed after playing and practicing, tired to the bone. The hard truth is I made myself who I am through hard work. Everything that happened out there in the woods, what I done…worthless. Meant nothing. Hi died for nothing. I could've practiced harder, could've been the skilled player Hi was if I'd just tried harder. My pa'd been right all along. Don't that just ice up your heart? Does mine."

Lenus lifted the bottle, took one last draw, set it onto the table near his bed.

"Was it worth it? Hell, no, kid. Is killing your brother, is killing anyone, ever worth it?"

Asa sighed. "I got nothing, man. Nothing. That story just… Think I better get off to bed. Gotta get up and check at the enlistment office tomorrow."

He stood slowly, weaved over to the door.

"Not sure I really needed to hear all that, Len."

Lenus nodded. "I understand, and I'm sorry, kid. Truly I am. But somebody had to. Popping that blister's been a long time coming, and you just happened to be here."

Asa said nothing, left the room, closing the door softly behind him.

Lenus listened to his footfalls down the quiet hallway, then fell back onto his bed, and was asleep within moments.

Len woke the next morning feeling better than he had any right to. He stretched in bed like a teenager, felt the light falling through the open window warm his legs. He sat up, dangled his feet off the bed.

On the floor was an empty bottle of Jack and a mostly empty bottle of Jack. Two bottles, two men. The odds seemed about right to him.

He padded out of the bedroom, to the bathroom. There, he peed, washed his hands, swished water around his mouth, spat it out. He dabbed more of the water to slick back his few hairs, then stared at himself in the mirror.

His eyes were bloodshot, and his skin looked as pocked and sallow as a supermarket chicken. But he felt good, despite what he saw. He felt great, in fact.

He stopped at Asa's door, thought about knocking, but could hear the young man's amazing snores coming from the room. He'd already missed whatever appointment he had with the enlistment officer, so best just to let him sleep it off.

Then, he sighed, because he knew this was it.

He was done.

Well, not just yet…

There was still one thing left to do.

He drifted back down the hallway to his room, where he stood before the mirror, looked at himself.

He emptied his pockets, putting it all on the sink. His wallet, the room key, a wad of cash he produced from his jacket. He twisted the ring he wore—an ostentatious lump of gold he'd won in a poker game from some rolling-in-the-dough Country star, he couldn't remember who just then—set it atop his wallet.

Taking his jacket and shoes off, he placed them in the suitcase. So much lighter now, without the bottles of hooch and the gun, the latter still slumbering under the pillow on his bed.

Seated on the bed, he slid his hand beneath the pillow, pulled out the gun. It gleamed in the afternoon sunlight of the room, all blacks and blues. He slid out the cylinder, checked it was still fully loaded.

He sat holding it, presently came to weeping.

Not for the fear of what he was going to do, not even, really, for what he'd already done.

No, he wept at the thought he might be allowed, by this god or that, to see his brother one last time. To apologize. Mayhap to play a tune or two with him, show him how far he'd come since…since…

Well, since offering him to that woodland god.

He lifted the gun, pulled back the hammer.

There was a knock at the door, then it opened.

"Len, wow, what a night. My head's still…Fuck, man!" he shouted. "What're you doing?"

Asa rushed into the room, skidded to a stop when Lenus waved the gun in the air.

"Shit, kid, why didn't you stay asleep for ten more minutes? My stuff is there on the sink. Take it all. And the banjo, if you're inclined. Put it to good use. If you still want to enlist, good luck, kid. Keep your head down.

"And try not to kill too many people."

Without another word, Lenus put the gun into his mouth and pulled the trigger.

A flat *crack!* reverberated off the walls, made Asa flinch.

Blood and gore sprayed the wall and window behind Lenus, and he fell back across the bed, the gun clattering to the floor.

Asa heard another sound, as grating as a choir of saws. The reverberation filled the room, becoming a keening wail cutting every nerve ending in his body.

He clapped his hands over his ears, but it penetrated his skull.

His teeth chattered, and he bit his tongue.

As the taste of blood flooded his mouth, something happened to the air above the bed where Lenus lay. It seemed to swirl in on itself, coagulating like spoiled milk. There was a flash of deep, purple light, and the air split in two, leaving a vertical slash hanging in the space above the bed.

As Asa watched, a clutch of purple-black tendrils pulled the sides of this apart, reached through and lifted Lenus' body gently, so gently from the bed. It held him aloft, his feet scraping the floor, blood pouring from the back of his head.

Before Asa could react, the arms pulled on opposite sides of the corpse, stretched him out, his head lolling limp as a boned fish.

There was a horrible, fleshy tearing sound, and the arms pulled Lenus apart, literally ripped him in half. Instead of the explosion of blood Asa expected, what came was a gush of purple ichor, thick and viscous as the air itself.

And, to Asa's surprise and shock, something else.

A boy.

A boy of about ten, clad only in white underwear, covered in purple goo.

The boy stared back at Asa, apparently as stunned as he was.

Asa tried to form words, but nothing came.

The tentacles withdrew into the split, taking the limp, lifeless halves of Lenus with them, as casually as they might a torn shirt. Before the cleft closed, dozens more arms emerged, each rooting like blind pigs, sniffing out every drop and spatter of Lenus' blood and lapping it up, from the bed, the walls, the window glass.

The purple stains hissed and disappeared into a foul-smelling mist, the cleft snapped closed. There was another detonation of light, then the air was clear again.

Asa stumbled forward, fell to his knees. Aside from the lingering ringing in his ears and the boy, the room was clear. Clean, really. Devoid of blood or purple goo, even of the gun Lenus had used to kill himself.

Crawling toward the trembling boy, Asa took him by the shoulders. He expected to see purple tendrils in the brown corona of his eyes.

But brown eyes, just brown eyes stared back at him, terrified.

"Hi? Hiram?" Asa asked.

The boy nodded, collapsed into his arms, sobbing.

Asa held him tight.

V.

Dan blinked, took a gulp of beer.

"Then what?" he asked, his eyes narrowed into slits.

"He was only wearing his underwear, and they was filthy. Covered in mud and whatnot. So, I took him down the hall, careful not to let anyone see us."

"Why not?"

"Jesus, Dan," Asia said. "Really? How'd you think it'd look, an older black dude creeping around with a white boy in his underpants?"

"Oh," Dan said.

"Yeah. Oh," Asia agreed. "Anyway, tried to get away from him while he took a bath, but he started to cry every time I made to leave. Had to help him get cleaned up. And then what to wear? And then…and then. And then how could I get myself outta that?"

"Well, you obviously didn't leave him."

"What could I do? From looking at him, he was still only eleven or so, not any older than Len said he was when the thing took him. How could I leave him?"

Instead, Asia explained how he put him in Lenus' room, told him to get in bed and not move.

"I ducked out to grab clothes for the kid," Asia said, swirling the beer left in his can. "Won't lie, though, every step I took, my brain screamed at me to leave, to head home. Forget about the kid, forget about Memphis, forget about the army. Just leave."

"But..."

"I took Lenus' money, which was a helluva lot, and bought the kid a couple pairs of jeans, a few shirts, undershirts, underwear, socks, shoes. A duffle bag to hold 'em. Carted it all back to the hotel, where he dressed.

"I figured he was hungry. I wasn't really feeling it, but forty-odd years stuck where he'd been, doing whatever he'd been doing must have made the kid hungry. I took him down the street to the luncheonette, filled him with food. Surprised myself with how much I ate, too. Almost no talking, from either of us. I guess as we were both stunned off our asses."

"No one think it was strange, seeing you together out in public?"

White people, Asia mused. They just have no idea.

"Back then? Nah, most people probably thought I worked for the family, out showing the young master around," he drawled, sarcasm even Dan picked up on. "No one cared or blinked. I needed that, because what I planned to do, watching Hi slurp down a second malted milk, cram French fries into his face as fast as he could, was crazy, and I knew it.

"I planned to take him home, to my momma, tell her this shit-crazy story, the whole thing, and see what she said. I was barely twenty at the time, what did I know? I needed someone to tell me what to do.

"We went back to the hotel, grabbed our stuff and the rest of Lenus', high-tailed it outta there. Lenus had already covered the rooms for the week, so I didn't stop at the front desk. We walked as fast as was seemly down to the Greyhound station, bought two tickets to Tunica, left that night."

Asia looked to the kids. Hi was helping them up the slide, riding down with him.

"And your mom?"

"Well, she was shocked as shit to see me, for sure. She barely had time to get over that when Hi peeked out from behind me. Liked to knock her over with a feather, as she was fond of saying…and probably did, though I don't remember anymore. Well, she heard my crazy story and didn't blink or say I was nuts or lying or whatnot. Eying Hi up and down, she said just three words.

"We're keeping him."

"Now, momma, this ain't no alley cat or abandoned dog we're talking about," I told her, suddenly afraid of bringing him here, what that might mean to all of us. "This here's a white boy."

By that time, my sisters had woken up, eyes bugging at this white boy sitting snug up again their momma, crying. Momma wiping his tears away and gently urging him to shush.

"Weren't all his kin dead? Where'd he go, who'd take him in? No, the good Lord said suffer the little children, and that, by God, is what we were gonna do. He'll live with us. None of the neighbors'll care, though it might raise eyebrows. And the whites? Most won't care because they don't pay us any mind. The ones who do'll just assume Hi has enough negro blood to make him negro in their eyes, his white appearance notwithstanding," she said.

"So, momma figures everyone'd leave us alone. You know what? They did. No one asked a single question, not even when we had to go and register him for school. Most probably figured it was some family shame on our part and let it go."

"You went back, enlisted, right?" Dan asked, draining the last of his beer. He'd stopped even pretending to keep up with Asia.

"Yeah, that was momma, too. She told me to just go on with my plans, she'd see to Hi until I got back. And she told me I damn well better come back, especially leaving her here with a white boy while I was away. So, I stayed a day or so, saw to Hi getting settled. Gave momma the wad of cash and Lenus' stuff—the suitcase with a few clothes, his hat and wallet, the banjo. Told her Hi might want those when he was older.

"I left with enough money to buy my bus ticket to Memphis, pay for a hotel and food if the good Corporal wanted to yank my black ass around more. But I didn't need it. I was inducted that very day, sent on another bus to basic training, and in eight weeks, I was wading through shit water in the jungles of Nam. So fast it made my head spin."

"Your momma raised Hi while you was overseas?" Dan asked.

"Yeah, when I got back, I got settled, found an apartment and got a job," Asia said, knocking a cigarette out, lighting up. "Hi wanted to come with me, live with me. So, I took him. Thought it were only right, ya know? Leaving him with my momma for years. Besides I was his only real link to Lenus."

Dan frowned, obviously chewing on a question.

"Go ahead and ask," Asia said, breathing out a cloud of smoke.

"Well, I mean, that was a helluva story, Asia. Helluva story," Dan said. "But does he remember what his brother done? Does he remember any of it?"

Asia drew deep on the cigarette, held the smoke in, blew it out.

"He remembers a little, not much. About his brother taking him into the woods, the strange monster he'd seen there. But, no, he don't remember his brother hurting him…murdering him. He does remember something of the time he spent with that creature, though fading away with every year."

"He does?"

"Yeah, I don't ask anymore, but when I have, he'd get this faraway look in his eyes, say, 'I played music underwater. The water was purple and green, and it was there. Others, too. Giants. Dancers with many legs.' That's all he could remember. Playing music and lots of many-legged dancers. I stopped asking a few years back, seein' as how I didn't really want an answer anyway. Don't really want him to remember. I figure it's a blessing."

Asia crushed out the cigarette.

The summer sun was sinking, and the cicadas were buzzing furiously. The barbecue fires were banked, and the aunts and older cousins were packing the leftovers, carrying sleeping toddlers to cars. Hi hefted his cousin Darnell, the boy's black-haired head nestled in the crook of Hi's blonde neck.

"After, well, I met Henrietta. Had to tell her about Hi. Course she didn't believe at first, thought we were just all pulling her leg, not wanting to tell her about the honky in the family tree. She eventually believed. Now she's as much Hi's momma as my momma was. As his real momma was."

"Guess that makes you his daddy," Dan said, smiling an unsettled smile, at best.

"Yeah, it does. Never really thought I'd be a father, specially not to a white boy," he said, stretching. "But that's about it. The whole story, so's you know."

"You seem pretty laid back about the whole thing. Not Hi, I mean what Lenus told you, what he'd done. What happened after. Is it the beer or are you really calm about it all?"

Asia stood, picking beer cans from the ground, lining the empties on the table. He stared after Hi, who turned and waved at his father, smiling a real smile there in the dusk. Hen stood near him, kissed his cheek as he climbed into the car.

Then, she motioned for Asia to join them.

Time to go home, she mouthed, then blew him a kiss, too.

"Calm? About Hi? Yeah, he's a good kid. Great kid," he said, sighing and waving back to Hi and his wife. "I keep thinking of what Lenus said. That one little thing buried in everything else he told me."

"What's that?" Dan asked, standing and stretching, too.

"I was over in Nam for a couple years. Killed a bunch of people, that's a fact. A lot," Asia said.

"And?" Dan said.

"Lenus said *Is killing anyone, ever worth it?* I gotta admit, through all of what he told me—the creature in the woods, killing his brother, what happened when Lenus shot himself. That's what sticks with me. That's what keeps me up at nights, what wakes me like an electric shock, sweating and gasping in my bed. What brings me to tears so bad at two a.m., I wake Hen, and she just holds me in her arms, rocking me while I sob."

"Why that, of all of it, Asia?"

"Because I see 'em, Dan. When I wake up. In the corner of my room, huddled there. Old men and young boys in their black uniforms, you know the ones? They look like ghosts in pajamas. I can smell the dank water, the mildew rot. I can hear their whispers."

He turned to Dan, smiled. Was it real?

"All those people I killed over there, men and boys. All gathered there in my bedroom waiting…waiting."

"Waiting for what?"

Time to come home.

"For me. To release them. Just like old Len. One thing holds me back, though. Just one thing."

Dan said nothing, waited for Asia's answer.

"What Len did there in that hotel room? Was that a mercy or a curse? An atonement? I just don't know. Expect I might never know if I learned anything from him. But Hi? I learn from him every day. He's teaching me some licks on the banjo."

THE END

FIN DE SIÈCLE

I. A Slumbering Eye, 1914

"This weather is an acquired taste, n'est ce pas?"

The grey sea churned under a grey sky as the massive *Carpathia* passed, throwing spumes as it cleaved through the water, leaving a sickly, colorless foam in its wake. The ship was on its way to Cherbourg, on the northern coast of France. From there, it would be just a short jaunt to Lyons-la-Forêt, just east of Rouen.

Orin hadn't noticed the questioner approach as he stood at the railing, but now he turned his attention to him. He was non-descript of feature, a short, stocky man swaddled in a long, dark wool coat, a scarf wrapped around his neck and a smart, stiff homburg atop his head. His skin was a curious, sallow hue, with undertones of yellow and pale green.

His eyes were dark black, with no delineation between iris and pupil. The effect was unsettling, as if they were widely dilated in constant shock or horror, already disgusted only twelve years into this twentieth century.

"You are Monsieur Orin Vance, come from America to purchase le grand télescope Parisien, oui?" the man asked, but it wasn't a question.

M. de Brau had promised to send his personal phaeton and a driver to collect Orin at the Cunard line docks. Orin had spent some of his considerable fortune securing first-class passage round trip. His money had also reserved a considerable portion of the ship's hold to transport back to the States what he'd come all this way to purchase.

The Great Paris Reflector.

He supposed this man might be that driver, but…already onboard? That made no sense.

"Oui, I am. Are you sent from M. de Brau?"

"Mais non," the man said, shaking his head sadly, either because he was not this person or simply from the mention of Orin's French contact. "I am…how you say…an interested party."

"Might I ask how you came to know my business and what concern it is of yours, sir?" Orin asked, turning fully to the smaller man. He noticed how uncomfortable he was in the cold, damp weather there on deck. He also took note of the man's plump form barely constrained under the folds of the thick, black coat he wore. How its curves seemed to be in all the wrong places, how the flesh seemed to…quiver beneath the material.

"We know, Monsieur Vance," the man. "We know."

Orin was unimpressed by enigmatic talk. He was accustomed to it, deeply inured to it. He'd heard such talk around midnight campfires, within ancient tombs, swaddled in incense, seated with legs folded amongst Hindu fakirs and Himalayan shaman.

His hands clenched at the wood railing on the observation deck. In the distance, barely visible through a thick pall of mist the same color as the sea and the sky, were the bleak, rocky cliffs of Cherbourg. This was what his money had bought him so far, grey seas, grey skies, grey rocks, grey talk.

This man and his bearing reminded him there'd be no Paris on this trip, no carriages down the Champs-Élysées, no night excursions up the Tour Eiffel, no lavish dinners or champagne until dawn or pretty Parisian women (or even, daringly, men). No festive cabaret nor dour Notre Dame. No cafes, no Louvre.

His money (his grandfather's really, from mundane American things like railroads and steel) had bought him plenty in the past. And not in the distant past. Orin Vance was still relatively young, only 32. Moneyed and unmarried, with his parents already in the ground and no siblings to dilute the terrific wealth they'd left him, Orin had traveled the world, ate the world, drank the world, screwed the world.

His money had bought him all that but couldn't prevent him from becoming bored with all that.

These adventures eventually took Orin into darker places, corners of Africa few white men had seen. Mysterious villages in the heights of Asia. Deep in the jungles of South America. Hidden caves in the Antarctic mountains.

He'd learned things from these trips, more than avoiding getting the clap from French chorus girls or uncorking champagne bottles with a sword or hiding money on his person to keep it from the artful thieves and cutpurses out in the Parisian night as he lurched his way through midnight arrondissments drunk on wine and absinthe.

Orin had learned there were deeper truths in the world, if one knew where to look, if one opened his eyes, his mind.

Mostly, though, he'd learned enigmatic talk was just that. Nothing.

Well, *mostly* nothing.

Orin sensed there was something profound, central to the things he'd heard, deeper, darker. Just out of reach, at the edges of the darkness it hid itself in.

Something he craved even more than the tickle of champagne bubbles, the smooth expanse of a cabaret dancer's inner thigh, the flutter of money flying from his fingertips.

Something this…*man*…and his kind were intent on thwarting.

What amused Orin more right now, though, about his new friend was he had bothered to adopt a French accent. It was a detail that struck him as strange, almost endearing.

"All right," he said. "So, you know. What is it, sir, you want?"

The man fixed him with a stern and penetrating gaze.

"Telescopes are wondrous devices, oui? Capable of showing so much, revealing, so much. Like opening a door. Do you take my meaning?"

"Not precisely."

Orin knew exactly what the man was saying, and his words made the chill, damp air out here on the deck all the more biting.

The man's mouth opened, his lips retracting into a smile. Orin was not surprised to see his teeth were tiny, almost as if they'd been filed down to pegs. And there was row upon row of them, arrayed like tin soldiers, one after the other, disappearing into the dark of the man's gullet.

Orin had seen smiles like this before, too.

"Some doors, Monsieur Vance, should remain closed. Closed doors are good for separating what is in one room from what is in another. *Things* in one room from *things* in another. Some things were not meant to mix."

"Wouldn't you agree locked doors simply taunt us into opening them, discovering what is behind? To learn. To *know*, as you just said."

"If the universe is a house, Monsieur Vance, continuing this delightful simile," said the plump little man. "One doesn't simply go to bed at night and leave the doors open to the outside, does one? There are things outside that need to stay outside. Irritating insects. Animals. Les criminels. Others with…nefarious intent. Doors, then, are useful things, wouldn't you say? Otherwise, why not just live on the lawn, non?"

"It's a metaphor," Orin said.

"Pardon?"

"You and your locked doors," Orin hissed, leaning into the man and smelling the smell of *them*, the subterranean reek of earth and sour milk this thing's kind exuded. "You can't prevent us from getting to know our neighbors, you know."

The man's smile slid away, and his face became sad, even wistful.

"Your neighbors aren't interested in you, monsieur," the man said. "They *are* interested in your house, though. Try to remember."

Shaking his head, he turned, slowly walked away.

Orin watched the odd little man waddle down the promenade and out of sight, then returned to the railing. Several stories beneath him, the grey sea churned.

Down the riveted side of the *Carpathia*, something caught his eye.

Up from the waterline, slithering past portholes in the black steel plates, was a congealed line of greyish jelly. It was thick and ropey, like mucus or a snail's trail, and it meandered from beneath the water all the way up to the observation deck just a few yards from where he stood.

Orin was not surprised to see it.

Looking out past the bow of the ship, he saw Cherbourg loomed.

Shivering just a bit at the damp cold, he made his way below to his cabin to ensure his things were packed and ready to go.

Two stewards from the *Carpathia* wheeled his cases past the crowd of other passengers, down the gangway and onto the docks. The weather on land wasn't much different than it had been at sea. Damp, misty, and with an oppressive, dank chill that sank through to the bone.

An automobile was idling a few yards away, long and powerful looking. A stiff, solid chauffeur stood beside the car, dressed in a grey frock coat and looking like nothing so much as the local weather personified.

Orin approached, the two stewards following with his cases on a handcart.

"Monsieur Vance," the man stated, barely turning his head to acknowledge Orin.

"Oui. Êtes-vous envoyé de Monsieur de Brau?" Orin said.

"Yes. I speak English, sir."

"Oh, well, splendid. Can we fit my cases into the auto?"

"No. A cart comes to collect your things. I will drive you to Monsieur de Brau's estate. If you will allow me."

The stolid man indicated the phaeton's passenger entrance, opened the door for Orin. Inside, completely isolated from the driver's cockpit, was a small chamber, sized for no more than two people. Plushly appointed in deep blue velvet, with touches of wood and leather. Orin had a few automobiles back in the States, none as opulent and plush as this.

"There are refreshments available in the side console should you wish. It will require about an hour to gain the estate. Should you need anything, there is an ivory button on the console to alert me. I trust, sir, you will be comfortable."

Orin gave instructions to the stewards as to the disposition of his things, tipped them, then climbed into the waiting phaeton. The chauffeur closed the door as Orin settled into the immensely comfortable seat. To his side, a wooden console held several cut crystal glasses, a decanter of what looked to be brandy or Armagnac and one uncorked bottle of a 1900 Chateau Margaux topped with a crystal stopper.

Orin's stomach rumbled. He hoped his host had arranged dinner for him, because it looked like he expected him to get drunk on the journey.

Or perhaps he hoped.

The ride seemed to take a very short amount of time, far shorter than the hour or so the chauffeur had indicated. Outside the phaeton's narrow windows, Orin watched the landscape slip past, rolling hills and deep, shadowed forests of thin, high-limbed trees packed densely together. The enshrouding mist lay over everything like a veil.

The phaeton's ride was remarkably smooth, given the tortured dirt roads, and Orin decided to partake of a glass of wine along the way. As the muted sun descended into the forest, Orin saw the driver had turned off onto another, much narrower road, really two ruts carved into the turf.

By leaning against the vibrating window glass, Orin could see, up ahead, a typical Norman-style chaumière, white-washed cob bright against the dusk, timber-framed windows all in a row. A low-pitched thatch roof with multiple stone chimneys stood out against the lush background of the forest, each with wisps of smoke curling into the condensed sky.

It looked snug and comfortable, an estate befitting a former member of la Chambre des Députés. Or what was of more interest to Orin, a current member of the Société d'Optique.

The phaeton growled to a halt on the crushed stone drive in

front of the house, and Orin replaced the empty wine glass into the console. He heard the chauffeur's door open, his footsteps crunching in the gravel. The driver opened his door, and Orin immediately smelled the damp air that rolled in, redolent of resinous trees and lavender, of rain and rosemary, burning wood from the estate's chimneys.

"Let me show you in to freshen yourself after your journey," the chauffeur said, leading him to the front door. "*Monsieur* de Brau will join you for drinks in La Salle Rouge at six sharp prior to dinner."

He drew the heavy, iron-banded front door open, motioned for Orin to step inside.

"My things?"

"Already settled in your room, sir."

Orin raised an eyebrow but said nothing.

The foyer of the house was dimly lit, a few candles guttering in sconces and a massive candelabra on an octagonal table in the center of the room. An ornate iron cage near the window held two large mynah birds, which squawked and called to the chauffeur as he came into the room and drew the door closed.

"Voici celui qui veut ouvrir la porte," said the one.

"Il ne sait pas que certaines portes sont mieux fermées," said the other.

"Calme, Roland, et toi aussi, Martine," the driver said. "Les oiseaux sauvages!" He clucked at them as he approached the aviary, took a candlestick from the table, and inclined his head toward Orin, indicating he should follow.

Orin walked behind the man down what looked to be the main hallway of the house, lined with paintings and tapestries hard to make out in the low light. They all seemed to echo the same theme: the dark forest outside the house, pressing in from all sides. And within that forest, all manner of beasts with mysterious form and illuminated eyes.

Outside a room on the main floor, the chauffeur stopped. Orin heard the rattling of keys, the click of a lock. The heavy wooden door was opened onto a large chamber, somewhat better lit than the rest of the house. It smelled tantalizingly of sandalwood inside and, of course, the roaring fire that lit much of the room. A writing desk sat before the heavily curtained window. A four-poster bed dominated the room, the thick, dark wood of its posts elaborately carved with sea figures—mermaids and mermen, conch shells and tridents, huge octopi with writhing arms.

Orin saw his cases stacked in the far corner of the room. An equally ornate armoire stood beside the fireplace, its doors slightly open. His clothing already hung inside.

"I will collect you at six and escort you to La Salle Rouge. Until then, relax."

The driver left, closed the door. Orin was bemused he didn't lock the door behind him.

Atop a table near the bed was a porcelain ewer of water in a basin, a cake of strongly scented rosemary soap. Orin stripped out of his traveling clothes, kicked off his boots and washed his hands and face in the basin. When he was finished, he stretched out onto the bed for a few minutes to relax.

The bed was incredibly soft and warm, and Orin lay there for a short time, afraid he might fall asleep. Grudgingly, he rose, went to the armoire, and dressed.

At six precisely, there came a smart series of raps on his door. Orin drew it open and found the chauffeur standing in the corridor holding a three-pronged candelabra, now dressed in the attire of a valet.

"Are you ready, sir?" he asked.

Through the main hallway, past the foyer, he paused outside a set of pocket doors, drew them open. Inside was a snug room, lined with bookcases. Persian rugs covered the floor and two heavy, rolled-arm leather chairs sat before a roaring fireplace, their backs toward the door.

"Monsieur Orin Vance," the chauffeur-cum-butler announced, drawing the doors closed behind them.

From one of the chairs rose a small, thin man in a well-worn Turkish smoking robe at least twenty years out of style. The man was mostly bald, a few wisps of dark hair pasted across the glistening pink dome of his head. His eyes were dark and deeply set, and his mouth was fleshy and saturnine.

He was smoking a cigarette, and he placed this into a huge porcelain ashtray sitting on a small table between the chairs.

"Ah, Monsieur Vance," he said, throwing his arms open wide. "Bienvenue, bienvenue chez moi, mon ami."

"Votre hospitalité me flatte, monsieur," Orin said, taking the man's hand and shaking it firmly. As he feared, it was tight and moist.

"Ahh please, sit, my friend," Monsieur de Brau said, indicating the seat next to his. "My English is…not…so very good. I am pleased you speak Français."

"My French is a bit rudimentary, but I'm sure we won't have any problem communicating," Orin said. As he sat, the butler appeared, holding a glass of red wine for him.

"Superbe!" de Brau said, taking a glass himself. "Je vous appellerai quand nous serons prêts pour le dîner, Hector."

"Oui, mon seigneur."

Behind him, Orin heard the pocket doors close.

"Ahh, monsieur!" de Brau said as he settled into his chair. "It is so very kind of you to visit an old man in his…how you say… dotage?"

Orin sipped at his wine, laughed. The wine was good, not great, but good. Probably one of the better bottles the old man still had left in his cellar.

"No, not at all. It is my pleasure. C'est mon plaisir."

De Brau took a swig of wine. "I must tell you, monsieur, in all honesty. I am…relieved to be rid of the thing. Je suis très soulagé. Things here on the continent are shifting, non? Perilous times. Tensions are high. Germany, Austria. Who knows what will happen in the days and months ahead? You are taking this back to your county at just the right time, I fear. I hope this does not…errr… drive down the price we have agreed on."

"Not at all, *monsieur*. In fact, I hope you don't find me impertinent, but I took the liberty while I was still aboard the *Carpathia* to wire the draft to your account at the *Banque deFrance*."

De Brau's bushy eyebrows rose. "Incroyable," he whispered, licking his lips. "The full amount?"

"Mais, non, monsieur," Orin said, taking another sip of the red. "Pas tout de suite."

The Frenchman's fleshy mouth pursed; his eyebrows lowered.

"Right now, half. Tomorrow, after I clarify a few things, the other half."

"Ahh, c'est tout bon," he nodded, mentally figuring just how many zeroes his depleted bank account now held. Gradually, his good humor returned.

"So, what is it you would like to know about le grand télescope Parisien?"

"Exactly how much of the original apparatus is my million francs buying me?"

"Tout. Tout cela."

"The entire thing?" Orin said, clutching the padded arms of his chair. "I'd thought most of the tube and mechanical parts were scrapped. The siderostat is in the Paris Observatory."

"C'est une copie. I have the original parts. All of them."

"How is that possible?"

"Ahh monsieur. Once I was somebody. But now...I fear my name wouldn't get you a table at the lowliest café in Paris. Ces jours-ci, je ne suis personne."

Orin was smart enough to know what de Brau meant was he no longer had the *money* to be important. Until today, that is...or tomorrow to be more precise.

De Brau saw Orin's confused look, poured another glass of wine for both of them from the carafe sitting on the table.

"Despret and Mantois each cast multiple mirrors and lenses. It took Gautier's firm several tries to grind and polish the optics successfully. Once the firm went bankrupt, it was easy to secure the entire assemblage. What I mean is there were so many duplicate parts, it was easy to secure the originals in all the confusion after the 1900 Exposition Universelle was over."

Orin still gripped the sides of his chair.

"Ahh, c'est comme je le pensais. You know the meaning of having the original instrument, eh, monsieur?"

Orin stared into the fire, nodded absently. He hadn't dared to think what he was buying was actually all the original parts of the telescope.

He instantly knew de Brau was a fool. He had no idea, none at all, how much Orin would have been willing to pay if he'd known all the parts were original. The old fool's bank account could have had twice or even triple the amount Orin was prepared to pay him.

This saved Orin a lot of legwork and, ultimately, a lot of money.

But Orin stared into the fire and betrayed none of this.

"Mais oui. Je comprends totalement."

"Were you able to see it? At the Palais de l'Optique? *Non*? It was… magnifique. Two hundred feet long. Fifty tons of steel pipe. The mirror's pivoting fork mount floated in sixty liters of pure mercury to smooth its motion. Flammarion himself came to use it. Antoniadi, too.

"Deloncle was an imbecilé. Fifty million people came to see it before he realized what it was…what it was capable of. Then, they took it down, tore it apart."

Here he sighed again, heavily, his brocade-robed shoulders rising, then slumping sharply.

"Fin de Siècle. End of the century. They thought… Well… Ce qu'ils pensaient être faux. That term, fin de siècle…do you take the meaning, sir? The real meaning?"

Orin frowned. "I'm not sure what you mean."

"Siècle has another, older meaning…deeper. Century, oui. But its older meaning is *cycle*. So, fin de siècle means *end of the cycle*. At least that's what they thought. And this telescope would usher it in. But as I said…Ils avaient tord."

"No, I never saw it in person," Orin said, answering his original question. "I was too young. I was only about twenty, still in university in the States. And not very interested in such things unfortunately." De Brau stirred in his chair. "But now?"

"Now," said Orin, feeling the warmth of the wine in his stomach, the fireplace at his feet. "Well, now, yes. Oui. Very much interested."

For a long while, neither man spoke. The only sounds in the room were the ticking of some distant clock, the crackling of the fire in the hearth. De Brau's wrinkled fingers tapped on his wine glass.

"Vous comprenez que c'est une porte, n'est-ce pas?" he whispered, almost to himself.

"Yes, I understand it's a door."

De Brau considered this. "And you understand the simple act of *seeing* influences the universe. Observation makes things so. It is…a spooky trait of physics that this is."

"I've learned this, oui," Orin said.

"Very well," de Brau said, lifting his glass and draining it once again. "It is all crated and no doubt already loaded into the *Carpathia* for your return to the United States."

With a hand that shook slightly, de Brau lifted a small silver bell near his chair, shook it. It rang so softly Orin was surprised Hector could hear it from wherever he was. But he instantly appeared, drawing the pocket doors open.

"Oui, mon seigneur?"

"Nous allons prendre dîner maintenant, Hector."

"Veuillez me suivre," de Brau said to Orin.

"One question, Monsieur de Brau, if you will."

The older man stopped, turned to his American guest.

"Did you ever use it?" Orin asked. "Pour son vrai usage?"

The old man's bushy eyebrows shot up at this question, then gathered like storm clouds over his eyes.

"I cannot… Je ne parlerai jamais de ça. Je suis désolé, monsieur."

Orin, still reeling from the shock of now actually owning all of the original pieces of the telescope, followed Hector and *Monsieur* de Brau into the dining room.

Dinner was a quiet affair, the two men at a table that could seat at least ten. Like the house itself and the wine he served, the silverware, the porcelain dinnerware all spoke of a family that had seen better days.

Orin wondered what had beset them. French politics were notoriously messy, and de Brau had served many years in la Chambre des Députés. But he was an old man, nearing the end of his life. Unmarried, with no direct heirs. A fortune, too, that had seen better days.

The second course were ortolans roasted whole on skewers served on slices of sturdy bread to soak in the juices.

"I think we can dispense with le théâtre des serviettes over the head, eh? With everything else we've discussed, I don't worry God cares how we eat these birds."

With that benediction, they began to eat. After a moment, though, de Brau stopped eating, placed his fork and knife beside his plate and stared at Orin for several seconds.

Orin, wrestling with the tiny, charred bird on the skewer, likewise stopped eating.

"Un problème, monsieur?" he asked.

"Where will you put it?"

Orin chewed his prickly mouthful of cooked songbird before answering.

"Underground," he said. "Where we can entomb anything that isn't…safe."

De Brau blinked at this answer, nodded, then went back to his plate.

The rest of the dinner continued in silence.

The next morning, Orin rose, made his morning toilet, then was led to a smaller orangery at the back of the house to eat breakfast alone. A note on his plate, in de Brau's spikey, hurried hand, explained he was called away on urgent business. Most probably a hasty visit to his bank, Orin guessed. He bade Orin stay as long as he liked. Hector would return him to the Cunard docks whenever he wished.

Orin dined on coddled eggs and beef kidneys with rusks and butter, raspberry jam and white coffee. He lingered at the table, staring through the orangery's glass walls into a manicured garden gone to seed. He suspected, in addition to driving and valeting, Hector also served as cook and gardener.

Perhaps that would change with monsieur's new influx of cash.

Hector came to collect him at around ten a.m., asked to meet in the front drive when he was ready to leave.

Orin went back to his room, noted his cases were already packed and ready. He splashed cold water from the ewer onto his face, dried with a hand towel, then made his way back to the front of the house.

In the foyer, he passed the aviary, which alerted the birds to his presence.

"Il faut se méfier à une porte à l'inconnu," croaked the bird he thought was Roland.

The other bird, Martine, fixed Orin with its sparkling, gimlet eyes.

"Les yeux des morts ne devraient jamais être ouverts."

Orin frowned at them, left the estate of Monsieur de Brau.

II. A Lidded Threshold, 1921

Six hundred feet beneath the rolling Missouri hills, it was always chilly. The air was heavy, damp, smelled minerally, felt gritty. And the darkness, when the lamps expired, was profound.

Orin thought of this as his driver turned the car onto the winding gravel road leading to the coal mine. A sign, listing on its two splintered wooden supports, announced *Farsight Mine Owned and Operated by Vance Consolidated. No Trespassing. No Soliciting.*

The car, a silver-grey Duesenberg Model J, turned heads as it passed. In an area of the country where few had seen cars at all, this might as well have been a spaceship. That wasn't to say the citizens of Corridon, the closest town, weren't familiar with Orin's car. He'd owned the mine for nearly twenty years now and had been visiting regularly for almost a decade.

Ever since he'd installed the telescope.

Not many at the mine or in Corridon knew about that, though.

Le grand télescope Parisien, purchased almost a decade ago, crated and shipped across the Atlantic, unloaded onto railcars and sent halfway across the United States. Unloaded and assembled underground in a coal mine in Missouri.

Who'd have even thought it possible?

It had taken nine years, but Orin learned recently they knew he'd accomplished this feat, knew roughly where the telescope was located.

Knew what he was attempting to do with it.

And they were none too happy about that knowledge.

The driver pulled the Duesenberg into a garage at the end of side road that veered away from the main office of the mine. A nondescript cinderblock structure, hidden by the trees, just big enough to accommodate the length of the car. Attached to the garage was a small office, again plain and unassuming. Just a desk, a single-file cabinet and three uncomfortable-looking chairs.

A small vestibule off this unremarkable office housed a tightly spiraled iron staircase twirling down through solid rock about twenty feet into a clean, spartan room painted bright white. One wall of the room was lined with wooden lockers and a low wooden bench, much as in the locker room of a gymnasium.

Orin's driver had seated himself at the desk, nodded as Orin entered the room with the staircase. Orin closed the door behind him, stepped slowly down the staircase. In the white room, he removed his suit jacket and donned a plain black robe taken from one of the wooden lockers. The robe was loose and made of black velveteen. It covered his body completely, had a hood attached at the back of the neck, that could be pulled forward over his face.

He kept the hood back, stepped through the only other door, on the opposite side of the room from the staircase. Immediately upon opening this door, there was a *whoosh!* of cool, damp air, the smell of crushed rock and damp earth. The sound of distant machinery clinking and clanging.

A rickety-looking, open-grate elevator car hung over a shaft just big enough to accommodate it. The shaft was unlit, and its darkness seemed to shine out from it, darkening the entire chamber.

Orin stepped into the car, closed and locked the gate, threw the control lever.

The elevator's mechanism groaned into life, the cables twanging like guitar strings.

The car gradually descended.

By the time the lift had brought him to the bottom of the shaft, Orin's eyes had acclimated to the almost total lack of light. The car was lit by one naked incandescent bulb that seemed as trivial as the tail of a firefly against the vastness of the night.

He was accustomed to it. When he traveled to Missouri, he spent much of his time down here, not at the beautiful country estate he'd built. That place seemed darker and colder to him, more of a mausoleum than being down here.

As the car lurched to a stop, the space his miners had carved out below the earth leapt into view. The huge passageways and chambers, the thick, roughhewn columns of dark rock. All of it as black and enigmatic as the robes swirling around him.

The air was dense and cool, closed, as compacted as the rock. Strings of electric lights snaked out in a few directions from the landing, long, loose constellations floating in space. One led to a wooden structure built during the assembly of the telescope almost a decade ago.

Another stretched off down a narrow, low-ceilinged tunnel disappearing into darkness regardless of its attempt at illumination.

Despite the darkness, Orin knew what lay that way.

Le grand télescope Parisien.

Once it had mesmerized crowds, astounded giants of astronomy in France. Now, it was buried here, deep below the earth in a coal mine in Missouri.

Where no telescope could function; where no telescope *should* function.

And currently, despite his best efforts, where no telescope did function.

Orin followed the string of lights to the subterranean office.

The office was almost as dark as the caverns outside. Orin didn't bother knocking. It was his mine, his office, his operation. Besides, Richard knew he was coming today.

Inside, the single room was plushly appointed. Heavy, leather-upholstered chairs and a couch. Thick oriental rugs lay over the floor, and weighty drapes of the same material as the robes Orin wore covered the few windows. There were several Tiffany lamps on a few low tables scattered throughout the room. An ornate iron stove crackled in a corner, providing a soothing warmth.

A row of bookcases covered the far wall. The weathered, cracked spines of antique books lined there gave the place the feeling of a cozy reading room six hundred feet below the Missouri ground.

A single person was seated there, clad in the same dark robes, feet propped before the stove, poring over the pages of an enormous book. The man looked up casually as Orin came in, closed the door behind him.

A beat, and the man abruptly stood, still careful to close the weighty book and set it on the side table.

"Mr. Vance, sir," the man said. "I didn't know it was you. So sorry."

Orin smiled. "I'm not a visiting general. No need for such formalities. And you are…?"

"Jim, sir. Jim Carolton. Mr. Haverly hired me a few weeks ago."

"Ahh," said Orin, gathering his robes and sitting on the side of the couch closest to the stove. "You're the professor translating the material."

"Yes, sir," Carolton replied, taking his seat. "Yes, from the state university in Cape Girardeau. You've got quite the collection of esoteric literature, Mr. Vance. It's a…well, a dream library for a guy like me."

"Me, too," Orin sighed, savoring the heat. "Have you found anything of note yet? Lord knows we haven't in years."

"Well, the relevant texts are in pretty poor shape, as you know," Carolton said, warming to the subject. "Missing pages, water-damage, smeared ink. And then there's the encryptions—easy stuff like Polybius squares and invisible ink, simple substitution ciphers. But it's really complex, algorithmic ciphers and homophonic ciphers, even hieroglyphics and ideograms I've never seen before. The people who wrote this stuff *really* didn't want it getting out."

"Mostly for good reason," Orin said. "Is Richard down here? Out with the scope?"

"Yeah, they tried another ceremony last night."

"And?"

"I wasn't there, but that bottle of Perrier-Jouët is still in the cupboard. So, I'd guess no success."

Orin considered this, then stood. "Nice to meet you, Professor Carolton. Please come by the house tonight about 6:30 for dinner, if you'd like. I would be delighted to speak in more detail about what you've found so far in your research."

"Likewise. 6:30 it is, then."

Pulling the robe's hood over his head, Orin left the office, followed the strand of lights leading to the telescope.

Richard was climbing a ladder near the siderostat, the two-meter mirror cocked at a thirty-degree angle. The polished glass reflected the dim electric lights and nothing more. Behind it, the slim length of the tube lanced into the darkness of the coal mine. More than sixty meters of steel weighing more than twenty-one thousand kilos, which had cost Orin a considerable sum to ship here from France. At the other end, Orin knew, was the eyepiece.

"I met Professor Carolton," Orin said.

"Ahh, good, good," Richard approached Orin, shook his hand. Richard was a bit older, perhaps fifty, with greyish red hair and a beard, sparkling blue eyes. He wore the same black velveteen robe Orin wore.

Slight of build but possessed of a frenetic almost manic energy.

Orin had hired him long ago, brought him from Toronto to manage this insane project.

"I suppose that's not why you asked me down here."

Richard tilted his head. "I think I can make the damn thing work…finally."

Orin nodded. "What was the key?"

"That book you picked up in Tayma was the key. The one supposedly acquired by Benjamin of Tudela. Sort of a secret addendum to his *Sefer ha-Masa'ot*. Gave us insight into how they might have opened portals in Nineveh and Pumbeditha."

Orin considered this. "Have you opened anything?"

Richard snorted, slapped Orin on the back. "Without my patron?" he laughed. "Of course not. You're paying for the band and the hall. You get the first dance."

"Fine then. Good. Good."

"There's a second key we're going to need, something you might have to get your checkbook out for."

"Oh, yay," Orin chuckled. "What's that?"

"Let's talk over dinner. I think Carolton should be in on this, too."

Orin looked into the darkness, the tube above them lancing off into it. How could a telescope buried hundreds of feet below the ground *see* anything?

The short answer: it couldn't.

The longer answer: it wasn't an eye.

It was a door. Just as the mynah bird in the cage at Monsieur de Brau's chateau had squawked at him more than a decade ago.

Il faut se méfier à une porte à l'inconnu

Something about the entire mechanism. Perhaps the steel or the iron or the mirrors, how they were ground. What strange metals went into their casting? Or the sixty liters of mercury the mirror's mount sat in to keep it steady? Perhaps the sheer size of the thing?

Who knew? Orin only knew that, as a telescope, the massive thing had failed, and failed grandly, ruining companies and reputations in its wake. Only a few suspected what the device was good at, and then only in the most hushed of whispers.

There was talk of the old gods, dark spaces between the stars. Colors that bent the mind. Other things, things to disturbing even for whispers.

Above all, one whisper caught Orin's ear,

Une clé d'une porte.

A key to a door.

"At dinner then."

Orin straightened his tie, looked in the oversize mirror in his dressing chamber. His face stared back lined, weary, even to his own gaze. The years, the travel, the expenditures, all of it was weighing on him. He was only forty-one, but he felt like an old man.

He felt like his father, long dead. The source of his wealth. The source of his drive for this hunt. Orin wanted this at least as much for his father as he did for himself.

He had no doubt his parents had been murdered. It had been a particularly hard realization to embrace. His father and his occult dealings, his search for a way *in*. It had consumed him and a great deal of his wealth. That had been his undoing. That's why *they*—whoever *they* actually were—had done it, killed them. They'd had to sink an entire ship to do it, but he knew that was the reason.

An iceberg…how absurd. But it had worked, and his parents'

corpses lay at the bottom of the cold North Atlantic, along with the wreck of that once mighty ship.

Orin had been very careful over the ensuing two decades to keep his own activities as quiet as possible.

But *they* knew. He knew they did.

They were watching him carefully, so carefully, fearful of what he was up to.

Now, with the crown jewel of his efforts safely hundreds of feet under the earth, they'd have to settle for guessing what he was doing.

That wouldn't last, Orin was sure.

In the end, his life was as in danger as his father's had been.

It was just a matter of time.

There was a knock at his door, and Orin stepped away from the mirror.

"Dinner is ready, mon seigneur," said Hector. Orin had brought him over when M. de Brau had passed a decade ago. Now, he served as Orin's personal aide. More than butler or a valet, Hector ran the entire household and assisted Orin in all things, large and small.

Where the years had weathered Orin, they had been remarkably kind to Hector. He looked no different than he had when Orin had first seen him in Cherbourg in 1914. Thin to the point of asceticism, with a calm, detached demeanor Orin had grown to depend on more and more over the years.

"Fine, Hector," he said, allowing the man to straighten his tie, the lapels of his jacket. "Go ahead and serve the brandy, and I'll be down in a second."

"Oui, mon seigneur."

Hector closed the door, and Orin strolled into the sitting room attached to his bed chamber. Bookcases filled with his personal library, a few lounge chairs, a writing desk. And sitting before the window that opened out onto the back lawn, an elaborate wrought iron aviary with two very old mynah birds seated on perches across from each other, watching him with what he knew was restrained amusement.

Hector had brought these two birds with him when he entered Orin's employment.

"Vous voyez comment il s'habille pour le dîner? Si fastidieux, si prim," croaked Roland.

Martine nodded, "La porte ne se soucie pas de la façon dont la personne qui la traverse s'habille."

Orin found the pen he wanted in the drawer of the desk, slipped it into his pocket.

"Chut, vous deux choses anciennes," he said, leaving the room.

When Orin came into the drawing room, he saw Richard and Professor Carolton sipping their brandies, exchanging words in hushed tones. Hector passed a snifter to Orin, drew the pocket doors shut.

"So, gentlemen, what soft voices from yon window breaks?" Orin said.

"Just exchanging ideas about the good Benjamin of Tudela and his secret volume," Richard said. "Coming to an agreement of what he meant, what we need."

"Oh-ho," laughed Orin, sipping his brandy. "I suddenly feel my pocketbook lightening."

"By a substantial amount, I'd guess," said Professor Carolton, rising. Orin waved him back to his seat.

"There are a few glyphs we need to decipher from an ancient Ninevite frieze in a museum in Baghdad. It's about a foot square, written during the Old Assyrian Period. A tablet depicting a worship scene from the Ishtar cult. We think it depicts the portion of the sky associated with opening a portal," Richard said.

"Alright," Orin said, leaning against the bookcase. "How do we get it? Can we get it?"

"We got it," Richard said. "I should say you do, since you paid for it. I had to bribe a museum official and the Iraqi director of antiquities. But it was packed and shipped last week. Should be here next."

"How much?" Orin asked, raising an eyebrow.

"Less than the telescope," Richard said, raising his glass in a toast.

"Well, that's at least a start," he said. "How do we aim a telescope at the sky when it's buried five hundred feet underground?"

"Simple," Professor Carlton said. "Once we identify what the star or cluster or object is, we can ascertain its right ascension and declination, adjust the altitude and azimuth for our location and time, then set the scope for those coordinates just as if it was above ground."

"What then?" Orin asked.

"Then?" Carolton asked.

"Yes, *then*. What happens then?"

"We'll have to wait and see," Richard said.

Hector drew the pocket doors open. "Dinner is served, seigneur, in the salon."

"Gentlemen," Orin motioned. "Squab tonight, Hector? Very well, let's see if we can speculate over dinner and fine wine."

They did speculate, through dinner, after aperitifs, and well past midnight. Orin sent the two away at about 1:30 a.m., walked up the staircase to his chambers. He undid his tie on the way up, tossed it onto the table in his dressing room, removed his shoes and socks.

A soft knock came at the door.

"Will that be all this evening, seigneur?" asked Hector, opening the door just a crack.

"Oui, Hector. Bon nuit."

The door closed, and he heard Hector's footsteps echo down the corridor. He removed the rest of his clothes, dressed in a nightshirt.

Orin entered his bedroom, put the pen back into the drawer of the writing table. One small light on the desk was the only illumination in the room. The air here was close and uncomfortably warm, so he decided to open the windows to hopefully let in a breeze.

He stopped short, though.

There was someone seated in one of the chairs near the window.

The figure, clothed in darkness, moved in the shadows slightly, just enough to register he was there.

"Good evening, Mr. Vance," the man said. He might have been the same man who had confronted him on the deck of the *Carpathia*. To Orin, all of these creatures looked the same.

"What are you doing in my house?"

"Excuse me," the man said. "The smell of your meal…squab was it? Delicious. I just couldn't resist."

Orin glanced behind where he sat, to the table with the aviary. Its ornate door was open, the inside littered with feathers.

"They were a bit old, no? A bit tough. Still," the man said, licking his lips.

"You son of a bitch," Orin whispered. His blood boiled at this intrusion, this death under his own roof.

The two old birds deserved so much better than to die this way.

He reached into the writing desk, brought out the loaded revolver he kept there.

"Tsk, tsk," the creature said, waving its pudgy, sharp finger at Orin. "You kill me, you don't get to hear what I came to say."

"Say it then," Orin said through clenched teeth.

"We know you have it here, le grand télescope Parisien. We know you brought it here, set it up in the mines. We know what you plan to use it for, the mistake you plan on making. We also know you lack one piece, the key to the puzzle, correct?"

"You seem to know so much, so why don't you tell me?"

"Mr. Vance," he said. "We're trying to help you. Can't you see? We're trying to prevent you from opening a door you should really want to keep closed. The Old Ones, they seek a way into this world. Don't offer one up to them."

"Why so concerned with this, with what we're attempting? Why shouldn't we be curious? It's in our nature as humans."

"They're not concerned with your curiosity, Mr. Vance. Your nature. *They* have their own purposes, they do things for their own purposes."

"And those are?"

"Believe me, Mr. Vance," the creature said, chuckling. "You don't want to know."

"But I do."

Orin pulled the trigger, shot the thing in the chest. It slumped in the chair, slid to the floor like melted night. He put one more bullet in it.

"One for Roland," he said, nudging the thing's body with his toe. "One for Martine."

"Killing me won't change things, Mr. Vance," said a wavery, ethereal voice coming from the corpse, but through unmoving lips. "We *will* stop you."

Orin stepped away, put another bullet into the body, just as Hector burst into the room.

"*You* won't."

A week passed. Orin floated through the days with nothing to do. He rattled around in the mansion, browsed books, ate three meals a day served to him at precise intervals by Hector.

Being at home was never Orin's thing. Travelling, searching for obscure texts, obscure relics, obscure people, that was his thing. He'd rather be just about anywhere except at home. It didn't feel right, like being cocooned in a suit two sizes too small. He strolled the grounds, took drives, went into town a few times to poke around the few stores there. They held nothing he was interested in, though he spent money here and there. He did it more out of a sense of obligation, knowing he was recognized, knowing they knew of his wealth. To not spend money with them seemed so manorial, so condescending Orin never even conceived of it.

He piled the parcels into the passenger seat of the car, drove the winding country roads back home. The weather was balmy, and he'd taken the top off his car. The cool wind and the hot sun agreed with him, and he took a longer route home than he'd intended. He knew he'd missed lunch, suspected Hector would have it waiting when he arrived.

When he pulled through the gates, a truck passed him, leaving the front circle. The driver waved as he went by, and Orin waved back absently.

Then he realized what the truck meant.

He sped into the circle, lurched to a stop spraying gravel everywhere.

Hector and another worker hauled a wooden crate through the front door. Orin ran up, helped as best he could.

It wasn't huge, but it was heavy and well-constructed, stamped on almost every surface with shipping instructions, taxes and port fees and cautions to protect what was contained within.

Orin sent the other man off for a crowbar, and they waited impatiently for him to return. When he did, Orin snatched the tool, sent the man to the mine to retrieve Richard.

By the time Richard arrived, breathless and covered in sweat, they'd pried the crate open, lifted the object from the meticulous wrapping and batting the senders had protected it with. It was a chunk of stone, broken from a temple wall or stela, depicting robed men—three on the left, three on the right—stiff bearded, hands upraised toward a grouping of seven stars. Some were carved deep to indicate their brightness, others barely etched into the stone.

From this constellation, twin lines came forth, heavenly emanations. They formed what was clearly a doorway over the heads of these men; a doorway slightly ajar.

The three men stood looking at the piece, knowing what it showed, knowing what it meant.

"Seeing it now, seeing those stars," Richard panted, "I could have done this with a picture."

Orin looked at him. "You're telling me I didn't need to buy this after all?"

Richard shrugged. "I'm sure it'll look nice in your library."

"Well, what is it? What are those stars?" Orin asked.

"The Pleiades. I'd know that cluster anywhere," Richard said. "It's the Pleiades."

To the Persians they were the Parvī, to the Babylonians, they were MUL. The Egyptians called them Ennead, and the Arabs called them Thurayya.

But to the Greeks, they were the Pleiades, seven sisters cast into the heavens as stars to avoid Orion's amorous pursuit. Myths say their names derive from the mother with whom Atlas fathered the daughters, Pleione. Scholars say the name of the cluster came first, and the mother was created after to explain the name. Most think now the name Pleiades comes from the Greek word plein, "to sail," in honor of the cluster's importance to sailors in the Mediterranean, who navigated by them.

They were a well-established navigation aid in the ancient world.

Of course.

Of course.

"Anyone else laughing at the fact we've spent millions of dollars setting up a telescope five hundred feet below ground, and now we're aiming it at a star cluster in the night sky?"

Richard leaned against the cold, black iron siderostat, mopping his brow and laughing.

"We spent millions of dollars?" Orin asked. "*We*?"

"Well, the professor and I helped," Richard said.

"I suppose you did," Orin said. "Do we have time to do this tonight? What time is it, anyway?"

"Just after two in the morning," Professor Carolton said. "It shouldn't matter. There's no specific time that's important for this. If the Assyrians were right, just the correct part of the sky and the ritual are necessary. That's it."

"If they were able to do it without a scope, why did I sail to France and spend a fortune for this?" Orin asked, slapping the solid iron of the siderostat.

"The Assyrians were only able to open a small peephole," Richard said. “You wanted a door. So, you paid for a bigger key. As far as a fortune, well, it’s simple inflation.”

Orin raised his eyebrows, looked down the tunnel where the tube of the scope disappeared into the darkness of the mine.

“Let’s head back to the office, raise a glass before we start in,” he said. The two men followed him to the little building, their way lit by a string of electric bulbs.

Inside the office, Orin pulled a bottle of wine from the locked bottom drawer of the desk.

“I always wondered what secret, arcane treasure was locked away inside that drawer,” Richard said as Orin uncorked the bottle.

“Nothing more mysterious than a bottle of Châteauneuf Calcernier 1892,” said Orin, taking three stems from the drawer and closing it. He placed them on the desk, filled each with a good measure of wine.

“What happened to the Perrier-Jouët?” Richard said, smiling.

“Drank it a few days ago when I was here reading. Anyway, this is nicer.” Orin handed each man a glass of wine, then lifted his in a toast.

“To meeting the neighbors,” Orin said.

They drank the dark red wine in their glasses. Orin opened the main drawer in the desk, removed a revolver. He undid the cylinder, spun it to ensure it was fully loaded. He locked the cylinder back in place, passed the gun to Richard.

“What’s that for?” Carolton asked.

Richard checked the safety, tucked the gun into his waistband.

“In case the neighbors aren’t friendly.”

“I made the last fine tuning to point the scope toward the Pleiades, so we have to act fast,” Richard said. “They’ll move out of acquisition pretty quickly.”

Professor Carolton lifted the book he carried, set it onto a lectern near the massive siderostat. "Richard and I will conduct the ceremony here. Mr. Vance, you'll want to be ready at the other end. If we're right, if this works, the eyepiece should...well, I'm not precisely sure what it will do. You'll want to be there for it. It's what you paid all this money for. But we don't know how long it will last."

Orin nodded. "Gentlemen..."

"Orin, get going," Richard said.

Turning, Orin raised the hood of his robe and strode down the tunnel toward the opposite end of the telescope. As he left, he heard Richard and Professor Carolton chanting the odd words from the ritual.

The syllables seemed odd in the cold, dense air of the mine, clunky, like jagged, mishappen chunks of ice tumbling through the darkness.

Od j'zanth R'yleh tak. Cor soc d'pren N'yog-Sothep jek Carcosa... jek Carcosa...

His feet crunching on the tunnel's stone floor, Orin made his way to the star chamber. Le grand telescope Parisien was so large, it didn't accommodate a telescope's usual single viewer eyepiece system. Instead, the eyepiece was a projector of sorts, originally casting its view onto a huge screen in a theater where hundreds of grand Parisiens could crowd in and marvel at what its out-size optics revealed.

Now, hundreds of feet underground in Missouri, its eyepiece pointed at a blank wall of stone, twenty feet high and forty feet wide. Orin had paid to have the wall smoothed and polished, to offer the clearest projection possible.

Orin could hear Richard and Carolton chanting, a ghost choir mumbling in the distance.

He stood in the star chamber and waited.

He didn't have to wait long.

A spectacular burst of light flashed into the chamber from the telescope's ocular, and Orin instinctively threw his hands over his face to ward his eyes from the blast. Turning from the scope to the blank wall, he peeked between his fingers.

There before him, the wall appeared to undulate, waver, ripples spreading out like a rock dropped through water. As if the very nature of the wall, its reality, were being warped.

The ripples slowed, stabilized, and Orin dropped his hands to his sides.

The entire blankness of the wall disappeared, and in its place was the universe. Stars and planets and gas clouds filled the cavity. Streaks of fiery plasma. Pulsing stars of blue and orange throwing out unimaginable bursts of energy. Exploding novae lit the night. Dense spheres of such concentrated black even light couldn't escape. Clouds of asteroids. Ringed planets, water planets, dead planets.

Through it all, behind it all, a vast black emptiness stretching on and on and on.

Yet…it wasn't empty.

Orin stepped closer to where the wall of stone had been, to where the vast chasm of eternity beckoned.

The blackness moved.

It wasn't empty at all, but composed entirely of tendrils, coils both mechanical and organic, corrugated, cold and menacing. All of it, all of that blankness between the stars, was this twisted stuff, like worms or writhing maggots.

Orin knew it was all one thing, all one creature coiled in every bit of space between the earth and the infinite.

All one vast, encompassing, entwining thing holding all of the universe together.

Exactly what Orin had hoped to encounter.

He stepped forward, sure he was now past where the stone wall had stood, out into the far reaches of space.

"Hello?" he cried, throwing back the hood of his robe. "Hello?"

There was no answer from the indifferent cosmos.

"Hello? Is there anyone there?"

There was an inaudible rumble, and another burst of light flooded the room. This light was no light, a null darker than night, blacker than empty space.

Orin felt a shift in the room, some presence shouldered in, unseen yet dwarfing the chamber, the space.

He shivered under its notice, ancient and condign. Not malignant, but uncaring certainly, unsympathetic.

Evil not in the sense it was out for his death. Rather, it was dismissive, contemptuous, indifferent. He knew intuitively he was less than an amoeba in its consideration. A pebble. An atom.

"Anyone?" a mellifluous, liquid voice responded. "I am here. I *am* always."

Always, Orin thought. *Or All Ways?*

"Who are you?"

"What would ask?"

"Orin Vance of Earth."

"Those words mean nothing to me. *It* means nothing to me. Why disturb my slumber with the ritual? Why open the door?"

"I…opened the door because of curiosity, because of mankind's… *my* kind's desire to explore, to know the answers to the universe's mysteries," Orin stammered.

"I slumber to hasten the becoming," the voice boomed. "It has awakened me, so now it must, too, be part of the becoming."

Orin saw the electric lights strung over the length of the telescope's enormous tube flicker. He could just make out Richard and Carolton cloistered near the siderostat, could hear them chanting the words of the ritual.

He swore he saw black shapes crawling over the iron shaft of the telescope, dropping to the ground, slinking back toward the two men.

"Its world will be made part of the becoming. Its world will suffer. Because of it. Because of *it*."

As Orin turned back to the star chamber, a storm of pseudopods unfurled around him, thin and sinuous. They emerged from between the suns and planets, through clouds of interstellar gas and out of the depthless mouths of collapsed stars. Their black was oily and iridescent, with shimmering scales of darkest violet and indigo. They pushed past him, palped along the length of the scope, blindly feeling their way down the tunnel. Under their blows, the iron of the scope's tube rang like a pealing of bells

Orin heard cries, shrieks from where Richard and Carolton were, well before the tentacles had reached them.

Orin raced back to the siderostat. What greeted him there was a horror.

Carolton and Richard had been torn apart, their black robes rent to shreds. Their bodies lay in pieces, strewn over the black earth floor. Puddles, streamers, sprays of blood just as black soaked into the earth, dripping from the iron of the telescope.

Carolton's head was nowhere to be seen, but Richard's…his lay near the base of the siderostat, face up. His eyes wide, mouth open as if he had just seen something so gruesome, so unimaginable its effect froze on his dying features.

The cilia had reached the siderostat now, and Orin stepped away, careful to avoid their touch, the puddles and spatters of his friends' blood.

"Does it think it can hide anywhere on its pitiful planet? My awakening comes at a price. It shall *become*. All its kind shall *become*, that I might rest again."

Orin heard the voice swirling into the tunnel from where the spinning cosmos filled the star chamber.

Fear rose cold within him, and he looked back to where the light bulbs strung overhead led—back to the lift, back to safety.

He considered that, rejected it.

He'd been searching for this for decades, spent millions of dollars, his life…

Why run from it now?

Slowly, he turned back, saw the black span of the universe now flooded the entire star chamber, a thousand cilia of it writhed across the telescope, towards him.

He closed his eyes.

The cilia closed, wriggled over him, around him, encasing his entire body.

They probed into his nostrils, wormed their way into his mouth, down his throat. They slid under his clothing, squirmed into his urethra, penetrated his anus.

They filled him, and he could not scream. His mouth opened wider, and more entered. They slithered over his eyeballs, into the sockets.

He never lost consciousness, couldn't.

Though they blinded his eyes, he could still see the image of the universe before him, spinning, filled with the same cilia, glutted with it. It looped around the stars and planets, weaved through comets and asteroids, became the very darkness between the galaxies.

Behind it all, that same presence chuckled gently as it returned to sleep.

Orin managed to crawl back to the lift, weakly manipulated the controls to rise to the surface of the mine. Blinded, mute and bloody, he pulled himself to the entrance to the mine shaft where Hector, standing by the car, rushed to him, took him home, called the local doctor.

Around eight a.m., with the morning sun fully over the trees and low mountains of southern Missouri, that same physician delivered the baby. A ten-pound, seven-ounce boy whose birth nearly killed his father.

III. A Seed in the Forest, 1945

V-E Day found us popping Nazis deep in the Fatherland around Giesenhausen, just south of Nuremburg. We were exhausted, elated, high on victory and blood. We spilled into the small town, crashed in barns and little homesteads, drank stolen bottles of *kirschwasser* and ate duck and goose eggs filched from farmers' coops. Whooped it up during the day in the ruins of shelled buildings, slept soundly at night under stars no longer glittering over a Nazi homeland.

One day my partner and I, a rangy New Englander by the name of John Foster, were walking down an alleyway in the main part of town. Hungry, hungover, with no desire to eat our rations, we were in search of something delicious and edible we could commandeer from one of the townspeople.

John stopped me with a tug on my arm, and I saw ahead in the alley approaching us a goose. A single, plump, living goose. It had stopped, too, as startled as we were. The town was mostly clear due to intermittent shelling, both from our side (just bored, really) and vestiges of the *Wehermacht*, still clinging to the idea they could still best us *Amerikaner*.

We'd been warned to stay out of town, but as I said, hungry and hungover.

As we stood eying each other, the whistle of an approaching shell grew louder.

John and I turned to run as the shell hit, farther up the alley toward where the goose had appraised us.

When the dust cleared, we walked to where the goose had been to find its head had been separated from its plump, delicious body by a well-placed piece of shrapnel. John, ever the New England pragmatist, scooped up the carcass, slung it over his shoulder.

As the sun set, we lit a fire, plucked, spitted, and roasted it. When it was finished, slightly charred, we hacked it apart with our field knives, shared it with a few other guys in our platoon. We ate it with a crock of pate someone had pinched, another bottle of clear *kirshwasser*, a jar of apricot preserves, sauerkraut and several loaves of fresh bread one of the guys had sweet-talked out of an apple-cheeked local *fraulein*. Probably not all he talked her out of, but all he shared with us.

It was the best meal I'd ever eaten. *Ever.* And I've eaten pretty fantastic meals. I grew up quite wealthy, to be honest. From old American money, steel and coal and railroads and such.

My name is Corey Vance, and I am not what anyone thinks.

Not at all.

It was pretty easy to drift away after the war was over. Europe was a mess, Germany particularly so. It wasn't difficult to just fade, disappear as the American presence didn't so much fade as evolve into an occupying force.

Many men disappeared during this period. Maybe they were

killed in unreported skirmishes, maybe they were murdered. Or maybe they decided it was time to start a new life, a fresh beginning in a land that was in the early throes of a fresh beginning.

I left for the same reason I volunteered for the army in the first place.

I was looking for something.

My earliest memory of my father was sitting in a wheelchair, bundled against the cool fall breeze, on the stone veranda overlooking the Mississippi. It was actually his parents' house—my grandparents who'd died long before I was born and left him unimaginable wealth.

The trees shook limbs scraggily filled with crisp, dead leaves. Hector, my father's valet, stood by, careful as always to make sure the blankets stayed put around my father's withered limbs, the drool flowing unceasingly from his lips was delicately daubed away.

My father never spoke, never really recovered from whatever mysterious accident had done the damage. He could never tell me what had happened, and there was no one else who might save Hector, and he offered little explanation.

At various times, he said it was my father's exploring that had done it. All of it, everything had done it.

L'univers a endommagé votre père.

I had no idea what he meant, and he offered no explanation, just muttered snatches of things in French I did not understand.

If you're looking for a father in this story, Hector would be that man. My own father was a lump in a bed or in a wheelchair, uncommunicative, dead-eyed, barely responsive to any stimuli. It was Hector who tucked me in at night, who read me stories, bought me toys, even did the American things like play catch with me in the yard of our expansive estate.

Mon père.

Orin Vance died in 1939, when I was just eighteen. I had come of age, as they say, entered into my inheritance, which constituted millions of dollars in several banks, estates across the United States and Europe, mines across Missouri, Illinois, Kentucky and Tennessee, even a railroad and a shipping line.

After he died, I tried to split the money with Hector, tried to get him to just retire and be my father, but he would have none of it. Gallic pride. Sheesh. He stayed on as he had my entire life, waking me, feeding me, looking after me. He'd been the one to see me through Harvard. He'd been the one to welcome me home. He'd been the one to shake his head ruefully when I told him of my plans to join the army.

It was 1944, and I'd been in possession of my father's papers for a few years at that point, trying to make sense of the mishmash of writings he'd left. My father had been an explorer, an adventurer of sorts, but he wasn't much of a writer. His journals were disjointed, much of them seemingly written under the influence of drugs and/or alcohol.

It was apparent he'd been looking for something.

Something he'd found.

Something I was sure had resulted in me.

My father hadn't succumbed instantly to the injuries that eventually left him catatonic. Hector told me he'd still been able to talk and eat and write on his own for several years after.

I remember nothing of these years since I'd been an infant, but Hector would tell me stories of my father's gradual decline. I was able to track this descent in his papers.

In his earlier papers, he seemed to be looking for something, whereas in these later papers it appeared he was looking for something else.

I now believe I was the first something he searched for.

That other thing, the one he apparently never found?

Yeah, I now needed to find it.

What was that saying I'd heard among my soldier compatriots? *Join the army. Travel to new and exotic lands.*

And kill people.

Yeah, Hector, I think, knew exactly what I was doing in joining the army. I'd be deposited in the European theater, fighting Nazis or maybe Italian fascists. If I managed to stay alive, it would be a lot easier to find the thing my father had been searching for. The *other* thing.

With a little luck and a judicious pulling of strings, calling in favors from my father's vast and varied experiences, I found myself in the 99th Infantry, "the Battle Babies" as they were called. We didn't see action until '44, but when we did, boy did we. Dropped into the European theater to form the key defense against the Nazis trying to enter Belgium in the Battle of the Bulge.

We fought and traveled at a quick pace, from Ardennes-Alsace in France to the heart of the Fatherland (hah!) and into Central Europe. My buddy John was still with me when the Germans surrendered in '45. We hung around a little, cleaning up the last pockets of resistance in and around Germany. Some of my unit were sent on to form a force for the invasion of mainland Japan, but that proved unnecessary.

V-J Day came soon after, and the war was won. The earth settled into a short period of relative peace, and I found myself, again with a little string pulling, discharged from the Army in mid-1945.

John and I had drinks in a bar in southern Germany. The army had taken over a small town on the edge of French occupied territory and had requisitioned housing from the locals to accommodate us. John and a couple of other guys took possession of a small cottage on the banks of a little stream right outside this peaceful, bucolic town.

We spent a week or so holed up there. Sleeping on actual beds for the first time in many months. Eating regular meals. Pissing and shitting in an enclosed structure rather than in the snow or under a tree at night, bullets zipping through the darkness, clipping leaves near your head.

As the war turned to occupation, my fellow soldiers drifted back to America and their former lives. Lennie to Secaucus, Matt to Akron, Jimmy down to Pascagoula, and finally John to New Hampshire.

I hung around for a while because, based on my father's fevered writings, I knew the thing he sought was near this town. He'd been unable to get to this place because of, well, whatever had happened to him. Then the war, and then, of course, his death.

Here I was, close to achieving whatever it was he'd devoted much of his life to, and I found myself anxious to close that loop for him. To offer his spirit, even after death, the peace that what he sought had been found.

By his son, no less.

But I was young and dumb and had no idea what it meant for a son to find the thing sought by the father.

A son who little understood the father's motivations, his true heart.

A son who barely understood his own.

A local widower, a farmer named Mathias, friend to the family who had lived in the house the army had sequestered for me, often came by to share a duck or sausages, hoarded bottled beir or Eiswein, and the town gossip. He was one of the few in town who spoke English.

One night, the lamps burning low, a bottle of the sweet Eiswein already empty, fallen over on the rickety table, we got into a discussion of the crops the local farmers produced. Now the war was over and the rations and hardship imposed by the dying regime were lifted, farm life in small villages like this was getting back to normal. Getting the food grown in these villages to the larger cities, many decimated by the advancing Allies and Soviets, was proving more of a problem.

Here, as in many other little burgs dotting conquered Germany, food was plentiful again. Mathias grew hops, wheat, sugar beets. His orchards grew apples and apricots and the grapes from which he made his sweet, thick Eiswein.

Mathias was lonely. His sons had been killed in the war, his wife died of consumption two years earlier. He had trouble finding laborers to work his fields, and I drunkenly promised to help him.

Loneliness made him talkative, and I let him do so at length. When the time was right, when he was thoroughly drunk and happy, I asked.

"What else is grown in this region?" I asked, topping our small glasses convivially.

"Oh, wheat and barley mostly," he said, slurring his words a little. "Cherry trees are popular. Couldn't get mine to take though."

I sipped at my glass. "Anything else? More exotic?"

He flashed a quick look that told me instantly he wasn't nearly as drunk as he was letting on.

"Exotic? Oh, there's a fellow a few towns over who grows corn. Exotic for these parts, though I guess you wouldn't think so, being an American and all. Doesn't everyone there grow corn?"

He was sipping from his glass, rather than pounding it down as he had been.

"Yeah, everyone has corn right in their backyard," I laughed. "No, I was talking very exotic. Secretive, in fact."

He flashed me that same look, but this time he realized I'd seen it.

"Secretive? Like what? For der Führer? Some wartime thing?"

I instantly sat up a little. The room suddenly seemed smaller, darker. The lamplight sputtered. Outside, I could hear the distinctive whine of a Jeep tooling off into the distance.

"Well, no, I don't think so," I said, wary about how to answer. Was it something Hitler found? No, if he'd have found it, he'd have exploited it for sure. "I'm not asking for the U.S. army; this is more for myself. Before the war, I was an explorer who sought out unusual things."

Unusual things? Wow, that sounded stupid.

Mathias took another sip, staring at me over the delicate rim of his wine glass.

"Unusual, eh?" he said, leaning in until his face was so near the burning lamp the flickering light uplit his features. "Well, there is a man I've heard of. He farms in a valley about ten kilometers from here. But he won't talk to you."

"How can you be so sure?" I asked. "Aren't I the most charming person you know?"

"For an American, ja." he said, not laughing.

"What's he grow that's so exotic?"

"Hard to say because he doesn't talk to *anyone*. Won't let anyone on his farm. Wouldn't even let the Nazis see what he was up to."

"How'd he manage that little trick?"

Mathias shrugged. "Who knows? But people say an entire contingent of Wehrmacht came to his village, doing a tally of all the farms and production in the area. He stopped them at the gate to his property. No one could hear what he told them, but they turned and left without so much as a cross word."

"Well, that is odd," I nodded. "Any thoughts on what he's growing?"

He was still leaning toward me across the table. Now, he spoke in hushed tones.

"Something unworldly," he breathed. "People say on nights with a new moon, his little valley glows ghostly blue."

Pushing back in his chair, he guffawed. "At least that's what people say!"

The measured looks, the guffaw were all theatrics I knew, designed at once to measure my interest and to cut it off.

"Where is he? What town?"

"He won't see you," Mathias said, the smile gone from both lips and eyes. His mouth was a thin, pressed line, and his eyes swam with fear.

"I know, I know. But what's his name and where is he?"

"Dietrich Sauer," Mathias grumbled. "He's an old man, probably won't even come to the gate to greet you. Go ahead and try, I suppose. You Americans never give up, do you?"

"No, which is why you and I are sitting here having a friendly drink," I said. "Where?"

"A kilometer or two outside Sosberg," he replied.

"In the French Occupation Zone?"

"We'll see if they'll let a Yank in to snoop around while they're in control," he said, sounding a bit too smug.

I wasn't offended. Not at all.

What I thought was simple.

I wonder what my money will buy me in war-ravaged Germany?

Turns out, not surprisingly, quite a lot.

Papers giving me permission to cross into the French Sector from an American commander who allowed his palm to be greased. For a little extra money, he even threw in the loan of a Jeep.

At the French command post, I was received by a weary Gallic commandant who made no pretense of listening to my spiel or reading my purchased papers. He eyed me up and down from behind a cluttered desk, then simply held out his hand.

The banking situation in the area was understandably spotty at best, and I didn't have much. But what I had was American dollars, the specie most desired. My bribe came to fifty bucks. I was cheerful to give it, and he seemed all too cheerful to take it.

He signed and stamped my papers, shooed me away, honking Gallically all the while.

I went back to my Jeep, flashing my papers to the two aspirants who had positioned themselves around the vehicle. Their expressions turned sour when they saw their commandant's signature. Apparently, they'd hope to get their hands on an American Jeep.

I had a basic map of the area, another gift of my American bribee, and it showed more or less how to get to Sosberg. I set off on a beautiful September day in southwestern Germany. The air smelled of lavender and a citrusy smell I assumed were hops.

Open air in the Jeep, with little worry of snipers, mortar shells or Panzers lumbering around a corner, it was almost a lark, a carefree summer drive back home in Missouri. I knew I shouldn't get my hopes up. My father had been searching for this for the greater part of his life. That I should stumble on it in a played-out theater of war simply because I happened to be in the area seemed too fortuitous, too easy.

The drive was uneventful, and by midafternoon, I came into the small village. The few people there seemed surprised to see me, going about their daily lives as best they could. Much of the town was in ruins, either due to us or the retreating Nazis. What did it matter now, especially to these people?

I used my basic German to inquire about Herr Sauer. Most eyed me suspiciously, turned away in distress at his name.

Instantly, I knew I was on the right track.

A small boy of about ten years old had crept over to the Jeep, was examining it with a humorous combination of caution (Kaugummifresser!) and curiosity. He was the embodiment of Hitler's Germany—tow-headed, blue-eyed, diffident.

"You like the Jeep do you?" I asked.

The kid jumped back a little, stared at me.

"I'm looking for someone," I said, reaching into the back in the vehicle to open my pack. "Herr Dietrich Sauer. Where can I find him?"

The kid crept back another step at the mention of Sauer. To counter, I waved the chocolate bar I'd taken from the bag.

"Willst du etwas Schokolade?" I asked, tick-tocking it back and forth before him.

"Herr Sauer?" he asked, no longer looking at the Jeep or me, fixated on the bar of chocolate. "Sein Hof?"

"Ja."

The kid gestured off into the distance behind him. "Zwei Kilometer rechts unten. Es gibt ein Tor."

"Danke schoen," I said, and tossed him the bar. He snatched it from the air, disappeared between two low buildings.

I climbed back into the Jeep and followed his less-than-specific directions. The dirt road led out of town, curving around the lushly greened foothills. At about the two-click mark, just like the kid said I would, I saw it.

The gate.

It was late afternoon now, and I sat at the entrance to what looked like a small, narrow valley or glen between the rolling hills. It was sealed with a stone wall about twelve feet tall, solidly built and appearing untouched by the war. The gate was a huge wooden affair, clad and hinged in black iron. Its doors were sealed tight. There wasn't even a handle or other handhold to open or close it from this side.

Hanging from one of the stone pillars securing a section of the gate doors was a great bell, a leather thong dangling from its clapper.

A bronze plaque behind the bell read simply:

Nicht klingeln.

Who puts out a bell and then tells passersby not to ring it?

I disregarded the plaque, rang the bell.

It peeled out in deep, resonant tones, echoing into the valley. I gave it three good pulls, then waited as the last of the echoes faded. Leaning against the Jeep, I fished a pack of cigarettes from my stash, lit up. I expected to be there a while, waiting for Herr Sauer to emerge. I thought it likely I would have to ring the bell a few more times, perhaps even try to climb the stone wall.

I was surprised when I heard the heavy clanking of heavy chains. The doors parted about a foot, and a bewildered, grizzled face peeked between them.

"Wer ist es."

"Guten tag," I said, tossing the cigarette. "Sind Sie Herr Sauer?"

The man's visage was mostly hair—a wild, tousled mane of grey hair and an equally unkempt beard—and wide, glassy eyes. He cocked his head, appraising me beneath bushy grey eyebrows.

"Amerikaner?"

I nodded

"I speak English," he said, surprising me for the second time. His words were accented, yes, but the thing I noticed most was the rustiness of his voice. This was a man who didn't speak much at all, English or German.

"Oh, well, great," I said, thrown off my stride a bit by this. "That'll make things easier."

"I don't entertain guests," the man growled, fading back into the darkness behind the gate.

"This world shall *become*," I said, not quite knowing which of the phrases in my father's journals might engender the biggest response.

That did the trick.

The old man stepped forward into the space between the doors.

"How do you know this?" he said, his voice filled with skepticism. "Who told you this?"

"A being who filled the space between the stars told me this," I said. "Rather, he told my father. Orin Vance. I'm his son, Corwin."

The man's eyes widened. But it wasn't at the mention of my name. It was my father's.

"You're *him*," he said. "You're the child."

I frowned. "Well, I mean, I was a child. At one point. Clearly not any longer."

He sidled between the doors, came to stand before me. He surveyed me up and down. He looked—*smelled*—atrocious, of stale tobacco, sour beer and unwashed old man.

He had the look, that indefinable aura of absolute, pure mania.

He held out shaking hands, tentatively, as if he wanted to touch me, to ascertain my validity, my realness, yet strangely afraid to do so.

I let him, felt his trembling fingertips graze my collar, my cheeks.

"By the ancient, you are him. You are real."

"I'd like to think so. Listen, can I come in? Can we talk?"

"Of course, of course," he cackled. "Of course. And why not? It's all for you, all for *him*."

I had a vague idea of what he spoke of, that same thing dancing at the edges of my father's journals, of everything he ever wrote, sought for.

Herr Sauer let me into a darkened gatehouse. As the doors banged shut, I found myself in complete darkness with a madman. Chains ratcheted, there was thump of heavy lumber, an ominous creaking.

A hand on my shoulder—shaking, so I knew it was his—pointed me in a direction then prodded me forward. I went through a narrow tunnel sloping downward, like the adit of a mine. The air was cold and clammy, and I almost see my breath swirl in the blackness.

Just as quickly, I felt the ground ascend. The hand on my shoulder stayed me, and I felt Sauer moved around me. More clacking and clinking, and a wedge of light appeared, fattened.

I blinked at the light's appearance, and as Sauer stepped aside, I saw his modest house about twenty yards in the distance, framed by the narrow slope of the valley hills on either side.

"Das schloss," he said, sounding sarcastic. "All I have is yours."

He turned to me, his rheumy eyes pleading with me to accept all that was his, pleading with me as surely not to.

"We must talk, Herr Sauer."

"Ja, ja. Ich weiß," he said, his hands fluttering between us like spooked birds. "Inside, inside. We sit. We eat. Kohl und knödel, ja?"

True to his word, he had a pot of cabbage and dumplings bubbling on the stove. Its sweaty, footlike scent slammed into me as the door opened. The inside of the house was filled with the kind of heavy, dark wood Germans seemed to favor. No baubles or geegaws, almost no decoration of any sort. I wondered if a woman had ever lived in this house, and then I knew one had. A small framed photo on the mantle of a stout older man and his stout frau.

Sauer's mother.

We sat at the table, and he handed me a steaming bowl. He served the stew with a hearty, black bread and a small dish of duck fat. We ate mostly in silence, him staring at me when I wasn't looking. When we were done—I shooed away a second helping—he took the dishes, set them on the board, disappeared behind a door.

I was wondering what he was up to when he emerged with two glass bottles of homebrew. He broke the seals, handed me a bottle. The bier inside was dark and heavy, a condensation of everything in Sauer's house. And it was delicious, going quite a way toward washing both the road dust and the taste of kohl und knödel out of my mouth.

"When can we see it?" I asked, drawing another mouthful of beer.

"Patience, ja? It won't appear to be much until after the sun goes down. We drink our beer and wait. It won't be long. Not long, not long."

He looked away, mumbled softly to himself. I couldn't make out a word of what he was saying, but it hurt my head if I focused on trying to decipher them. So I let them go. They seemed to drift, floating about his head like a miasma.

Through the lead-veined glass window in his kitchen, I could see the sun had dipped below the crest of the hills. The shadows of the trees had lengthened, casting the valley into darkness though the sky was still indigo.

"Finished?" he asked, holding his hand out for my empty bottle. I handed it over, and he placed these on the sideboard next to the dirty dishes. "We go now, ja?"

I agreed, and he led me through the house to a back door opening onto a courtyard paved with flagstones. It was a jumbled mess out here. Farm implements lay willy-nilly. A broken cart, hay tumbling down its sides, one wooden wheel missing. Dozens of wooden bushels, hand tools, what looked like a broken door removed from the house.

On the opposite end of the courtyard was a ramshackle barn. A horse stood at its entrance, an enormous, swayback nag that had seen better days. It cropped a tuft of grass or weed that had sprouted along the side of the stones. It lifted its head and gave us a desultory look, then went back to eating.

"This way, back to the field," he said. "Yes, yes, you will see. You will see. If…"

"*If?*"

"If you are the one," he responded, turning away and cackling.

Behind the barn, Sauer's land opened, the vista expanding left and right to the hills, stretching far into the distance. The sun was very low now, and the shadows stretched across the valley, filling it with an almost wet, cobalt light. The sky above was bruised violet, fading to a rose gold at the tops of the hills. Stars had begun to show, glittering like diamonds scattered over velvet.

"How long have you farmed here, Herr Sauer?" I asked, traipsing along beside him. We were crossing a wide verge, just grass and scrub weeds. I could see a dark mass of ahead, tall, huddled, swaying in the evening air.

"Generations," he said. "My father's father's father farmed here, and generations before. We've grown the food, waited, oh yes, we waited. So many years. Centuries, ja? Patient, oh, so patient. My grandfather died waiting, miserable and defeated. My father, too, wretched and angry. But I will not die unfulfilled, no. Nein! I have lived to greet you and take you there, to show you our fidelity, my family's long patience."

"Yes, well, you'll be rewarded, I'm sure," I said, having little idea what he was raving about.

"Your father, he bought le grand télescope Parisien?"

"Yes, he did."

"And he put it back together. He *saw* through it."

"Yes."

The man stopped in his tracks. I thought he might drop to his knees, clasp my hand, kiss the back of it in abject worship, abject terror.

He didn't, just regarded me through the veil of his wild hair.

"You came through," he muttered. "He sent you through."

"What are you talking about?" I asked. "He? He who? And sent through from where?"

"From the one who curls around the cosmos, abides."

"I can assure you, I am not sent from any such…person," I said, wondering if that was a bit too much to blurt out to this insane man. Would he stop here, so close, and not take me to see what I came to see?

He just cackled, stared into my eyes and mumbled nonsense syllables.

Od j'zanth R'yleh tak. Cor soc d'pren N'yog-Sothep jek Carcosa… jek Carcosa…

The words smacked into my head like pebbles hurled one at a

time, leaving me more and more disoriented. My sight waivered, my legs felt wobbly.

I looked down at my feet, my legs, was horrified to find they were no longer mine. From my waist down, my legs had become one solid, fused, tubular mass, slick and smooth, glistening like an aquatic creature hauled from the depths of the ocean.

That trunk terminated where my knees had been minutes before, and from there the mass of my body was held upright by a clutch of tentacles, pale, ochre-colored, perhaps a foot or a foot-and-a-half long. Writhing, palping the ground.

"Wha…?" I muttered. "What are you doing?"

"Your true nature, ja? I am showing you, perhaps for the first time?"

"Nonsense. I'm Corey Vance, son of Orin Vance."

"Your mother?"

"She…died. Never knew her."

"Never had one is more like it. No mother. You were born of man, yes, but not woman."

I genuinely had no idea what he was talking of, and the moment of dizziness had begun to pass. The illusion of my legs waivered, the sheath and tentacles fading. I passed a hand over my eyes, my forehead, wiping at the sweat gathering there, rubbing the vision away.

"Don't do that again," I said, with perhaps more force than I intended.

Sauer fell to his knees before me, finally, grasping for a hand that, for a moment, looked like a clutch of small tendrils.

"My lord, I meant no offense," he cried. And he really cried, I mean with little gasps of breath and tears dripping through the mop of his hair.

"I'm not your lord or anyone's," I said. "Get up, Herr Sauer. Show me what I came to see."

"Of course," he sniffled. "Of course, the fields, the crop. Oh, the crop, my…Herr Vance. You'll be so proud of my lineage, what we've accomplished. For you. For him."

"No doubt, but let's see it."

"Yes," he said, jumping to his feet faster than I might have given him credit for. "Yes, it is time. Finally."

Ahead, in the deepening night, I saw a strange bluish glow had filled the "V" of the valley ahead, a low and creeping noctilucent fog. It hung over the darkened hump of whatever the Sauers grew here for generations.

We walked toward it, and at some point I lost all sense of Sauer walking near me. It was if I was alone in this strange twilight, on another world, far away, eons away, so ancient the earth itself was still an accretion disc whirling around a fiercely newborn star, hot and raging.

I stepped forward, straining against veils, forcing myself elsewhere. The air became rarified, as if I were ascending a great mountain.

The aural blue glow grew, floating in the air, above it, the great wave-wall of the plants now visible, swaying to a music I was beginning to hear now, playing at the edge of my senses.

Banjoes?

Why would I hear that?

Against that distant, ghostly twanging, I heard the crisp rustle of the leaves, like the leaves of a book turning, flipping over, one by one, revealing knowledge, quiescent, ancient, unknowable.

Words appeared before my eyes in a script far older than our knowledge, characters scraping my brain like razors, left weals across my consciousness.

Now, the wall of plants stood before me, and the stalks bent aside as if to say *Enter, Enter.*

I entered.

Sauer was gone, completely absent from my senses now as the plants accepted me, closed around me.

There was nothing now, just the plants, the darkness between, the blue glow above.

I could see the individual plants clearly now. Their stems looked tree-like, hard and solid with leaves growing from them, blade-shaped, serrated and sharp enough to cut flesh.

The bluish glow came from the plants themselves.

Underneath these brutal leaves, pods, two or three to a plant, disturbingly familiar. Their bluish outer covering appeared fleshy; a veiny, pulsing sack resembling a scrotum, heavy with fluid.

I went to one, hefted it, cupped it gently in the palm of my hand.

As if hypnotized, I fished a pocketknife from my trousers. I slid the blade delicately over the pod's taut skin, and a gush of indigo fluid, the blood of night itself, gushed from the wound. I shifted uncomfortably as one of my fingers entered this slit.

I squeezed out a bluish thing, about the size of a cicada, writhing in the pool of amniotic fluid formed by the cup of my hand. Thick as a big toe, segmented, glistening in its slick, mucilaginous coating. It seemed to have no tail, no head, no mouth or features, simply tapered away on each end.

It made a tiny sound, a small, barely heard mewling that made me shiver in disgust and fear.

I'm ashamed to admit, in hunger.

"Taste of it," Sauer said from nearby. "They're the food of the gods."

My stomach lurched, but my mouth watered. It smelled of almonds and some barely remembered, savory spice.

"What is it?" was the last thing I said before my lips closed, teeth squelched into it.

"They're *shuggoth*," Sauer said, but the word tangled itself on the air between his tongue and my ear, deforming my ability to hear it correctly. "Their larval form."

Shuggoth was a name I'd heard. My father's journals…

The tiny thing burst between my teeth, thick liquid rupturing from it, flowing over my tongue like strange jelly, sweet and ethereal in taste. Its gentle cries became a sharp, brief shriek in my brain before being silenced.

Its husk dissolved on my tongue, and I swallowed it. It left a musky, though not unpleasant, taste, redolent of that dimly recalled spice.

"Tricky to grow, you know," Sauer continued conversationally. "Never been tried on our world. Took my family countless generations to get it right, *ja?* Many, many ancestors failed, failed, failed. Today, you are here, and they grow. They will feed you and others. For the Becoming. Yes, the Becoming. Tastes great, ja? So sweet."

I nodded, closing my eyes, savoring the taste of it. Words came to my lips from some part of myself I had no understanding of.

"Happy they grew so well, because we'll need a lot of them to feed him when he gets here. He'll be here soon. The world will change."

As I spoke, I *saw*…

The universe opened, burst into being in a cramp of nauseous, violet light. Clouds of cosmic gas ignited, expanding to envelop planets, moons, stars. Tendrils of fire moved between them, blistered, laval snakes slithering with intelligence, winding from world to world, snuffing them out.

It wasn't just one, it was many, each winding in a hundred, a million different directions against the black velvet of space, seeking, destroying…

"We'll bring him here. We'll help him save us."

Did Sauer say this or did I?

It didn't matter.

I trembled with a larger realization.

These weren't snakes but millions of pseudopods, each connected to the next, all leading back to one great, amorphous shape, a bloated, many-eyed thing hanging in the vastness of space, reaching across the universe, across time, across the dimensions, feeding on worlds.

It hungered. It wanted.

It wanted me. It wanted this planet.

And everyone on it.

I was different, I knew now. I wasn't of earth, of my father.

I was of *it*, a part of *it*.

I myself was a tendril, reaching out, burning on the inside.

These…*shuggoth*…they would feed me, sustain me until…

The Becoming.

I plucked another from a plant, then another, and another, squeezing the pulp out of each, the tiny larvae. I ate them one after another, like nuts.

With each, I became more myself, more *it*, less of earth or indeed any planet.

I, too, was of the dark stuff between stars.

All of my *father's* life, his explorations, his notes, journals, all the stuff he'd collected, the secrets he'd penetrated. All of it seemed simultaneously clear, yet completely meaningless, as a tiny sliver seen through a keyhole suddenly coming into fine focus. Still a sliver, though, just a meaningless part of an incomprehensible whole.

But I *saw* now.

I saw the whole thing, the insignificance of this little planet, my little role.

A role nonetheless, and I was happy for it.

"I need to take this back with me, back to my home," I said to no one in particular.

"But, lord, these…this is my life," came the sputtering reply from the gloom there in the field.

"Your life is nothing," I said. "You will become."

I followed him back to the barn, the night sky blazing down onto us, glowering its disdain for all beneath it. In the quiet of the barn, he passed me a small leather pouch of seeds. The pouch hung like a bag, a scrotum, like the fruits of the things it would grow back on my home soil.

"America is for growing things," I told him, imagining these night-blue flowers sprouting in vast numbers on the prairies of the United States, radiating their indigo aura so fiercely they outshone the lights of the country's cities, so bright it would be seen from space, far, far out where cold, dispassionate eyes searched for such things.

"The Becoming will start there, spread across the planet." Sauer had fallen to the floor, weeping, perhaps understanding finally, awfully the full heritage of his family, what they'd striven for across the gulf of centuries, devoted their lives to.

All that came crashing through the thin floor of his madness, like a great weight through cardboard, like a drunk faced with something horrible that instantly sobers him.

For me it was as if a light snapped on inside, illuminating hallways, rooms I never knew existed.

Shining a light on a path, a purpose.

I would go home to the red, white and blue.

Mostly blue, though.
Mostly blue.

THE END

HER MOUTH WAS FILLED WITH SECRET SOUP

"I shouldn't ask for your help, and you damn sure shouldn't be offering, kid. Leastways not to me, leastways not if you know what's good for ya, so…scram," the barker said, fingering the dusty brim of his hat, which slouched on the cold, marble counter beside his plate. "Believe me, you don't want to get involved in this."

But I did.

Just an hour or so earlier, I'd watched his performance outside the railroad stop in the small Missouri town of Corridon. Their troupe pulled the wagon to the side of that ramshackle building, a wooden structure barely able to hold up the tin roof shielding those unlucky enough to unboard a train in that dusty, forgotten burg.

The music was what attracted me, for I couldn't see from a distance over the heads of the crowd who had gathered. I'd been inside the General Store on the main street, surreptitiously filling my pockets with apples, stick candy and a slice or two of jerky when I'd heard it.

The store had a radio playing, entertaining the kid behind the counter, probably a year or two older than me, as he watched the store for his dad or his uncle. Fiddlin' John Carson, who'd stopped recording music a few years before, was back in a big way, and no radio ever seemed without his new tunes these days. He sawed away with abandon now, the pimply clerk perched atop a stool tapping his toes and slapping his knees in time with Old John's rendition of *Barbara Allen.*

I listened to the song absently, Carson being sort of the background music of the time in small towns like these. But as I lingered, watching the stupid clerk close his eyes and screech along in a raspy falsetto, debating whether I should press my luck and try for a pickle from the barrel set in front of the cash register, I heard another pulse of music.

It came from outside, at first sweet and sensuous on my ear, quickly increasing until it muscled that other, more familiar tune aside.

I patted the wooden pickle barrel ruefully as I passed to the front. The jingle of the shop's bell as the door shut behind me barely registered. I stood on the wooden boards trying to tell where the music was coming from, like a hungry fairgoer sniffing at the rapturous odors of cooking meat.

The crowd had gathered around a wagon, painted all in carnival reds and golds and blues. *The Incredible Dr. Alatryx and his Mysterious Persian Cure! By Way of Egypt, India, The Orient, Persia.*

A medicine show. I should have known. I considered going back in, trying for that pickle, but the music was strangely insistent. A banjo accompanied by a fiddle, bass. Someone sang, but I realized the banjo was the hook here, the thing that seemed to sink into my brain.

I stepped off the walk and into the street without looking. Lucky for me the few cars in this small town were stopped, either by the crush of people or, like me, by the music.

Parting the people in front of me like a curtain, I finally stood before the hastily erected wooden stage, even more rickety than the worn boards of the main walk.

A canvas banner was draped behind this stage, having seen better days. Its garishly colored paint was faded and dusty, done up in the style of the medicine shows from forty years ago or longer. This one showed a mustachioed man, larger than life, looming over the pyramids and an Oriental palace. His right hand was thrown wide, his left held an amber bottle of liquid splashing fluid onto a crowd of small, beseeching figures.

The eponymous Dr. Alatryx ministering to his flock.

The music that had called me came from a Negro girl, perhaps twenty or so years old, sitting on a plain, wooden chair at the center of the stage. She wore a simple blue gingham dress, her hair straightened and pulled into two dark pigtails, tied with bright, red ribbons.

Her feet were bare, calloused and large, and they tapped the stage in time with her music. Her hands, also rough and big for her age, picked at the banjo she held with unbelievable dexterity, plucked at its strings, patted its drum.

I was unfamiliar with the song, but the two men behind her, good old boys if I'd ever seen them, kept pace easily, one with a fiddle, the other with an upright bass. To the other side of the stage, the barker stood, also tapping his feet to the music, swiping his perspiring forehead with a handkerchief he kept at the ready.

The two musicians behind the girl sweated liberally as well. It was a hot afternoon, and I felt sweaty myself. Something about that unknown song made me feel all the clammier.

But, and here's the thing, the girl didn't exhibit as much as one drop of perspiration on her dark skin. *Nothing*. It was as if the heat of the day, the exertions of her musical efforts, didn't touch her at all.

It might not have affected her, but the music certainly had a strange effect on the gathered crowd, myself included. Everyone seemed enraptured by it, tapping toes, slapping their thighs like the idiot who'd let me steal about a buck's worth of food. A few older women and children danced in the dust at the foot of the stage, kicking up their heels, raising their skirts almost as high as the gentlemen's eyes.

A few flounces from the fiddler, a hard line from the bass, and the girl's fingers stopped as if caught by force, and she slapped one hand on the instrument's taut drum.

The strain of her voice, the twang of her banjo faded on the air, cleared like a fog. The dancing women and children stopped like marionettes whose strings were cut, and they faded back into the crowd, looking perplexed.

The Negro girl sat motionless, then she snapped her eyes open.

I was surprised, and so was the crowd, too, as a gasp went up to fill the quiet left behind.

Her eyes were a milky white, almost silver in the afternoon light.

She was blind.

The barker mopped his brow one last time, strode onto the stage stuffing the handkerchief inside his jacket.

"Ladies and gentlemen, I give you Rashida, the prodigy I procured myself from the very depths of blackest Africa! Saved her from savages whose practices were so horrendous I cannot discuss them aloud in proper society," he said, then raised a hand to his lips, leaned to stage left where a few young men huddled. "But ask me later and I might share the more delicate details."

Laughter erupted, harsh and discordant.

"That concludes our afternoon performances," the barker said, standing to his full height, sweeping off his bowler hat. "We appreciate your patronage and hope to see you all under the stars tonight just outside town, near the Old South Bridge."

He went to the girl, offered her his hand. She rose slowly, slung the banjo over her shoulder.

"Wait a sec, there, doc," someone from the audience shouted. "What about your patent medicines?"

I scanned the crowd for the person who shouted this, sure as anything it'd come from a plant, a ringer.

The barker hesitated, smiled, turned back to the crowd, still clutching Rashida's hand.

"Tonight, my friends! Tonight we will sing and dance and share the most incredible cure-all you will ever encounter in your lifetime. Bring your dancing shoes, your best guy or girl, and most important…bring money! Tonight!"

With that, the crowd dispersed, and I watched the tall man disappear behind the canvas. The bass player and the fiddler leaned against the end of the stage, one smoking, the other chewing.

I walked over to them. "Great show, fellas."

The bass player said nothing, just chewed and looked at me. Such are bass players. But the fiddler sized me up, poked me in the chest with his bow.

"Well, thanks, boy. You just showed real taste there. Rare in these parts, ain't it, Pinkney?"

The bass player screwed up his mouth, spat a large wad of oily phlegm at my feet.

"Mayhap we'll see ya tonight, right, scout?" the fiddler asked.

"Can I talk to the barker, Dr. Alatryx?" I asked. That set them both to laughing, brown drool trickling down Pinkney's jowly face.

"I 'spect you'll have to find the good doc," the fiddler laughed. "Probably off having lunch or whatnot."

"Or whatnot," Pinkney said, spitting again.

Scowling, I turned away, caught a glimpse of the barker's hat bobbing above the heads of the dispersed crowd.

I dashed after him.

"You don't want no business with him, scout," the fiddler shouted after me. "His business means business."

That was how I found myself plunking a penny down for a glass of Coca-Cola at the Emporium next to the General store, sitting beside that same gentleman.

As he ate, I struck up a conversation, letting him know I'd seen the show, how much I enjoyed the music. He answered in grunts between bites of his lunch, eying me cautiously, fingers drumming on his hat.

Those fingers stopped when I asked him for a job.

I didn't babble or explain or whatever to fill in the silence that followed, I just let him think on my request. Truly, I didn't expect him to be agreeable to my proposal, but I had learned from a year or so on the road now it never does hurt to ask.

"I shouldn't ask for your help, and you damn sure shouldn't be offering any, kid. Leastways not to me, leastways not if you know what's good for ya, so…scram. Believe me, you don't want to get involved in this," he said, as I'd related earlier.

But he continued staring at me, almost daring me to respond.

"That's the kind of job offer I just can't turn down, Dr. Alatryx," I said, grinning ear to ear.

The man sighed at the mention of that name, pushed his plate aside and reached out to grab the collar of my shirt, pull me near. He smelled of sweat and alcohol in equal parts, as if the stuff oozed from his pores. He also smelled of dirt and tobacco, bad breath and something else, hard to describe, almost as if he had a disease that wafted from him in alternating currents of sweet and sour.

"You wanna travel, boy? See the world? Be in show business like those people you hear on the radio?" He pronounced *radio* strangely, with a long ah sound: *rahhdio*.

I nodded, but he wasn't listening. His free hand had already grabbed for his hat, but his other stayed curled in the fabric of my shirt.

"I do require help from such as yourself. I can pay, as well as feed you and put a roof over your head. But it's hard work, damning. Not for the squeamish. So, think twice before you commit."

He pushed me away, not roughly, and made his way toward the door.

"If you still think you might, see me before tonight's show, out near the bridge. Say around 7:30. Got a watch? No? Then, figure it out, boy. Won't be the last time I tell you," he said. He winked and disappeared outside.

I saw he'd left money for his meal and my soda on the counter. The soda jerk scooped it away before I could touch it, and I followed my new employer out the same door, found a quiet place to eat an apple and two leathery straps of jerky.

I stayed within sight of the clock atop the town's city hall. At around seven p.m., I picked myself off the curb and walked toward the bridge on the south side of town. Past the main street of shops and businesses, there was a row of huge, fancy houses, the kinds with two stories and a wraparound porch. Probably owned by the bankers, business owners and politicians. I could almost see them lounging within, dressed in their seersuckers and boater's hats, sipping lemonade (or what passed for it), playing records on their Victrolas.

They weren't, though the houses were mostly lit from the inside, twilight deepening the farther I walked. It was 1934, and not too many people were interested in partying, at least not conspicuously, at least not in small towns. Even the bankers, business owners and politicians were having trouble making ends meet. Well…maybe *not* the politicians.

Past this, the town faded back into the landscape, just rolling hills along a gravel road twisting along with them. After a few minutes, I saw the girders of the bridge spanning the Eleven Point River. It was a narrow bridge, the river not a particularly large one. Its floor was rough wooden timbers that twitched ominously when a car went over.

More than a few did as I crossed. Apparently, Dr. Alatryx was drawing quite the crowd this evening.

As I crested the top of a rise on the opposite side of the river, the landscape opened. I stood on the lip of a shallow, natural bowl amidst the Missouri hills. It was gently carpeted with thick, green grass. Toward the far end, tucked against the hills forming a natural boundary, was Dr. Alatryx's wagon and a couple beat-up, black Ford Model As.

The stage I'd seen near the railway depot was set up out here, strings of lights draped over the canvas banner and hung from the foot of the structure. The warm, yellow light flushed the little glen, like the glow of fireflies against the spreading night. It pushed back the blackness of the hills, lit the trees as if in a fairy tale.

I marveled at this picture. Even the cars parking on the grass a dozen or so yards away, their headlights wavering, horns blowing occasionally, didn't ruin it for me. I'm not much for church or anything. I grew up poor in a poor family, one that tried to send me down into the lead mines with my dad or ship me east to work in the Tennessee coal mines with my uncle, to send my meager pay back to support them either way.

I figured god never cared too much for me. Never saw why I had to feel any different.

But I saw the Bible prints those traveling salesmen tried to sell us over the years. How they'd stand dripping sweat in our parlor, paging through full-color prints from Europe, old wood cuts from copies of the Bible hundreds of years old. I remember seeing those with a kind of hushed awe my parents probably saw as proper piety, but it wasn't. It was just something about those pictures, with their impossible grandeur, with light that made the simplest things seem to glow from within.

Those pictures made me seem impossibly large and impossibly small at the same time.

Standing there atop that rise, I felt the same thing.

Not religious, mind you. Well, at least I didn't think it was religious, not that, as I said, I knew much.

No... *occult* seemed the right word. Not in the sense of those Ouija boards or people in turbans reading fortunes in crystal balls. *Occult* as in the sense of hidden, concealed from sight or understanding.

I traipsed down the hill, through a grove of mulberry trees. Passing within their branches, I paused to pluck a handful of the sweet, blackberries before I headed in. Dodging cars and trucks and even the occasional rider on horseback, I made my way to the stage. People were already crowded there, standing, seated on folding chairs they'd brought themselves.

Kind of felt like an old-time tent revival, same atmosphere. People spoke, laughed. A few danced, though there was no music yet.

I saw the fiddler slouched to stage right, smoking again. He was alone, and he watched as I approached, neither smiling nor frowning.

"Well, if it ain't the wet sock," he drawled. "Heard you's just the joe to get this operation running smoothly."

I'd met plenty of guys like him during my time on my own. They pretended to like you, but really didn't. All they wanted you to know, ultimately, was they were higher on the ladder than you.

"Doc Alatryx asked me to see him," I said.

«*Doctor* Alatryx," he corrected, this drawing a smirk. "Did he now? Well, go on then, I suppose."

He gestured with a hand, and I went to pass him. He grabbed my shoulder, leaned in close. I smelled alcohol on his breath.

"Don't get above your raisin' there, kid. And don't gum up the monkeyworks here, or…»

"Or what? You don't seem to be the one calling the shots," I said.

He withdrew his hand, and for a second, I thought he was going to pop me. Probably was, and it wouldn't've been the first time someone had taken a swing at me. But a strange expression crossed his face, and he pulled out his pack of cigarettes, knocked one out, lit it instead.

"So, he's expecting you," he said, breathing a cloud of smoke toward me. "Take a powder, why dontchya?"

I eased around him, back behind the banner. The wagon was parked there. Alatryx's figure painted on its side seemed Biblical, too. Like a great prophet of old preaching to the masses.

Warm light spilled from the open door at the rear of the wagon. I smelled burning, spicy and aromatic. I crept closer. A short set of steps led to the door, set off by a beaded curtain.

"Come in, boy, if you mean to start your job," called a voice from inside.

It *wasn't* Dr. Alatryx.

It was smoky inside, powerfully filled with that smell I'd noticed outside. Deeper than cinnamon or anything I was accustomed to, almost peppery. Clouds of it filled the small, cluttered chamber.

There was another smell underneath, a smell I'd come to know very well. It was dense and smoky, like the other, softer note. But this had the tang of a skunk, that sour, burnt fart smell you get from a distance.

I felt the one smell was being employed to cover—or at least diminish—the other.

The walls of the wooden wagon were covered in Persian carpets. Some scattered over the floor, too. A single circular table sat close to a bench built into the wall. On the table were a profusion of candles and a fist-sized iron pot belching smoke that filled the room. It was the source of the nicer of the two smells.

Seated at the table were Dr. Alatryx and Rashida, and they looked on me with a species of detached humor. Alatryx's hat lay atop the table, and he fingered its brim just as he had at the diner. Rashida, for her part, wore an air of weary aloofness, still clad in the gingham dress she'd worn earlier.

They each had cigarettes in their mouths. The skunkier smell came from whatever it was they were inhaling.

I also saw, close up now, Rashida wasn't nearly as young as I'd thought. She was small, true, maybe just about five feet. I think she dressed and acted, on stage at least, such that people would think she was younger.

All part of the act.

So much, looking back now, so much of it all was illusion, sleight of hand, tricks.

But not everything. No…not *everything*.

Rashida was just a bit older than me. If I had to guess, perhaps thirty or so years old.

"What light through yonder window breaks," Alatryx intoned, languidly inclining his head toward me.

"He sees, but through a glass darkly," Rashida said, and it was the same voice I'd heard from outside, beckoning me in. She smiled, blew a cloud of pungent vapor toward me.

"Have a seat, egg," Alatryx said, motioning to the one empty one. "I expect you're here to get the lay of the land, see what this job is you so rashly accepted."

"Why he's just as cute as a bug's ear," Rashida said, looking at me, her cataractic eyes glowing silver in the candlelight.

"Now, now, young lady," the doctor admonished. "We'll have none of that."

"Can she see or not?" I asked, confused.

"Why, what an impertinent question," Rashida said, chuckling.

"She sees things beyond the ken of you or I," Alatryx said, his booming, barker voice filling the wagon.

"Dr. Alatryx…»

Rashida giggled, the focus of her eyes still on me.

«…you offered me a job, and I come here to accept, sir."

"That I did, boy. That I did. So, tonight we'll do our full performance, not the brief musical interlude we offered this afternoon. At the appropriate time, the lovely Rashida here…»

Rashida inclined her head coquettishly at me.

«…will play with Mr. Staunton. At which time you and Mr. Pinkney will go into the crowd with boxes of our patent medicine."

His hand disappeared under the table, and then reappeared, tossed something at me. I caught it, fumbled it, brought it into the light.

It was an amber glass bottle with a paper label glued to its face.

Dr. Alatryx's Mysterious Persian Cure! Good For ALL AILMENTS! Indigestion! Headaches! Tooth Pain! Gout! Piles! To be taken internally and liberally.

"You'll be selling these at a buck a bottle. Go ahead and take a snort, if you want. But not too much. Shouldn't drink up all the profits!"

I uncorked the bottle—cork, not the newfangled steel twist caps most medicines had nowadays—and sniffed at it. It smelled of alcohol and not much else.

I took a sip, and it took my breath away. I knew what it was immediately.

Corn liquor. Sour mash. Hooch.

"Okay," I said, trying not to cough as it burned down my pipe. "All right. I get it. I get it."

"Oh, my dear girl. He *gets* it. He's on to us," Alatryx said.

Rashida's smile had faded. "He is, I believe. Watch this one."

"Why?" Alatryx said, giving no hint he actually cared. "Is he a G-man? Working for the Treasury Department, egg?"

"No, sir," I said.

"No," Rashida repeated, keeping her attention on me. "Just watch him."

Alatryx cast a side eye at her, then smacked the table.

"That's your job. Sell the product, collect the money. After, you'll help clean and pack. We'll leave here tonight, off to… Where did you say we're headed, my dear?"

"Siloam Springs, doctor," she said, investing that last word with just enough irony I heard it. Was meant to hear it.

"That's all for now. Just stand ready until I call for the product sales to begin. And be ready should I require something."

"Like what?" I asked.

"Like anything at all, boy. Now skedaddle," he said, shooing me out.

I smiled shyly at Rashida, but she'd gone back to not seeing me.

It was cooler outside, the air mostly clear of the smoke in the enclosed wagon. I could hear the sawing of the crickets, the murmur of the crowd out front. As I stood there wondering what to do, the bass player, Pinkney, emerged from the darkness carrying a wooden crate whose contents clinked.

He bumped purposefully into me, nodded behind to where he'd come. A small stack of similar crates stood near the wagon. I guessed I was being asked to move them to wherever it was he was moving them to.

I hefted a crate, followed him into the gloom.

The beginning of the show was pretty much what I'd seen back in town. A few words from the good doc, then Rashida, Pinkney and Staunton came on stage. They immediately kicked into a version of *Barbara Allen*, then *The Little Old Log Cabin in the Lane*, then *The Lost Child*, where Staunton proved he wasn't just a smartass. He really could play the fiddle.

After a few more words from Dr. Alatryx, the three came back and played through *The Wreck of the Old '97*, where the normally silent Pinckney sang in a pleasing, deep baritone, then *Keep My Skillet Good'n Greasy*, and finally *Risin' Sun Blues*.

About midway through the last number, Alatryx motioned to me from the side of the stage. I stopped tapping my toes and moved quickly to him.

"Get a case or two of the stuff and carry it to the back of the crowd," he said without looking at me. "When I say, go ahead and come forward—slowly, now, slowly, mind ya—and give people a chance to buy. That's what your job is from here on out. Sell as many bottles of this stuff as you can. Buck a bottle. All monies collected come to me. Don't give it to either Pinkney or Staunton. *Me only*."

"What about Rashida?" I asked over the music.

He looked at me and smiled. "Kid, she ain't interested in money. Or you, for that matter. If you were wondering."

He winked, strode onto the stage before I could ask my other question, which seemed more important.

I wasn't wondering about Rashida's interest in me, so that gave me a pause. I walked to where the crates were, deep in thought.

There looked to be about thirty or so people out there now. And I'd only seen four crates, each holding about ten or so bottles of the elixir. What did we do if we sold out, which seemed likely to me?

I picked up two of the crates, hefted them to the rear of the crowd. Two of the town's police cars were parked there, the cops enjoying the music or waiting for something untoward to happen, I wasn't sure. I nodded to the officers and waited as instructed.

I didn't have to wait too long. They finished up on *Risin' Sun Blues*, and Doc Alatryx practically ran back out on stage. I saw Pinkney set his bass aside, then come down and pick up the other two crates, walk to the rear at the other side of the crowd.

"Ladies and gentlemen! Weren't they great? Fantastic performers all, and here entirely for your entertainment this evening."

This drew a second wave of applause and cheers from the crowd, and Alatryx let this subside before speaking. Because now he leaned toward the crowd, put a hand aside his mouth as if we were whispering to them.

"Now they's here for your entertainment," he said in a soft voice. "But I ain't. I'm here for your health. YOUR HEALTH, LADIES AND GENTLMEN!"

He shouted that last line so loudly those who had leaned in to hear his whisper recoiled in surprise.

"That's right, your health. I am one-hundred-percent all about your health, ladies and gentlemen. Who do you know who can say that? Your local doc, mayhap. Sure. Who else? Your momma, if you're lucky enough to have one still here on earth. But who else, I ask?"

He paused dramatically. "NO ONE, I can promise you. Not a single other soul. Not your neighbor, not your government, not no one. Me! So, let me share a little secret with you, a secret of indefatigable health."

He pronounced every syllable of *indefatigable* as if there periods between them.

From within his jacket pocket, he produced a single bottle of the elixir, thrust it into the air. Rashida, still seated on stage behind him, strummed her banjo back and forth manically, with no real tune, just a loud braying of strings.

It had the effect of everyone paying rapt attention to the bottle Alatryx held aloft.

"This is, as promised, the answer to your HEALTH. Your WELFARE. Your VERY LIFE.Got headaches or toothaches? This can help! Got indigestion or insomnia? This can help! Got piles or scurvy, bad teeth or bad breath? This can help! Got weak eyesight or a weak heart? Piles or rickets? Shingles or miasma? THIS LITTLE BOTTLE CAN HELP!"

He turned from the crowd for a moment, then slowly back.

"And it asks so little in return. One dollar, folks. One measly, crummy dollar. That ain't much, is it? Nah. I suspect most of you can scrape up a dollar from your pin money," he said, winking over conspicuously. "Or gents, your beer money?

"I almost forgot, ladies," and here he squatted at the foot of the stage, put his conspiratorial hand near his mouth. "It's also good for your lady issues. You know, that monthly curse and all. Pain and headaches and bloating. NO MORE!"

He barked this last line while leaping to his feet.

As I watched all this, I began to notice folks in the audience begin to root around in pockets, in purses, in jackets. Men were hauling out little-used wallets, and instead of their wives giving them the stink eye—as wives are wont to do with the things men like to spend money on—they prodded them, nudged them to move faster, get that money out.

I was surprised, shocked at how easily these people reacted to the doc's sales pitch. I mean, it's not like these shows hadn't been around for decades. Not like charlatans and mountebanks of all kinds hadn't crisscrossed the country's backroads and highways, filching money from people in all different ways.

These people pulled money out like they's rich, which I knew they weren't. But it looked like we were about to make a good fifty or sixty bucks that night, for a couple of hillbilly songs, a little carnival barking and a few ounces of moonshine.

"One little dollar, folks, and you'll be springing out of bed in the morning, racing to work in the factory or out in the fields, racing home at night. You'll have more energy with your kids, with chores, hell, even with the family dog."

The aside hand again. "And gents, before I forget, it can give you more energy for that lucky lady. Even," he said, this time putting out a fist with one pinky wiggling. "Put a little lead in your pencil. Strictly for those who need that sorta thing, of course."

A wink, his pinky straightened, and ribald laughter rippled through the audience. Wives gave their husbands demure side glances. Younger men elbowed each other in the ribs.

"A dollar for all that, you might ask? ONE AMERICAN DOLLAR. That's it. One single dollar, and all this health, all this vibrancy, all this LIFE is yours. So, there are gentlemen out there with a limited quantity of this miracle brew. LIMITED means when it's GONE, unfortunately, it's GONE. I wouldn't hesitate were I you. I'd buy. Buy two or three, as we might not be back this way for a while. And you DON'T want to run out, folks, now, do ya?"

Doc Alatryx's eyes found me, nodded.

I took one step, just one, into the crowd, and was mobbed.

As I tried to make sense of the bills and coins people were pressing at me, I heard Rashida and Staunton begin to play again. This wasn't anything I'd ever heard, didn't even really seem to qualify as music. There seemed no tune, no structure to the piece, just a lot of caterwauling fiddle and weird, jarring chords on the banjo.

Rashida sang counterpoint to the notes, halting and full of thick, tripping consonants. In a language I'd never heard, held no meaning to me.

They felt greasy on the air, made my mouth parched.

I grabbed money and passed bottles as quickly as I could, jamming wads of bills into my pockets, along with coins and really anything people thrust at me. My other hand doled out bottles from the crate, clinking against each other as the mass of people jostled me.

My first crate was quickly emptied, and I bent to drop it, pick up the next.

As I rose, tucking the filled second crate under my arm, I saw something over the stage, over Alatryx and Rashida and Staunton, maybe twenty or so feet in the air. It was flat, spinning lazily, illuminated from within, perhaps the length of a single railcar. And it seemed sorta here and sorta there, if you take my meaning. Kinda dreamy and foggy, like a ghost that ain't exactly real.

I pushed it aside because I had more immediate concerns. Dozens of hands still pushed money at me, and I could feel other hands trying to lift bottles out of the crate, unpaid. Well, that insulted my skills as a shoplifter, I tell ya. I slapped hands as much as I was taking money from 'em.

One, three, ten, soon all the bottles I had were gone, and disgusted people drew away, no more to be had. I stood there confused. Never heard of a medicine show running out of medicine. I mean, it's what they *did*.

I looked across the crowd to Pinkney, saw him upend his crate, let it fall to the ground.

As if a signal to Alatryx, he barked a single word.

I didn't know then what he said, but the sound of it—and I don't just mean the volume he shouted at—hit my ears as if I'd just taken a roundhouse to the side of my face.

The jarring music reached a crescendo of screeching and wailing, and something unbelievable happened.

Everyone—every man, woman, and child—fell to the ground as if poleaxed. There were no cries or screams or even sighs. They all just collapsed wordlessly to the ground, like someone snatched their skeletons right out of 'em.

The cops had collapsed, too, one slumped across the hood of his cruiser.

Pinkney, paying no attention to me, navigated the crowd, collecting the bottles of Dr. Alatryx's Persian Cure, nestling them carefully back into the crates.

"Hey genius, collect the bottles, quick like," Alatryx yelled from the stage.

It was a job, right? No one looked hurt or dead or anything. Yeah, I checked to make sure they were breathing as I took the bottles back. As I bent here and there, like a mad chicken, I saw Pinkney also stealing money from the wallets and handbags of the unconscious people. I even saw him pull a ring from a finger or two.

On stage, Staunton and Rashida played on, if you can call it that. From here, I could see Staunton sawed at his fiddle, eyes shut. I could see the crow's nests at either side of his eyes, squinched tight.

Rashida, though, had thrown her head back, and she looked… well, she looked like one of those ladies in the churches my parents dragged me to when I was a kid. Some were moved by the holy spirit, or so they said, to gabble like turkeys or throw themselves on the floor and wriggle. Some even handled snakes and such, claiming the Lord protected them from poison.

I expect most of them died. But they all had that same head thrown back, eyes wide, mouth hung open look communicating either something too big to get in.

Or too big to get out.

Blind or not, Rashida had that same look about her.

"Hurry, gentlemen!" Alatryx yelled again, his voice filling the darkened glen. "Get those crates stowed and get this stage struck! Time waits for no man! Once that door is opened, he ain't likely to be too picky 'bout who he takes."

He? I thought. *He who? And what door?*

I kept my head low, filled the crates until every bottle had been returned. I looked back, and Alatryx was impatiently tapping his feet.

"Best get movin', egg, unless you wanna take a trip I guarantee you don't wanna take."

Still having no idea what he was referring to, I hefted both crates, ran as best I could, following Pinkney behind the stage. He loaded the crates into the back of the truck that pulled the wagon, barking at me to load mine, too. I did, then watched Alatryx and Staunton strike the banner, roll it up quickly, stow it above the wagon.

There was a sound, a sort of scratchy, needle-raked-over-the-record sound that came from above. When I looked up, I saw that ghostly pinwheel above the stage.

The thing seemed to be stretching, pulling itself wider like cotton candy at a fair. It was wispy, slightly purple in color. Bursts of lightning leapt across what was becoming a hole at its center. It took on the appearance of a huge, ghost doughnut, still not quite there.

The hole at its middle...that drew my attention.

The sky around this thing was clear and starlit. The air was cool and still, and there weren't any clouds at all. The moon had peeked above the horizon, just over the trees behind the stage, not high enough yet to come near this strange thing. It shone brightly in the sky, which looked a deep, dark blue-purple.

The middle of that thing, where the night sky should have showed, was as black as a darkened room. No stars, no sky.

It was if the sky behind it wasn't there anymore, didn't exist.

I couldn't wrap my mind around what was happening.

If that wasn't the sky, what was it?

I looked back across the stage, but aside from Rashida, none of the others paid it any mind. They acted as if they'd seen it before. As if it happened all the time. Instead, Staunton and Pinkney scrambled here and there, stowing and packing parts of the stage. Only Alatryx looked elsewhere, out into the slumbering crowd.

I watched a man's fedora roll across the foot of the stage, caught by the wind and carried over the treetops.

"Help me with Rashida," he yelled, as the wind strengthened. I didn't know if it was a normal wind or one kicked up by the spinning disc of violet clouds.

Alatryx took one arm and I took her other. Her banjo hung from its strap around her neck. Her head was upraised, mouth open, still singing discordant, nonsense syllables. Now I was closer, I could hear them, thick with twisted consonants.

We carried her limp form off the stage, up the steps and into the wagon, where we lowered her into the seat at the round table. Alatryx settled her head, cheek down, gently onto the table.

He went to the door, turned to me.

"You stay here with her," he said. "Make sure she doesn't get rattled around too much."

"Where are we going?" I asked, raising my voice. The wind

outside had begun to howl, and I could hear the tree limbs creaking outside.

"We're leaving, egg!" Alatryx shouted.

"But the storm," I protested. "All those people…"

Alatryx stood framed in the wagon's doorway, turned his head toward me.

"They got nothing to fear from a little wind," he said. He stepped down the stairs, grabbed the door. "It's what comes *after*…that's the worry."

With that, he closed the door, yelled at me to bolt it from the inside.

Instantly, the trailer was plunged into darkness. I fumbled along the wall until I found the table, sat as the wagon began rocking from side to side. I slid next to Rashida, put my arm around her shoulders to keep her from knockin' about.

The truck started, and the wagon was yanked into motion. There were a few moments of wild lurching and jumping until I guessed the cars found the main road, then we accelerated away.

Outside the darkened trailer, the wind still shrieked, debris struck its sides.

Once or twice, I saw flashes of purple light under the jiggling door frame.

What kind of lighting is purple?

We pulled into the outskirts of what I assumed was Siloam Springs at about two a.m. Rashida was out cold in the wagon, and I had nodded off after leaving Corridon, filled with emotions and questions I could neither contain nor answer.

I was awakened when the wagon's jouncing stopped. I could

hear car doors slam, shouting voices from outside. It was pitch black where I was. Reaching out, I made sure Rashida was okay. She sat beside me, slumped onto the table, snoring noisily. I fumbled my way to the door.

The sky outside was clear, no clouds, certainly no swirling mass or strange, eldritch flashes of lightning. The car with Pinkney and Staunton was pulled just behind the wagon, its headlights on. Dr. Alatryx came around the front of the wagon, from the truck that pulled it.

“Nice trip, egg?” he asked, slapping me on the back as he walked by.

I followed him, saw the two other men had already started a fire, had a small campsite erected. A trivet set up over the fire held a coffee pot, a skillet and a Dutch oven. I could smell bacon cooking.

Alatryx sprawled onto a blanket laid on the ground. Pinkney sat on a stone, glowering over the fire, poking the embers with a stick. Staunton ducked into the car to turn the headlights off, then leaned against the hood, twirling a cup in his fingers, evidently eager for coffee.

“Hungry, kid?” Alatryx asked. “You must be. Didn’t eat much at the soda fountain this morning.”

“Yeah,” I said, coming forward. I hadn’t eaten bacon in a long time, and its smell was intoxicating. “What’s in the pot?”

“Beans,” Pinkney barked. “Last night’s beans is in the pot.”

“Before we go to bed tonight, we’ll slide new beans in. Then we’ll have beans for tomorrow,” Alatryx said. “That’s the way it works. Beans today, beans tomorrow.”

“Life on the road, kid. Better get used to it,” Staunton said.

I sat on a spare blanket on the other side of the fire from Alatryx. “Bacon every night?”

Pinkney snorted, Staunton laughed, but Alatryx seemed insulted.

"Every night, he asks? What a question. No, not *every* night. Sometimes we do well enough to have a nice chicken or even a couple steaks. Other nights, there are just beans. It pans out, as they say."

"How'd we do tonight, then?" I asked.

"Oh-ho, now he wants to know his cut from the evening's proceeds," Alatryx laughed. "Well, let's just see. Gentlemen, empty your pockets and bring the results here. And I adjure you not to keep a single penny!"

I'd forgotten my pockets were crammed with money. I stood hurriedly, stuck my hands in and pulled out what I had. I took this to Alatryx, and he gestured me to dump it onto the blanket before him. Staunton and Pinkney did likewise.

When we were finished, there was quite the mound of bills, coins and jewelry. Alatryx separated the money from the baubles. He counted out the bills in a pile, then the change.

"Well, gentlemen, it looks like steak tomorrow," he said. "We made nearly fifty dollars. And when I pawn the rest of this stuff, we might make another twenty or so. Enough for steaks and maybe a bottle or two, if it can be had."

Staunton and Pinkney hooted. Alatryx peeled off a few bills each, wadded them up and tossed them over to the men. He eyed me carefully, tossed me something.

Surprised, I fumbled it, almost knocked it into the fire. I saved it, peeled apart two dollars. I sat on my blanket, mesmerized. I couldn't remember if I'd ever held two dollar bills at once.

"Kid's in shock," Staunton said, then laughed.

"More where that came from, egg. If you play your cards right," Alatryx said.

"Bacon's done, coffee's brewed," Pinkney said.

Alatryx climbed to his feet.

I jammed the money back into my pocket, stood.

"I'll go get Rashida," I said.

Alatryx looked amused. "Whatever for?"

"For supper."

The three of them laughed, Pinkney sloshing a little of the beans into a tin bowl.

"She ain't missing anything she'd want, trust me, egg," Alatryx said.

I ate beans and bacon off a tin plate, sipped strong, black coffee from a tin mug and thought myself a prince of the world.

When I awoke the next day, the sun blazed in a blue sky. I blinked up into its vast emptiness, then shielded my eyes, rubbed them. I was alone, the other blankets around the fire, now just ashes, rolled and stacked.

The truck and the wagon were still there, which gave me relief. I honestly thought they'd all picked up and left me in the middle of the night. But the other car was gone.

I stood, stretched, headed off into the tree line to pee. When I returned, I examined the coffee pot and beans on the trivet over the fire. There was coffee left, though cold coffee was not appealing. Ditto a potful of cold beans.

I went to the wagon, wondering what time it was. I had no idea how long I'd slept or where the others were. I climbed the steps, listened at the door, then knocked quietly.

"Come in, cute boy," whispered Rashida.

I hesitated.

Cute boy?

I drew the door open onto air dense and humid as a held breath. Light flooded the darkened room, casting its contents into stark relief. No candles burned or lamps lit. She'd been sitting here in the dark.

"You coming in or what?" she asked. She was seated at the table, as she had been when I'd left her last night. She had risen at some point, because now she was wearing a spectacular oriental silk robe, bright with turquoise and red and orange and gold stitching. Her hair was pulled back from her face with a violet kerchief. Her face was smooth and unlined, her eyes bright and clear.

"Should I leave the door open or will we just sit in the dark?" I asked.

"You afraid to sit in the dark with me, cute boy?"

Her tone was curious. It was open and mocking, yet still gentle and joking.

"Nah, I ain't afraid of the dark, though I don't know what we'd do," I said, trying to sound all manly and brave.

"Don't you now?" she asked, and that had an edge to it, biting and daring.

I stepped into the wagon and closed the door, holding her eyes all the while.

The room was dipped in black, and for a moment I cursed myself for looking—*being!*—so dumb. But instantly, a light flared.

Rashida held a match to one of the lanterns hanging from the ceiling over the table, and the room swam in yellowed illumination, the light that seemed to suit it best. She shook the match out, lit another, touched a few candles with it. Soon, the entire interior was alight with flickering flames.

"You gonna come sit here or stand there with your mouth hanging open," she said, laughing a little.

Of all the things that happened in that room, then or later, her laugh is the thing that bothers me most. It was a slow, languorous laugh, oozy and slithery, and it made gooseflesh raise on my arms.

I went to the table, sat beside her.

She was beautiful there in the candlelight. I think I'd never noticed up to that point. When I thought she was just a little girl, I didn't pay attention, and by the time I knew she wasn't, things were moving too fast to care much.

Here, in this wagon, she was beautiful.

She smelled fantastic, all of sandalwood and musk and roses and something peppery and spicy but unplaceable. I inhaled deeply as I sat, and she seemed to notice, giggling again.

"Breathe deep, sweetie," she said, leaning into me a little.

Confusion washed over me again. I was like a dumb beach where this wave crashed over me continuously.

"You're wondering what we're doing here," Rashida said, her silver eyes flashing in the candlelight. "And I don't mean you and I, right here."

I kinda was more wondering about her and I right there, but I let it pass. Mostly because it scared me for the conversation to veer in that direction.

"So, what are we doing here?"

She turned to me, waggled her eyebrows suggestively.

"What's your view of the world, cute boy?" she asked, reaching out to take my hand. Hers was big for her size, but soft and warm.

"My…view?" I said.

"What is the world to you? What does it mean?"

"I'm not sure…I mean, the world is the world, isn't it? All of it, the land and the oceans and stuff. People," I stammered. "Animals."

She nodded enthusiastically. "Yes, all that. But what about the sky?"

"Sure."

"And what lies beyond. Space and the stars and planets."

"I guess so."

"And what lies beyond?"

Confusion.

"Uhh…heaven?"

She beamed at me.

"Okay, sure. Heaven. So, what lies beyond?"

I wasn't sure what she meant.

"Beyond heaven?" I asked. "Nothing."

That last word was meant to be both a statement and a question, because I truly had no idea what she was getting at.

"Nothing. And that's your worldview, sweetie? There's all this around us. Then, heaven. Then, nothing."

She was definitely mocking me now, but I was lost in the forest of her words.

"Think for a moment of shows you've seen. Plays perhaps. Or movies. You seen a picture show?"

I nodded. I'd seen a couple as I'd passed through bigger cities like St. Louis or Memphis.

"Think of, well, this little show you're helping with now. All of these shows are directed toward the audience, right? Everything we do, every song we play, everything you see up there flickering on that big movie screen. It's all for the audience."

She touched my cheek, stroked her nails gently to my hairline.

"But even with just one night in, you know what goes on before and after—even during—the show. You know stages have to be set, props provided. Concessions sold and money collected. It's the same for everything, cute boy—shows, movies, churches. Reality."

I closed my eyes at the feeling of her fingers toying with the edges of my hair. She leaned into me, put her lips to my ear.

"Remember. There's always stuff going on behind the curtain, backstage. Always people needed to keep the show going."

I shivered at the feel of her breath, and then there was a disturbance from the other end of the wagon. Light burst in, and my head jerked up. I shielded my eyes but saw a dark shape in the light.

"Aww, hell, kid," came Alatryx's voice. "I was gone for an hour. Just one hour, and you're already screwing up."

"Dr. Alatryx!" I said, trying to sidle away from Rashida. But she held my hand, kept me close. "I...umm...woke up and no one was here, so I came in to say good morning to Rashida and..."

"Spare me the details, egg," he said, coming into the wagon and frowning. But he wasn't directing that at me, leastways not like he was his words. No, the frown was for Rashida.

"Why don't you leave the lovely Rashida to her own devices, hmm? Come on out and help me scout for an appropriate area for tomorrow's performances?"

I saw Staunton and Pinkney behind him. Pinkney stared at the ground, disinterested. Staunton, though, lounged on the hood of the car, smirked.

"Sure," I said, a bit too energetically. I launched myself away from Rashida's grip, pushed from the table with enough force to rock the wagon, several of the hanging lamps swaying crazily. I lost my balance, stumbling into Alatryx.

He caught me roughly.

"Ready?" he said, steadying me. I nodded, and he leaned past me to address Rashida. "We'll leave you be. I know your beauty sleep is vital to your wellbeing. Wouldn't want you to appear tomorrow in a disheveled appearance, my dear, now would we?"

Rashida smiled thinly. "No, I expect no one would enjoy that."

"We'll see you tomorrow, then," he said, pulling me out and

down the stairs, then closing the wagon's door on her. The sunlight nearly blinding me, the last thing I saw was Rashida blowing me a kiss I don't think anyone else noticed. The candles reflected in her silver eyes.

"Don't bother her while I'm not around, egg," Alatryx frowned

"Why? We were just talking, that's all," I said, starting to feel a little defensive.

"Talking opens all sorts of doors better left closed," he said, almost airily. Then, he turned to the other two. "We're going to scout for a location for tomorrow's show. Who wants to stay here and guard the wagon and who wants to come to town?"

"I'll go to town. He'll stay," Staunton said, sliding off the hood and hooking his thumb towards Pinkney.

"It's settled then," Alatryx said, getting into the car. "You ride shotgun, egg."

Staunton, who already had the front passenger door open, glared at me as I took the seat. He closed the door mock gently, then got into the backseat.

We drove a short way into Siloam Spring, down dirt tracks almost overgrown with weeds. It was a cool day, and the cicadas droned lazily. We passed a few houses here and there, ramshackle cabins most of them, with listing porches, warped boards and tarpaper siding.

A few children, dirty and missing teeth, played in these yards, stopped to watch us dumbly as we drove by. In one or two, a slovenly mother—wrapped in a worn, soiled dressed, barefoot, with lank hair and sunken eyes—would stand on the porch and glare at us, not waving, not smiling. Blank as an old stain.

With no transition, we were suddenly in the main part of town. Just a single street, unpaved, a few low buildings and a church at the far end of the street. Post office, a general store, a gas station, what looked to be a Grange Hall. A small café.

A few men milled the street. Two were hunched over the open engine of a truck, hard at work within. They lifted their heads at the sound of our car, watched with narrowed eyes as we slid down the street. Two dogs lay sprawled in the road, didn't move at all as Alatryx steered around them.

"Stop here and let me out. Fancy a hamburger at that place there," Staunton said.

Alatryx stopped the car, and Staunton got out, came around to the driver side.

"We'll be back by in an hour or two," Alatryx said. "Might stop at the general store there, see about supplies and such."

"Gotcha," Staunton said, slapping the side of the car as Alatryx put the car back in gear, drove away.

We were down the street and past the church before Alatryx spoke.

"So, what were you talking to Rashida about, egg?"

I had my right arm cocked over the open window, and I'd stuck my head out a little, to let the wind blow across my face. When he said this, I leaned back into the car.

"What did I what?"

"Talk about with Rashida?"

"Nothing much. I hadn't been in there long when you opened the door."

"What was the nothing much you two discussed?"

The road had wound its way out of town now, circling up a small hill.

"About what I was doing, helping the show and all," I said.

Alatryx considered. "And what *are* you doing, egg?"

Was I supposed to be the innocent rube here and not let on I knew or was I supposed to just come clean?

"Helping out with a traveling medicine show. We move from town to town playing music and selling patent medicine."

"And…?"

"And we fleece people of their money, take the product back and move on," I said, opting for the latter approach. "I mean, I'm not dense, doc."

He looked away, but I saw him roll his eyes as he did.

"Okay, kid," he said, chuckling. "Just as long as you know what you've got yourself into."

I waited for him to say something else, but we drove on in silence for quite a while. I thrust my head out the window again, hearing nothing much but the rush of wind, feeling the warmth of the sun on my face, when I felt him nudge my arm.

"Not to put too fine a point on this, but before you get dingy on the canary back there, watch yourself. My advice is stay away, particularly when I'm not around."

"I told you. We weren't doing anything at all," I said, getting angry.

"You just don't get it, do you?" he said. "I'm trying to protect *you*."

"I can handle myself," I said, I guess a bit to off-handedly, and he reached over and gripped my shoulder tightly.

"Okay, genius. Just think about this, though. We've been doing this show for a while now. You suppose you're the first stagehand we've ever had?"

He turned his attention back to finding a suitable spot for the show.

I sat quietly, thinking about what he said.

What he *meant.*

Wasn't long after we found what Dr. Alatryx pronounced as the "perfect" place to set up shop. Like back in Corridon, the spot was a secluded little glen right off a dirt road about two miles outside Siloam Springs. A series of gentle, sloping hills formed a little bowl, with a broad, grassy field spread out before it.

We drove back to camp, hung around all evening until dinner time, which was beans and coffee and four thick steaks Staunton had procured for us. No steak, I noticed, for Rashida. She, in fact, stayed inside the wagon by herself the entire day and evening. No one, including Alatryx, went in to check on her.

Aside from a few other essentials—soap, coffee, salt, flour and more beans—Staunton produced two unmarked glass jugs of what he called white whiskey, procured from a person he'd struck up a conversation with in town. We sat around the campfire after eating our steaks—also a first for me—patting our bellies, groaning, passing the glass bottle around and taking nips from it.

"Careful there, egg," Alatryx said, handing the bottle to me for the first round. "This ain't like bottled beer you're accustomed to. And we got a show tomorrow."

He winked to the others as I took the bottle, swallowed a far bigger mouthful than I intended. It burned like fire in my throat, but I was able to keep it down without coughing or gagging. My eyes, I'm sure, bugged out of my skull, though.

I gave the bottle to Pinkney, and so the evening passed.

The next morning, we rose, had coffee, then rode into town, wagon and all. As when I first saw them in Corridon, Alatryx parked the wagon in a conspicuous place—in front of the church—and the warm-up show began.

They played a few tunes, Rashida sang and strummed the banjo, and Alatryx invited all to come out to see us that night. There weren't many people, certainly nowhere near as many as in Corridon, and both Alatryx and Rashida seemed out of sorts about it when they came offstage.

That night, the weather was warm and dense. There were only about a dozen or so people in the audience. Nonetheless, the trio played much as they had the night before last, bouncing their way through *Blue Yodel No. 3, Ragged but Right* and *Sugar Baby Blues.*

I thought they'd do more, but they almost seemed eager to get tonight's show over. After *Sugar Baby Blues*, Alatryx came back out, rushed through his patter, and then I was out in the crowd, alone this time, dispensing bottles.

Nothing like the last performance. There were a few people asking to look at the bottles. A few asked if they could sample them. Unsure, I told them no.

I sold maybe a half dozen bottles, Alatryx all the while frowning sourly from the stage. This time no spinning wheel appeared over the stage, no weird portal at its center. Rashida kept singing, but while it was not really words—more like jazz scatting—it wasn't anything approaching what I'd heard previously. This wasn't all clunky consonants and weird patterns. And it didn't hurt my ears to hear it.

After I'd collected all I was likely to collect, I stood holding the mostly filled crate.

Alatryx nodded, then left the stage. They stumbled through their last numbers—*My Blue Ridge Mountain Home* and *Chicken Reel*—though with no great urgency or energy. When they were done, they were done. Staunton and Pinkney took their instruments off stage to a smattering of applause.

Rashida stood and looked out into the crowd, found me.

Surprisingly, she smiled and winked.

I felt funny, as if the rest of the audience had seen this—as if Alatryx had noticed it—and lurched into motion, banging the crate against my hip as I hurried it back to the wagon.

The people and the few cars dispersed quickly. I helped Staunton and Pinkney roll the banner, take down the stage, stow everything away.

When I finished, Alatryx was standing near the front of the car, talking with Staunton.

"…try a little bigger, mind you. How about Doniphan, down near the Arkansas border? After, we can head down there or over into Tennessee. Don't make much of a difference."

Pinkney and Staunton nodded, said nothing as I approached. I emptied my pockets of the money I'd collected—three bills and a handful of change—and held it out to Alatryx.

"Keep it, egg. Like everything else about tonight, it ain't worth bothering with," Alatryx said, as Staunton and Pinkney drifted away, into the car. "Come on. You ride with me in the truck tonight."

"I want him," came Rashida's voice. She stood at the top of the steps into the wagon, turned back toward us. "He's gonna ride with me."

Alatryx sighed. "You remember when I said you shouldn't be offering to help me? Keep that in mind."

I had no idea if that was permission, a warning or both, so I stood rooted to the spot.

"Well, go on. Mustn't keep a lady waiting," he said, then lowering his voice. "But mind yourself, kid. Really."

I walked away, took Rashida's waiting hand, and we drifted into the darkened wagon.

"Longer drive tonight," she said, settling in as the wagon began moving. "Plenty of time to get to know each other."

I sat next to her. The tin lanterns hanging over the table swayed and bounced, the holes punched into them casting constellations that jumped and spun cross the ceiling.

"Where you from anyway?" she asked, putting her hand over mine I had placed atop the table to steady myself.

"From southern Illinois, around Makanda," I told her. "Out in the middle of nowhere, really."

"Why'd you leave?" she asked.

"Weren't nothing to do anywhere around there…except coal mining. And I didn't want to do that. I'd seen my dad and my uncles all work the mines. They thought I'd follow. Not because they particularly wanted me to, mind you. What else was there?"

"So, what'd you do?"

"I left is what I did. Set out on my own with clothes and a few books. Been doing odd jobs and stuff, farmhand, field picker, that sorta thing."

"Until you saw our show in Corridon."

"Yeah, I guess. Just a spur of the moment thing, really. Me talking with Dr. Alatryx at the soda fountain. Lucky for me, you guys evidently needed a new hand to replace the one you lost."

Rashida seemed surprised. "He told you? Told you about Roy?"

"Well, he didn't mention a name or anything. And he was pretty vague about it."

"I see."

"What was he like?" I asked, weirdly, stupidly feeling a pang of jealousy twang through me.

"Roy? Oh, he was fine, in his way. No one I paid much attention to, mind you," she said, looking at me from under her eyelids as if knowing what my reaction would be.

"What happened to him?"

"Moved onto to bigger and better things. Least, that's what I understand. Not my concern," she said, subtly moving into me, covering my hand with both of hers. "What's the goal here, cute boy? What's your plan?"

My mouth went schoolboy-dry. "My errr…plan?"

"Yeah, your goal."

"I…well…I'm not sure what I mean…I mean you mean…I mean…"

She left me hanging there for what seemed an eternity, then laughed that little bird-trill laugh of hers. "I mean for your life. What do you want out of life? What do you want to do?"

"Oh," I said, swallowing, trying to get the spit to every corner of my mouth to lubricate my words. "That. Well, I'm not sure. I wanted to get out and see the country, ride the rails. Try my hand at a bunch of stuff to see what I like, what I'm good at. Other than that, I don't know."

"Family? Kids?"

"Sure, back in Makanda, a sister and two brothers. Mom and Dad."

That laugh. "I mean for you. Ever thought of a family, having kids of your own?"

The dry mouth came back in a rush, and I could feel sweat leap out the pores of my body.

"Kids? *Me?* No, never thought of that. I mean…"

"Well you'd have to have a girl first, I suppose," she said, squeezing my hand.

I squirmed, tried to think of what to say.

"Dr. Alatryx warned me away from you," I stammered, instantly regretting.

"Oh, he did, did he?" she giggled, turning my hand over in hers, clasping it tightly. Her grip was soft and warm, and her fingers…her fingers felt strange entwined in mine. They were so soft and pliable, and it felt as if there were so many of them.

"He's probably right, you know," she said, then leaned into me, found my lips with hers.

I've never been much of a ladies' man. I've had one or two great loves of my life, but I sorta lucked into them. It wasn't because I'd been a great swain or spectacular lover.

What I'm trying to say is girls always made me nervous, especially back then, young as I was. But Rashida…she made me so nervous I could scarcely see straight.

And that kiss. That kiss stirred deep within, uncoiling inside and spreading out, as if plumbing the dimensions of my body for the very first time.

She pulled away slowly, leaving me puckering there in the air like a freshly caught fish. I'd closed my eyes but opened them to see she hadn't. Her silvery eyes regarded me as if she saw directly into me.

"Where are you from?" I asked.

She touched my temple, moved away a lock of my hair.

"Oh, nowhere you'd know, really."

"Try me."

"Carcosa. A great city. Far removed from here."

"Carcosa? Sounds like a place in South America."

She giggled, covered her mouth. "Exactly. Deep, deep south."

"So, how'd you end up with Dr. Alatryx?"

She stared at me without answering, as if she were measuring me.

"You really have no idea what we're doing here, do you?"

"Selling bootleg whiskey to the rubes."

"That's part of the act, cute boy," she said, pursing her lips as if pouting at me. "And just as there've been other stagehands, there've been other Dr. Alatryxs. Other Stauntons. Other Pinkneys.

"But just one me."

I considered that, tried to fathom what she was saying.

"I don't get it."

Because I truly didn't get it.

She leaned in, whispered into my ear.

"Press gangs."

I drew away, frowned at her.

"Huh?"

She giggled, pulled me near, stopped my questions with kisses.

As we kissed and kissed, I fell into a swoon. My lips kept moving over hers, my eyes still closed. Her tongue moved inside my mouth, startling me. Never had a girl do that, and it was weirdly arousing. But, man, her tongue seemed to grow in length and in girth, flicking back and forth, until it almost filled my mouth.

I began to worry it would snake down my throat. But I was lulled into a trance. I don't know if it was the hypnotic swaying of the lamps or her cool, soft hands moving over my cheeks.

Or the taste of her, redolent of spice I'd never savored, earthy, salty, but also brackish and mildewed.

I passed out.

I woke to her hands on the nape of my neck, stroking, tickling me with her nails.

I groggily lifted my head from the pool of spit gathered under my cheek. The lamps still burned, but they weren't swinging anymore.

The wagon had stopped.

There came a rap at the door.

"Get up, egg," shouted Alatryx. "We're here."

"We're in Doniphan already?" I croaked, blinking dumbly at Rashida. It felt like only a few minutes had passed since we'd kissed.

"My how time flies," she said, still toying with my hair.

Alatryx eyed me suspiciously as I climbed from the wagon, closing the door behind me. We ate dinner around a campfire too hot for the warm night. When I looked up, I almost hallucinated I was still in the wagon, the pin-pricked tin lanterns casting their jittery stars against its ceiling.

We ate in silence, bedded down in silence.

We set up late the next morning in Doniphan. Not as big as Corridon, with its railway station, but bigger than Siloam Springs. At the dusty end of the little burg, just past the town hall, we parked the wagon, unfurled the banner, set out the stage.

Noon saw Dr. Alatryx bound onto the stage to announce the show to the few people who'd gathered to see what was up. By the time Rashida, Staunton and Pinkney had launched into the first song—*Who's Been Giving You Corn?*—we had a crowd of about thirty people. Probably damn near everyone who was in downtown Doniphan at the time.

The trio plucked and sawed their way through two more songs, *Nellie Dare* and *Big Bend Gal*, before Alatryx returned to announce we'd be playing (and selling the patent medicine) just outside the city limits, near the cement plant.

The crowd dispersed quickly as we put everything away. Alatryx disappeared onto the main street, as he had in Corridon, probably to find something to eat or drink. Rashida went into the wagon, and Staunton and Pinkney drove off in the car, leaving me alone.

I remembered I had about six or seven dollars in my pocket. I had never held that much money in my life, and it floored me. I was hungry, too, and tired of beans. I walked down the main street to see what was available.

It was a pretty small town, so the answer was not much.

There were two restaurants, though. One was a diner-type place, and when I looked inside the window, there sat Alatryx chatting up the waitress. I didn't want to eat with him, and I'm sure he shared that sentiment, so I sauntered down to the other place.

This was attached to the general store, and looked to be really more for the town's working men, whatever trade they were in. Small tables covered in gingham with a counter that also served the store.

I went in, the little bell ringing over my head. A few of the workmen hunched over their lunches turned to look at me, just as quickly went back to eating.

"Go ahead and sit where you want, hun," came a voice. I turned and saw a girl about my age, dark hair, slim figure, wearing a pair of overalls, her hair tied into a ponytail. She was behind the counter, ringing an old biddy up.

There were stools, so I sat.

When she was finished, the old woman left, giving me a hard glance as she went through the door.

"Don't mind old Gladys," the girl said, coming toward me. "She has a dim view of your people."

"My *people*?"

"You show folks," she said, then she saw I still didn't understand. "You're with that show just played out there by the town hall, right? I mean, I saw you hanging 'round and didn't recognize you. So, I just assumed you were with them."

She was breathtakingly pretty up close. As fresh-faced and rosy as only a country girl can be. Her eyes were startlingly grey-blue, and her hair was black as night.

I, of course, reverted to the stammering idiot I was around girls.

"Well, yeah, I'm with the show. I mean I'm not *in* the show or anything. I just help out is all."

She smiled, and it was like the sun coming through the clouds on a cold winter's day.

"I thought so. What'll you have?"

"What do you recommend?" I said. "I got money and all."

She crinkled her face as if I were joshing her. "Well, that's good. My daddy frowns on me giving meals and such away."

I blushed then, don't know why, and she laughed. But it wasn't like Rashida's laugh—knowing and a little mocking. It was friendly and warm.

"I recommend the hamburger, if you're that sort. Meatloaf's good, too," she said, then leaned in conspiratorially. "But it's from last night."

"Delilah!" came a coarse voice through the narrow kitchen window.

"Sorry, daddy," she called, then turned back to me and winked.

"I'll have the hamburger and fries, if you got 'em. And a Coke."

"Great. Grab one yourself from the machine over there. I'll just go and put this order in before daddy growls at me again."

I nodded and watched her walk away. I think she noticed I was watching—or at least seemed to hope I was—for she turned back to me after speaking through the window and winked.

I stumbled to my feet, feeling the heat rise on my cheeks, to get that Coke. Sitting back down, I sipped from the ice-cold bottle, wanting it to last. Then, I realized I had enough money to get several Cokes if I wanted. So, I started to guzzle it. When I was finished, I went and got another.

"Whoa, there, boy. Slow down," Delilah said, setting a plate before me. I could smell the hamburger, and it made my stomach rumble. "Save some for the other customers."

"I will, I promise," I said, reseating myself. "Thanks, Delilah."

She stayed there as I ate, pretending to clean the shelves of canned goods behind the counter. "Call me Del," she said. "No one calls me Delilah, only my daddy."

"Okay, Del. You can call me Baker. My real name's Bakewell, but my folks and friends call me Baker. Or Bake. Whatever you like."

"You're having a show tonight, right, Bake?" she asked, her back to me.

"Yep," I said, scarfing another bite of the burger. "Outside of town near the cement plant."

"I know where that is," she said, dragging the rag over the counter around my plate. "What time?"

"Seven sharp. Doc Alatryx likes to be prompt and all."

"I'd like to come see it," she said, and I noticed she'd stopped pretending she was cleaning.

"Oh, well, you should. Definitely," I said, stopping the flow of fries to my mouth. "You'll have fun, if you like that kind of music."

"Course, I might have to bring my daddy," she huffed.

"Well, that's fine."

Like I said, pretty dumb.

"I expect he'll be so caught up in the music he won't notice if I wander off," she said, lowering her voice and looking over her shoulder at the kitchen window. "Maybe you might have time to wander off with me?"

One single girl from age zero to twenty, then two in a day.

"Yes, ma'am. I ain't got a lot to do while they're playing," I said.

"Great. I'll tell my daddy we need to go tonight," she said, then flounced away.

"Okay, Del."

"I'll see you tonight, Bakey-boy," she turned and whispered.

I swallowed my last bite of burger, felt like an electric cord had been plugged into me.

"Hey, Del" I said.

"Yeah?"

"Can I get another burger?"

She smiled, disappeared into the kitchen.

That night was crowded, almost as many people as had been at Corridon. Maybe fifty or so, including the obligatory cops. I stayed behind the wagon with Pinkney, topping off the bottles of patent medicine with a couple of mason jars filled with hootch they'd finagled from wherever it was they'd visited that afternoon.

Pinkney was normally silent around me, so I nearly jumped out of my skin when he spoke, hunched over the crates of bottles.

"You get anywhere with Rashida?" he asked, corking a bottle and sliding it back into place.

I jerked up, stared at him.

"What's the matter, kid? Snake bite ya? Rashida bite ya?" He laughed then, at least I guess that's what it was. A low rumble like a car engine trying to turn over.

"Get anywhere?" I asked, as if I didn't know what he meant. "No, I mean…we might've kissed, but that was it."

I had no idea why I told him, other than he'd shocked me by speaking.

"Well, at least she didn't *send* you anywhere. She must like you better'n poor old Roy," he said, shaking his head, then hefting his crate and carrying it into the growing crowd.

"What'd she do to Roy?"

Pinkney shook his head, relapsed into his silence as he walked away with a stack of crates. I watched him leave, feeling a little uncomfortable.

At least she didn't send you anywhere.

Send?

What the hell was that supposed to mean?

I had little time to think, as I heard Alatryx's voice boom from onstage. I had to get into the audience with my crates and do my job.

But I was beginning to wonder exactly what my job was.

They were playing *Big Rock Candy Mountain* by the time I reached the back of the audience. The crowd was singing along and swaying, laughing, smiling. Rashida's voice was high and clear, and she even whistled during part of it. I put the crates down, scanned the backs of the gathered people to find Del.

There she was, seated next to her mountain of a father on a blanket. She was singing and clapping, too, but she was looking around. I hoped she was looking for me.

When she found me, it was as if as she'd speared my heart, wriggling like a fish in my chest. She spoke to her dad, kissed his cheek, then came to me.

She wore a red gingham dress, and her hair was down, night black against the paleness of her skin. She wore lipstick and there were subtle dots of rouge on her cheeks. She smiled shyly as she approached, and my heart beat so hard it threatened to leap from my throat and toddle off down the lane.

"Well, hello there Bakey-boy," she said, coming near and kissing my cheek demurely. Where her lips touched my skin, they left burning weals.

"Hi," I croaked, not knowing what else to say, how to stand, where to put my hands, and dozens of other inconsequential things.

"So, this is what you do?" she asked, her eyes telling me she was teasing.

"Well, I help put the stage and everything up, tear it down. And I sell the patent medicine during the show," I said, bending to pull one of the amber bottles from the crate. I held it out to her, and she took it from my hands, turned it over and over.

She surprised me by uncorking it and taking a sniff, then a large swig.

"Let's take a bottle of this and head over into the woods there. If you want, that is."

I wanted.

We crept past the police cars and into a thin stand of woods. The lights from the stage shone through the branches, giving wan illumination. Del leaned against a tree trunk, pulled me close. As the musicians played *The Fate of Talmedge Osborn*, she locked her lips with mine. I tasted the raw alcohol on her breath, dense and metallic, felt the waxy smear of her lipstick against my mouth.

I was barely able to catch my breath when she took my hands and put them onto her body, one on her waist, the other cupping a breast. She breathed heavily into my mouth, while her hands fumbled with my pants.

Up to that point, I was pretty inexperienced. Been with one girl, did little more than heavy petting, as they said in those days.

Now she was unzipping my pants. Her hand, her unfamiliar hand, dove into the opening and grabbed a part of me had never before felt another's touch. And it took notice.

She hiked up her dress, pushed my hand down to touch her *there*. She wore no underclothes, and my hand trembled as it passed down the smoothness of her belly, into the thatch of her own woods.

She jumped up a bit, wrapped her legs around my waist, guided me with her fingers. And suddenly, I was engulfed in warmth, in tightness I'd never felt before. I had no idea what to do, but my body seemingly did, and I moved into her, pulled away, back and forth, bouncing her against the tree trunk.

"Take me with you when you leave," she panted, her lips near my ear. "Take. Me. With. You."

I think I agreed, not sure now with the passage of years. And my brain had sort of detached itself from every other activity save the one I was engaged in.

But I know my answer would have been *yes*. Would be *yes* if she was here, asking me today. She should have come with me. I should have gone with her.

We finished on a wave of heat and gasps. I lowered her to the ground, stepped away on shaky legs.

"You'll take me? You really will? You promise?" she said, still breathing hard.

"I will. Promise," I said, finding my own voice.

I stepped in, kissed her again, hard, and she returned it.

Dr. Alatryx's voice boomed through the trees.

"Ladies and gentlemen! Weren't they great? Fantastic performers all, and here entirely for your entertainment this evening."

"Shoot!" I said, zipping my pants up hurriedly. "I gotta go."

"Okay. You go do your show. I'll wait after. And we'll go, right?"

I could almost see her eyes there in the darkness, pleading with me louder than her words.

"We'll go," I said, pecking her once more on the cheek before racing out of the woods and back to my stack of crates.

I saw Alatryx looking for me as he did his patter. When he finally found me, a frown passed quickly over his features.

When he reached the part where the sales were supposed to begin, I moved into the crowd, handing out bottles and taking money. Del had returned to her father's side, and he bought two bottles of the stuff himself.

As I finished, I heard Rashida's nonsense singing start, the hard, ungainly syllables, the strange melody-less melody. I saw the air congeal into a flat, spinning disc, like a phonograph. That strange purple light. The hole of darkness at its center.

I remembered, then, what was about to happen, and I rushed back to where Del sat with her father, my hands stuffed with money, coins that dribbled out along the way.

As I neared, I saw Del's face, rapturous, bobbing and weaving to Rashida's discordant tune. Her eyes were the same shining silver as Rashida's, nearly glowing in their sockets. Del's father's were, too.

I looked around the gathering, saw everyone's eyes were metallic silver.

"Best be moving, egg," Alatryx shouted to me from the stage. Then, he looked up at the swirling mass above him. "Looks hungry tonight. Don't want to be caught down there with them. Leastways, I wouldn't."

I took his words in a panic, looked over to Rashida. She was still in a trance, still singing. Staunton and Pinkney stood on stage behind her, smirking.

I turned to where Del had slumped over onto her father.

"No, no, no," I said, threading my hands under her arms. I had hefted her over my shoulders when I saw the other folks in the audience rise from the ground. Most of them had fallen over, asleep. Now, their prone bodies lifted into the air, as if grabbed by their waists.

I glanced up, saw the pulsing, vaporous light above. From the dark heart at its center, ghostly appendages slithered down snakelike. They were a strange purple green, about the thickness of a baseball bat, and semi-transparent.

There were a lot of them, and each had latched onto an unconscious person, lifted them toward the dark pupil at the heart of the spinning clouds. The people floated on their backs, their limbs dangling limp beneath them.

I felt Del's body lift, too, and I tightened my grip on her, slapped at the phantom tentacles grabbing her. My hands went right through them as if they were mist, yet their grasp on Del was strong.

I gritted my teeth, watched her father's huge, prone form ascend, higher, higher, until it disappeared into the darkness.

I would not let that happen to Del.

I could not prevent that from happening to Del.

The tentacle pulled, inextricable, until I lost my grip, watched her body sail beyond my straining fingertips, up, up, her dark hair fanning from her head until she vanished, too.

And then I felt a tentacle grasp me.

It pulsed around my shoulders, slid down to my body. I saw it, semi-transparent in the light, circling me, tightening.

No, not a chance.

I broke into a run toward the stage, and the thing—momentarily confused—loosened its hold. I dashed up the steps, and it lost its grip, vanished in a puff of grey smoke.

Staunton and Pinkney laughed, and Alatryx came toward me from across the small stage.

"Did you think I was just bumping gums when I told you to...," he shouted.

I drew back and slammed my fist into the side of his head. He looked at me funny as I swung, but the punch floored him. Pinkney didn't move, but Staunton went to his side to check on him.

He was out cold.

The wind picked up, and jagged bolts of purple lighting flashed. All of the people from the audience had disappeared, and the stormy eye overhead seemed to be closing, collapsing in on itself.

"Now, look, scrub, before you go off half-cocked, you better get it straight," Staunton shouted over the whine of the wind.

"Shut up or I'll deck you, too," I said.

Staunton looked over to Pinkney, who didn't move.

I went to Rashida, pushing past Staunton. She sat on her chair mid-stage, still sort of strumming the banjo. Her head was thrown back on her neck, her face pointed up toward that spinning nexus. Her eyes flashed silver with each burst of lightning.

"Rashida!" I yelled, laying hands on her shoulders and shaking her. "Rashida! Whatever you're doing, stop! You gotta stop!"

But she didn't. She still strummed, she still babbled. The clouds spun overhead.

"Rashida!"

I leaned over her face and saw something I had no way of identifying.

Her mouth moved around those strange, unwieldy syllables, but inside, back behind her teeth, where her tongue floated, there was yellow-green liquid bubbling up from her throat, like a thick soup.

She didn't (or couldn't) swallow, but it didn't seem to inhibit her sing-song cadence.

I reached out, put my hands to her face, held her cheeks. They felt flushed and damp.

I touched her lips, opened her mouth a little more. The stuff inside spun lazily, as if it had been stirred. Spun like the clouds above.

I opened her mouth more, pulled her chin down to get a better look. It unhinged like the jaw of a snake, literally fell away to clump onto the wooden stage floor.

I stepped back in alarm, and Staunton stumbled across the stage. Alatryx lay still, even as Staunton kicked him.

Rashida's jaw stretched a good three feet from her face to the floor, drooping open like a wet bag. But nothing spilled out. All of that greenish soup stayed inside her cavernous maw, swirling in rhythm with the clouds overhead.

I stepped forward carefully, reached for Rashida.

Now it was Pinkney's turn to warn me.

"Are you whacky, kid?" he said. "Don't do it!"

I thought of Del, her kisses, her beautiful face and dark hair.

I took hold of Rashida's mouth, pulled it apart horizontally until my arms were stretched to their maximum. Her mouth held its shape, she still sang, and not one drop of stuff spilled from her. Her mouth was now the size of a small door, that stuff churning inside.

"Kid, really," Pinkney shouted.

Holding on to either side, I stepped forward, put one foot into her distended mouth, ducked under her teeth and lips, holding them out like the flaps of a tent.

Went *through* her...

...And stepped into a landscape I'd never thought possible. The first thing I noticed was the sky, although it was only the sky in the sense it was what stretched over me. I had half-expected to look up and see Rashida's teeth, her upper palette.

But no.

This was a striated, swirling mess, like melted rainbow sherbet over a schoolroom blackboard. As I stood there eyes raised, it moved, pulsed and writhed. It was impossible to tell if that background blackness was the night upon which these oozy colors moved or just another twisting pigment.

A city rose against this, perched on a distant hill. It thrust up in a series of towers, strange, mushroom-shaped, with tall, thin spires and broad caps. The buildings, if that was what they were, swayed like blades of grass in the wind.

Lights shone from their windows, irregular and changing shape as I watched.

I instantly realized even though this was clearly a city, there were absolutely no straight lines anywhere, no ninety-degree angles. All spirals and curlicues and weird, bulbous shapes, squamous and bloated.

The ground beneath my feet oozed and squirmed, short-shorn grass the color of a corpse's skin swaying like seaweed in a tide, grasping at my shoes. I tore my feet away, walked with exaggerated, high steps.

The sky vibrated like a struck gong, and something stunned me immobile. Eyes in the sky, huge, each as large as the full harvest moon on a crisp, clear autumn evening. They were carious, yellow slits filled with hatred and venom, and they seemed to be looking directly at me.

Rashida?

But no, these eyes were ancient, completely alien, almost reptilian, cold and calculating. I looked away because their gaze made my skull pulse in pain. My brain, overtaxed with all of this, felt like jelly sliding around a mason jar.

Forms emerged from the cluster of fungi that was the city, rippling shadows at first, but they coalesced into figures. Three of them, each more hideous than the next.

The first was a bit shorter than me, with a solid, stooped body. It wore no clothing, and its skin was various shades of green, covered in warts and pustules. Its head was blunt and amphibian, with speckled gold eyes that mimicked the loathing I'd seen in those eyes in the sky.

The second was a thin squiggle of thing, like a vertical earthworm, probably no thicker than a broom handle. It was the color of raw meat, with no eyes but a pair of what looked like nostrils, flaring in anger as it came.

The third...well, the third made my eyes water as I looked. Hard to focus on, its form was hidden behind a wavering haze, glimpsed only in fits and starts. It seemed to be a rolling mass of gelatin, transparent. Inside, I could see its organs glowing, ablaze with inner fire. It left a trail of slime behind it that glowed yellow green.

I backed up a step or two, my shoes squelching in the mucilaginous earth.

"Del!" I shouted. "Del!"

But I couldn't find her in the shifting scene, like colors painted on the surface of boiling water. I turned and ran from the three monstrosities pursuing me, wondering how to leave.

"Del!" I shouted again, and I heard the sound of my voice slide away from me, echo in the far reaches of this world, then come back as deep, booming laughter.

The eyes above me flashed. I could feel the whole weight of their gaze.

I had to get out of here.

I had to find Del.

But where could she be?

Where were all the people who had floated up into the sky of my world?

Where were all the people who had floated away during all of Dr. Alatryx's shows, before I even met him?

I ran as best I could, and I thought about *The Incredible Dr. Alatryx and his Mysterious Persian Cure! By Way of Egypt, India, The Orient, Persia.*

I realized the entire point of the show hadn't ever been to sell the bottles of doctored hootch. Hadn't ever been about the money.

It had been about *this*.

Getting people *here*, wherever this place was, for whatever reason.

I passed a grove of tree-things, thick, red trunks sprouting balloon-like appendages that bounced together in the light breeze. The squeaked like balloons, too, and some ruptured as they rubbed, a curdled, yellow custard spilling out. The ground underneath grew mouths to lap up all that rained down.

The trees behind me now, the three creatures still in hot pursuit, I ascended a slight hill armored in iridescent slivers like fish scales. At the top of the hill, I looked upon a wide valley. In the distance, another line of hills moved, fell and rose like the humps of a great serpent.

Down in the valley, I saw a crowd of people—*humans!* There were thousands of them, tens of thousands. It was a like a small city had disgorged its inhabitants on this broad, flat swath of land.

I scrambled down the hill, the goo of it sucking each of my steps. At its bottom, I caught my breath, instantly in this horde of people. They were yoked together by rusted chains with thick links connected neck and waist to cruel collars.

They walked together in almost dreamy step, eyes glazed, hands limp at their sides. I could see the line of them stretch into the distance on this arid plain. Far past them, maybe a mile or so, the chains connected to a large structure, a pylon or obelisk. They appeared to be dragging it behind them. Astounding since the structure was enormous, even from this far away. And even though there were thousands and thousands of people dragging this behind them, the task seemed insurmountable.

Still they trudged, step after step in the dust.

Other figures hovered around this chained horde, outside the lines, unfettered. I approached three of them, who took no notice of me. When I neared, I saw why.

Women (though it was hard to tell), crones, dressed in dirty white vestments, a wimple framing their withered faces. They held cruel, hooked whips in each hand, cattails with barbs on each lash, and they beat those nearest them savagely, for no apparent reason.

They didn't react to me because, I saw as I got closer, they were blind, their eyes sewn shut with barbwire. The gore of that blinding remained on their cheeks, dried, rust-colored blood like tears, streaked with the grey dust.

They were blind, but not mute. I heard them chanting in a dull, wavering monotone. The syllables of their nonsense words were slick on the air, felt like a corroded liquid dripping into my ears, scalding my brain.

Od j'zanth R'yleh tak. Cor soc d'pren N'yog-Sothep jek Carcosa… jek Carcosa…

I fell to my knees, clapped my hands over my ears, but the words found their way in, pummeled my brain.

Where the hell was I? Where was Del?

And more important, how was I getting back?

I heard the crunch of feet in the dust, looked up into the face of a creature bending down to me. It had the head of a horseshoe crab, blunt and featureless, with a long, stiff, spiny tail at the rear. No eyes, no mouth, no ears.

Its body was birdlike, feathered in pale sky blue, with wise, diminutive hands. Long, banded legs were thrust into what looked like water jugs made from clay.

The thing offered me a hand, and I cautiously took it, stood.

"Who…who are you? Where am I?"

"The Scaffolding," came the thing's screechy, high-pitched voice. "Where you weren't meant to be."

"The Scaffolding?" I asked, raising my head to the eyes that still glared from above. "What the hell is that?"

"Behind the scenes, where the fly system is kept. The cogs and gears, the pumping fluids and the vast mire of veins."

"*What?*"

"As with any machine, there are things operating in the background, things you never notice. Things you're not meant to see. Things vital to the order of reality," it said.

"Why are all these people here?"

"The machine requires operators, people to pull the levers, operate the gears."

"These people aren't pulling levers or operating gears," I protested.

"Some levers are larger than others."

I tried to clear my head. "Who are you?"

"You don't know me, cute boy?" it said.

"Rashida?" I blinked. "*Rashida?*"

"Of course. Am I so different?"

I was stunned, silent. This was Rashida, *this*? Not the young banjo player I knew from the medicine show?

This?

"What are you doing?"

"Is it so hard to understand? This place, this Scaffolding, requires workers. I help provide them."

I looked everywhere but at her. I couldn't address the smooth shell of her face, its passivity, its stern blankness.

"You're kidnapping them? Forcing them to work?"

"Okay. Yes," she nodded. "But it's important, didn't you listen? I told you…"

"I heard that, but...*here*? They don't even seem to be alive."

"Oh, they're alive."

"But look, their faces, their eyes," I said, reaching out to the nearest to shake her bonds. "The chains."

"So, they can't run off," Rashida said. "Wouldn't you, if you could?"

"Absolutely I would!"

"You think your life is any different, cute boy?" she said, stepping toward me, trying to take my hand again. I swatted hers away, and she cocked her crab head in a way that deftly communicated sorrow.

"You think you live your life knowing what you're doing, the hows and whys of it all? What's to come? No, you humans are blinkered, either here or there. Don't you think, if you weren't, you'd also run from the things that could be, will be for you in the tiny stretches of your lives? You'd run, too. And then what would happen? What would get done? The universe would collapse into chaos.

"So what if we pull your blinded forms from one world into another? So what if we force you to work at the gears and pistons of reality? It must be done. And you and your kind were made merely to serve. And you do. Here or there."

"My god, Rashida," I muttered. "My god."

"Your god is *not* here," she said, her tone becoming solemn. She raised her domed heard toward the sky. "Only the old ones, the ancient ones. I'm one of their many doors, and you must return through me. Back to your plane."

I must admit I was relieved to hear it. At first.

"But Del...what about Del? I'm not leaving without her."

Rashida cocked her head, this time in confusion.

Then, "The girl? From the audience?"

"Yes!"

"No," she said. "She has been impressed; she cannot go back. This is her life. She is a hand. She turns the wheels now."

"I'm not leaving without her," I said, turning away from Rashida, scanning the chained crowd, their faces, trying to find the dark-haired Del. But it was an impossible task. I knew it. There were far, far too many people for me to find her.

"Then, you must remain here, cute boy," Rashida said. "Choose. Remain and turn the wheel. Or go and live your life, knowing what you know now. Which is easier, I wonder?"

I felt like tearing off, running up and down the rows and aisles of chained people, searching for her face, her hair, her eyes. But I knew it would take a lifetime. I knew I would never find her.

I knew, sooner or later, those blind nuns would beat me down, collars would be welded around my neck, my waist, heavy chains latched to them. I, too, would join this stumbling horde. Or another catatonic, lurching mass of humans occupied with another monotonous task.

For the rest of my life.

"Send me back," I said. "Send me back. At least I understand what's happening back there."

If her smoothly armored head could have smirked at me, it would have.

"Take my hand," she said, reaching out.

"But your mouth?"

"Hand, mouth. It's all the same," she said, and I took her small, rough, cold hand.

The eyes above me flared in loathing.

Then all was swirling, eddying black.

I came to face first on the ground. I felt queasy, disoriented, and I didn't move for a while. My head pounded, and as I lifted it, grass and clumps of dirt adhered to my cheek, fell away.

I wasn't sure at first if I was still under the striated sky or the more familiar blue one.

Wherever it was, the sun was out, bright and warm.

I sat up, got my bearings.

Alone.

I was back in the clearing outside of Doniphan, where the medicine show had played. The sun was high in the sky, the air clear, the light warm on me.

No one was with me. Not the audience, of course, they'd floated up, floated away into… Certainly not Dr. Alatryx and his performers.

Certainly not Rashida.

I sat there most of the afternoon, trying to decide what to do, where to go. Tell someone? Who, exactly? Who'd believe such a thing? Sure, they might think it odd so many of their neighbors had disappeared, but really, would they? It was a different time then. People pulled up stakes and moved where the jobs were all the time. Wouldn't be hard to believe they'd set off to the farms of California or the oil fields of Texas or Oklahoma.

Anywhere but right here, where they were.

I stood, felt something in my pockets. I stuck my hand in and found all the bills and change I'd collected before…

Must have been about twenty bucks or so. I still had money left over from Alatryx paying me the day before. But suddenly that money, all of it, felt dirty.

I walked back into town, looked in the windows of the general store. Dark and empty. The entire town of Doniphan felt the same way.

I went inside, grabbed a bag, filled it with groceries. A few loaves of bread, cheese, as many bottles of Coke as I could carry. Who'd miss them? Certainly not Del or her very large floating father.

I ate two sandwiches at the counter, with ham I found. Drank a few of the cold Cokes. When I left, I plunked two dollars onto the counter, more to assuage my conscience than pay for anything.

I walked. I kept walking until I came to a town with a bus. Wasn't even sure what state I was in. I bought a ticket and rode that bus as far east as it could go, all the way to New York.

Tried to forget all of this, what I'd seen.

What I'd *helped* with.

I volunteered during World War II, came home, drifted.

In 1950, I met a woman who was as far removed from either Rashida or Del as possible. Beautiful, sensible, practical. Who would never have to feign belief in what had happened to me so long ago.

I never tested that by telling her. I just tried to forget it had ever happened.

And I did forget, for about thirty years, until the summer of 1964.

The weather in Long Island had turned early that year, from a fresh, cool spring to a torrid summer. I'd just started my new job with the ad agency, and Carolyn and I decided to take the kids out to Coney Island. Let the boys ride the rides. We'd laze on the beach, eat dogs, drink beers.

The island was on the downswing then. Most people were heading out to the World's Fair in Queens. Not a lot of people at Coney. This was right before that great shit Fred Trump bought it, went about trying to gentrify the neighborhood, evict the poor and screw the city. Multitasking assholery. It's the Trump brand.

Carolyn raised an eyebrow at the choice of Coney Park, but the kids were excited. I knew there'd be few people on the beach, easy parking. So, we piled into the car and went.

The boys got a few dollars each and strict instructions to meet us at around noon for lunch. They then disappeared down the boardwalk, gaggling up a torrent.

Carolyn held my arm as we walked slowly past the shops with their touristy paraphernalia—the T-shirts and snow globes, the ice cream and saltwater taffy, the rides off in the distance, most of them motionless.

The boardwalk seemed rundown and in disrepair, the beach littered. There were more than a few vagrants and disreputable types hanging around. Carolyn asked about the boys, if we shouldn't find them and keep them near, but they were ten and twelve, and I thought they'd be okay.

This part of the story isn't about any worries about my boys. No, this part of the story goes back to the beginning, back to me in distant, almost forgotten Corridon, Missouri so long ago.

Carolyn and I walked hand in hand down the boardwalk, almost to its end, and there was a ramshackle building, a small theatre of sorts that had seen better days. One of its windows was broken, giving it the look of a beaten prizefighter. The lights on the marquee were mostly burnt out.

The Alhambra.

My heart shrunk in my chest as I saw the playbill slapped near the ticket booth.

A mustachioed man, larger than life, looming over the pyramids and an Oriental palace. His right hand was thrown wide, his left held an amber bottle of liquid sloshing fluid onto a crowd of small, beseeching figures.

The Incredible Dr. Alatryx and his Mysterious Persian Cure! By Way of Egypt, India, The Orient, Persia.

It was the same sign, exact down to the garish colors and carnival type font.

Could it really be the same show?

I turned to Carolyn. "You want to duck in and see the show?"

"No," she said, then she looked at me carefully. "Are you serious? *Really*?"

"We've got all day, and this is…what? A buck a ticket? Why not? It'll be fun."

I twisted my face into a grin, but I knew in my heart it would *not* be fun.

"Okay," she sighed. "But you're going to owe me a nice dinner."

"I can do that," I said, approaching the ticket window. An old man slumped atop a stool behind the window, looking as if he were part of the collapsing building. He trembled to life as I knocked on the glass.

"Two tickets, please," I said, pushing the dollars through the slot at the bottom of the window. I looked at him closely. Staunton? Pinkney? Dr. Alatryx himself? Possible, I guessed. It had only been thirty years. But, no, I saw no glimmer of them in this man's lined features.

He said nothing, waved us in.

Carolyn flashed me a dubious look but walked through the door I'd opened for her.

There was a small, threadbare lobby, an unused popcorn machine. A single set of doors opened onto a small theatre, seating no more than about fifty people. No one was there.

The stage sat about two feet off the floor, draped with a dark blue velvet curtain, moth-eaten and covered in dust. The benches were arranged in a cup around the stage. The floorboards were squeaky and dirty, sticky in places, probably with all the dried residue from the popcorn butter, sodas, lemonades and cotton candy dropped there over the years.

I wiped the seat with a handkerchief before Carolyn and I sat.

Almost immediately, there was a ratcheting sound from the stage, and the curtain parted.

There was nothing there, no backdrop or banner. Just the rear of the building with a few conduits and breaker boxes.

A man bounded onstage, dressed in a wrinkled tuxedo, a top hat.

My heart lurched.

But this man was not *my* Dr. Alatryx. This man was portly, probably no more than forty, pale and jowly. No beard or mustache.

"Welcome, ladies and gentlemen!" he roared, or tried to. His voice was too reedy and thin, but Carolyn started a bit anyway. "We've got a great show for you this morning. Great music! With our fantastic players. Mr. Daly on the upright bass! Mr. Carlson on the fiddle! And our star, our nightingale, the lovely Miranda playing the banjo and singing."

The three came onstage, and I watched them carefully. None of them were recognizable.

Until Miranda sat centerstage and placed her banjo on her lap.

Her eyes were the same flat silver as Rashida's had been.

They launched into a rendition of *Barbara Allen*, then segued smoothly into the *Risin' Sun Blues*. Carolyn eventually started clapping her hands in time, seemingly enjoying the music.

I didn't. Nor did I tap my feet.

I stared at Miranda, who took no notice of me.

The trio wound their way through three more numbers, and then it happened.

As they played their version of *The Brakeman's Blues*, a light above them fell, dangled by its cord over their heads.

The music faltered, then stopped, Carlson and Daly looking up at the light.

Dr. Alatryx rushed onto the stage, offered his apologies as they paused to fix this problem.

But Miranda…she was looking right at me now, fixing me with those reflective eyes of hers. She smiled thinly, as if recognizing me.

I looked up to the proscenium, half expecting to see that flat, ghostly spinning disc with its black center. As I watched, the light was jerked back into the loft by someone yanking its cord.

"Well, sorry about that, folks. But remember there's always stuff going on behind the curtain, backstage. Always people needed to keep the show going," Alatryx said, sidling offstage.

As soon as he was gone, the music continued, picking up just where it had stopped.

I waited a beat, then took Carolyn's hand in mine, led her out of the theatre, out into the bright afternoon sun.

I wasn't about to wait for the sales part of the show, whatever they might be selling these days. Wasn't about to wait to be sucked up into that spinning disc, chained and forced to work in that other place with the wobbling towers and the staring eyes.

We could hear the music continue as if we were still seated inside, fading as we walked away.

"What was that all about?" she asked. "You're the one who wanted to go in there in the first place. And I was just getting into it."

"I know," I said, struggling to find an answer for her. "I used to like that kind of music. I guess as I don't much anymore."

"Okay," she said, confused.

It was behind us even more so than the receding theatre.

"How about taffy? The boys might like a box of it to take home, and we might actually get a piece or two before they find out we have it."

"Sounds great," I said, then I cast one final glance behind me at the Alhambra, slumped and derelict on the Boardwalk. "I've had enough of show business."

THE END

IN THE DIM MEADOWS, DESOLATE

"She's coming," Hough said, plucking the cigarette from his mouth and grinding it against the warped wooden boards of the porch. "She's coming and I wish she wouldn't. I don't think I can hold out any longer. That's the truth of it."

Tim McCurry sat on a wooden packing crate behind Hough, reading from Franzen, *The Corrections*, maybe. It was a cool, early April evening with the kind of gentle breeze that turned nights with the windows open into a sleeping pill. The golden light from the rising three-quarters moon spilled syrupy over the hills and the greening land.

"I'm tired…you have no idea how tired of running a man can get."

"*Who's* coming?" Tim asked. He bent a corner of a page down, folded the paperback closed against his lap. Hough hadn't spoken much to Tim, so this was a kind of revelation.

Houghton Reef was a tall, thin man of indeterminate age, wiry, thinly muscled with skin darkened and leathered by the sun. He was quiet, laconic, with a dry sense of humor and a drawl that made him sound like an Okie of old, a character ripped from the pages of *Grapes of Wrath* or *Of Mice and Men.* He'd been here for a few days, having just turned up for work again this season on the Gallider farm.

Quiet and unassuming, Reef had come into the bunkhouse unannounced, tossed his duffel bag onto the empty cot farthest from the door, and held his hand out to Tim. Tim's hand was engulfed in it, as dry and tight as an abandoned gopher hole.

Tim had settled in just a few days earlier. He was a friend of Mike Gallider from college, and had been invited to come up and make some cash by working a season on the Gallider's sprawling property in central Missouri. The patchwork farm had been sewn together over several generations through hard work and cagey business deals by the great-great grandfather, Theodore J. Gallider.

These days, the operation was actually made up of several farms, tied together by the multi-generational family and the ever-changing cast of migrant workers the Galliders employed each year to plant, tend and harvest their crops—everything from corn and soybeans to wheat and rye, and even side crops like pumpkins and watermelons.

Each year, the family hired on a shifting crew of about 50 workers to help out. Some stayed all the way through, until the last of the winter wheat was harvested. Others, like Hough, stayed only for a specific time, for specific crops. Most went on to other farms farther west and south; into California or Florida or even Texas. Some went back to Mexico for the winter.

Tim didn't know Houghton Reef well enough to know what he did in the offseason. Didn't know him well enough to ask. Judging from the depth of their conversations so far, he never would.

Perhaps the man lived in a cabin in the mountains, a fishing shed on the banks of a river. Or maybe he was like Tim, just taking time from another life to remind himself what it was like where the sweat of one day's work was barely dry on your skin when the next day began.

Whatever the reason behind his appearance, Reef was a returning employee of the Galliders. Joey, one of the farm's blacksmiths –they actually had two—said Hough had been coming around now for about fifteen years.

"Hough's a hard worker, keeps to himself," said Joey while shoeing a horse. "He never stays the season through...always leaves right before it gets too hot. Has a girlfriend, I think. Seen her a few times. Pretty young thing."

Tim had considered this for a while, thought about someone as old and weathered as Houghton Reef having a beautiful, young girlfriend, then dismissed that thought almost casually. It was like the Marlboro Man or an older Clint Eastwood having a pretty young girlfriend.

More likely a daughter or even a granddaughter, he supposed.

All of this passed through Tim's mind as Hough (pronounced *How*, as the older man told him upon meeting) crushed his cigarette out that cool, breezy spring evening.

The man looked at Tim's face, breathed out the remaining smoke from his last cigarette of the evening.

"You believe in the gods?" he asked. He closed his mouth into a tight, dry line across his face, waited for Tim's answer.

"*God*, you mean?"

Hough chuckled softly. "Sure."

Tim considered this for a moment; a weighty decision for a man his age to blurt out. Only old men answered this question quickly. "I guess so."

"Think he screws with you?"

That wasn't the follow-up question he'd been expecting, and he placed the book down beside him, sat back against the dry window frame.

"Screws with *me*?"

"You. Me. *People.*"

Those words came out in a toneless staccato, falling as baled and dry as hay.

Tim frowned, not sure where this was leading. "Not really, I guess. I'd hope he's got better things to do with his time."

Hough paused, felt at the pocket of the leather vest he wore, patted the pack of cigarettes there; comforting it or being comforted by it.

"Well, maybe *him*...there's only one of him," he said. "But *them*...they screw with each other so much screwing with us is like a vacation."

With that, he pushed the rickety door to the bunkhouse open, disappeared inside.

Tim thought about asking again who was coming.

Was it his daughter? His girlfriend? His wife?

The door closed behind him. Tim heard the creak of the bedsprings after a minute, then went back to reading his book.

Over the next two months, Tim learned working on a big, busy farm didn't leave much time to get to know your co-workers or their views on god and gods. Most of his fellow hands weren't really interested in him, anyway. Or, as Tim found during the first few weeks trying to make small talk, interested in English.

From sun up to sundown, the day was comprised of work; hard, physical work that left little room for much else in a day than eating, drinking and sleeping.

Tim did find time for two things. One was talking to Hough, whom he gravitated toward, despite the older man's initial reticence, because he was one of the few hands who spoke English. Once he was able to haul more than two words out of Hough, which was quite a feat in and of itself, he was fascinating, an endless store of knowledge and information and tales that seemed to reach back, way back, past even the man's weathered years, into some dim, forgotten recesses of history.

The second thing Tim found time for was Mike Gallider's older sister, Tina. She lived in the main farmhouse with Mike and his parents. She was tall and willowy, with honey-colored hair usually in ponytail, long, brown graceful limbs and an energetic, coltish attitude Tim found mesmerizing.

Tina often hung around after work was done, when Tim went up to the main house for the family's evening meal and a few beers on the front porch. While Mike and Tim shot the shit, Tina listened to their college tales, made witty interjections. Tim found it hard to tell whether this was just her personality or if she were flirting. He also found she was increasingly occupying his thoughts, filling the hot, sweaty length of his days, the sometimes hotter, sweatier length of his nights.

Mike noticed the interest on both sides, and found it both humorous and harmless. Tim's fellow workers noticed it, too, and began to whisper when he was around, as if the Spanish wasn't proof enough against his decipherment of what they said.

Hough noticed it as well, and one evening—after more than a few beers, more than a few half-lidded looks exchanged between Tim and Tina, the touch of a finger or two when a beer was passed, the innuendoes becoming less and less vague—Tim staggered down the gravel road from the farmhouse to the bunkhouse, head swimming,

As he approached, he saw a dark shape on the porch of the bunkhouse, the glowing ember of a cigarette floating in the air. Tim mounted the creaking wooden steps, prepared to mutter a "good night," push through the door and flop as quietly as possible into his bed.

"You love her?" came Hough's voice from the darkness.

Tim lurched to a stop, his body swaying, one hand reaching for the doorknob.

"Huh?"

There was the sound of a draw on a cigarette, dry and crackling, the breathy expulsion of smoke.

"It's all fluttery stomachs and sweating palms and tripping tongues. At night, you dream and hug your pillow like it's her. What you're really doing is putting things off…waiting for a sign from the world that says it's okay to proceed, it's okay to love her."

Tim's beer-soaked mind wondered for an instant if Hough were talking to him, then wondered what he was talking about.

"Are you talking to me?"

Hough chuckled, deep and low. "Yeah. You love her."

"I love *who*?" Tim asked, the liquor swirling in his gut, his brain starting to make him feel a little angry; angry because he knew exactly what Hough was talking about, exactly *who* Hough was talking about.

"The farmer's daughter," Hough laughed, took a draw on his cigarette so deep the glow of its tip eerily under lit his face. "Your friend's sister, Tina."

Like most drunks over aware of their pride, Tim drew himself erect. "I don't know what you're talking about. I'd never…"

"Sure you would, kid. We all have or will or would," said Hough, dropping the cigarette to the floor and grinding it into the wood with the toe of his boot. "And everyone knows. Everyone can see it. Christ, you wear it like part of your work clothes."

Tim felt a flush of heat rise up in him, alcohol or anger or both. "What business is it of yours or anyone else's for that matter?"

"Shhh," Hough said. "You'll wake our *amigos* inside. Besides, I'm not trying to piss you off. It ain't my business, not really. Just asking. Trying to help, that's all."

"Help?" Tim said, then belched. "How?"

"Think you're the only person who's fallen in love with the farmer's daughter? Where do you think the joke *came* from?"

Tim swayed, blinked. He really needed to sit, let the beer drain from his head. In fact, he really needed to take a piss and let the beer drain from his body.

"What would you know about it?" Tim asked. "You hardly talk to anybody here, barely seem to *like* anyone."

There was silence for a moment, and in that silence, Tim thought he might have angered or even hurt the man with those words.

There was a long sigh, then, and Hough backed toward one of the rocking chairs on the porch, as much collapsed as sat. He fumbled with his shirt pocket, knocked out a pack of unfiltered Camels, lit up. He took one or two long drags before he spoke again.

"I was like you once…seems a long time ago. Christ, it *was* a long time ago, why pretend? Young kid, making my way in the world, trying new things. Finding out about myself, my place. I fell in love…fell hard. Yeah, I found out all about love…especially what it costs."

Tim crept closer, one hand braced against the columns of the porch to steady himself. "*You* fell in love with the farmer's daughter?"

Hough motioned to the rocking chair sitting next to his.

"Kid, I fell in love with *the* farmer's daughter."

The first time I saw her was, oh, back in '33. In a little town in Kansas called Crete. You don't see the irony in that name now, but you will…you will.

Nothing little town, just a single street with a post office, a drug store, a feed store and a church. On all sides, pressing in like a deep, green sea were fields. Fields of wheat. Fields of corn. Fields of hay and rye and oats.

I'd moved west, through Illinois and Missouri, restless and mostly unemployed like any man of my age during that time. The Depression was in full swing, and the entire country was moribund, as Eliot said, like a patient etherized upon a table. I spent the early Thirties drifting across the Midwest like a fog.

My own family had died early. Dad was a coal miner back east in the days when a coal miner's life span was pretty short. Ma died pretty soon after he was in the ground, as much, I think, to avoid the responsibilities of raising six kids as from the disease she allowed to kill her.

Once she was in the cold, hard Appalachian ground next to dad, the family—us kids anyway—came apart like a cheap suit. My older brother went north, into Canada, into logging. My older sister grafted herself like a barnacle to the nearest eligible man who'd whisk her away from Virginia. The three youngest were taken in by a distant cousin in Indiana, to help work the family farm.

Me? I slid away with few farewells and even less tears. None of us seemed really broken up about being broken up. Strange. It seemed, in those days anyway, family ties—of blood or sweat or genes or whatever—were easily rent, giving way to the stronger tides of economics and reality.

West…always west. Didn't have too many skills to offer in those days, just a young man's muscle and strong back and seemingly endless supply of energy. I went from farm to farm, hiring myself out as a day laborer. Whatever mindless labor needed to be done for a few bucks, I was there.

I lived in a succession of bunk houses and boarding houses, sometimes for a few days, a few weeks. Ate what I was fed, slept where I was allowed to sleep. There were days without food, sure, and nights spent in culverts or on the banks of rivers.

Always alone. As much by choice as circumstances. Even at that age, and, I musta been twenty or twenty-one then, I never really saw the need for companionship, of either sex, for whatever reason. I didn't need other mouths to be responsible for. Christ, that's what split my own family apart. I knew it would be much harder for two to find work than it was for just one.

Just me.

"Wait a sec," Tim said, stomping out a cigarette against the rough boards of the porch and chuckling. "You didn't think I'd notice?"

Hough leaned back against one of the support posts, narrowed his eyes and smiled. "Notice what?"

"If you were twenty or twenty-one right before the Dust Bowl, you'd be about a hundred years old by now. I may not have been to college, man, but I'm not stupid."

"No, no, you're not," Hough drawled, in a tone that definitely said *Yes, yes, you are.*

Silence between the two for a minute, where Tim looked on Hough expectantly.

There was no denial, no explanation. Hough just stared out in the distant night.

"Okay," Tim said, finally breaking the silence. "Go ahead with your story."

After a few years of drifting like that, I washed up in Crete.

Just that little main street, like I said, and about a dozen or so family farms pressing alongside it. From just a few acres all the way up to a thousand or so acres owned by the local big fishes, the Karabas family. They grew a little bit of just about everything and a helluva lot of wheat and corn.

Of course, being the big fish in a small sea, and what with the waves and waves of people just like me constantly lapping at their shore, getting hired there was purely a matter of luck. But I was lucky…I guess.

I stumbled across the farm even before I stumbled across the town. I was walking down a dusty road, just heading west. I'd left another job thirty or forty miles east just a week or two before, and I was tired and hungry. As I crossed what looked to be a service road, a caravan of tired, overloaded vehicles sped by, kicking up a trail of dust streaming behind them into the distance.

I lowered my face, clapped a bandana over my mouth as they passed, each rickety vehicle laden with people and junk—furniture, tools, ropes, chains, spare tires. As the final truck lurched through the turn, I looked up. The open bed was filled with more of the same and at least half a dozen young boys, all dirty and hollow-eyed and bedraggled.

One, a scraggly boy who looked to be fourteen or fifteen, barefoot and clad in a pair of ill-fitting overalls, hung across the wooden sideboard, his feet dangling over the tailgate. He flashed me a wide, gap-toothed smile as they passed.

"Ain't it your lucky day, Jasper!" he called out to me. "Best farm in the county, and they shore gonna be needin' a lotta help with us leavin'."

I waved, looked back the way they'd come.

"Watch out for that Percy, though, if'n you know what's good for ya!" he yelled back at me as the truck receded into the distance, blotted out by the dust it raised.

I shielded my eyes from the setting sun, from the blowing dirt, so I couldn't see the boys, but I heard peels of their rough, bawdy teenage laughter.

Smiling despite myself, I made the turn onto the road they'd just come from, saw a complex of buildings what looked to be a mile down the road, set off in that direction.

Another half hour of walking brought me to a side road that snaked across low hills, more like rucks in the broad expanse of flat carpet that is Kansas. Down this road, surrounded on all sides by crops, I saw a tight compound of structures—a farmhouse, a couple of barns, a silo, a few low outbuildings. Looked like the place.

The sun had almost set when I arrived. The sky was a dull, bruised violet giving way to absolute night. A crescent moon hung in the sky like a fingernail paring, a sailing ship against a sea of stars.

The farmhouse was lit against the dark, and a few strings of lights hung between it and the main barn and what I knew would be the bunkhouse for the hands. Evidently the owners were well-off enough to get electricity out here.

A few people milled about, carrying items from here to there, leading horses into the barn. The place had the feel of settling down, settling in. I didn't own a watch, but I figured it was around 7 p.m. The owners were no doubt enjoying their evening, preparing for bed, while the hands were probably just back from the fields.

I knew the routine. Wherever you were, whatever the operation, the rhythms were the same. Early to rise, wash up, breakfast, out to work, stop around midday to have a quick meal, some water, then back to work. Stop just before sundown, head back, wash up, eat dinner, hang around for a while shooting the shit, then to bed. Repeat every day. Forever.

Not much time to sit your ass down or kick your heels up. An hour or two in the evening, mainly spent playing cards or checkers, listening to the radio. After working hard all day, who had the energy to do any more?

Generally, it was a peaceful, if exhausting existence. Lonely in its way. Sure, there were always a few in every operation—the drinkers or gamblers, the fighters or the lovers. My experience was these men were usually threshed out pretty soon. They upset the rhythm.

While these farmers seemed to tolerate a lot to get their crops planted and harvested and tended to, none I'd ever encountered would tolerate a disruption of the rhythm.

Rhythms, as I would learn, were the backbone of everything—farming, living, believing…

…*loving*.

I went straight to the bunkhouse, a low, sturdily built structure set off behind the barn. A few men glanced at me as I walked by, but no one said a word. We were of a kind, I knew. And so did they. No need to ask.

I clomped on the porch of the bunkhouse, heard the clink and rattle and voices of dinner. More electrical lights burned inside. The door opened onto a clean, well-lit expanse of space…and what seemed to be a party.

About twenty men sat around a long trestle table large enough to seat about twenty more. They were eating off tin plates, greedily loading them to towering heights, stuffing their mouths with food. Plates were piled high with biscuits and chicken. Bowls and bowls of fresh fruit were scattered about, apples and grapes and all sorts of stuff I hadn't seen before—pineapples, oranges, bananas, melons of all kinds.

The men laughed and sang, morsels and dribbles spilling from their lips. They served themselves from great lacquer-ware pots and pans of food. I smelled the distinctive aromas of greens and beans, knew there'd be more distinctive aromas that night.

"Sorry to interrupt, boys," I said, taking my hat off and stepping into the room. "Looking for the foreman."

None of the rest of the men paid me any attention, and the revelry continued unabated. A fat, hairy little man at the head of the table, though, pushed back and got to his feet.

"Well, ain't this your lucky day, mister," he said, his gingham napkin tucked tight between the neck of his stained and stretched shirt and his sweaty jowls. One great, fat-fingered hand was closed around a huge tin mug, with dark red liquid sloshing from it. "Name's Bull. I'm foreman for the Karabas farm. Whatchya looking for?"

I took the man's doughy hand, moist with perspiration and chicken grease, shook it firmly. "Work, sir. Honest work's all."

"Like I said, today you're one lucky sumbitch," he laughed, releasing my hand and leaving a clammy, slick residue.

"That's the third time I've heard that."

"Oh yeah? Who told ya first?"

"Some kid in the line of trucks leaving here 'bout a half hour ago."

Bull nodded energetically, picked at corn caught in his teeth. "Yep, that'd be the Waldingham clan. Fuckers. Whole mess of 'em up and quit today. So we're down a dozen and a half hands or so, and we got work out the wazoo, if you know what I mean."

"Well," I said, looking at the table of food, at the men hunched over it, ignoring this exchange. "I guess as how I'm lucky, then."

Bull clapped me on the back. I caught the pronounced odors of chicken grease and alcohol drifting from him. "Son, you ain't got no idea how good goddamn lucky you are. You know how hard it is to get on here at Karabas?"

I shook my head, but I could guess.

"Hard as my pecker on a cold winter's morning," he laughed. "By that, I mean hard as shit to get, but pretty damn easy to get off."

This brought a raucous round of laughter from the table. He saw me looking at the ridiculously large spread of food laid out there.

"You got experience as a hand, son?"

"Oh yeah," I replied. "Coming east, making my way for a while now. All sorts of farms, all sorts of jobs."

Bull nodded, looked back at the table, obviously eager to return to his meal. "Well, shitbird, son, let's getchya seated, get some food and drink in ya, and we can get ya a bunk and talk later."

He pushed me toward the table, and as soon as I sat, bowls and pots were passed to me. I filled my plate first, my belly second. The stuff in the great tin mugs the men drank from was wine, which surprised me greatly. On all the other farms I'd worked, there were strict rules against drinking. I mean, it was Prohibition, remember? They didn't seem to care. The men poured it eagerly from great pitchers stranding on the table amidst the food, and soon I didn't care either.

I'd never been one for drinking much, and when I did, it was usually cheap beer. But the wine was good…sweet and cold, and my mug was refilled just as soon as I drained it.

I never saw anyone refill it, never saw anyone refill the pitchers.

Damn thing was, as long as I was there, I never saw anyone bring the food to the bunkhouse, lay it out across the trestle tables, clear the dishes and the scraps when the meal was over.

Still, I drank the wine and ate the food and didn't ask questions.

Lucky sumbitch, yeah.

That night, my head swimming with wine, I slept on a clean bed, with sheets and a pillow smelling of soap, and not the unwashed body of whatever migrant worker had preceded me. Mr. Bull told me a little about the operation, the schedule, what was expected of me and what I'd be paid. Nothing I hadn't heard before, though the pay was pretty good for those days. Obviously the food and board were first rate.

I was up at the crack of dawn the next morning, surprised at how good I felt. Surprised my head wasn't splitting and my ass dragging from the previous night's drinking. Got a nice breakfast of eggs, biscuits, redeye gravy and hot coffee.

Then, off to the fields. As the new guy, I did most of the shit work that first week or two; mostly moving heavy equipment, hay bales to feed the animals, cleaning stalls. In that time, though, more men came in as I'd done, stood before Mr. Bull there at our evening feasts as he told them how lucky they were.

And they were. The place had the same rhythms as the other places I'd worked, but it was more organized, less stressful. You were expected to do your job, but no one seemed to have to yell or holler at anyone to ensure this. The pay, the food and board...they were all the motivation that was necessary. It was as slick an operation as I'd ever worked at, and I began to see myself staying there for a while, perhaps returning next season.

As the workforce was replenished, I moved up in the ranks and became a field hand, out on the wagons every morning to whatever field, whatever crop we were working. Could be corn or wheat or oats or rye, hay or some of the huge vegetable crops grown there—carrots and radishes, cabbage and potatoes and turnips and lettuce and peppers and rhubarb. Remember, this is back when farms grew everything, for their own use and for sale.

It was a busy life, pleasant and relaxing in its own way, though even back then, young as I was, I fell into bed every evening and slept night after dreamless night. My body might have ached, but my belly was full and my mind was at peace for the first time in years, for the first time since my dad and mama died.

I'd been there about three weeks before I met anyone from the Karabas family. Most of them kept to themselves, had their own chores to do around the farm. I seldom saw Mr. Karabas, and when I did it was from a distance out in the fields, in his Model A, a straw hat shading his features. Mrs. Karabas kept mostly to the house, but I'd see her hanging linen out on the lines to dry. I knew from the other hands they had a four kids, an older boy who was away at school, a girl just out of her teens, and two young school-age boys.

It was just my luck the first Karabas I met was the girl.

I saw her the first time one morning about a month after I'd begun at the Karabas place. I'd stepped out after breakfast to smoke, then decided to take an apple I'd pocketed over to the barn to give it Old Bill, an ancient horse who'd been mostly retired from serious labor. He and I had become friends over the weeks. Horses, I have found, are great judges of people, and to be loved or even liked by one is a tremendous recommendation, akin to a dog's.

Anyway, it was dawn yet, with that lovely pink-rose sky and the quiet shadow of the awakening land. Few birds chirped, there was still little ruckus from the workers or their equipment. A single light burned in the main house. It was that innocent, sleepy time, when the world is rousing, and the night's dreams are still as much within one's grasp as the day's possibilities.

I walked to the barn, entered into its quiet, almost hallowed enclosure. A few lanterns hung in its midst, like candles in a cathedral. That sharp smell of hay, of old wood and new dung, hung impossibly pleasant on the cool air. James, a stable hand, passed me on the way, nodded happily at the apple I carried.

Old Bill's stall was at the very end, a little larger than the rest. Bill had earned it, having worked for the Karabas family for twenty some-odd years. I heard him stir within as I approached, as if he knew I'd be coming or could smell me or the apple.

He nickered a little, put his head over the stall door and nodded as I neared. His old eyes were rheumy with age, his chin grizzled by a scraggly mass of wiry, grey hairs.

"Hey, old man," said, running my hand along the side of his head, over his neck. "How's life treating you today?"

Bill put his head onto my shoulder and huffed a little, bumped into the stall. He wanted the apple. I held it up, then removed a knife from the pocket of my jeans. Bill's old teeth were not up to the task of eating an entire apple whole anymore, so we'd prolong our visit by slicing it into quarters or even eighths.

I made the first cut, Bill watching me quietly as I did, then cut the half again, held the quarter piece out to him. He sniffed at it, opened his mouth around huge teeth the color of corn, took it gently from my fingers, crunched it thoughtfully.

"You know," came a voice from behind me. "Apples are for people. Carrots are actually better for horses."

I turned more quickly than I'd intended because the voice was something I'd not encountered a lot of, particularly lately.

It was *feminine.*

She stood behind me, and though the barn was dark yet, she was…*radiant.*

I don't mean purely because of her beauty—and before I go any farther, let me tell you she *was* beautiful, gloriously, terrifyingly beautiful—but because of something intrinsic, something within that was utterly of her nature.

It wasn't as if she emitted a glow or radiated light, but she did seem to dismiss the shadows, to lessen the darkness around her.

She was a tall, tall lady, with a fine figure and flowing chestnut hair. Not brown, no, too ordinary, too drab. Chestnut, with all the shades of gold and honey and mahogany within those strands. Her eyes were deep grey, too light to be blue, and I saw within them they could flash with anger like storm clouds.

She smiled at me as I turned, wearing just a simple chambray shirt and a pair of jeans, and my mouth went as dry as a Temperance meeting. Let me stress to you I'm not a wallflower. Even at that age, I had dated plenty of women…bedded a few, too. I wasn't shy nor retiring, and my tongue was not one that tied itself in knots over the prospect of talking to a woman.

My tongue shriveled like a nickel's worth of bologna left on a summer sidewalk, cleaved to the roof of my mouth. I fear she heard it as I unpeeled it from where it was stuck, tried to moisten it to say something.

"Did I scare you, mister…?"

"Reef," I finally croaked, with all the coolness of a teenage boy. "Houghton Reef, ma'am. And no, you didn't scare me. Just feeding Old Bill, here."

She looked at me, and I mean *really* looked at me. These days, I guess, it's not so unusual for a woman to look a man over. Back then, though, well…times were different. Women didn't ogle men. But she ogled me. Or not ogled really, that's kind of a low-class word for what she did.

I guess it was more like she…*appraised* me.

That's not even right, because there was something in that look, in how she studied me.

I didn't know what it was then, though it did begin to make me sweat.

I know what it is now, because I am more…*directly* acquainted with it.

Hunger.

"I've seen you around," she said, ignoring what I'd said. "One of the new hired hands?"

"Yes, ma'am," I said, trying to swallow away the dryness in my throat. "Came on a few weeks ago."

She narrowed her eyes at me, lowered her head in a strange, measured way. "Will you stay the season, Mr. Houghton Reef?"

I found the words crossed my lips before my brain had fully formed them. "Yes, ma'am. The season and perhaps a little more, if you'll have me."

I didn't know where that had come from, and the sudden forwardness of it made me blush…blush, like a schoolboy.

She stood silent for a moment, still watching me through narrowed eyes. She looked as if she might reach up and touch the red of my cheeks, and, oh, for a wonderful moment, I wish she had… wish her cool hand had touched, just barely, my heated skin.

"We just might," she laughed softly, then turned away, back toward the barn's entrance. "We just might at that."

"Wait a second," I said, finding myself now her piercing gaze was not focused on me. "What's your name?"

She didn't stop, just turned slightly over her shoulder.

"Percy."

And with that, she was gone, out the door, out into the dawn.

I licked my dry lips, worked up enough spit to moisten the leather of my tongue, my throat, swallowed.

Percy.

Watch out for that Percy, though, if'n you know what's good for ya!

I thought on that for a moment, how I thought on that.

I realized I still had the apple pieces in one hand, my knife in the other. So, I turned back to Bill to feed the rest of the apple to him.

He no longer pressed against the stall's gate, straining for the apple. No, he huddled in the far corner, packed as tightly as he could get into the shadow. He looked at me, looked at me with those big, rolling old horse eyes glazed with fear. His breathing was hard, too.

"Here ya go, Bill," said, clicking my tongue for him to come, holding the apple out to him. Bill's eyes just rolled from the apple to me, more of their whites showing than I thought was possible.

He wouldn't come, so I ended up leaving the apples atop the gate for him to get later.

When I think back on that now, I realize both that dirty, rangy kid in the truck and Old Bill had warned me about Percy.

I should have listened.

"A vampire," Tim chuckled from beside Reef.

"What?" the older man said, awakened from the reverie of his story.

"You're gonna tell me she was a vampire, right? Something like that. Telling me ghost stories?"

Tim waited for Reef to respond, waited several seconds where he felt anger might be building up in the other man.

"A *vampire*?" Reef said, echoing Tim's low, derisive laughter. "Why'd you say that?"

"You said she was hungry," Tim said. "That's like code for *vampire* these days."

Reef fished another cigarette from his pocket, lit it.

"Vampires aren't real, though, are they?"

Tim snorted. "Nope, not even when you were young."

Reef drew on the cigarette, held in the smoke, let it out in a long sigh.

"You think only monsters can be hungry, kid? No, there are only two kinds of folk who are hungry, in my experience. They're both completely real, but to each, hunger is a completely different thing."

"What two kinds?"

Reef drew in again, pushed the smoke out through his nose.

"Poor people. And gods. One needs food. The other, love."

I knew she was hungry when I kissed her.

I could taste it on her full lips, feel it on her smooth skin, as taut as a drumhead. Her muscles quivered with it, like exhausted horseflesh. Her mouth tasted of desire and need…for what, I didn't know. Love, perhaps. At least I'd hoped it was love. Desire, maybe. Dreamed it was.

First was the kiss…I get ahead of myself.

After that first encounter in the barn, I saw her more often, but always at a little distance, as if she was teasing me, testing me. I'd see her standing near the edge of the fields in the morning or out by the flapping linens on the line.

Always she managed to be where she knew I'd see her. Always positioned to catch my eye.

I started to wave the first time I saw her, then thought better of it. I was a hired hand, nothing more. I wasn't a friend of the family or whatnot. Just a hand. A paid worker. I knew—knew not from personal experience but by seeing this kind of thing played out at other jobs, on other farms I'd worked—this wasn't a good idea.

You see, it might seem funny now, but back then, for good or ill, there was still a way of thinking that discouraged things like "rising above your station."

For a guy like me, at that particular place in time, that meant losing a job, probably being roughed up and run out of town on a rail. The roughing up and running out, I could handle. I didn't want to lose my job, though...particularly not this one.

But one night, after dinner...

You're a young man, so you're going to appreciate this part of the story, appreciate how a young man can...how's it put today?... think with his smaller head instead of his big one?

How you can know it's wrong, bad for you. Know it right through to the depths of your bones, but still...it's not precisely a bone, anyway, is it?

Anyway, after the nightly chaos of the dinner feast, I pushed back from the table, went to my bunk to grab a pack of cigarettes I'd bought in town. I walked back past the table toward the door, and noticed Bull watching me carefully.

As I passed, he reached out, encircled my wrist with his plump, wet hand.

"Where to, boy?" he asked, his eyes narrowed to doughy slits atop his flushed, red cheeks. His strange, all-purpose smile stayed on his face as if painted there.

"Just outside for a smoke's all."

He looked at me carefully, then squeezed my wrist hard before releasing it.

"Don't stray," he whispered. "Or better yet, don't mistake the need for love for love itself. They ain't the same…no, not nearly so."

I nodded, not precisely getting what he was after, but pushed outside, let the door close behind me.

The night was still young, quiet at it always was around the place at this time. The sky was clear and high, unblemished by a single cloud. Even though it was a warm evening, the stars blinked down coldly, and a breeze stirred the shores of the sea of green corn pushing against the edges of the compound.

I went to the corner of the porch, leaned against the wall. Through the wood, I could feel the noise and the heat inside—the kind of manic energy the dinners always had—could feel it pulse through the walls like a living thing, fluid and seeking to fill any space it encountered.

I lit the cigarette, and had drawn in its first, heady breath—why doesn't tobacco seem as strong anymore as it did then?—when I saw movement on the side of the building. A shadow detached itself from the greater shadows there.

"Smoking is like a sacrifice, an offering," her voice said, light and clear as the night air and cold as the stars.

"What?" was all I could think to say.

The shadow stepped closer, moved its arms.

Beckoning.

I stepped off the porch, the sounds inside cutting off as if clipped by a knife.

"Smoking is a burnt offering…a sacrifice to the gods," she said as I approached her. "Is that what you're doing…offering yourself for me?"

I came to her, stood beside the shadow, and I could see her clearly now. As before, in the barn, something about her, while not necessarily luminous, seemed to dispel the shadows.

"I don't know what you're saying," and that was the god's honest truth.

She put her hand across the back of my neck and it was so unexpected, so sensuous I shivered at its cool, cool touch.

"Breathe it into me," she whispered.

I didn't stop to decipher what she meant, just raised the glowing cigarette to my lips, drew on it deeply. When my mouth was filled with smoke, I lowered my face to hers.

Our lips touched, and the smoke spilled from me into her. I felt her quiver a little at the touch of our lips…or perhaps it was the smoke? I don't know, though I have my thoughts on it now.

Like an electric current or the shock of being dunked head first in cold, cold water. A shudder rippled through me, arched my back. Her hand on the back of my neck clenched tightly, held me there.

That convulsion passed through me, ended…well, it ended below the belt…if you know what I mean. If you don't, let me be clear, because this is important.

I shot off in my pants like a schoolboy, like a virgin, shot off and filled my underwear. It wasn't pleasurable at all, not really. Maybe it was so pleasurable it crossed over to pain, just as it can be so cold it feels hot.

Oh, it startled me, shocked me, surprised even my body. But it was about as pleasurable as shooting razor blades.

I gasped, pulled away, breathing hard. I was embarrassed, yes, ashamed even, as if she could know what that one kiss, that one touch had done to me.

Even more, I was *afraid.*

Our mouths separated by only an inch or so, I could see she knew. Impossibly, she knew.

And it delighted her.

She smiled, pushed me away, powerfully but not roughly.

As she did, she exhaled, and a cloud of silver vapor passed between her lips, rose like a phantom into the sky.

"Your offering has been accepted," she whispered.

Laughing gently, she disappeared behind the bulk of the bunkhouse without another word or a backward glance.

I felt the cold stickiness in my underwear, still vaguely embarrassed, still vaguely afraid. In that moment, I thought of Mr. Bill, cowering in the shadows of his stall, looking out at where she'd been with wide, wary eyes.

Realizing I still held the glowing butt of the cigarette, I dropped it from my limp fingers, ground it into the dust.

A little shakily, I walked back to the porch. As I raised one foot to step, hands shot out of the darkness, yanked me up.

It was Bull, and he lifted me to stare directly into my face. His eyes were bulging with anger, and sweat seemed to squeeze from his pores. Strangely, though, he was still smiling, but now it seemed thin and brutal.

"I warned ya, didn't I?" he rasped, and I could smell the wine on his breath. "Warned ya not to stray! And with *her*…oh, son, you got no idea…no idea what kind of shit you've started."

I grabbed his pudgy hands, twisted in the material of my shirt, plucked them away, straightened myself with all the exaggerated dignity I could muster.

"I don't know what you're talking about," I said, preparing to push past him.

For the second time that evening, something entirely unexpected happened.

He grabbed my privates, grabbed all three of the main parts and squeezed, not hard enough to hurt, mind you, just hard enough to make a point. He pulled me a step closer, lowered his head, lowered it toward my crotch.

He snuffled, snorting like a pig, sniffing between my legs.

I felt my dick and balls squeezed together hard, sliding around each other covered in their cold jelly. I was so shocked, so immobilized I didn't move.

Bull gave one more lingering squeeze, then pushed away, stood.

"I see you know exactly what I'm talking about," he said, raising his hand to his face and licking his palm with broad, lascivious swipes of his tongue. "I can taste it."

He leered at me, rearing his head back and roaring with laughter.

"That don't taste like love to me. Tastes like…*need*. You men… you've always gotten the two confused. *Always.*»

Flushing, and not only with anger, I pushed past him, went into the bunkhouse.

Inside, it was quiet already, the lights dim.

The table was cleared, the food gone.

I stumbled to my bed, didn't bother to change my drawers, take off my clothes or even kick my boots off.

Sleep came like a hammer to my forehead.

Or a hand cupping the back of my neck.

After that, the other men avoided me. I'd never been overly chummy with any of them, but now they seemed to purposefully leave me alone. Conversations died when I approached, became whispers when I departed.

Only the evening revelries continued unabated; the excess of food, the wine, the laughter, the songs. The men ignored me. Bull, though, seemed to pay more attention. His dark, beady eyes followed me everywhere, watched my every move, from the moment I woke, all day at my job, to when I closed my own eyes in bed. He said little to me, just what was needed for the job.

Instead of anger or suspicion, however, he treated me with slightly detached humor. I couldn't reconcile this demeanor with his invigorated attention of me, so I eventually ignored it.

After a few days where nothing happened, I drifted away from dinner one night back to my cot. It was at the rear of the bunkhouse, as far from the dinner festivities as I could get. As men had come and gone over the weeks, I'd changed bunks until I got this one, which offered a little more privacy.

On waves of laughter, sounding more forced and desperate these days, I went to stretch out, perhaps turn in early. As I approached, sitting atop my pillow was a piece of fruit.

It wasn't like anything I'd ever seen. About the size of a softball, a mottled red color, almost like an apple, with a tiny crown at its top. I looked back at the diners, who ignored me, and wondered what this thing was, why it was here and who'd placed it on my pillow. There was only one entrance to the bunkhouse, and I hadn't noticed anyone unusual coming in or going out.

I picked up the fruit—I still didn't know what it was—and a slip of paper fell from beneath it. Sitting on the cot, I unfolded it. In spiky, feminine handwriting it read, *Meet me tonight in the fields behind the barn. Bring this fruit.*

My heart and breathing stopped almost simultaneously. I looked back toward the dining area with guilt, folded the paper and stuffed it into the pocket of my jeans.

I brought the fruit into the light, turned it in my hand. It was lighter than it seemed. I sniffed it, but could smell nothing. I fished my knife from the other pocket, drew open its blade and made a small incision in the thing. The rind was leathery, tough, and wine-red fluid seeped out, startling me. I dabbed my finger in the flow, staining the swirls and eddies of its pad. Hesitantly, I sniffed my finger, smelled a deep, floral tang. Then, I tasted the juice.

It was sour and sweet and like nothing I'd ever tasted. I made another cut into the fruit, split off a narrow wedge. What I saw seemed alien and weirdly biological. There was a clump of crimson seeds, bright and plump with that bloodlike fluid, between which twisted a bone-white curl of papery material.

I broke off a few of these seeds, put them in my mouth. Bursting them with my teeth, I tasted that same sweetness, that same acrid tartness at the back of my throat. Drops of the nectar spilled from the cut fruit, dribbled onto my hand, down my wrist.

I licked it off my hand, my wrist, licked the blade of my knife to clean it before putting it away. Standing, I hid the fruit in my hand, left the bunkhouse.

I didn't even pause to see if Bull had noticed any of this.

The night outside was hot, humid. A full moon glowered in the sky, bathing the landscape in its silver glow, limning everything in argence. I stepped from the porch, walked past the barn to the dark wall of corn just a dozen or so yards beyond.

I watched the silver-tipped leaves sway in the heavy breeze, smelled the sweetness of the corn, the green, green sap of the leaves.

Whatever it was, it quickened my pulse, seemed to concentrate and focus the heat of the air inside my lungs with each breath. My blood grew hot in my veins, and I found myself panting, sweating, nearly crazed.

For a moment, I wondered what I was doing, standing before the fields of corn, panting and perspiring, clutching a fruit I'd never seen or tasted before, nearly rabid to see this girl. Where would I even find her in all this corn?

Whatever had ignited the blood inside me shoved all this aside, roughly stamped it out. I drew the cornstalks apart like a curtain, stepped into the fragrant darkness, pushed forward.

I walked for many minutes, parting the stalks before me, their fronds whipping my face. I stumbled into a clearing, corn silk caught in my hair, sweat making my shirt stick to my chest.

The stalks here were twisted, tamped, and merged to form a deep, green bowl within the corn. At its center stood Percy. She was radiantly, terrifyingly beautiful. Her hair was swept up, glittering in the fell light. She wore a short, simple shift of white that glowed against her skin. Her eyes flashed in the moon's silver blaze, and she raised her arms to me, drew me to her.

I came, because...well, what choice did I have, really?

As I went to her, whatever held her hair in place fell away, and it spilled out, across her shoulders. At the touch of those tresses, the shoulders of her shift came loose, and it slithered down around her form, pooled at her feet like a puddle of white gold.

I was upon her, drew her to me. Our lips found each other, and that expression of the fire within me seemed to light the glade a golden-green, pushing the silver light of the moon aside as if negligible.

My hands played with her hair, slid down the curve of her back, cupped her smooth, tight ass. My lips searched hers, traveled across her cheeks, the hollow of her throat, the delicate skin of her neck.

Hers, too, moved. With no conscious awareness of how it happened, suddenly I was bare assed. I felt her hands—so cold and light compared to the hot and heavy air within this bower—skate over my shoulders, my chest.

I felt nails trace my arm, take the fruit I still clutched there.

She brought it between us, her eyes flashing.

"You brought the pomegranate," she whispered, turning it in her hands. Then, she saw the wedge I'd cut from it. "You ate of it?"

I nodded.

"Do you not know what it is?"

"No. Never tasted one before…never even seen one before."

She licked her lips. "It is the food of the dead."

I wanted more of her lips, more of her skin, more of *her*…and less talk of the fruit. I leaned in, bit into the thing, tearing off a large chunk of its flesh, feeling the pips within burst against my teeth, the cool, sweet fluid run down my throat.

Percy tossed the thing aside, where it was swallowed by the cornstalks.

She took my face in both hands, yanked my head to hers, kissed me, kissed me, kissed me. She trailed these kisses down my neck, my chest. She fell before me…and, well, I'd never had *that* kissed before.

Soon, we were entwined on a smooth, golden carpet of corn silk. She moved against me, and I thought that I'd never been hotter, never been harder. With each caress, with each kiss, I seemed to grow and grow, to solidify, as if, before her, I had only been smoke.

When I entered her, it was like rutting an oven. We were both bathed in sweat, or she was bathed in mine. Our slick bodies moved atop the corn silk, and I lost all track of time. My muscles ached, my throat was raw from the screams that I had first thought, with all my male ego, were hers, but were actually mine.

Within her, I was a brand, a torch, rock that was fast becoming magma.

When it did, when the heat finally melted me and what was left flowed into her, I collapsed, shaking. I passed out for a while, awoke to her beside me, her body twisting to my conformations. Her skin, of course, was cool against mine, cool against the night, as the sweat dried on my limbs, my shaking chest.

We lay there for a while and said nothing, her head on my shoulder. I kissed her hair, smelled apples and sweet, dry wheat. Giggling, she lifted her face to mine, kissed me deeply. I saw that her lips, her chin were stained red, perhaps from blood, perhaps from the seeds of that fruit she'd given me.

Red lines twisted across her breasts, her hips. Smears of the stuff mottled my chest, spattered my belly as if our exertions had ruptured an artery.

"You are of the dead, now," she said, and it sounded sad yet filled with expectation.

She snuggled in the crook of my arm, and I closed my eyes.

The green-gold light turned red seen through the shades of my eyelids, and I fell asleep.

I awoke, alone, that morning in my bed back at the bunkhouse.

"So, it *is* vampires," Tim interrupted, shaking his head ruefully.

"Kid, stop it with the vampire crap," Hough snorted. "It ain't vampires. And quit interrupting. The night's only so long. Besides, this ain't a story about monsters, like I said. It's a story about love."

Reef stared into the distance, turned something over in his mind.

"Okay, it's about love," he said, not facing Tim. "But I guess love's a monster, too."

Our meetings continued for a month or so. Not every night—none where there was a new moon. She let me know by placing a pomegranate on my pillow. A note wasn't necessary any longer. We both knew where to go, what we'd be doing.

What started as a compulsion, I think for both of us, turned into something else over those weeks. I mean, we weren't *dating*, not in that sense, certainly not in the sense of the word in those days. I didn't take her to the movies or to the drugstore to get a soda. We didn't walk arm-in-arm down main street, window shopping, trading small talk, kissing shyly. We didn't hold hands and watch the sunset.

We screwed, though. Lord, how we screwed. Things, I guess, worked in reverse from there. We found an intimacy beyond that of our bodies. The first few times we met, it was animalistic, feverish, and we generally lay there when it was done slicked in sweat, exhausted, spent, silent. I would wake in the morning in my own bed, with little idea of how I got there.

After, we lay there and talk. At first, she let me do the talking, and though that was a bit strange for me—I wasn't then given to speaking about myself—she drew it out of me, interested in my life, my lost family, my dreams.

Eventually, she allowed me to draw her out, too. When she spoke, she held me rapt. She told me of her family, of their history. She told me of her loneliness, her isolation. She told me stories of such exquisite, crystalline sadness that I had no choice but to fall in love with her. Because I knew I had to be the one to hold her, to comfort her, to wipe the tears from her face and stroke her soft, brown hair.

After a while, she fell in love with me, too.

I realized *that* had been her hunger all along. She was hungry for love. She'd known it on a greater scale before, long ago. Never, though, in this more intimate way. She had been stripped of both, the big and the small, by time and forces beyond her control. It'd taken ages to realize that she still needed one or the other.

For her—for all of the Karabas family, she made me understand—that greater love was gone, never to return. It seemed, to her at least, that the more singular love, the intimate kind, was denied now only to her.

Things changed when her mother found out.

We'd been meeting for nearly two months, with only the occasional stink eye from Bull, when it finally happened. One evening in midsummer, we lay together in the field. It was quiet, only the rush and rustle of the corn whispering in the night air.

I was getting ready to say something—to this day, I have no idea what—when it all changed. The atmosphere in our little glade altered, took on weight. The air became sweet, almost overbearingly so.

Percy leapt to her feet, stood breathing hard. She was naked and afraid, yes, but also defiant in a curious, childlike manner. As if she had been awaiting what was coming, had planned for it.

I pulled myself up to sit beside her, absently kissed her smooth, soft calf as it presented itself.

The corn stalks all around were moving, twisting in unfelt wind. They seemed in pain, writhing hideously, and growing taller as I watched. I could hear their growth, and it sounded like torture, a creaking, groaning sound that set my teeth on edge.

Something pushed through them…*she* pushed through them.

"Mother!" Percy said

Mrs. Karabas, for that was how I knew her, stepped into our bower on a wave of frenetic green fronds and tendrils that reached before her, parting the corn, forming a dense, fecund carpet that softened her footsteps.

Like Percy earlier, Mrs. Karabas' hair was upswept. She wore a simple shift of dazzling green, and her feet were bare and unadorned. She came several steps into the bower of corn, stopped. She spared barely a glance at me, turned all of her powerful, palpable ire onto her daughter.

"You dare, child?" she hissed. "You dare break the covenant… and for one such as this? In my time, Pan wouldn't have found him worthy to boil the meat from his bones to make a pipe. You betray us all for *him*?"

Percy, for, again, that is all I knew her as, straightened her shoulders, and threw her head back with a careful, studied haughtiness.

"You speak to me of betrayal, mother, yet you bargained with the life of your own daughter to achieve…*what?* You've left me nothing. No love at all.»

Mrs. Karabas was still, but the plant life around her writhed in frustration, twisted and grew and pressed into the clearing, restless and desperate.

«*He* will know," she finally said, whispering and urgent. "*He* will find out."

"So?" Percy responded, though her answer seemed tinged with fear for the first time.

"When he does, his anger will be great," her mother responded. "Do you think he will take it out on you?"

Percy swallowed, looked down at me.

"No, he will take it out on them. On *him*.»

Percy cried, softly. I saw tears splash down her naked, upturned breasts.

"You are a fool, Persephone," her mother said. "You always were. What are your days spent below compared to our months here? His love for you keeps him at bay, chains death to his own realm. And you would smash that all to pieces...for what? Your own selfish love?"

Percy sniffled, dashed the tears from her eyes.

"You don't know what you're talking about. You don't have to spend any time there. It's cold...he's...*cold*. His love is...*death*. Only death."

Mrs. Karabas sneered at her. "The two are inseparably entwined, Persephone. All love is death, child. All death is love. How can you have lived so long and not know that? After so many millennia, it's all we have left. This world no longer holds any love for such as us. Our time here has become a slow, slow death. You buy us time."

Percy approached her mother, wringing her hands. "Time? For what, mother? There are no offerings, no belief. There is no love for us, surely. But for me? For you? Where is the harm in us finding our own love?"

"They cannot love us, child. Not in that way. You think this one will love you? That he will do all it takes to keep that love alive?"

"Why shouldn't I try? What does it matter if I stay here and find my own love? What does it matter, mother?"

Mrs. Karabas took a few steps, turned back to where she'd come in. The living mass of the carpet swirled and reformed around her, pushed back the corn before her.

"You never think of anyone but yourself, child," her mother said without turning. "That is the lesson I attempted to teach you. You simply will not learn. Perhaps when all the world is dead, when all around is cold and dust, perhaps then you will learn.

"It will be too late. For all of us. For all of them. Your love will have slain the world."

She moved off, and the corn closed behind her.

"Mother!" Percy shrieked, her arms flying up to reach out for her, beckon her back. But she was gone, and all the light and heat that had been in the clearing vanished with her.

Now only the silver light of the moon shone around us.

I looked at Percy—*Persephone?* Where had I heard that name before?

She looked at me and shrieked again.

It was loud and lonely and lost, and it spiraled up and up and up until it filled the clearing, filled my head.

I passed out.

I didn't see her for many days after that.

The rhythms of the farm carried me away, took my mind off it, off her. Each evening, as weary as I was, I dashed into the bunkhouse anxious to see a pomegranate on my pillow.

Bull's attention waned, and he joined the group of other workers who basically ignored me. I worked hard all day, ate my evening meals amidst the laughter and singing, took myself to bed early.

When I slept, I dreamt of her, under the moon, within our green and golden bower. I dreamt of her, the crisp apple smell of her skin, her hair like sweet corn, her breath like honey. I dreamt of her cool hands, and me engulfed by the fire within her. My nights were as long as my days, and twice as lonely.

I tried to tell myself I didn't love her, *couldn't* love her. I barely knew her, certainly not at all outside the corn. But I did…I did love her, I knew. It made me profoundly sad. That love…I knew it would never amount to anything. Could never amount to anything.

I thought of moving on, of leaving the Karabas farm, of

continuing west, always west. Always away, from the past…from the pain, I guess.

I gave up, sought out Bull on a late summer evening, after the work, before the strange revelry of the evening feast, to find him and tell him I quit. He gave me a wide, wine-stained smile, clapped me on the back.

"It never woulda, ya know?" he barked. "Never woulda amounted to anything! The love you think you got for her…it ain't the kinda love we need."

He paid over my last bit of wages, and I tucked that into my knapsack with all the other money I'd earned since coming on. There was so little to spend it on, so little reason to even go to town, I'd managed to hang onto nearly everything I'd made. It made for quite a little bankroll.

I'd take this money, set out west, find the next farm, perhaps in Kansas, perhaps in Colorado. Maybe it'd be farming or ranching, who knew? Just to get me away from here, away from this awkward, painful love.

The electric bulbs strung between the bunkhouse and the barn cast their yellow-white light over the ground, pale and diffuse. The air was thick, humid, but the heaviness of the summer heat had already been squeezed from the air. I crunched down the gravel driveway, breathed in air that already had the first tang of fall on it. The spice of falling leaves, the flat, damp smell of decay.

At the bottom of the drive, where it met the dusty road, I turned, spared one last look back at the place.

My last mistake, really.

In every story, all the old ones that begin with "Once upon a time," there's always heartache when you look back.

What I saw were headlights, the headlights of the old Ford truck as it jounced down the drive toward me. It pulled alongside, stopped.

"Get in," she said, and it wasn't an offer or a promise or a plea.

It was a command.

I slung my roll into the bed, pulled the door open and climbed inside.

She turned to me, and her face…oh, her face there in the early evening glow, in the dim and greenish radiance of the dashboard lights, was beautiful. Awesomely, horribly, terribly beautiful.

My mouth went dry, my legs began to shake…shake like a scared boy's.

I yanked the door closed.

She said nothing, turned the truck out onto the road. I watched the Karabas farm in the side mirror receding into the distance.

I thought, for a few heady moments anyway, that we were leaving together, going away.

Going west.

Because, you see, they were all going west, the entire Karabas family. All going west, west for a thousand years, two thousand years, three thousand years. Following the same promises, the same false hopes, the same dreams we all were back then.

I know now that west leads nowhere, leastways not anywhere better than east or north or south. It's just a direction, just somewhere to run to avoid things, life, love, the decline of things.

Death.

Love.

I knew that she wasn't coming with me. I think, then, that had been her plan, at least initially, to follow me, to run away with me west, always west.

As we drove away, as the farm and her family and everything faded behind us, she realized what she was doing, the futility of it.

She slowed, turned off onto narrow dirt road that plunged into one of the farm's surrounding orchards. Tree limbs batted against the truck as it shot between the rows. Leaves stuck to the windshield wipers and apples clunked against the truck's body, the windows.

The truck slewed into a small clearing in the orchard, fishtailed to a stop. The trees were dense on all sides, and the road split into a fork, angling off left and right and disappearing into the foliage.

Still without saying anything, Percy stopped the truck and got out. I did, too, following her around to the back of the vehicle, where she leaned against the battered bumper and looked at me through narrow eyes.

I realized we weren't going anywhere.

I was. Oh yeah, I would be going.

She would stay here with them.

Have you ever looked back on a moment, a moment that is captured and imprinted on your brain in all its glory, in all its drama, in all it colors and meanings and implications?

Have you ever looked back on such a moment with the rue, the ache that comes from knowing you got it all wrong?

All completely wrong.

She was crying, her head bowed, the low sun sparkling gold and yellow like fire within her hair. I reached out to touch that hair, expecting that she might push my hand away, look up at me with those tear-smeared eyes and curse me, tell me to leave.

God, god…how I wish she would have…

Instead, she took my hand softly, touched the back of it gently, then sat up, stood still holding my hand, and flowed against my body like something liquid, conforming to the very length of me, every hollow, every declination.

She brought her head up, catching the last few rays of sunlight in her hair, in the pores of her smooth skin, in the swirls and eddies of her blue, blue eyes.

When we kissed, it felt as if she passed that fire into me, where it barreled through my veins, igniting my insides, my muscles, my sinews.

My heart.

It was like a concatenation inside me, an explosion that tore me apart, pieced me together in a way that was close to my original form, but not quite.

I pulled away slowly, so I could look at her face.

Her eyes were still closed, and her lips, still moist from our kiss, were barely open.

I could smell her breath, and it smelled of apples and sweet, growing things.

"I'm coming with you," she said, her eyes snapping open.

That was all.

That was enough.

The wind picked up out of nowhere, and the gentle whisper of the trees turned into the horrified murmuring of a crowd, aghast at what it had heard, what it had witnessed.

What was to come.

She stiffened in my embrace, and I saw her eyes go wide.

The wind was a tornado now in the grove. Leaves torn from the trees. Apples flung into the night. Trunks bent and creaking around us.

From a distance, a tearing, an awful rending sound, rose above the howl of the wind, came closer.

As if the sun had been tamped down behind the flat horizon, all light was extinguished and darkness oozed between the apple trees, spilled out, swirled between us.

Loud pounding now, rhythmic, shaking the earth.

From between the forked road, the apple trees parted with

a horrible keening of split wood. Darkness, inky black and impenetrable, congealed between the two ravaged trees.

Percy clung to me, her fingernails digging into my arm, the back of my neck. She buried her face in my chest and whimpered.

I don't know what I expected, really. A man oddly muscular for his age, exuding power and quiet dignity. A bearded man swaddled in flowing robes, ancient and wise and maybe even benign.

What came forward was about twelve feet tall and wasn't wearing clothes, certainly not robes, but the gloom that carried into the clearing churned around it, covered and revealed its body like the movement of clouds against the dark of the moon.

It was generally shaped like an incredibly big human.

Except for its head.

Its head was nothing remotely human, a great inverted chevron, elegantly curved and formed from a glistening, yellowish-gray, chitinous material. Its uppermost two points arced up and back, while the single point was directed down, like a sharp, sharp chin.

Dozens of dark ebony spheres lay in rows along both sides of the chevron, glittering in the no light like spider eyes. There was nothing that resembled a nose or a mouth or anything that made the head look like a head.

It was a head, and it turned to focus on us…on *me*.

It appraised me quickly, dismissed me utterly.

Then that head turned insect quick to focus on her.

"You," it said, and its voice was thin and reedy, mellifluous in a high-pitched, almost scratchy sort of way. "You would dare? All this…all this? For a man? *A man?"*

It said the last two sentences in a kind of mocking, falsetto way that struck me as particularly insectile, though I've never heard an insect speak.

"Surely you know how fickle man's love is? Is not our current life, our current plight signal enough of that?" he asked. "You think love from such as him would be strong? Would be steadfast? Would he love you, my dear, were he to see your true form?"

She lifted her head sharply at that, turned to him.

"You are cold, Hades. So cold. How can you expect me to love you?"

The figure emitted a grating, chirping sound that could only have been laughter.

"You speak to me of cold, dear? Your heart is darker and colder than anywhere I have taken you."

"I cannot…cannot go back. With you. Cannot. Will not."

I felt her entire body shiver in fear.

The figure threw its head back, until its pointed chin was aimed at the dark, unseen sky above. A keening wail issued from a hidden orifice, and it thrashed its head back and forth.

"Then this world dies, dear one. *Dies*. Because of you. Because of your…*love*.»

With that, it turned its attention back to me.

When its twin row of black-jeweled eyes rolled in their orbits toward me, I stiffened, stood taller, felt as if all the air in my lungs were being drawn from me.

"Except this one. Except him."

He took two steps toward me, so quickly that I flinched. His movements were smooth and gracile, and his hands weaved the air in front of me.

He crouched, lowering his strange head to mine.

I stopped breathing, but could smell him, an odor of ash and attar, dry and bitter like crushed aspirin and dirt.

"Do you know me, *man?"* it asked.

My mouth was dry, completely unable to form words.

Did I know him? No…yes…

My head swiveled bonelessly atop my neck.

"I am the Receiver of Many Guests," he said, his voice close to my ear, a sibilant whistle. "But not for you. I will not receive you."

He flowed back to stand between the hulking wrecks of the two trees his entrance had destroyed.

Percy pulled from me then, rushed to him.

"But you cannot…must not. He has eaten of your food. You must take him."

The darkness that cloaked him parted and one withered, human hand came forth, stroked her cheek.

"I may not command your love, but I still rule within my realm. I decide who comes and who goes. And who does neither. You would do well to remember this. You would do well to remember that you did this for *love*.»

His voice scratched out that last word derisively.

The darkness receded, like the ocean at low tide. The sky returned, a thin line of rose-pink etching the far western horizon again.

Percy dropped to her knees, wept.

I hitched in a breath, pulled the air inside of me as if re-inflating my lungs.

The air of the clearing was sharp and sour, like apples left too long in the cider house.

Looking back to the sky, I saw the coral fire of the setting sun was gone, replaced by a sinuous band of darkness that mounted the sky, devoured it.

There was a sound, too, grating on my ears, rough and raspy.

She stood.

"I would go with you wherever you will go," she said, taking my face in her cool, cool hands. "Let him do what he will. I love you."

I couldn't.

Couldn't take her with me, couldn't leave the world, this world, to his rough, unkind hands.

At least, that's what I thought…*then*.

I covered her small, soft hands with my own as the darkness roiled behind her.

"No," I said simply. "I can't. Your place is here. With him."

She looked away, saw what was coming behind her.

"With two words you damn me more surely than my own mother."

Behind her, the darkness mounted in the sky, began to blot out the stars.

"I love you, but not this way. I can't ask you to give up everything for me. *Everything*. I can't even know what that means for you. I can't ask you to go west when there won't be anything there for me…for us."

I smiled at her, stepped back down the road between the shadows of the apple trees.

I heard her weep as the dust spilled from the sky, obliterating the stars, the moon, the night.

After a few steps, I could no longer see anything before me except the thick curtain of dust.

A few steps more, and it filled my eyes, my nose, my throat.

A few more, and I sagged against a tree, slid to the ground, stopped breathing.

That was the last time I saw her for at least seventeen years.

Houghton Reef leaned against the porch railing and took a tremendous pull on his cigarette, held in the smoke for a long while, let it out.

Tim watched the man in silence, still fairly drunk.

"That was the dustbowl," Reef said, blowing out another mouthful of smoke. "At least the beginning of it. When I woke up the next morning, I was covered in grey dust. The orchard was destroyed, laid waste. The trees stripped of leaves, limbs bare, ruined fruit strewn across the blasted ground. Nothing. But I was alive. I'd made a choice."

Tim seemed held in rapt silence by Reef's story.

"What did you do?"

Reef seemed to be thinking, not about Tim's question. No, he turned over something deeper, far deeper in his mind.

"What did I do?" he finally snorted. "I got up, dusted myself off and continued west. I shoulda been dead, that much I knew. But he wouldn't take me. He told me that. I thought, I was running before, why stop? So, I went west. Alone."

"Percy?"

Reef stared into the distance of the night. "Oh I didn't see her for a while. A couple years or more. In '47, she found me in Montana. In '54, in Wyoming. In '63, I finally reached Southern California, and she found me there, too.

"Each time I ran. Been running for nearly eighty years now. I don't get sick too much, don't hardly age at all. I can't die. Bastard won't let me. But I'm tired, lord help me. Tired of running, tired of being alone, tired of…well, of carrying this choice around inside me."

He stood in silence, considering.

"I ran *from* her when I thought I was running *for* her, running for all of us. But she kept looking. Each time, she found me."

Tim mulled this over.

"Did you…do you love her?"

Reef let the cigarette fall from his lips, ground it out with the toe of his boot against the rough wood of the porch.

"Love? Well, sure, I *love* her. And your next question is does she love me? Yes, I'm sure of it. Absolutely. He knew it, that's why he did what he did, sent the dust storms to destroy the things that she and her mother loved the most. To destroy the things that we depend on to live."

"Why?"

"Because I'd taken from him the thing he needed to live. He thought I'd taken what they all needed to live. But in the end, though he didn't realize it, I took it from him and him alone. They can't understand that singular kind of love, the love between two people. It doesn't register for them. But they're just as susceptible to it as you and I are, probably more so these days," Reef said.

"Over the centuries, we fell out of love with them. We all, all of us, took from them what they needed to live. What I did…what she did… that only personalized it for him. Only made it hurt that much more."

He fished in his shirt pocket, pulled out his pack of cigarettes.

"Does she love me? Yeah. Why else would she chase me across the country, across the decades? Sure, at first it was because of fear, of death. Over the years, it became just as much about love. Sooner or later, it's all about love, and death takes a backseat to everything.

"Love means sacrifice. Why do you think we used to give up things for our gods? Love requires giving something up. I've learned that much. He knew it all along, and his fear of that knowledge made him angry."

Tim considered this for a few moments. "What would you be giving up, precisely, to be with her?"

Reef knocked a single cigarette from the pack, looked at it as if he had no idea where it had come from.

"Everything. All this...," he said, making an airy gesture with the hand holding the unlit cigarette. "*Mankind.*»

That last word dripped with contempt.

"What have I learned in eighty years of running?" he grunted, staring at the cigarette. "Sounds bitter, but I'm running from her to save...*what?* This crappy world? Where husbands beat their wives, where children starve? Where people shoot each other over spare change? Where there's a new war every week?

"I'm trading my love to save that shit?"

"What about everyone else? What about their love?"

"Hell, kid, there's no love left in this world to save. We don't love our gods anymore, and we damn sure don't love each other. We've thrown it all out like yesterday's garbage. Why throw mine away, too?

"It's like I've been standing there in that desolated orchard for eighty years, weighing love against death. Knowing what the right answer is, just too damn afraid to make it."

Tim waited, thinking that he might say more, but Hough stared off into the distance, as if he could see something there, just below the horizon.

"Will she find you here? Will she come?" Tim finally asked.

Hough flicked the cigarette out into the night, then chucked the entire pack after it. "She's here already, kid. She's just biding her time is all. Biding her time and hoping that I'll change my mind. Waiting for me to change my mind. Like all of 'em, really. They're just hanging around now hoping we'll change our minds, hoping that one day we'll love them again. But we won't. We can't."

He turned and opened the bunkhouse door, went to step inside.

"Will you?" Tim asked. "Will you change your mind?"

Reef paused in the open doorway.

"You don't understand, do you? I changed my mind eighty years ago, kid. Right there in that orchard. Been runnin' from that choice ever since. That's the hell of it. Good night."

Tim went in and fell into bed, images from Reef's story spiraling through his head, then floating through his dreams.

Through it all, behind it all, was Tina. Tina Gallider. Her face, her body, her spirit.

She was Tim's farmer's daughter, and she had begun to haunt him in much the same way that Percy haunted Reef.

Did Tim love her?

Yes. He thought so.

She was Mike's sister. She was the farm owner's daughter. He was just…what?

A man the same as Houghton Reef.

Tim slept a restless sleep, cast his covers away at the morning call and got dressed slowly. He smelled the breakfast being laid out in the mess hall of the bunkhouse, nothing like what Reef had described, but still a sturdy farmhouse meal of eggs, sausage, biscuits, gravy, hot coffee.

Tim finished dressing, looked down the row of bunks to the one Reef had claimed as his own. He could see, even from this distance, the bed was made, unslept in.

He ate his breakfast quickly, pushed back from the table and stepped out onto the early morning porch.

A tight cluster of people huddled in the space between the outbuildings, all looking west, all pointing at the sky.

Half of the sky was blue, clear, blameless.

The other half, the one that started on the western horizon, was a roiling, black mass, moving toward them, piling atop itself, expanding.

Tim saw arms of lightning rip inside the cloud, illuminating it from within in in lurid purple flashes.

Dust storm.

There hadn't been dust storms in this area of the country in decades…

Tim caught movement out of the corner of his eye, turned to see two figures silhouetted in the remaining sunlight between the buildings.

One was Reef, tall, thin.

The other was tall and thin, too, a woman with chestnut hair shimmering in the fading sunlight.

He moved to kiss her, slowly, lingering, then parted.

Tim thought he saw their shadows look his way, and Reef lifted his hand, waved briefly. Then Reef took her hand, and they disappeared behind the barn.

Overhead, the billowing mass had moved higher, closer. Tim heard the pattering of the dust particles. He tasted its grit on the cool morning air, a harbinger.

He looked to the main farmhouse, the family house.

A few people stood on the porch looking at the approaching storm.

Tim couldn't tell from this distance if Tina was one of them.

He thought of Houghton Reef and his long, long decision.

Tim debated for only a moment, moved off toward the house as the storm descended.

THE END

TELL ME WHAT IT MEANS TO ME

Officer Bill Tyson heard the sound three times.

Twice in this world, once in another.

The other world was Midnight Land, and it was this world that, ultimately, would claim him.

It was a little after two a.m. Clouds across a cold moon in a clear, sparkling sky. A few night birds cooing, the hoot of an owl. Miller's Grove was mostly asleep, as any small city in America would be at this time. Just a few cars out, a cluster of them waiting for their drunken owners to stumble out of the Regal House bar on the edge of town, its neon signs flashing brightly into the night. An ambulance headed back toward Memorial General Hospital, its lights tellingly off.

And, of course, Bill's cruiser, a 1951 Ford Deluxe Fordor, black and white with a siren and a single red light perched on the roof.

In other words, a police car.

And him a black man. A black *policeman* in a mostly white town in a mostly white state in the mostly white United States of America. In the year of our Lord nineteen hundred and fifty-eight, no less.

Bill had been on the force for just two years, and only by the grace of his best friend Sheriff Mike Pilot. Bill had grown up with Mike, both on small farms bordering Miller›s Grove and the dense forest cupping it on three sides. They hadn›t gone to school together, what black and white friends did?

Mike Pilot had attended Millard Fillmore High School, four whole names for the place. It was clean and well maintained, with crewcut boys and smiling, ponytailed girls wearing soft sweaters and poodle skirts and saddle shoes. Fillmore sported porcelain drinking fountains, seats for every student, and a gymnasium with real locker rooms. A neatly clipped football field, and baseball diamonds where the plates were regularly swept free of dirt and the baselines were kept manicured.

Bill went to a Negro schoolhouse with no name, mostly dilapidated. The older students had to stand some days as there weren't enough seats. There were no drinking fountains, no textbooks, no football team, certainly no neatly clipped fields.

Bill's school wasn't even in town proper, it was tucked away in The Club, the black part of the county north of the main square, near the crook of the river forming the town's eastern border. The one side not framed by the forest.

The Club.

It was the name given to the black neighborhoods by the white community, and it was a derogatory one, as most names for black things given by white folks tended to be. Truth be told, the real name most whites gave the black neighborhood was The Coon Club. Fake gentility, though, had cleaned it up to just The Club. The white folks thought they were being discrete, thought the black folks weren't in on the joke, but they were. They very much were.

The "club" part of the name came honestly, at least. During

Prohibition, there were a few social clubs there, where black and white mixed freely, if uneasily, to hear the very best jazz and blues musicians, and swig cheap, fiery hooch some said was produced in stills hidden away in The Outside since Prohibition.

The Clubs were gone now, burned down more than three decades ago during an almost legendary racial altercation that began (supposedly) with a young black man who'd whistled at a white woman. The oldest one in the playbook of white supremacy.

The stalwart white men of Miller's Grove razed The Clubs to the ground looking for him, so the story went. And in the process, they also torched about twenty other homes, killing a half a dozen or so black men and women.

Some weren't just killed, though. No, not just killed.

Lynched. Hanged. Burned alive.

But that was thirty years ago, and Ike and the Supreme Court had spoken above the din just a few years back, and black and white students now attended Woodrow Wilson Elementary School and Millard Fillmore High School together, if a little uneasily. Bill's old schoolhouse—the one with the rickety desks, a leaking roof and one room into which crammed about seventy-five kids, ages six to seventeen—fell into ruin, collapsed in on itself, was quickly covered in kudzu and weeds and all but forgotten.

Sure, there were black-only water fountains at Fillmore and Wilson. And parts of both beautiful locker rooms and showers for the girls and boys at Fillmore, if not signed as such, were understood to be *solely* for the black athletes.

It was a détente of sorts, though a forced one, an uneasy one. Bill, being the first black police officer in town, was in a unique position to both appreciate and loathe it. The high school—and even the elementary school, Bill figured—were just microcosms of the town.

Its citizens, just like its students, trying to figure out this new social order where people of all color could live and work together.

It wasn't perfect, not by a long shot, but just the fact Bill could have become a deputy in the Sheriff's department in Miller's Grove with no cross burnings or lynchings or angry mobs of people taking to the streets was something. Certainly, when Bill was a child, he had no aspirations to be a police officer. Why would he? It was as farfetched as…well….as someone walking on the moon. Why even dream of a thing so silly?

But when his friend, Mike, was elected sheriff five years ago now, he'd promised Bill—working at a scrap yard—he'd make him a deputy in good time. Just give him a couple of years.

Mike, as always, was as good as his word. It took him three years to get the Sherriff's office organized the way he wanted it. To root out the officers who were dead weight or just plain bad. To streamline operations and build up a level of trust with community leaders.

When he brought Bill in, there was an uproar, to be sure. They were just getting accustomed to the idea of segregated schools for their children…and now *this?*

Black cops? people asked Mike on the streets, in the MaryRose Diner, in Joe Schlutter's Hardware store. *Are you kidding, Mike? What's next? Teachers? Doctors? A judge?*

Mike answered all of these questions with a smile and the same two words.

Hope so.

After a few months, as Mike had predicted, the rancor faded to hushed whispers and backroom chats far away from Bill's—and even Mike's—ears. It was the way of such things for the angry voices to fade, to become a mutter in the background of daily life. Most townsfolk, if not exactly accepting of Bill's position on the force, were at least aware it was a done deal and there was nothing, not a damn thing they could do to change or affect Sherriff Mike Pilot's mind.

Mike had spent the previous three years making sure of that. And though he was up for re-election next year, no one was seriously calling for him to be voted out over this.

Bill turned the cruiser around the corner of Dunstan Road, just off the main drag. His windows were rolled down and early summer air blew through the car. Crickets and cicadas hummed their songs into the night, droning like a lullaby.

Not that it affected Bill in the least. This was *his* time, and he loved having these late-night shifts. He had no wife, no children, so no real calls to be home for dinner or any particular time. So, he took these shifts from the other guys who did have families. He loved the night and the stuff that happened during these shifts. All the really interesting things, all the best stories to trade with the other cops happened during the night shift, and Bill wanted to be there for whatever happened.

Down Dunstan Road, ahead in the distance, was the forest, a great bulwark of black clouds, frozen in space like an enormous tidal wave ready to crash over the town. It rose from behind the buildings to eat at the horizon, swallowing the sky and the stars.

With little to do on this quiet night, Bill switched the radio on softly, just enough to hear Rita, tonight's dispatcher, if she called. Louis Armstrong's "I Get Ideas." His fingers drummed outside the driver's door, keeping time with the baseline.

Dunstan Road twisted around the southern part of town, snaking its way eventually southwest. Just as it seemed it would plunge into the woods, it veered sharply to the right, took a miles-long detour around the edge of the trees, as if deflected or repelled by the forest. It finally spilled out in the flatland of the farms both he and Mike had grown up on. From there, Dunstan Road went to Kobalt and Reinerton and eventually to other, bigger towns Bill had never been to, never even hoped to see.

But not *through* the forest.

Only one road went through the forest, an old logging trail, now abandoned and mostly grown over, from when they actually logged in there. But that hadn't happened since right after the Civil War, and it had been a short-lived venture at that. Seemed the loggers hadn't liked being in there.

As Bill drove around the forest early that morning, it was featureless, a black scrim drawn over the stage of the world, hiding something deeper and dark. Funny, he thought (and not for the first time), it doesn't even have a name. It doesn't even have an agreed-on placeholder for a name. It was, variously, the Woods, the Forest, or the Timbers.

Most white people called it the Thicket, as if it were little more than a few trees clumped together.

Most black people just referred to it as the Outside, and that only in passing, to warn kids away from it, like the boogeyman.

Now you stay away from the Outside, you mind me? Things in there don't need no disturbing.

What black and white folks both seemed to agree on, though, was it was best left alone. No one hiked it or camped out in it. No one plunked around the streams flowing into or out of it. No one logged in it or built houses in it or too near it if they could help.

It was rarely ever discussed, either. There just seemed to be some tacit agreement among the denizens of the town to stay out, stay away. It had been like that for as long as anyone could remember. No one knew exactly why.

Bill thought back to his childhood. He and Mike had gone into the Outside on several occasions because…well, what child hasn't gone where they're not supposed to? On each expedition, Bill remembered, they didn't go far, and they didn't stay long.

Usually, it was Bill who chickened out. Something about the Outside unnerved him terribly, even just the mention of its name.

When Bill and Mike had gone in, they didn't see or hear anything weird. There were no ghosts or monsters or deranged madmen waiting to capture and eat little children. It was a forest, almost like any other in their experience, it was just that the atmosphere inside was different, as if the air were weighted and adhesive. The light filtering through the leaves seemed altered by its passage, weak and sickly as it oozed across the forest floor.

It was quiet…deathly still. No birds chirped, no insects buzzed. No dogs barking or cars passing in the distance penetrated the canopy of trees.

Each time they'd gone in, they'd left quickly, within minutes usually. Just a feeling, a disquiet they each felt, yet didn't communicate to the other.

Bill thought of this briefly as he drove by its black bulk.

He hummed the tune on the radio, The Platters "Twilight Time."

Out of the mists now, he sang, and then his voice broke. His mouth and throat felt scratchy and dry, and he remembered the Thermos of hot coffee he'd packed with the ham sandwich, hardboiled egg and a few cookies for his late-night lunch.

Scanning for an area of road to pull over on, he saw a wide shoulder ahead, just before the sprawl of the water treatment plan. He nudged the steering wheel, and the car slowed, came to a stop in a crunch of gravel and a cloud of silvery, ethereal dust.

Bill put the car in park, reached into the passenger floorboard.

His hand closed on the warm metal Thermos, and he hefted it. He turned the volume on the radio up—and the volume on the dispatch to compensate—then stepped out of the car.

He poured a cup of coffee, set the Thermos on the hood, drank staring at the dense, blank wall of the Outside.

The coffee was hot, sugary, and black, and it scoured his throat as it went down.

The Platters finished their song and up came Jimmy Clanton and His Rockets with "Just a Dream." It was now about three a.m., and Bill guessed the overnight disc jockeys liked to joke around with their music selection.

He sipped at his coffee, thought about reaching back inside to find the crumpled paper sack with his sandwich.

The sound crept up on him. At first, he ignored it. Seemingly far off, it was dim and hard to place, just background noise. But it continued to build, ratcheting up in the relative silence.

What was it?

Hard to tell. The sound grew to be full and complex, almost like a bank of televisions tuned to different channels, their volumes turned all the way up, a cacophony of sounds and noises and screeching music sounding like war movies, laugh tracks and music all run together, underpinned by white noise.

As the sound (sounds?) increased in volume, though, it became less variegated and more homogenous. Like a series of high-pitched tones or a symphony of screams, cycling up and down. Sort of like the wobbly flying saucer sound effects Bill remembered from some of the science fiction flicks he'd seen over at The Rialto in town.

The volume continued to increase, louder and louder until it blotted out all the other night sounds completely. Bill slapped his hands over his hears, grimaced. The Thermos danced across the hood of the car, vibrating until it fell off the front end, flashing in the headlights, spraying coffee.

Then the headlights went off, and he was swallowed by the night.

The sound was so loud now, so close, Bill looked up, expecting to see a low-flying plane of some kind or even the flying saucer it sounded as if it came from.

But nothing.

In an instant, it was gone. Not fading away or gradually lessening, just gone.

Bill now heard only his own rough breathing, his quickened heartbeat.

Slowly, he lifted his hands from his ears.

He didn't notice, at first, they came away wet and tacky.

His feet scrabbling in the dirt, he caught himself, yanked at the car door, practically fell inside. He wished he had that coffee now, even something stronger than that.

He sat there, still hearing the echo of the sound in his ears. He noticed the engine was off, the radio, the dispatch.

After a few attempts at fumbling with the car keys, the engine coughed and sputtered, then rolled weakly over once, twice. Caught. But it idled roughly, threatened to stall again.

It didn't, and while he waited to see if it would continue to run, he snapped the interior light on, looked at himself in the rearview mirror.

A dark trail twisted out of each ear, hard to see in the washed-out light of the overhead. He touched his right ear, brought his hand away.

Blood.

Not waiting for anything else, he yanked the lever into drive, pushed the pedal down hard. The car fishtailed, spraying dirt and gravel.

There was a good-size jounce before the car found its footing, squealed away back down Dunstan Road.

Only later, back at the station, did he realize he'd run over his Thermos.

Bill was at his desk at the back of the office when Sheriff Pilot came in. The door jingled, and there was a brief burst of cool air, early morning traffic sounds from outside.

He'd taken time once he'd returned to the station to wash the blood from his hands, his ears, and cheeks, to peer at his haggard face in the fluorescent bathroom light. Now he sat slumped, his head held in his clean hands. He briefly looked up when his friend closed the door behind him.

"Well, don't you look like a sorry sack of shit," Mike said. "You drinking on the job again, Billy?"

Groaning despite himself, Bill lifted his head, smiled thinly. "Only because you drive me to it."

Mike ducked into his own office, just behind Bill's desk, shrugged out of his coat, dropped a few things onto his desk. All the while, Bill knew, keeping an eye on him.

"What's the matter, hoss? You feelin' poorly?" Mike asked, leaning around the doorframe. "Need a few aspirin, maybe a Bromo Seltzer?"

Bill took a deep breath. "Took some a while ago. Hasn't helped. Had something weird happen last night. Left me feeling…odd."

"Looking odd, too," Mike said, stepping fully from his office, now sounding concerned. "What's up? One of our wonderful citizens giving you trouble?"

Bill looked at his friend, unsure of where to start. "Nah, nothing like that. I was out driving, 'bout three a.m. Stopped to drink a cup of coffee out off Dunstan near the water plant. Heard something."

"Heard what?"

Bill's mouth moved for a second without much coming out. Finally, "I don't rightly know."

"You don't know? Well, what'd it sound like?"

"That's just it. I don't know. Sounded like everyone in town had their television sets all turned up. Sounded like people screaming. I dunno, but it got pretty damn loud before it stopped."

Mike leaned against the jamb, a strange look on his face. "Had to gas up this morning over at Norb's Sinclair," he said. "You know old Norb lives in a room at the back of the garage. Told me he heard something last night from the Outside, screams and such. His power went off for a while, too. I thought he'd been drinking. Probably had."

Bill looked away.

"What?"

"My car stalled while I heard it. Took me a minute to get it started after. Drove straight back here."

Mike's eyes narrowed.

"One more thing," Bill said. "My ears started bleeding."

Mike thought about this, then nodded. "Janey wasn't feelin' well, so no breakfast this morning. I'm gonna stop by the MaryRose for some eggs. I think Doc Gilbert's up and about. Whyn't you head on up there, have him give you a once over. Then meet me over there. Breakfast's on me."

Bill opened his mouth to say something.

"Now, don't argue with me."

"I wasn't gonna argue with you, Mike. I was just gonna suggest The Sparrow instead."

"What's wrong with the MaryRose?"

"They don't exactly like me over there."

Mike shook that off. "You'll be with me. You don't pay them no nevermind."

About forty-five minutes later, Bill walked through the door of the MaryRose. It was steamy inside, smelling of greasy, cooking food, sharp, black coffee, and cigarette smoke.

Bill noted, though he pretended to ignore it, all of the white heads in the place turned incrementally toward him as he let the door close. But no one greeted him, not a "good morning," a tip of the hat, or a nod of the head.

Sheriff Pilot was sitting on a stool at the counter, sipping from a cup of coffee, looking impatient. Bill sidled up to him, pulled off his hat.

"So, what'd the doc say?"

"Oh, some inflammation of my ear drum, that's about it. He noted I was tired, too, if that's helpful," Bill said, sitting next to Mike. "Did you order yet?"

"Nah, just coffee so far. I was waiting for you."

"Why'd you wait?" Bill asked, but he knew the answer to the question, just as he knew why Marge at the counter hadn't been down immediately to bring him coffee.

"Couldn't order bein' worried about you and all," Mike said, smiling.

"Ahh, mother hen. I'm alright."

Bill surveyed the room. Pretty much the same faces he saw everywhere, every day. Old Bob Purcell in the corner, overalls and denim shirt, jawing away with Tim Javitts, the head of the farm bureau. In the opposite corner, Terry Quinn, Jimmy Nelson and Pete Baskin, the VFW contingent. At the opposite end of the front counter were Dan Corley and Jack Oakley from the fire department. Bill nodded to them, and they nodded back quickly and unobtrusively, went back to their breakfasts.

Meanwhile, Marge stood near the open kitchen window, speaking softly to Manny, the cook, who happened to be her husband and the owner. She was the eponymous MaryRose, though no one but Manny called her that.

Mike drummed his fingers on the counter as they waited. It was all a game, Bill knew, to see how long they'd wait.

Bill hated this place, didn't much care for the people who frequented it. And, he knew, they all felt the same about him.

Finally, Mike raised his voice. "Damnit, Marge. We gonna do this every time?"

Marge spared a last word to her husband, then lurched over to the coffee pot, plucked it from the counter along with a thick, white mug, drifted over to them. She plunked the cup down in front of Bill, sloshed some coffee into it.

She didn't look at Bill at all.

"I'll have two eggs, easy over, bacon, hash browns, toast. Tell your hubby not to break the yolks this time. What'll you have, deputy?"

Bill picked up his coffee cup, drained it, set it back down.

"Sheriff, I think I'll have some more coffee, this time with cream," he said.

Marge refilled his cup, spun to walk away.

"Oh, and I'll have two eggs, over hard, sausage, rye toast."

Marge stopped, flashed him a brutal look, continued on to the kitchen window. She scrawled something onto her pad, ripped the sheet off, slapped it onto the windowsill. That accomplished, she returned to lean against the counter near the firemen, saying nothing, staring into the distance.

"You know they don't like me in here, Mike. Why you gotta push? Probably find a hair in my eggs. Or worse, Manny'll just spit on the plate."

"Calm down, Bill." Mike scooted around on his stool to try to get comfortable. "Jesus, my ass is too big for this stool."

"Your ass is spreading from sitting at your desk all day," Bill said, sipping his coffee, knowing he'd probably get no more.

"Look who's talking." Mike said, looking at his friend askance. He sighed. "Listen, if you're good enough to be a deputy in their police department, you're good enough to sit in their restaurant and eat their damn food."

"They don't think I'm good enough for either. That's the problem."

"Look, do I gotta fight you, too, about this? Hard enough to fight all them."

"Then why bother?"

"Don't you want all this to change?"

Bill considered this. "I guess so, yeah."

"Well, how's it gonna unless those who can, push?"

"All it seems to do is make 'em talk, Mike."

"So? Let 'em talk."

"They talk behind *your* back, but to *my* face."

Mike slugged back his coffee, rapped his cup on the counter like a judge calling court to order, hard enough to make Marge jump. She grabbed the coffee pot, rushed over, filled both of their cups. No cream still, Bill noticed.

"They don't mean anything by it anyway. Not really," he said, loud enough for Marge to hear as she departed. "You just gotta ignore what they say, Billy. Don't let it bother ya none."

The '53 Bel Air, two-toned white and sky blue, shot through the four-way, all-stop intersection at two in the morning about a week later. They were on the north side of Main Street, near The Club, at the corner of Busy Bee's Bakery and The Sparrow, the black diner Bill was fond of.

Bill had pulled into the empty lot of the Busy Bee to eat his lunch when the car shot past, windows down, radio blaring.

Kids.

White ones.

Bill thought about it for a moment, leaned toward letting them skate. Pulling over white folks—even kids—was problematic and not really worth the hassle.

Besides, he was eating.

They breezed through the four-way, and another car—who'd have thought there'd be two out here at this hour of the night?—squealed to a stop to keep from plowing into them.

Bill heard the throaty engine of the Chevy accelerate, the whooping of the young men, and put his half-eaten ham sandwich aside, screwed the lid back on his brand-new Thermos.

Lunch would have to wait.

He turned the ignition, flipped the lights on, and rolled the cruiser out onto Main. In the distance, receding fast, he saw the red taillights of the Chevy.

He took off after them, slowing to let the other car creep carefully through the intersection before pushing his own pedal to the floor.

Catching up to them a few blocks north of Dunstan, he flipped the sirens on for good measure.

He saw the dark shapes of their heads highlighted in the flashing red lights. They were turning back and forth between looking at Bill's car and gesticulating wildly at the driver of theirs.

Bill knew they weren't arguing with him to slow down and stop at the sight of a cop. No, he knew they were egging the driver on, telling him to step on it, they could ditch him.

The car turned on Dunstan without slowing, tires shrieking. It fishtailed, then rocketed off down Dunstan.

Annoyed now, Bill gunned his engine and took the turn just as fast, just as recklessly. But where these boys hadn't been driving long, had probably never been involved in a high-speed chase, Bill had been driving for nearly twenty years now and had done this dozens of times.

In less than a minute, he was right back behind them, flashing his headlights and honking in addition to the siren and flashing Beacon Ray atop the cruiser. None of it made the kids stop or even slow their car. If anything, they accelerated, taking turns almost on two wheels.

Bill thought again about letting them go, riding off into the night, but the fact they ignored him—a deputy sheriff in the Miller's Grove Police Department—picked at his sense of personal respect.

As the two cars shot past the huge, dark bulk of the Outside, Bill floored the accelerator.

His windows were down, and wind buffeted everything in the car. His hat and his lunch circled on the passenger floorboard. The Thermos rolled off the seat to join them.

That's when it struck, the sound.

A howling cycled up through the rushing wind, like a static scream. The dashboard lights flickered. The dispatch radio erupted in a burst of white noise then snapped off.

The engine backfired, sputtered, died.

Ahead, the taillights of the kids' Chevy stuttered, went dark, and the car slowed to a crawl. The car veered onto the shoulder, where it shuddered like an animal, stopped.

Bill drifted in right behind them, the crunching of gravel barely noticeable under the torrent of noise ripping through the night.

Bumping the door open with his thigh, he spilled out of the cruiser, hands moving to cover his ears for all the good it did. The sound seemed to disregard any attempts to block it, burrowing straight into his brain.

He felt a runnel of blood seep between the fingers of both hands.

As the sound pulsated in his head, he staggered to the other car. Four doors flew open, and five boys tumbled out. The driver, a teenager Bill recognized as Ricky Birsha, fell to his knees and vomited extravagantly onto the gravel.

Feeling wobbly, his head thrumming from the noise ricocheting within his skull, Bill braced himself on the trunk of the boys' car. As Ricky slumped to the ground, practically in the dark pool of his own puke, Bill saw the faces of the other two kids on this side of the car. Both had trails of blood running from their ears, their noses. One was even weeping blood from the corners of his eyes.

Then, just as suddenly as it had begun, the sound stopped. The air rang like a struck gong after its silence.

Bill lowered his head, felt a thick runner of drool streaked with blood slide from his mouth down the side of the car.

He waited until he was sure the sound wouldn't unexpectedly start again, until he caught his breath. Then, he lurched over to Ricky, put a hand on the boy's shoulder.

"Come on, son," he said, his voice cracking despite his best efforts. "Get up."

Ricky stirred, a blank expression quickly melting into fear. Not fear of a police officer, Bill realized…not even a black one.

Fear of whatever that sound was.

Bill helped the kid to his feet, propped him against the car, stopped him from sliding back to the ground. Then, he went to check on the others.

On the driver side, hunched over, braced against his knees, was Jim Thompson, the school quarterback and a big young man. He nodded at Bill, waved him away.

On the other side of the car, three boys lay in the weeds, moaning. Bill recognized Ed Allen, Pete Lee, Vince Cushing. All seniors at Fillmore. All white boys.

All troublemakers.

Bill peered inside the car. Beer cans and at least one bottle of booze, which had spilled onto the floorboard. The inside of the car smelled of liquor and Brylcreem and cigarettes. And now vomit.

Shaking his head, he walked back to the driver side, waving the other boys along.

They climbed to their feet, looking at each other, noticing the blood on their faces.

"What the fuck?" asked Ed, daubing his fingers in the blood lining both sides of his face.

"You wanna shut that mouth and get over here, Allen," Bill said, a little rougher than he'd intended.

The boys listened, lining up dutifully alongside the car, leaning against it for support. Bill wished he could join them, talk about what had just happened, perhaps even just climb into the cars (if they still worked) and race out of here every bit as fast as they'd come.

But he couldn't. He had a job to do.

Clearing his throat, he looked up and down the line of them. Right now, in the moment, they looked very much like a row of boys, perplexed, nervous, scared. But as the seconds ticked away, as the memory of the razor cut of the sound faded, their shields came back up, the masks went back on.

"Why'd you have to go and do that for...*officer*?" Allen again. The others tittered at the inflection he'd given the last word.

"I didn't do anything, and you're pretty damn lucky I didn't."

"We weren't doing nothing," Cushing muttered. "You have no right to pull us over. We was just...drivin' around, havin' fun is all."

Bill walked over, stood before him. He took this kind of attitude from the white adults of Miller's Grove all day. Be damned if he was going to take it from their snot-nose kids at night.

"You'd better watch your mouth there, boy."

"*Boy*?" Allen snickered. "I only see one *boy* here."

Bill waited a second, then moved toward Allen, twisting the front of his shirt and yanking him up, slamming him into the car.

"Who you calling *boy*, cracker?" he said, pushing his face right into Allen's. "I'm a deputy sheriff, you little shit. You treat me with respect."

Allen's carefully manicured smile faltered as Bill held him.

"How'd you turn off our car like that?" one of the other boys asked.

Bill gripped Allen's shirt a bit longer, then released it. Allen fell back onto the car, slid to the ground. He picked himself up with no help from Bill, glared at him.

"I didn't," Bill said, stepping back. "I don't know why our cars stopped."

"Yours did, too, huh?" Ricky asked. "What was that...noise?"

Bill shook his head, searching for words.

"It sounded like it came from the Thicket," Cushing indicated, motioning toward the dark wall of the forest.

Bill looked where the kid pointed. He didn't expect to see anything really, and he didn't. Just the dark black silhouette of the forest against the navy backdrop of the night sky.

Bill turned back to the boys. They were all standing now, no more leaning on the car. Their eyes held a look…a look Bill was intimately familiar with.

What are you gonna do about this anyway? You can't touch us.

You wouldn't dare touch us.

Remember what happened on that night, long ago?

Yeah, you wouldn't want to go causing any trouble like that.

Would you?

Sighing, Bill wiped away some of the blood on his face, stared at it for a second.

"Look, I dunno exactly what happened tonight, but it got to us all. I think maybe it's best if you boys took that car of yours and went home. Straight home. No more messing around tonight.

"You do that, and we can just forget what happened earlier. The underage drinking, the drinking and driving, the numerous traffic violations. Just go home and we'll call it even."

The boys looked at each other, most nodding, counting their lucky stars that Bill didn't seem inclined to push the matter.

Allen, however, cocked his head at Bill.

"What if we're not ready to go to bed just yet…*officer*?"

"Look, I'm more than happy to let them all go and throw *your* stupid ass in jail, if that's what you want. Have your parents come down in the morning. Maybe save a couple of those cans and bottles you've got in the car. Show 'em what you've been up to tonight. I'm sure Sheriff Pilot would love to host a little show and tell. You up for that, tough guy?"

Bill felt slightly sour at having to mention Mike's name, but let it go.

Allen's cocky mien faltered, and the other boys climbed back into the car.

Bill stepped to the driver window, waited for Ricky to turn the ignition. The car sputtered to life. The headlights snapped on, and Bill slapped the windowsill.

"Straight home, you hear? I'm on duty until seven a.m., and if I see you out, all bets are off. Got it?"

Five "Yes, sirs" came, some less enthusiastic than others.

Bill looked at each of the boys, then stepped back from the car.

"What're you gonna do?" Ricky asked.

"Never you mind. Just head on home."

The car pulled away, turned around, headed back toward town.

Bill heard them laughing and hooting as they left.

Was sure of at least one of the words ringing out to him across the night.

After they'd left, Bill went back, sat in his cruiser and tried to settle down. He fished the Thermos from the floor, unscrewed the cap with a shaky hand. He drank two cups of coffee, staring at the Outside through his window.

The night had returned to quiet. Crickets buzzing, a train whistle from somewhere miles and miles away.

Not much else, certainly no brain-jarring noise emanating from nowhere.

Nowhere?

They'd said it, too. It seemed to have come from the Outside.

Bill, already sure of what he intended, shivered. Might have been the night air, might have been what he was thinking.

He drained the last of the coffee, screwed the cap back onto the Thermos, wrestled his big flashlight out of the glove compartment. He rolled the windows closed, turned the car off and climbed out.

As he stood surveying the forest, he withdrew his sidearm, opened the cylinder, checked the bullets. All accounted for, he reholstered the weapon, decided against turning the flashlight on just yet.

He'd certainly need it later.

With that, he crossed the weed-choked culvert on the other side of the road, tramped across the relatively narrow swath of scrub grass, then into the dense stand of trees.

Into darkness.

Bill lost some of his forward momentum about twenty feet inside the forest.

It was dark in here, much darker than he might have thought before entering. He gradually slowed, then stopped walking. The sky above was completely gone, blocked by the dense canopy of trees. No stars winked playfully above. No moon glowered through the branches.

Beneath his feet, was soft, dry earth, covered with a mat of pine needles, leaves and other detritus.

When he finally came to a stop, he listened. There was a brief susurrus of wind, the rustle of leaves. But no other sound, no crickets or night birds or road sounds. Nothing. Certainly no brain-scrambling bursts of static overlaid with screams. Or whatever that sound had been.

Bill heard nothing more than his own breathing, the whoosh-whoosh of blood through his veins.

Feeling the need to press on, he lifted the flashlight, thumbed its switch.

The beam leapt out, illuminated the dense trunks of trees and underbrush with a hyper-real light. But the beam didn't penetrate far. Within maybe four or five yards, it seemed to diffuse, swallowed by the forest.

Where it struck, each bough, each leaf seemed isolated, as if painted by itself onto a black backdrop, independent and unaffected by the rest of the woods.

Bill raked the beam around, searching for…what? He didn't know precisely. A path? Perhaps. Whatever was making that noise? Ultimately.

He fleetingly wondered why it mattered so much. He really should be headed back to his cruiser, headed into town to make sure those white boys weren't hoopin' and hollerin' and racing through town.

Instead, though, he began walking again, and not in the direction of the cruiser.

Deeper into the woods.

The farther he went, the more disassociated he became with what lay outside the woods—his police car, sure, but also Miller's Grove, the Sheriff's Department, his life. As the stars above him fell away, so, too, gradually did his strong feelings about himself, who he was, what his life entailed.

It was as if he were becoming another person entirely.

Here, in the woods pressing in on him from all sides, like the dark waters of some primal ocean clamping down on a deep-sea diver, his life outside all seemed so distant, so pointless.

Ahead, through the vertical blinds of the trees, he saw a light. At first, he thought it must be reflection, a trick of his eyes in the near total darkness. As he approached, it grew, coalesced.

It was a sign, a lit, neon sign.

Through the trees, nearer now, he could see it, read it.

Midnight Land, vertically in red neon script.

The sign was affixed to a building, low, its shape and size impossible to see in the darkness. It hung above a darkened door, closed.

Surprisingly, a man stood outside this door.

Bill considered this, weighed his options.

Stumble through the woods to his cruiser to call someone to back him up.

Or press on.

He thought of the tales of the Prohibition bars up in The Club decades ago, but he could remember no stories of anything other than random bootleggers here in the Outside. Leastways not any places *admitting* to being out here.

Touching his sidearm, he took a deep breath, walked forward.

As he stepped out of the dense line of trees, the gentleman at the door turned his head slowly to look at him.

Bill switched the flashlight off, holding it the ready, though, should he need a weapon other than a gun.

The man, thick and solid and dressed in unremarkable clothes, watched him approach, said nothing.

Bill stopped before him, opened his mouth.

"Look familiar, Deputy Tyson?" the man asked.

Bill couldn't really see the man's features, but he was large, impassive.

Something about him caused a shiver to race up Bill's back

"They're expecting you inside."

The man turned, drew the door open, stood so Bill could pass him and enter. He saw red light, smelled thick cigar and cigarette smoke (and maybe just a little Mary Jane), heard soft music dense on the air inside.

Bill put his hand on the butt of his holstered weapon, stepped into the room.

The man closed the door behind Bill, sealing off the woods.

It was dim inside, as shadowy as the woods, just in different ways. The predominant color was shaded rose, from the illumination behind the bar and the pink footlights around a small stage across the room from where Bill entered. A stool sat next to an upright piano, both unoccupied.

There were a few people in the place, though. A bartender wiping down the bar, two guys playing cards at a small table near the stage. A man and a woman seated at the bar, both turned toward him, giving him a thorough appraisal.

What really caught his eye, though, at the end of the bar, seated alone, was a man.

He was naked, absolutely nude, and he bled from any number of wounds, lacerations, welts, scrapes. Around his neck was a twist of thick hemp rope, coiled several times, then rising into the air behind his head like an Indian fakir's magic trick.

Disappearing utterly about a foot in the air.

That wasn't all.

His legs, from his thighs down, were on fire, fully engulfed by flames. The fire curled around him, bluish at its tips, white-yellow near his skin. Horrified, Bill could see the flesh through the flames, curled like paper in a fire, charred at the edges, angry red underneath.

It didn't seem to concern him at all, neither the noose nor the flames. And the fire didn't seem to consume the man, just flickered and sputtered over skin already ruined.

"Silas does give a man pause, don't he, deputy?"

Bill took a step back, his legs encountering the edge of a table, and he faltered.

"Whoa there, sugah," came a voice from behind. A hand touched his shoulder gently. He felt its warmth, nails through his uniform shirt.

Turning, he saw a beautiful black woman, almost as tall as him, her hair dark and heavy and loose over her shoulders. Her eyes were dark, too, her lips and fingernails very red in the scarlet light, as was the very tight silk dress she wore.

"What's going on here?" he stammered, trying to draw away from the woman's touch, but he was right up against the table. "What is this place?"

"Why, Midnight Land, hun," she laughed, then lowered her voice mockingly. "You wanna dem dere niggahs who cain't read?"

"He kinda looks like he can't read," called the bartender, pausing from wiping the counter. Bill flashed an angry look at the man, the only white person in the room, who also appeared vaguely familiar.

"Oh, but lookee here at this shiny badge," the woman cooed, lifting her nails from Bill's shoulder and fingering his Miller's Grove Police Department Badge No. Seventeen, pulling it gently from where it was pinned to his shirt. "I don't think they give these shiny badges to negroes who can't read. Unless you's a house negro."

"I can read," Bill said. "And don't use *that* term. I don't like it."

She snickered, dropped the badge back to his shirt, sat at the table behind him.

Bill sidled past, toward the door he'd come through, still gripping the handle of his pistol. "Is this some kinda illegal bar? I know for a fact the town hasn't licensed any liquor establishments in the Outside."

One of the card-playing men near the stage stirred. "The Outside, he says," the man harrumphed, snapping a card onto the table. "He's got no idea how far *outside* he is. Maybe time for him to come back inside."

The smaller man at the table opposite him threw back his head and laughed like a hyena at this, but kept his attention focused on the cards.

"Some kinda illegal bar? Why yes, sugah. Some kinda," the woman said. "Some kinda speakeasy. Hooch palace. Gin joint, watering hole, or even…a tavern."

The bartender hooted, and hyena-man barked out laughter again.

"If we gettin' high class, that is," the bartender said. He stared at Bill as if he knew him, too, daring Bill to recognize him.

"If," the lady agreed, and she patted the seat of the chair beside her. "Whyn't you take your ease, deputy? Explain to us how a readin' black man got himself a shiny badge."

Bill looked at her, looked at the offered chair, shook his head.

He looked back at the man seated at the bar.

Silas, legs aflame, head surmounted by a taut rope halo, lifted a glass of some pale amber fluid toward Bill, knocked it back.

"What the hell's going on here?" Bill said, unsnapping the brass catch of his holster, his hand shaking on the gun's handle. "Am I dreaming?"

"You generally have dreams like this, deputy?" the larger card player asked.

"No," Bill said.

"Sugah, you heard the music, and you came," she said, smiling. Bill saw some of her red lipstick had smeared on her teeth.

"You found us."

"Music?" he asked. "I heard a noise…something… Made my ears bleed. Stalled my cruiser."

"It's music to us. Now *sit*, deputy."

Her voice had an unpleasant edge to it this time.

Bill found it hard to take his eyes off Silas, but managed to look away, draw the chair out, drop slowly into it.

"There, now can we talk all proper like," she said. "Introductions all around. I'm Bernadette, but folks call me Bernie. That there's Ed and Floyd."

The two men playing cards each gave Bill an absent wave.

"Rick behind the bar. And I believe you've met Silas."

Rick nodded, Silas saluted him with another drink.

"Miss Bernadette," Bill said. "Bernie…where the hell am I? I mean, I gotta be dreaming. Probably fell somewhere, knocked unconscious."

Bernie considered this, smoothed at the dress' material across her legs. "Dreaming's just an altered state of consciousness, lawman. So, yeah, you're participating in an altered state of consciousness."

The other men guffawed, even Silas this time.

"This place seems familiar," he said, looking around. "But there's nothing in the Outside. Leastways nothing like this."

"And how'd you know? You ain't never been in those woods before, save for a few times with that white friend of yours, Sheriff what's-his-name?"

"Pilot. Sheriff Pilot. Mike," said the bartender, still absently wiping down the bar, scrubbing out glasses. The air about this man smoldered, shimmered like heat haze over summer pavement, as if he were every bit as on fire as Silas.

"Mike," Bernie nodded, as if considering something. "Besides, who said we're in the Outside anyway? No one here surely did."

Bill blinked. "I walked into the Outside from my car. Where else would I be?"

"Walking takes a body anywhere," she said. "Everywhere."

"Home," said one of the card players, and Bernie flashed them an angry look.

As Bill attempted to decipher that sentiment, a drink was plunked onto the table before him, sloshing liquid over his arm.

"Drink!"

He lifted his arm, looked up.

Silas, the hanged man.

The curse Bill had been about to utter died as a croak. He looked at Silas closely now, could hear the crackling of the flames, could see the truncated end of the noose weaving in the air, back and forth like the head of a cobra.

He hadn't been this close to a fully naked man since his days in the high school locker room. He wasn't sure what discomfited him more—being eye level with Silas' particulars or the fact they were as fully engulfed in flames as his legs.

Silas nodded toward the drink again, pulled out the seat opposite Bernie, sat.

Bill shook his head. "I can't drink. I'm on duty." "Never stopped you before," Silas said, winking. "Anyway, you ain't on duty now. 'Sides, you gonna need it if you wanna hear this story."

He looked at Silas, could see the way the rope bit into his neck, furrowed into his skin. He could see every cut in the man's flesh, the way the blood beaded on his dark skin like rain on a freshly waxed car.

Reaching out, he grabbed the glass, downed the liquor.

Bourbon, neat.

It floated into him, spread out like warm fog.

Strangely, rather than making him relax, accept what was happening, what he was seeing, the whisky was like a jolt of reality injected into his bloodstream. Suddenly all he could think about was his job, Mike, his parents, his grandfather, his tidy little house in The Club.

His other life.

"Welcome back to Midnight Land!" shouted Bernie, throwing her hands wide and laughing. The others looked on, laughing in unison.

"Why'd they give you a badge anyhow?" Silas asked as the laughter died away. "In my days, they wasn't passing out shiny badges to folks like you, they was handing out rope."

Bill set the empty glass onto the table. Silas looked familiar… damn familiar.

"Who did this to you?" he asked.

Silas narrowed his eyes, and the flames along his lower half crackled and snapped, almost avid with anticipation.

"Oh, you know it happened a while back. Since I been here, I can't hardly remember how long it's been." Silas turned toward the bartender with a distant, sorrowful gaze.

"Did this happen here?"

"Wha…? In Midnight Land? Lord, no! Things like that don't happen *here*. Things like that are what *end up* here," Silas said, snapping back to face Bill.

"But you might know some who did this, even though you left before it all went down. Sure, some are still out there, goin' 'bout they business. Sipping coffee, maybe patting they grandkids' heads with the same hands tightened this noose. Mayhap lighting they hearths with the same hands lit me up as I choked 'n spun. Mayhap kissing they wives with the same lips screamed at me.

"Mayhap eating meals at that very same diner you eat at with y'friend, that Sheriff. The very same men who cut me down like a Sunday ham from the smokehouse, all crisp and smellin' of hickory."

"Was it a hickory tree they strung you up on, hoss?" Floyd called over his shoulder, still focused on the seemingly never-ending card game.

"I think it was a hickory tree at that," Silas said, slapping the table and causing Bill to start. Bernie giggled, sipped at her drink. "Up there in old Mr. Boussard's yard in The Club. Beautiful old tree, never really was the same after a few strange fruit, though."

"Aye-ya," Floyd and Ed both answered.

Bill frowned. "Mr. Boussard's? Wait…that's my…wait. Do you mean Joseph Boussard?"

"Yup. Old Joe Boussard. His place is where I hung. Well, me and a few of my contemporaries, that is," Silas said.

"*Contemporaries*," Floyd echoed, then laughed his hyena cackle.

"That's my grandfather. His yard. His house. Where I live now," Bill said, almost to himself.

"Yeah? How's Old Joe, huh? He must be…what eighty some-odd years old b'now," Silas said. "Good, long life. Glad to see it paid off for him."

"Paid off!" screeched Floyd. Bernie turned to him, frowned.

"No one ever told me the lynchings took place right in my front yard," Bill said, standing, holding himself leaning over the table, propped on his fingertips. His voice increased in volume and pitch with each word.

"Nah, not quite the kind of thing he'd tell ya, now would he? Selling out his own for a little slice of theirs. Buying his safety by shutting his mouth while they roasted some strange fruit in his front yard. But that stink don't come off, now do it?" Silas said.

Bill stood fully, stepped away from the table.

"No, that can't be true. Can't. "

He turned, made his way back to the door he'd entered through.

All of them watched him leave but made no effort to stop him.

Shoving the door open, he brushed past the bouncer, still standing in the dark beside the door.

Overhead, the neon sign flashed.

Midnight Land.

"You'll hear the music again," came Bernie's voice just as the door closed. "You'll be back."

Bill heard the door thump shut behind him, and he dashed into the woods. He crashed through the darkened underbrush wildly, not looking for a path of any kind or the route he'd taken to get there. He simply ran through the trees, pushing branches out of his way, stumbling here and there, never completely falling, though.

When he came to the edge of the Outside, he ran full tilt, his shoes sliding on the dense mat of leaves and pine needles.

Suddenly, he was outside the tree line.

He continued running for few yards, slowly stopped, bent, resting his hands on his knees and breathing hard.

When he'd caught his breath, he looked up at the sky.

It was bright, clear daylight.

Across the road, his cruiser was gone.

It was about four in the afternoon when Bill came dragging into the Miller's Grove Sheriff's Office. He was hot and exhausted from the walk down Dunstan and through town. Thirsty, hungry, confused and a little disoriented.

Plenty of people gave him strange looks and second glances as he hoofed it down Main Street, not unusual.

When he pushed open the door to the office, he was glad for the rush of cooled air rolling out and over him. He stepped inside.

Betsy Vreeland, the sheriff's secretary and the dispatcher, almost ran him down, evidently leaving for the day. She let out a little yelp of surprise when they collided.

When she saw who it was, it became a scream echoing in the small office. She dropped her purse, took a step away from Bill, her hand flying to her mouth.

"See another mouse, Bets..."

Sheriff Pilot's genial voice faded away, and he stared at Bill.

"Where the fuck have you been?" he said, and it came out in a strangled croak.

Bill tried to answer, found his throat strangely dry and constricted.

"I..."

Sheriff Pilot came around Betsy, still standing hands-aflutter near her desk, and grabbed Bill in a tight embrace.

Still a little dazed, Bill returned the embrace. After a moment, though, Mike pushed him away, scrutinized his friend.

Then, "Betsy, honey, you head on home now," Mike said, holding Bill at arm's length, still studying the man. "And not a word to anyone about this. Not even to Carl. Betsy, *especially* not to Carl, you hear? I don't need the town gossip tree starting up just yet."

Carl was Betsy's husband, and a well-known purveyor of talk.

"Y-yes, Sheriff," she said, snatching her purse from the ground and sidling past the two men and out the door.

"Are you alright?" Mike asked, letting go of Bill.

"I think so. A little confused, though."

"Okay...we can work with confused. Come in here and sit. Can I get you anything?"

Bill considered. "A Coke'd be nice."

"You sit. I'll be right back."

Going to Mike's office, Bill sat in one of the two chairs before the cluttered desk. Mike came back with an ice-cold bottle of Coke, already dewing in his hands. He passed it to Bill, who took a pull from it, closed his eyes as it cooled his throat, then drained the rest.

"I'll get you another," Mike said, disappearing. Bill didn't argue.

When he returned, Bill sipped at the second Coke. Mike sat on the edge of his desk.

"I don't know whether to hug you again or punch you in the face."

Bill looked at his friend.

"Sorry. Don't know if anything I say is gonna help you decide."

"Jesus, Bill, where've you been? I mean we looked everywhere, talked to everyone. I don't think there's a person in town we didn't speak with. Not a place we didn't scour searching for you. And then you just waltz in here looking right as rain on an April day?"

"You must not have looked in the Outside," Bill said, turning the soda bottle in his hands, feeling its cool perspiration wet his fingers.

"The Outside? Well, shit, no. Not really, at any rate. We had old Stanley Boykins' dogs sniff around near where we found your car. They seemed to have found your scent, but of course no one, not even the damned dogs, wanted to go in there. Are you saying that's where you've been?"

Bill nodded, took another swig of Coke.

"Yeah, but it's…complicated."

Mike narrowed his eyes, stared at his friend.

"Bill, we've known each other since we was kids. You're like a brother to me, you know that, right?"

Bill nodded again.

"Listen to me and listen good. You…you just tell me who the sons of bitches were did this, and we'll take care of it. No worries. I don't care if it's the town aldermen or the assholes in the white bedsheets. We'll take care of it. This kinda shit will not stand in my county."

"It's not like that, Mike. I walked into the Outside on my own. I walked out on my own."

"I don't understand," Mike said. "What're you saying? If someone didn't force you, then where have you been all this time?"

"I pulled over some delinquents in a car last night, then heard something…that sound coming from the Outside again. You know, the one I told you about. I let the kids go, then followed the sound into the Outside. Musta gotten turned around, lost. When I found my way back out this morning, my cruiser's gone. I walked here. End of story."

Mike considered his friend blankly, then leaned into him.

"This morning?" he whispered. "Mike, it's been eight days since you disappeared. Eight fucking days."

Mike ended up letting Bill drive his cruiser back to his house in The Club, despite plenty of misgivings. The two men had ended up talking in Mike's office for almost two hours, hashing and rehashing Bill's experience in Midnight Land.

At first, Bill was hesitant to give details, fearing Mike would think he was crazy…or worse, had been drinking. And at first, Mike did suspect these things. But as Bill walked him deeper and deeper into his story, Mike realized whatever had happened, Bill was being a cop. He was telling his friend what had happened as dispassionately as possible, leaving out no details, no matter how small they seemed.

The last detail Bill shared, the one he still found it difficult to reconcile, was Silas.

When Bill finally broke through that last barrier and shared his matter-of-fact description of the man, he noticed Mike's jaw set, then begin to clench.

"That sounds…well, I'm not gonna shit ya, pal. That sounds flat-out unbelievable," Mike said, barely getting the words through tense lips.

"How it was, Mike. He was sitting there, as close as you are now, on fire with a noose around his neck."

"A noose disappeared in the air above his head? Do you know how crazy that sounds?"

"Do you know how crazy it was, sitting there with him? Talking to him?"

Mike looked away, shook his head.

"Did this man have a name?"

"Silas."

That single word is what set the muscles of Mike's jaw to twitching.

"Let's call it an evening. I can't process any more of this. Go home, get some rest. Take tomorrow off and do it all again. I'll spend the day handling this, letting people now you're back. If Carl hasn't already started the process."

Bill stood, walked out of Mike's office.

"And Bill?"

He turned back to his friend.

"Not a word of this to anyone, okay? Not yet, anyway."

"Sure," he said, then left the office, drove home.

Bill parked the car in the dirt driveway running beside the house, sat for a while with the lights off. It was full-on night now, and it seemed so bright in comparison to the night he'd spent stumbling around in the Outside.

Drinking in Midnight Land.

He was suddenly bone tired, a kind of immediate exhaustion he'd never experienced before, as if he'd been clotheslined in a football game. He sighed, lowered his head onto the cool plastic of the steering wheel.

Turning his head to the right, he saw it, outside the passenger window.

The dark form of the great hickory tree twisted out of his front yard like a gnarled fist, balled in rage against the sky. He remembered seeing that tree through the window of his childhood bedroom, in this very house. Could remember how it scared him, especially at night, especially in thunderstorms, where it seemed almost to move against the backdrop of lightning.

It was old now, crooked and bent, as crippled as an arthritic hand. Ancient and condign.

He imagined it as it once was, stately, with a magnificent spread of branches, offering shade and shelter in its day.

But then he also imagined it as he knew it now to be, malignant and ripe with the kind of fruit that seemed almost native to America, but whose full flower was particular to the South.

Pulling himself from the car, he lurched into the house.

Locking the front door behind him, he started off to the kitchen, to see what might be left in the icebox. Something hopefully. His grandfather, with whom he shared this house, was not the most attentive grocery shopper, but Bill hoped there would at least be some milk, maybe some ham.

He reached around the wall to find the kitchen light switch, and when he snapped it on, he didn't even see the figure of his grandfather seated at the kitchen table.

Instead, he shuffled to the fridge, drew it open. Inside, blessedly, was a bottle of milk, a plate with a small chunk of ham left on it. He took these out, along with a jar of mustard, put it all on the counter.

"They's bread in the breadbox, good rye. And a few good 'maters left there on the counter," came his grandfather's voice, startling him.

"Better fix me a samwich, too, I s'pect," his grandfather said, stifling a yawn. "Been waiting up for you 'bout a week now and hadn't much appetite until tonight. Funny how it's all come back t'once."

Bill unloaded everything onto the counter, went over to kneel before his granddad, give him a hug. The old man's crabbed hands—so much like the tree branches outside, Bill couldn't help but think—patted at his back.

"You go off and get you some strange, that it?" he said.

"No, that's not it…not by a longshot," Bill said, standing.

"What then? One of these fine outstanding citizens catch you up in something?"

Bill went back to the counter, opened the breadbox, lifted out the rye loaf, began assembling two sandwiches.

"No, not it either."

His granddad watched him for a minute, cutting the tomatoes, laying them over the thick slices he carved from the ham. He slathered all of this with mustard that seemed too bright under the kitchen lights, sealed the sandwiches with another slice of rye.

When they were assembled, he slid them onto small plates, cut them in half. He brought them to the table.

"They's chips in the tin atop the icebox, and a glass of milk'd be good to wash this all down."

Smiling, Bill lifted the tin, set it atop the table, removed the lid. Then, he went back to the fridge, grabbed the cold bottle of milk and poured two glasses. He sat at the table, pushed one of the glasses to the old man.

Bill noticed he was dressed in his tatty old brown terrycloth robe, holes in the elbow, and the ghost of a partially squared-off tear marked where a pocket had once been. He looked exhausted, hadn't shaved in a few days. His eyes were narrow and rheumy.

He lifted a half sandwich and took a careful bite, favoring the right side of his mouth where he had more teeth. Bill tucked in too, demolishing his first half sandwich in three enormous bites.

"Wherever you been, you must notta eaten," his granddad smiled, chewing thoughtfully. Bill knew he was waiting, biding his time. His old granddad was a patient man, always had been. A big picture, long road kind of guy.

"No, and I'm starving," Bill replied, tearing into the second half. He knew there was at least one more whole sandwich in his future before he went to bed. And probably the rest of the milk. He'd no doubt have to get some groceries tomorrow.

"So, out with it, young'n. If it ain't a woman or the white folks what lead you away, where were ya?"

Bill chewed, considered.

"What if I were to tell you I was in Midnight Land?"

If Bill was hoping for a reaction, he had the wrong man. His grandad took another bite of his sandwich, mustard squirting down his chin. He set the rest of the sandwich down, daubed at his chin with a napkin from the holder on the table, nestled in with the salt and pepper shakers.

"Midnight Land, eh?" he said, and Bill noticed the old man's hands did seem to shake a little more than usual. "I'd say you were plum crazy. Or onto something you have no business bein' onto."

Bill pushed in the last bite of his sandwich, followed it with the last of the milk in his glass. He turned back to the counter, went there and made another sandwich. When he sat back at the table, his grandad was chewing on potato chips, feeding them into his mouth slowly, one after another.

"Well, that's where I was. In Midnight Land."

"Boy, that place burned long ago…long ago," he said, a touch of rue on his words. He waved one hand in the air. "Nothin' left of it but the stink, after all these years. Nothin'. Leastways nothin' left you could go to. Who even tell you about that place anyway? Michael?"

His grandfather's face twisted into a mask of dim disapproval, as it always did when Mike or his family came up in discussion. Bill supposed the old man wasn't even aware he did it anymore.

"No, not Mike, grandad. *Silas.*"

His grandfather stopped chewing, and his mouth opened to say something, but no words came out. Instead, he pushed his plate away, covered the rest of his sandwich with the napkin he'd used.

"I'll be headed to bed now. Suddenly bone tired."

He stood, waved off Bill's offer of assistance, then clumped down the hallway. Bill heard the soft sound of his bedroom door closing, pushed back from the table. He reached over, grabbed the milk bottle from the counter and poured himself another glass.

He wondered about the old man's reaction to Midnight Land and Silas' name.

But at the moment, he had more pressing concerns. He lifted the napkin, ate the other half of his granddad's sandwich, alternating bites with fistfuls of chips and swallows of milk.

When he finished, he set their dishes in the sink, returned the food to the icebox, turned off the kitchen light.

As he passed his grandad's room, he listened. He couldn't hear him snoring on the other side of the door, so imagined the old man stretched atop his bed, staring at the ceiling.

Mike went into his own room, drew the door shut quietly behind. He removed his belt, its holster, set the gun atop his dresser. Sitting on the edge of his bed, he kicked off his shoes, peeled away his socks.

Another minute, and he was clad only in boxers, slipped beneath his sheets.

His dreams, and he did have them that night, were of a wailing, ululating sound that scraped at the inside of his skull, struck his mind as inherently wrong.

Outside, as if conducting this symphony, the contorted fingers of the tree palped at the dark sky, insect like, cast grasping shadows onto the shades of his closed window.

Bill woke when the sun, yellowed from its journey though the old roller shade covering his window, warmed his face.

He stretched, pulled himself from his bed, padded to the bathroom. Having no idea what time it was, he took his time in the shower, letting the hot water fall across his shoulders, pound on his neck.

Later, dressed in his civvies, he went into the kitchen. No grandad in the front room nor the kitchen. And, he remembered, no more milk in the icebox. Black coffee was the order of the day, and he found his grandad had started a pot already in the battered silver percolator.

He poured himself a cup of coffee, slid a piece of bread into the toaster. When it was thoroughly buttered, he carried it and the cup of coffee onto the porch.

His grandad was seated in his rocker there, staring out across the yard, across the acres and acres of farmland stretching into the distance as far as he could see.

The morning was bright and already warm, and the insects droned the monotonous white noise soundtrack to southern summers. Heat shimmered in the air around them. It was oppressively humid already, and grandad kept his handkerchief clutched in one hand, ready to mop head and neck when necessary.

Bill sat in the metal chair next to him, set his cup of coffee onto the small wooden table between them, next to the old man's cup.

"Mornin'," Bill said, stretching his legs out, feeling his joints creak and pop satisfyingly. He stared at the same scene his grandfather studied silently, over the green ocean waves of half-grown corn.

"I s'pose, being a police officer and all, you got lots of questions you ain't gonna let loose of until they's answered."

Bill sipped at his coffee, said nothing.

"Well, there was no way I's gonna talk about this at all, leastways not at night," the old man sighed, turned to fix his grandson with his kindly, yellowed eyes.

"But you gonna hear it sometime, best be from me. Least thataways, you get the whole, unvarnished truth. What I'm about to tell ya, ya momma and daddy don't even really know. Oh, they suspect, for sure. But they don't hear nothing but whispers, because people don't talk about it much anymore. White folk or black. Like we been keeping each other's secrets for so long, we don't know how to tell the truth anymore. Think it's gonna be a long, long time before we all manage to get singing from the same hymnal."

The old man paused as if resting, gathering, then took a sip from his cup.

"I knows you find this hard to believe, but I was a young man once. Heh, younger than you, to be sure. I felt things, more strongly than I feel 'em now. Time, well, it has a habit of squeezing those feelings outchya, like you's a lemon and it's making lemonade. Toward the end, you're all squeezed up, dried like a rind left on the counter.

"Back when I was young, I was fulla juice, tart and sweet. You hear me? Plenty of folks, though, don't like they lemons black and tart."

When you get a buncha hepped up young people in a room, dancing and listening to music and generally carrying on, sparks is gonna fly. Don't matter if they's black and white or yellow or red or whatever. Young blood is young blood, and it calls out each to each, regardless of the skin a'swaddlin' it.

I was, oh, lord, probably twenty-two years old when this all happened. Twenty-two, dear god, what a lifetime ago. I ain't done much in life at that point, no sir. Little schooling in that same schoolhouse you sat in counting flies on the windowsill. Little carousing and carrying on, sure. Drinking. Smoking, too, if we's gonna be honest, and I guess as we have to. Stepping out, too, let's not forget that. Lord, how I loved to go dancing or listening to music. More often than not, a pretty girl on my arm. Yeah, your granddad had style back then, a swagger I ain't had in many, many a year.

I took all that youthful energy to The Club.

Anyway, The Club in those days was called that because we had a few mixed-race speakeasies outsida the town proper, where folks could go and hear some good music, dance a piece, drink. Mix it up, ya know? Mostly it was nice and quiet like. A few raids here and there, only for the Grove police to keep a presence, keep their hands in.

More to keep their fingers in, as in the tills, you know? So, they got they's cut and made sure people knew they been watched. Kept the fighting and ruckus to a minimum. Also kept the mixing to a minimum, you understand?

Well, at least keeping the black swains mixing with the white girls. A lot of the fine, upstanding white gentlemen had their black trixies, mistresses they could bop on the down-low, without too much tongue wagging. But that, to them, was different.

It's always different when it moves that way. Always has been.

The Clubs…oh, I do miss them now. The music was fantastic.

All the best black acts from the time. King Oliver, Sidney Bechet, Willy "The Lion" Smith," even the Wolverines and Duke Ellington. Stuff you just don't hear as much these days. Live, right there.

And out here in the boonies. There weren't much to do for colored folk in town, but out here, away from the white folks, we had plenty. A few restaurants, long gone, and all the music joints in The Club.

They's just shacks, you know? Nothing like the taverns today. Some board walls, a tarpaper roof, but man, what palaces. The After Hours was the big one, used to stand just down the road a piece. The Corn Ballroom. Ida's Place. And Midnight Land.

That's where it happened, where it *all* ended. Midnight Land.

See, over there at the far end of Thompson's Field yonder? Back there where the air makes everything looked fogged with heat? Tucked back there in the corner, that's where it stood. Midnight Land was mayhap the shackiest of 'em all. Rickety goddamn place, with sawdust over dirt floors, a bar made from fruit crates, and a stage weren't nothing more than old house doors up on cinder blocks. Place was a disgrace, no argument. But it was the place I loved the best of all. Mostly, and I'm a little ashamed to admit it, because it was the least patronized by white folks.

Now, don't you be looking at me with your narrow-ass eyes, young'n. I like white folks jess fine, some of 'em, anyway. From a distance. They's fine when keeping to they own concerns, but when they stick their noses in on us, well, it usually means the worse for both.

And don't think for a second it was a different time back then. Everyone says that, but it ain't true. Sure, things was different, but what was right out in the open back then is exactly the same, just with a few coats of varnish slapped on now to gussy it up a little, that's all. Same old boards underneath, rotten and warped as hell. All that decay and ricketiness? That spread from the ruins of The Club, right back into town.

Anyhow, Midnight Land had all the best acts tromping through, a well-stocked bar, for the time anyway. Miss Bernadette even cooked some nights, depending on how she felt. Things didn't get jumping until about eleven, which was when the white boys usually started showing up, being that was when they's parents were in bed…or they wives.

Things'd been pretty bad around that time, all over the county, but Miller's Grove in particular. The Klan had been pretty active all over, burning crosses, staging rallies and the like. Most of the fine, upstanding white men in town belonged. The mayor, the council, even the preachers and teachers. All of 'em was in it because it was like a club itself, 'cept most white folks thought membership was mandatory.

So, they were all respectable during the day, wearing their suits and ties, their preaching clothes. At night, though, they took their white sheets out the closet and raised hell.

Yeah, they kept busy alright. Strung up a few men around the area, mostly those trying to organize, unionize you know.

Most people didn't cotton to that too unions, not for white men and specially not for black. That and Prohibition was in full swing, and drinking was being looked at more and more cross-eyed. When it first came, people was a little more tolerant of a few drinks taken in private, particularly if taken with the coloreds down in their clubs. Ya know, away from respectable folk. Particularly if those who needed their palms greased got 'em greased real slick.

But with all that, they was beginning to crack down. The drinking, the unionizing, the race mixing. All of it. And in our community, we was getting tired of it, too. The discrimination, the threats, the violence. Treating us one way when they was lifting they wrists in our clubs and ogling our girls, and another when we were out shopping for groceries or trying to make a living.

Miss Lee had even taken to hiring a man or two to act as a bouncer, big guy named Hiram who kept the peace at her place, made sure fights were kept to a minimum. He was a big boy, oooh, lord. Big man. Just looking at him was usually enough to make folks behave. I seen him once pick up a man and throw him 'bout twenty feet across the parking lot. People say he was likely packing, too, but I never saw him with no gun. Never needed it, as far as I could tell.

Anyway, I was there that evening. It was a hot one, hotter than this. Humid like only a night round here can be. Air so thick it's like moving through soup. I'd just done a thirteen-hour stretch down at the mill, and I was hungry and thirsty, even more so than bone tired. I knew your grandmom would be asleep with your momma, just a tiny baby at the time, so I thought I'd pop into Midnight Land, hoped Miss Bernadette would be cooking that night. Stretch a little. Have a few beers.

Got more than I bargained for, I guess.

Or did I?

Thought about that night, what led up to it, for, oh, three decades now, and there's not a part of it I don't regret. The stuff I was responsible for, the stuff I wasn't. The stuff no one was responsible for, though truth told there weren't much of that.

Best start with Silas Johnson.

Old Silas…boy, do I remember him. Everything 'bout that boy was *fire*.

Everything.

He was a few years older'n me. Taller, nicer looking, I guess I should say, if I'm being honest. Fair looking, with smooth features and nice skin. Broad smile, smiling eyes, as they used to say. Always whistling a tune, least when he was a young boy. Life drove a lot of that out him by the time he was a man, and he became sharp and cynical.

Silas was one of a group of young men who was trying to unionize the black folk at the mills, mostly the colored who's working the yard, unloading the cotton bales, loading up the finished goods into the boxcars. The white men was trying to unionize, too, with a little more success. But they wouldn't have us colored in they union, no sir. So, Silas and his men were trying to form our own.

The rich men who owned the mills didn't much like the poor white workers forming up. But they were up against it. Not a lot they could do, and what they tried didn't work. Roughing men up and such is about all they could really think of to do.

But they *detested* the thought of the black men trying for the same. That wasn't going to happen, as far as they were concerned. They was some brawls here and there, paid union buster thugs brought in to rough people up. Got worse over the years. A few men were really busted up. Few houses burned.

And the lynchings.

Hmmm…not so much of those these days, Lord praised, but it always seem so close to me, so close. As if they's just a little bit away, waiting…waiting for some signal to come on back, pick up like there's been no pause. Like the tinder is here, always been here just waiting for a match.

Lynchings were not exactly an everyday occurrence, but they was common then. Sometimes some poor kid who got caught with his hand in the whites' cookie jar, and I mean that plainly as well as not, you understand? Sometimes it was a rough old guy, someone who killed or raped or whatever.

But mostly it was just some unfortunate Joe who really pissed off the white men.

Maybe leered at some woman, sure. But maybe he was being polite or friendly. Most like he just smiled or winked or offered some other normal, human response. All used as an excuse to lay hands on him, see some blood flow, light a fire in they veins. All of 'em.

But then they's some like Silas, they did to silence. To shut up an uppity black who was trying to unify his folks, bring 'em together to better 'em, better us all. And you know, it weren't the mill owners themselves I blame. Nah, they mighta been wealthy, but they weren't as wealthy as the bankers and the politicians who was pulling the strings.

They's the ones who really did it, though they'd never actually sully they hands with rope or gas. They didn't pull any triggers or slash any throats. No, they hands was too delicate. How can you blame the knives and bullets for what was done and not blame the soft, smooth hands wielding them?

Anyway, old Silas was there that night. The place was already packed when I got there, white, black. I nodded to big ole Hiram as I came in, and he nodded back at me, sweating and sweating in his suit as he kept an eye on things.

Inside it was all jabbering, all dancing. Miss Bernadette saw me when I came through the rickety door, pulled me aside.

"'Spect you wanting something to eat?" she asked me, wiping her hands on her apron. "I got neck bones and beans, some cornbread. Think I can rustle up some buttermilk. Cain't have you start in to drinking without something on your belly. Nadine'd likely kick my ass."

"She might just at that," I laughed. She waved me to a table, and I waited for my meal. It didn't take her long. She returned with a steaming bowl of beans, a basket of cornbread, a glass of buttermilk. Putting these down absently, she disappeared back into the crowd, shouting at someone or someones to *Stop it right there!*

I ate quickly, bodies jostling my elbows. I wanted to finish as fast as I could. I could smell the food, but I could also smell something on the air, something electric like right before a thunderstorm. It was metallic and brittle and scared me a little…more'n a little.

No drinking, no dancing, no music for me. I wanted to eat and be outta there.

Shouldn't have even done that.

I saw him outta the corner of my eye, leaning up against the wall with a couple of his friends. There was Manny Durwin, Bob Cushing, Danny Birsha. The town toughs. They all hung together, caused trouble not just with us blacks but with whites, too. And they leader, well, you'd best be sittin', now.

They leader was Rick Pilot.

Your best friend's daddy.

"Rick Pilot?" Bill said. "I remember him. The town tough? He was still alive when I was young. Kinda a quiet and gentle man."

"Quiet and gentle," his grandfather chuckled. "Yeah, I guess he could afford to be, in his later years."

"He died a good man, at least I thought so."

"Yeah, he's dead now, and I shouldn't speak ill of the dead. But I gotta tell you, son, hell's the better off for it."

His grandfather continued the story.

When he was alive, he was someone apt to give you pause if you passed him on the street, day or night. Mean a man as I ever met. He was in the Klan, oh yes. But none of us colored took that much to heart, seen as he pretty much hated everyone equal.

Trouble is, he could only get away with so much against white folks without involving the law. They was well aware of him and his antics, so he didn't have much he could do to terrorize white folk.

What he did to black folk, though? Well, nobody much gave a damn, leastways not anyone with a star on they uniform. He could steal, beat, and even rape, and no lawman anywhere around here would do much more than slap him on the wrist.

Anyway, most of us working at the mills believed the owners was paying old Rick Pilot to terrorize us into stopping all the agitatin'—for voting rights, equal treatment, unionizing, all that. He and his boys got all round the county, roughing black workers up, burning crosses here and there. Even burned some houses.

The law hadn't bothered to connect him or his gang to any lynchings, but we all figured, come on, he had to have a hand in 'em. Though he was a fervent believer an' all, as many of 'em were—still are—a lot of it was done in secret, under dark, under hoods, where no faces could be seen.

Then there was ole Silas. He seemed to be the opposite of Rick, and not just in color. Silas was a whirligig. He lived his life loud. Wore the best threads, pomaded his hair, slicked his little mustache. He wore jewelry, flashy rings and such. Dude was handsome and cool as they come, and most everyone in our community loved him.

But he stood out like a sore thumb to white folks. He was too loud for their tastes. Dressed too nice. Was too friendly, always a smile. What was he hiding? What no-good was he getting up to? Black people just shouldn't be so happy and social.

Silas grated on white people's nerves something fierce.

Well, there'd been a few attempts on Silas' life over the years. Someone shot up his car. His house was firebombed, but they was able to put it out before it did much damage. He'd been beaten more than a few times. But it was apparent none of it was working. Silas still strode down the street bright as a penny, tipping his hat to one and all, smiling as he saw fit. Trying to get the mill workers to band together.

So, there I was eating my beans and cornbread in Midnight Land. I'd just slammed down the rest of my buttermilk when it started.

The band was playing "Bye Bye Blackbird," and I tapped my foot as I ate. Thinking all the while of creeping back to my house, slipping into my bed with my wife. But that wasn't to be, at leastways not like I thought.

As to "Bye Bye Blackbird," never will forget that tune. Never could listen to it again. Always made me sweat a little, shake a little.

I heard a ruckus from over by the bar and seen Pilot and his boys had circled old Silas, had him by the scruff of the neck, hectoring and hollering. Some punches had obviously flown. Blood on Silas' chin and a sort of crazed scared look in his eyes despite his smile.

Pilot's boys were standing in a circle around the two men, and some of the other white men had begun to push in, elbow'n the colored folk outta the way, clearing them like cattle.

Hiram had waded through the crowd, on his way to break up whatever was fixin' to start.

I stood, upset the table s'badly it tipped, sending my dishes to the dirt floor in a clatter that registered with no one. I wasn't quick to leap to Silas' aid, mind you. No, I was quick to go home to your grandma, slip away, slip away.

I heard some of the words.

"…we can't have one of 'em eyeing up a respectable white woman, can we boys?"

A chorus of "No!" rang out, and that stormy feeling I'd noticed in the air earlier seemed crackling and alive now.

I ain't ashamed I moved toward the exit then. I didn't need to be involved in trouble like this. I had a wife and child asleep at home. A job.

"We ain't gonna put up with this no longer!" Pilot shouted over the murmuring of the crowd. "We gotta stop this before things get outta hand. Am I right? I am! We gotta put a stop to this now. Tonight! Right here!"

I passed Miss Bernadette, standing in the doorway to the kitchen, her hands clenched in her apron. Bernie was a tough lady, tougher than most men I'd known. She looked at me, and I saw fear. Something was different, and she could tell it, just as I could smell it in the air.

I took her hand, wrestled it from her apron, and told her, with my eyes, to come with me, follow me.

"Where's Hiram?" she asked. "This is exactly what I pay his fat ass for. He should be putting a stop to this 'fore it gets out of hand."

I wanted to tell her that it was already well out of hand, when I noticed the music had stopped.

Over at the stage, the last of the musicians—the big old bass player—disappeared out the back door. A large shape shadowed him, turned back just as he was about to leave, too.

Hiram.

I saw Hiram follow the bass player across the parking lot, through the fields, and into the night…never saw him again, either.

I heard the rattle and cough of a few car engines outside turning over, tires spraying dirt and gravel as more people shot outta the parking lot.

I took Miss Bernadette's hand firmly, pulled her toward the door.

"Best way to end this all and start anew is with fire," I heard Pilot fairly shriek, like a Baptist minister from the pulpit. "Block the doors! Find me some matches and gasoline! Let's start with this place and put the rest of these clubs to the torch! Make an example."

I was in the doorway when I felt his words directed at me.

"You there. Boy! Stop him, stop him or anyone from leavin'!"

I yanked at Miss Bernadette to move, but she was frozen in fear, and it was like trying to uproot a tree. She just wouldn't budge.

Before I could say anything to her, a number of men rushed from the crowd, shoved her aside, laid hands on me.

Miss Bernadette fell to the ground, and just like ole Hiram, I never saw her again…*ever*. Some said she moved off to Atlanta or Chicago, but I never knew for sure. She just disappeared into the night. Got away like I'd wished I did.

Those white boys held me, tussled with me. I coulda taken a few of them. Truth be told, I'd held my own plenty of times with small packs of white boys itching for trouble. But I was tired, and there were so many of them. Moreso, it seemed different now. They'd always been a pack of wild dogs, yes, but now they were a pack of dogs with rabies.

Someone punched me, sharp and hard, cross the mouth, and I stopped fighting and just stood there bleeding.

"Where you goin', boy?" Pilot asked, stepping close. "You in cahoots with these other coons? You an agitator? A pervert? A coward who assaults white women? Or were you runnin' off to fetch the law, get them involved?"

"No, sir," I answered, seeing where all this was headed. "Just stopped in for dinner, now I want to go home to my family."

Pilot's eyes narrowed at me. "You Joe Boussard, aintchya? Work down at Crosser's Mill? You got a house near here, big old Hickory in the front yard? I know the place."

"Yes, that's my house," I babbled, feeling the fear rise in me, too. "But I ain't involved in nothing, sir. Just stopped in…"

"You ain't one of them agitators, are you, Joe? One of them black boys fussing to unionize their at the mill? I think I seen you in the crowd a time or two."

"No, sir. Just want to work and do my job. I ain't no agitator."

"Well, it ain't no nevermind. At any rate, you got a nice house with a big tree there, Joe. Seems as good a place as any, don't it, boys? To show them a lesson so's they keep in their place?"

I couldn't do much but stare back at him. He seemed transported, like a tongue-speaker in church.

"Bring that old boy," he said, hooking his thumb back at Silas and smiling. "Joe's invited us all back to his place for a barbecue. And we're bringing the meat! Let's get the party started!"

I saw the white boys behind us set on Silas, beat him until he stopped resisting, so's they could get him to the parking lot. By the time they'd finished with him, he hung between the men, limp as wet laundry on a line.

After I saw that, I didn't fight 'em. I just let the wave carry me out of the building, where I was jammed into a car with Pilot. I sat next to him the entire way, feeling that heat wash off him waves. His breathing quick and rough, like someone who's just run a spell. He never once looked at me, though. Not even a glance.

The driver took us pell-mell to this very house, just a few blocks from Midnight Land.

All the while, Pilot—sitting in the front passenger seat but turned to look out the window—kept telling me, "Don't worry, don't you worry. You're not the one we're after tonight. But we gotta make a point, don't we? Yessir, a *point*."

I turned to look out the rear window.

Midnight Land was fully in flames, and I watched thick, black smoke curl up, smudge the blue-black sky. Wasn't much too it, so it didn't take long for it to brun to the ground. I suppose it was mostly gone by the time we'd reached this house.

Didn't take long to get away from there or get here.

When the two white boys sitting either side of me wrestled me outta the car, I could still see the glow of the fire at Midnight Land on the horizon, like a sun that would never rise again.

They was already gathered round the hickory tree in the front yard. It was a magnificent one back then, in its full growth. Probably sixty feet tall and limbs spread just as wide. Beautiful old tree, planted there, so's I was told, by my great grandfather when he first got this land, right after Emancipation.

I loved that tree. Climbed it as a boy. Courted your grandma under it. Took picnics in its shade with her and your momma when she was young. One huge old limb stretched away from the house, about ten feet from the ground, and I shivered as I saw it, as if for the first time.

There was already a rope thrown over it.

Silas stood in the flatbed of an old Ford truck, held upright by two men who looked exultant.

Silas'd been beaten extravagantly.

He was bleeding, his eyes were swollen shut, looked like purple goggles. His mouth was swollen, and more blood dripped from it. His clothes had been torn away, and he was stark naked.

I remember, as dazed and in pain as he was, he was still trying to cover his privates. Still trying to retain some dignity in the indignities that had been heaped upon him.

Blood flowed from his privates, too, and I wonder even today if he was trying to protect his modesty or if they'd done even worse to him on the way here.

A crowd had gathered, probably fifty or so people, mostly whites, but they's a few black folk scattered here and there, brought here against they will, held in place to pay witness to what was goin' down. Take that news of fear back out into our community.

The rest of the evening is a bit of a daze, but I remember little flashes of things.

Torches lighting the expectant faces of the white men organizing all this.

The ripe, eager smell of gasoline.

The whispered murmurings of prayers from some of the colored ladies.

The feel of the hands holding me tight, shaking against my skin.

I was glad to notice, through my own fear, no one had broken into my house. I didn't see your grandma's face in the crowd, heard no cries from you momma.

That gave me some relief, knowing they's safe, at least at that moment. My fear then was not that these white boys would do to me what they were fixing to do to Silas. No, it was that they'd grab your momma and your grandma, do worse to them.

I hoped your grandma would have the sense to stay inside, not come out and see what all this was about.

Stay in the house and keep safe, even when they strung me up.

Cuz I just knew, knew I was set to follow Silas under that tree, swing amiably next to him, bulging eyes raised to heaven, feet kicking at the earth.

So, I stood by, watching the front door of my house, praying to Jesus it would not open, as they doused Silas with gas, cinched the rope tight, hefted him from his feet.

The driver of the old Ford revved the engine.

The rest of the white boys leapt from the bed of the truck, stumbled away.

The truck whined like a beast, anticipatin'.

Pilot stepped forward, smacked the side of the truck as if it were a horse, and it clunked into gear, lurched away.

The rope around Silas' neck sprang taut, yanked him up from the bed of the vehicle, left him twisting and kicking in the air.

Someone passed Pilot a lit torch, and he set it against Silas.

Flames *whoomphed!* over him, wrapped him like a caul around a newborn.

I didn't turn toward him, didn't watch as the flames engulfed him, didn't watch as his neck strained, as his eyes bled tears, as his skin charred and sloughed embers onto my front lawn.

Or maybe I did.

Maybe I kept one eye on him and another watching the front door of the house, praying it would stay closed, no one would come out...*or go in.*

I didn't realize Pilot had come to my side, pressed his lips to my ear.

"You wanna keep all this to yaself, boy. No telling anyone what happened here tonight. No telling who was here, who did this to your burning friend there. Clean up this little bonfire and go about ya business all quiet like, and your family can remain safe and sound. You can keep that nice job down at Crosser's.

"Or we can string you up right next to him, rightcheer on your own tree. And your colored wife and little colored child can follow you up, one after the other. They'd enough room on that branch , and we got enough rope and gasoline for all y'all. Your call."

"I'll never tell. No one."

"Just remember that word. *Never.* Cuz we can always come back. Somethin› tells me this tree gonna be here a long time. A nice long time."

He stepped away, and I realized I was crying.

Not because of what he said.

Not because everyone ran off, but I got caught up.

Not even because I realized I was being spared.

Spared…hah.

No.

It was because the door to my house had never opened.

Bill looked away from his grandfather to the hulk of the tree standing a few yards away. It had been there, right there, all his life, and he'd ever spared it a single thought. Never once thought it had been the scene of such a horrific incident.

It was just a tree, twisted and cramped, like an arthritic hand.

He tried to picture it soaring into the sky, with limbs young and broad, reaching into the clouds. Leaves all bright green, swaying in a light breeze, catching the rays of the sun.

He tried imagining it with a rope tossed over the one limb stretched away from the porch, across the yard.

Tried imagining it with a body kicking and swaying from the limb.

"Why'd you never say something until now, grandad?" Bill asked, his voice softer than he thought the question deserved. "Why am I just learning this *now*?"

"Doesn't seem so long to me, all those years piling up like waves on a beach. Like it happened yesterday. I can still feel Rick Pilot's beery breath on my face, the spittle from his tongue flecking my cheek. I can feel his hand clamped on my arm, like it was burning a circle there."

Bill found he was breathing hard. He swallowed, and his spit tasted warm and bitter.

"How could you have just let that happen? All of you? And here…right here in your own yard?"

His grandad turned to him, his wrinkled face set.

"I got enough regret piled on my shoulders, so don't you sit there and tell me what I shoulda done, how I shoulda felt. That's what they do, what they all do. Tell us how we should feel about stuff and how we should act. What's acceptable and what isn't. Besides what exactly you think you'da done different?"

"Something. *Anything.* Why didn't you just cut this damn tree down afterwards?"

"Yeah? And how was that supposed to happen? He watched over me, made sure I didn't breathe a word of what they'd done to nobody. Not to the sheriff the next day, not to anyone for years and years after.

Bill shook his head, at a loss for words.

"Cut the tree down? You think he wouldn't have taken that as a sign I was about to say something? Tell someone what'd happened that night? That I was about to name names, point fingers at a bunch of white boys in a police line-up? Shit, might as well have followed them one night and pulled the hoods off their robes."

"So, you just left it? As a reminder of what they'd done. Right in our front yard of all places, grandad."

"You don't understand, boy. I didn't leave the tree here as a reminder of what *they did*. I don't need no cussed reminder of what they did. It's burnt into my brain. I left it as a reminder of what *I didn't do.* The price they made me pay to keep my family safe. Never wanted to forget that lesson, no sir."

Bill was starting to feel less and less charitable to his granddad, and it made him restless, fidgety in the uncomfortable chair he sat in on the porch. He'd never seen his grandad in this light, never thought of him in this way.

A coward? Was that too rough or too charitable, Bill couldn't decide. He knew, though, that was he was angry at being put in the position of needing to decide.

"How could he have kept an eye on you for that long? Long enough for your tongue to shrivel up? It doesn't make any sense."

The old man, evidently, felt just as hot.

"Sometimes, Bill Tyson, you're a damn fool. Why you think his son showed up on your doorstep? Just to be your friend? He just decided on his own he'd pal around with some colored boy? The colored grandson of the man whose tree he hung and burned a man alive on? It had nothing to do with me, just with you. You were just so wonderful he couldn't help but be your friend?"

Bill's heart slowed, stilled.

"What're you saying?"

"I'm saying Rick Pilot *sent* his son to you, deliberate like. To hang around our place, to watch me, to make sure I stayed quiet. Even after all those years had passed, Rick was still worried I'd spill the beans. He put his son with you in order to remind me he had eyes on me, if his son heard or saw something Rick didn't like, well, he could snap his fingers and I'd be twitching and kicking from that very same tree."

Bill found himself standing without realizing he'd done so.

"Mike Pilot was deliberately planted here. He's as much a part of all this as is that tree there."

"That's a cussed mean lie, grandad," Bill said, taking the two steps from the porch down to the lawn. "Mike's my best friend, been so all my life. Never said a cross word toward me, called me a name. Never hung out with any of the white boys causing trouble. Never. Once."

"You best believe it, boy," his grandfather shouted after him. "That white boy may be your friend, but he ain't nothing but his father's eyes still on me after all these years. Still on me even after he's dead!"

Bill silenced his grandfather by climbing into the cruiser and slamming the door.

He yanked the transmission into reverse, peeled out of his driveway, spraying up an enormous cloud of dust as he did.

Looking in his rearview mirror, he saw his grandad's frail form slumped over in his rocker, his shoulders heaving.

The next time he saw him was at the mortuary, laid out in his best suit that Bill had taken from the back of his grandad's closet, as if the man were saving it for something special.

At least he was no longer sobbing.

The open door—the one closed all those long years—was closed once again.

A few weeks later, back at the station, Bill shuffled papers on his desk, stapled a stack of them together, slid them into a manila file. This he handed to Betsy, who filed it all away in the three-drawer near her desk.

"Hey, Bill," came Mike's voice from his office. "Come on in here."

Bill smiled at Betsy, strolled into his friend's office.

"Close the door and sit down."

Bill did as he was asked, sat in the chair across from Mike.

"What's up?"

"Just getting ready to head on out," Bill said.

"We gonna talk? I mean, like friends, not like sheriff and deputy?"

"Not sure what you mean, Mike."

"I'm just thinking I musta done something wrong, though I don't know what it is. You been awful quiet for an awful long time now, and I've let you be seeing as how your grandad passed. But let's settle this between us. Whatever it is, I'm sorry."

Bill shifted uncomfortably.

"Out with it."

Bill saw, over his shoulder, a framed black and white photo of Mike getting his sheriff's star pinned to his chest by his father, old Rick Pilot. Saw how the older man had beamed at his son. Saw how the younger man favored the older, how much he looked like his father, that very same man he'd seen tending bar in the dreamworld of Midnight Land.

"You know the name Silas Johnson?"

He watched Mike's face for a tell, some clue Mike knew something more than he'd given him credit for. There was nothing, though Mike shifted in his chair.

"Silas Johnson? Colored guy who disappeared back in the twenties?"

"He didn't disappear. He was lynched."

Mike said, "Your grandad tell you that?"

"Yep. He was lynched, set on fire and hung right in that very tree still in my front yard."

"*Your* front yard? Your grandad's place? Why there?"

"As a message."

"To who?"

"My granddad. To the other colored folk who were at Midnight Land that night. To keep their mouths shut about what had happened. Right there at his own house and all over The Club that night."

"A message from who, Bill?"

Bill stopped fidgeting, faced his friend. His mouth felt dry, his lips chapped. His tongue cleaved to the roof of his mouth as if unwilling to form the words he was fixing to say.

"I want to know if you know, Mike. I want you to tell me you *don't* know. I need for you to tell me that. I think, after all these years, you owe that to me."

"Well, shit, Bill. Then we're both lucky, because I have no idea what you're talking about. I'm supposed to know all this ancient history? No one talks about any of that. There aren't any files from that period, thanks to that old asshole, Sheriff Baetz. They never wrote any of that shit down, what they did, who they did it to. And any that existed were most likely cleaned out. Maybe burned at one of their midnight cross burnings. Expunged, I'm sure, to protect all the white folks involved. Make 'em all feel good in the light of day about what they done most nights."

"And you don't know…don't have any guesses as to who did it all? Never heard anything, never wondered?"

Here, Mike blushed.

"Heard a lot, Bill. Same as you. People whisper a lot of shit. Talk in hush tones in bars or VFW meetings. Over lunches or cocktails. Most of 'em don't know what they're talking about. Just rumors or third-hand stories. Never put much stock in any of it, and you shouldn't either. At any rate, why you suddenly so concerned about what happened thirty-odd years ago?"

"Because things haven't changed much, have they?"

Mike waved his hand. "Come on, man. Things haven't changed? You of all people are telling me of all people? You're a goddamn deputy now. Think that'd happen back then? Think that'd happen with Sherriff Baetz?"

"Sometimes I wonder..."

"Bill, for chrissakes, out with it. What'd your granddad say to you anyways?"

"He told me what happened that night. Who started things... who ended things. How old Silas Johnson finished up on fire, swaying from a rope over the tree in my front yard."

"Who, Bill?"

"Mike, I think you know. Even if you don't *know*, you know. The way a cop should."

Mike's flush deepened, the red dipping beneath his collar. His gaze drifted away, and Bill almost thought old Rick Pilot had opened the door and strode in, ready to knock him upside the head, cart him off and hang him, too.

But Bill didn't turn, and the door remained shut.

"I see no reason to lie and tell you I ain't never heard that. Because, I have. I've heard all about that. Long ago. He'd whisper about it sometimes with his cronies. Or worse, laugh about it."

"Why'd you never say anything to me?"

"Because it happened long ago. Because we've moved past that now. Why dredge it up? Besides, I had no idea up until a few minutes ago that you knew anything about it, much less it happening right there in your front yard."

"It might seem long ago to you, but it wasn't to *us*."

"*Us*?"

"Colored folk!" Bill said, thrusting his bare arm forward toward Mike, holding his skin out to his friend, as if revealing something for the very first time.

"Ahh, well, shit," Mike said, launching himself back in his chair.

"Evidently my granddad lived in fear of all of this since it happened. The last thirty years of his life afraid of your dad, your family. You, Mike. *You*."

"Me? Christ, what›d I do? Not like I was there."

"He said you were your father's eyes," Bill said, a growing sadness in him as he felt his friendship with this man curling at the edges, fading and shriveling like old paper. Could it survive the damage burning it now?

Mike's face fell.

"Well, I gotta be truthful, that's a hard thing to hear, Bill. Hard."

"He felt your dad brought us together to keep an eye on him, to remind him to keep quiet about he'd seen, what your dad had done."

"And what do you believe? Because you shouldn't. You shouldn't believe *that*, Bill." Mike pinched at his eyes, ran a hand over his forehead. "At least you shouldn't believe that of me, that I was in on that anymore than I was in on what happened at The Club. We became friends because…well, shit, I dunno. Why does anyone become friends, man? I can only say my dad never forced you on me or me on you. You can take that straight to the bank."

Bill gripped the arms of his chair, stood. He hesitated, measuring his words carefully, believing that in the final moments of this discussion, that it could end, their relationship, as easily as if it were hanging by no more than a thread. One false word from him or Mike, and it would sever years of memories.

"After the last few weeks, I'm not sure what I believe anymore. But I do know one thing, Mike."

He opened the door, stepped through. Outside, Betsy went back to pretending she was doing something rather than straining to hear what the two men were arguing about.

"What's that?"

"Getting real tired of people telling me what to think about shit."

Bill left the office, got into his cruiser, and drove.

He'd turned the dispatch radio off.

Later that night after his shift was over, Bill drove home slower than usual. Without his grandfather to greet him, he was in no hurry to get there. It was just an empty house without him. An empty house with an empty room

No, it was worse than that. Even though his grandad was gone, the house still seemed filled with his secret, literally bursting with what he'd done. As if the house itself were holding its breath, holding in the secret his grandad had been forced to hide for decades.

What he'd done.

What he *hadn't* done.

Mike drank milk from the bottle, leaning on the open icebox door. Its small interior bulb was the only light in the room, and he was okay with that. It kept him from seeing any of the hundreds of little touches throughout the house that still reminded him of his granddad. The photos, the knickknacks of his grandma the old man had kept carefully dusted. A jacket hung near the door; a sweater carefully folded over the back of a recliner.

He suspected that would never change, that he'd certainly never change any of it. He he wondered how he could continue to live in this place if that was the case, if he had to look at all this in the harsh light of day, every day.

Funny how that also seemed to apply now to Miller's Grove.

In his room, he stripped down to his skivvies, slid between the sheets. He thought he might not sleep, weighted down as he was by all he now knew.

But he slept that night, soundly.

Even though the shadow of one grasping tree limb raked across his window all night, he didn't dream of it at all.

He was up early, showered and dressed, drinking coffee over the sink. There was still no fresh milk in the refrigerator, so he drank it black.

He already knew what he was going to do, had known since he'd snapped his eyes open that morning.

When he'd drained the coffee, he rinsed the cup out, set it in the rack next to the sink. He went outside, to the detached shed that served as a garage in the winter. What he was looking for was propped against the back wall, sheathed in a leather sleeve.

His granddad's axe.

Hefting it, he slid the blade free. It looked oiled and sharp, well cared-for.

The tree out front was thick around its trunk, but not as tall as it once was. Decades of storms and age and rot had whittled it down to around thirty feet tall. No soaring limbs, no enormous, shady canopy.

As he eyed it, he felt something for this tree. Empathy? Sympathy? He wasn't at all sure. But some kind of strange kinship that rankled at him. There was no way he could ever love this tree anymore, but certainly it had no choice in the role it played that night.

That didn't matter. His mind was set. It'd take him some time, but he felt he'd be able to drop it today, lay it out in the front yard. Then dissect what was left, use it for firewood.

He found a pair of work gloves, worn and comfortable, took the axe into the front yard. Giving the tree one last look, he set about his work.

Later that evening, exhausted, he stood over the corpse of the old hickory, shirtless, the sweat dripping from his brow, down the small of his back and down into his drawers. What remained of the tree sprawled across the entirety of his lawn. So much larger on the ground than it had looked standing upright.

He'd been able to drop it away from the house, chop off a few of its limbs, stack them across the length of its trunk.

The woody smell of the raw hickory was thick, only slightly hidden now by that other, richer aroma.

Gasoline.

He struck a kitchen match, tossed it onto the tangle of limbs, the fallen trunk of the tree.

Flames bloomed from it instantly, leapt into the indigo twilight of the sky. Eager, avid flames, as if they, too, were eager to see the end of this tree.

Funny how it had only taken one match to undo the work of one match.

He pushed the box of matches back into the pocket of his jeans, lifted a bottle of beer to his lips. Watched the flames crawl over the tree, consuming its corpse, sending its ghost into the heavens.

Embers leapt from it, spun in the air like fireflies, more stars joining those spangling the skies.

Its bark sloughed away, glowing, and he remembered the skin of Silas' legs, cracked and limned with fire.

As the fire grew, he had less and less pity for the tree. It was just a thing. A thing used for an unspeakable act. He went to the porch, sat on his grandfather's chair and felt the heat of blaze on his naked chest. He watched the thing burn, felt as if he'd done a good thing that day.

As if he'd put part of his granddad's shame to rest.

Pulling on the last of his beer, he stared past the fire, off across the field to where his granddad had said Midnight Land had once stood.

He wondered if it had burned as prettily.

Monday morning, and Bill came into work a little later than usual. When he drew the office door open, Betsy gave him an odd look, stopped sipping her coffee. He was never late, so this was out of character.

Mike leaned against his doorway, gave him a silent, apprising look.

"Let's go grab some breakfast."

"MaryRose, I guess."

Mike nodded sharply, reached over to his desk to grab his hat.

He held the door open as Mike passed. They climbed into Mike's car, drove the short way to the diner in silence. Once there, they went inside, the little bell over the front door at MaryRose's tinkling their arrival.

Bill saw all the white faces perk up when they saw their sheriff enter, set again when they saw Bill come up behind. Like the ebb and flow of a tide, in and out.

Not today. Lord, not today. My guard's not up for this today.

They sat at the counter, as they usually did, both removing their hats.

Marge loitered near the kitchen window, eyeing them both, whispering to her husband, Manny. Otherwise not making any effort to acknowledge them, greet them, take their order. Bill wondered if they said the same things to each other each time Mike dragged him in here.

After a minute or two of waiting, Mike turned, his face flushed.

"We gonna do this every time we come in, Marge? Every goddamn time?"

The entire place lapsed into a hush, and Marge's mouth, which had been compressed into a thin, pink line, fell.

"Now, you watch that language, Sheriff. I don›t need you talking to my wife like…" came Manny's voice through the kitchen window.

Mike stood, and Bill grabbed at his sleeve, to get him to sit back down.

"Like what? Huh? Like I›ve got no respect for her? Is that what you were going to say, Manny? Because you best be thinking of how you and she both treat me and my deputy every time we come into this place," Mike said, his voice steady and low, but loud enough in the suddenly quiet diner for everyone to hear plainly.

"Then don't come in here," some wit from the assembled diners said, quietly enough to make it impossible to place who.

Mike spun, making eye contact with every single person in turn, his head swiveling to take in the entire room.

"Last time I checked, this was the *United States of America* not the *Confederate States of America*, as some of you evidently think. They lost, got their asses kicked a long time ago. So, if you got a problem with me bringing my friend into this place for a meal, then I suggest we step outside and discuss it…now!"

Mike yelled the last word, unsnapped his holster and placed his hand on his weapon.

Bill eyes widened, and he put his hand on his friend's, hoped to stay him from drawing the weapon, doing something rash. Or at least ruining his career.

Until he heard someone say something in the dining room, something almost lost in Mike's rant.

"…coon…"

Bill pushed Mike›s hand down hard, snapped the holster›s brass button closed, stood on his own.

"You're an old man, Durwin, so I'll let that go," Bill said, stepping in front of Mike. "I just lost my grandad, about as old as you, see? But he told me about you. About a few of you kindly folks gathered here. You, Mr. Cushing, and you, too, Mr. Birsha. You was all there. All you fine upstanding white Christian men. All three of you still alive and my grandad dead. Don't hardly seem fair, but that's where we are. So you get one, Durwin. Another and I'll lay you out for talking to me like that."

The gathered white faces, mostly old, all gawped at him, wondering where this was going. Most couldn't remember a black man ever speaking to them like this. Not and getting away with it.

"What'd we ever do to you, boy?" came Mr. Cushing's reply. Bent over his cane even at the table, he sounded so much like his punk grandson.

Bill turned slowly to him. "You best watch that tongue of yours, Cushing. I ain't your boy. I'm a lawfully recognized deputy. You mightn't done anything directly to me, you piece of shit, but you done plenty to my granddad, done plenty to my folks, yes, sir."

Cushing fell silent again, and the room took on an expectant atmosphere, holding its breath.

"That's right, I don't go back that far, but *our* memory does. We remember you all hectoring us constantly, beating us, burning our houses, our crops. You think all that stuff just goes away, is forgotten? Do you think a little change here and there makes us forget what you done? Do you think this...." Bill pulled at the star pinned to his chest, just as Bernie had in Midnight Land.

"...gonna make me overlook what you done? Because, let me tell you, it ain't."

"Forget what? What is it you think you know?" Cushing asked.

"Name Silas Johnson mean anything to you fine, upstanding men? Midnight Land? Burning down all the colored clubs, maybe even a few unfortunate negroes along the way? Ring a bell? Threatening a fine man like my granddad not to say anything about hanging a man from a tree right in his front yard, burning him alive? Where his wife, his own small daughter could watch? Remember? Because, I promise you even if we don't talk much about it, *we* remember. Yes, we do. We remember it all."

Uncomfortable shifting among the patrons, a paper-thin silence.

Then, "'Twas a long time ago. Things is different. You oughta just let it go, forget about it all," Birsha chimed in.

"Don't tell me how to feel about this," Bill said, turning toward the door. "Don't you goddamn tell me or any of us how we *oughta* feel about what you did. What you still do!"

"Bill!" Mike called after him.

But Bill let the door shut behind him, the little bell tinkling ironically as it closed.

He was up the street, walking fast, when he heard it again.

"Bill!" Mike shouted. "Wait up."

He didn't.

Beating Mike to the office, he hopped in his patrol car, sped off.

He passed Mike in the sheriff's cruiser. They turned to each other as they passed, and Bill swore he saw something in his friend's face.

Sadness? Regret?

It didn't matter.

Funny after so many years, it didn't much matter.

Bill drove directly to Dunstan Road, made the turn without thinking. Stopped the car by the water plant, without thinking.

Entered the Outside before he even knew clearly what he intended.

Would he be able to find it, Midnight Land, in the light of day?

He parked the cruiser along the shoulder, just down from the water plant. He turned off the ignition, left the keys on the seat when he got out.

Sunshine filtered through the high-up tree branches, pulsed atop the forest floor like light reflected off the surface of a swimming pool. Without much sense of exactly what direction he needed to be going, Bill moved forward.

The trees seemed even more densely packed than they had at night, almost as if they stood shoulder to shoulder, blocking his way. But he picked his path between them, and they snagged at him, clawing at arm and leg in an effort to impede his progress.

But he persisted.

He seemed lost, maybe not headed in the right direction. He didn't see anything in the distance, nothing that looked as if it might be that strange nightclub in the middle of the Outside.

After nearly a half hour of walking, though, he saw it up ahead.

The bland façade, the vertical sign bolted to it, the neon pale and unlit.

Midnight Land.

He thought this was an imperfect representation of the actual club. He'd bet money its building never had walls like this, brick and mortared oh so nice. Never had a neon sign spelling out its name.

There was no bouncer standing by its door this time, and Bill wondered what that meant.

Was it locked up?

Would he be denied entrance again?

He touched the handle, it was cold, oh so very cold out here in the warm air of the woods. He closed his hand tightly around the handle, drew the door open.

Inside, it was dark. His eyes, blinded by the summer sun, took a moment to adjust.

He let the door shut slowly behind him, and that little wedge of brightly lit reality seemed to recede into the distance as it did. Bill knew that it wasn't just an illusion, knew that his world, his reality was receding, falling away. He wondered if he'd ever find his way back there.

If he really wanted to, after all.

It closed with a loud click, and Bill froze.

When his eyes had adjusted, he saw it wasn't completely dark inside. The same dim, rosy light he remembered from before bathed the interior.

He stepped forward, came into the main room of Midnight Land. Arranged just the same, the little rickety stage over to the left, bare of musicians but with one upright bass leaning against a stand near an empty folding chair.

In this room, the scattering of small round tables, each with a chair or two. The bar with the kaleidoscope of liquors in various bottles.

Amazingly, the people were still there…if they were, indeed, people.

If this was actually a place.

But they were asleep, seated and slumped atop their tables or their stools.

Bernie, Ed & Floyd, even Silas, the flames still guttering around his legs, the noose still snaking into the air. Bill could see that, as he breathed, he blurted out little squibs of flame.

"You back so soon? We ain't even open, strictly speaking," said Rick, coming in from someplace behind the bar. He had a cloth in his hand, absently polishing a glass, as if Bill had interrupted him doing chores.

"Well, I'm here, Rick. Surprise you?" Bill said, approaching the bar.

"Mr. Pilot, if you please, boy. Show your elder some respect." He set the glass down in front of Bill, braced his arms against the back of the bar.

"I got no respect for ya, so I think we'll stick with Rick."

Pilot smiled thinly. "What'll you have?"

"The truth, Rick. Hows 'bout we start with that, work our way up?"

Rick snorted. "You think you can waltz in here, all high'n mighty and order me around? You think that tin star on your chest means something to me? It never really meant anything to me pinned to the chest of white man."

"I expect it doesn't," Bill said. "But you'll tell me nonetheless."

"And why is that?"

"First, because I think you want to. Actually, I think you *need* to. I think that›s the truth of Midnight Land, at least the one that stands here. Wherever *here* is."

Rick's face didn't change, but Bill was sure he saw something in his eye, a spark of something.

"And two for the friendship I bear your son. For his sake, if for no other, you'll tell me what happened that night."

The bartender's demeanor softened at the mention of his son, and his shoulders sagged a little. He looked away from Bill.

"Fine. What is it you wanna know…that you should already know?"

"Why?" Bill said, without hesitation.

Rick opened his mouth to answer, but Bill cut him off.

"And I don't mean why you did what you did to Silas. I know *that*. I mean, what you did to my granddad, to me. To my momma and grandma. Hell, what you did to your own son."

"You think you know why I did what I did, to Silas or anyone else? You don't know nothing about my whys, boy. You can't even decipher your own. Go fuck yourself."

"I already had it out with one white asshole this morning. That's the last *boy* I'm allowing. One more, and we're gonna have more than words."

"You don't know nothing about me or any of the others, old Manny, Bobby, Danny. How they getting along anyway? Man, ain't I glad I didn't hang around to get old enough for my balls to touch the toilet water or my ass hairs to go grey."

"They're doin' fine as can be expected, for a group of old racist assholes."

"Oh we's all racists, Bill. That much is for sure. But we were so much more. And by *so much more*, I mean so much less."

"What's that supposed to mean?"

"One thing I've learned over here is the danger in trying to figure out evil is most truly see it as one one-dimensional. You got a bad guy. You think *He likes to steal.* Or *He likes to hurt people.* Or whatever. The truth is, he›s one big ball of bad things, all rolled up together. Trying to figure out which one drives him is like trying to suss out one thread of a carpet. And some of those threads—*some*, mind ya—are good ones."

"You trying to say you were actually a good man? Because...," Bill chuckled.

"Hell no," Rick said, almost chuckling himself at that notion. "I *was* an asshole, but so much more'n asshole than you could ever possibly give me credit for being. You just have no idea, though you think you do. Me, Manny, Bobby, and Danny, too. There was good in all of us. Not for one minute, though, does that outweigh the bad we did…we *were*."

"Well, I gotta agree with you there," Bill said. "But why my grandad? He didn't do anything."

"You saying you think old Silas over there *did* something? To deserve what we did to him? Do honestly believe the bullshit reason we gave for lynching him? Jesus Walking Christ, you must be dumb. And even if it were true, do you think that'd be reason enough?"

"No," Bill shook his head.

"Your grandad had enough standing in town to get me into hot water if he blabbed, if he pressed it with the right authorities. Killing a colored, excuse me for saying, was a crime then, but not mucha one. Certainly not one most white folks particularly wanted to prosecute, 'specially if it was a white man did the killing. But if you was to rub it in their faces…"

"You were afraid Joe would rub it in their faces."

"Yep."

"So, hanging Silas, setting him on fire in our front yard…"

"Was a reminder."

"Yep."

"Like your son?"

Rick's face grimaced at the mention Mike.

"Leave my boy out of it."

"Why? You didn't."

"I don't see what you…"

"Bringing us together, almost forcing friendship on us."

Rick sighed. "You're not gonna like my answer, just saying."

"Try me."

A deep breath. "I forced Michael on you to protect him, not me."

It was Bill's turn to be confused. "How's that, again?"

"You think black folk took kindly to what I done? What we all done that night? Do you honestly think there weren't repercussions for what we done? Might not've been anything on the level we *earned*, but there were some over the years. Here and there. Threats. Property damage. Maybe one of us jumped out on a country road or behind the store in town, beaten to a pulp. Not enough to kill any of us, mind you. Just enough to remind us people still remembered."

"Good! You all deserved that and a lot more," Bill snapped.

"I'm not whingeing about it, just stating a fact, Mr. Lawman," Rick said. "At first, I had no real family to worry about. To protect. I didn›t have kids until much later, when I was older. I›d like to say wiser, too, but we›ll just stick with older. By the time I got around to it actually wanting one, my pecker didn›t work all that well. Shirl popped out old Michael, and that was it.

"By then, I was old enough to appreciate him. And I did. I treasured that boy in a way I'd never valued anything else before, not e'en my own life. I wanted for his happiness. Wanted to keep him safe. And I thought…"

"You thought keeping him close to me—close to the very black folks who were threatening you—you could keep him safe."

Rick nodded.

"And now you're here."

"We're here," Rick corrected.

"What is this place anyway?"

"Why, sugah, it's Midnight Land," said Bernie, awakening behind him.

They were all awake now, all watching this interchange between him and the bartender.

"That place burned down long ago. That's the reason we're all here, in the Outside," Bill said, turning back to Rick. "So where are we? I take it not really in the Outside, surely."

"No, surely not," said Silas.

"This is regret," Floyd said, and laughed his barking laugh.

"Regret?"

"We all build our own regret through life," Bernie said. "Things we done, things we didn't. All of us, black and white. We, though, we share this particular regret, along with quite a few others. Some of 'em visit from time to time, and some will be by presently, I'm sure. They'll all be here one day, even if the stay is short. But *we* share this one. And we call it Midnight Land, as much to remind us as for any other reason. Though there's not much way we'd forget at this point. Even if we wanted to."

"We recently got a new member, before you go on too long," Ed added.

Bill stiffened, felt his stomach flop. He sensed what was coming… what had to happen now.

There, over on the small stage, seated in the chair. He had the bass pulled up between his legs, and he plucked absently at the strings, produced a series of low, solemn notes like distilled sorrow.

"Grandad?"

Bill left the bar, staggered toward him.

He was young…what had he said? Twenty-two? Twenty-three. Handsome and thin, with a straight back and sparkling, mischievous eyes.

"Hello, Billy!"

Bill climbed the step to the stage, fell to his knees before the man, who looked down on him, reached out to stroke his head.

"Shhh, now, hush y'self," he whispered. "Ain't no way for a deputy sheriff to carry on."

"But…you don't play the bass," Bill said, scrubbing the tears from his eyes. "You never played any instrument."

"Not very well, at least," Ed commented, and Floyd laughed.

"Shut you mouth, you ignorant drummer. What'd you know about music anyways, just rap-tap-tapping on those skins? Anybody with a palsy can do as much."

The rest of them laughed. Bill saw even Rick laughed.

"Fact is after that night, I never did play the bass or anything else ever again. Not even records. Couldn't abide what had happened. What had been done…what I did. Music only served to remind me."

Bill remembered the story his grandad had told him the morning before he'd died.

"*You*? You were the bass player that ducked out? You didn›t come there just for a meal before going home. You…*played* there?"

"Played there and all around the area. Something of a local celebrity. Hometown colored boy makes good. Played with some of the very best, for a little while at least. Until—"

"That's why…"

"That's why I did what I did at *his* house," Rick said from the bar. "He was a *somebody* in a community that didn't have many somebodies. I wanted to send them all a message, not just your grandad. People knew who he was, knew what had happened in his front lawn. They'd remember."

"And that's my regret," his granddad said, helping him to his feet. "Not just that I tried to duck out, that they caught me anyways in the parking lot. But that I didn't say anything, do anything *afterward*. I was one of the few who might have, but I didn't. Because I was afraid. For my wife and my daughter. For me. I shut up. Shut down. I regret it all, every last piece of it. S'why I'm here. Why this place draws us all back. It's like…regret has a dark gravity, sucking everything back to it.

"That's Midnight Land. Dark gravity."

Amen, someone said.

Bill looked back toward Mike.

"I can't judge you, any of you," Bill said, stepping off the stage, away from his granddad. "Though I think some of you merit it. Though I might like to. I can›t…can›t even tell you not to regret whatever it is you›re regretting. Doesn›t seem right to me."

"It ain't," Silas said. "Why do we let those who aren't hurt say what hurt is supposed to mean to those suffering? Know what defines things for people? *Pain.* Pain alone gives a person the right to feel any which way they choose. And if you ain›t the one hurtin›, you need to sit down and shut your mouth."

A round of quiet *Amens*.

"Even," said Bernie, "if pain is self-inflicted."

"Regret," Bill said.

"Even if," Bernie smiled, nodded. "Time for you to slough off your own regret now, too, wouldn't you say?"

Bill frowned in confusion.

"Me? What do I have to regret about all this?" "Each of us, all of us, done things or didn't do things that night, right or wrong. And each of us carries they own regret for it. It's a personal load, you hear? Ain't God or the universe or anyone or anything else placing that weight on our shoulders. And now it's time to shirk that weight, move on," said Floyd, no longer laughing or even appearing amused. "Don't you think? Finally?"

"So, you know it's time, sugah, to come on home, come back to Midnight Land?" Bernie said. Unbidden, tears pooled in Bill's eyes as he anticipated the next word spoken to him.

"It's time," Bill's granddad said. "Hiram."

A huge, sobbing shudder wracked Bill's form, and he staggered, propped himself against a table. His vision clouded, waivered.

"Hiram?" Bill asked, scrubbing at his tears. "But that's the bouncer who disappeared, that's not—"

"You," his granddad said, coming to him, patting his heaving back. "It's you."

"What happened, what you done, what you didn't do ate you up. After you took your beating, you fled Midnight Land, fled Miller's Grove, fled the county, left it all behind ya," said Miss Lee, coming to stand beside him. "Least you thought you did."

"But you couldn't leave it behind, no matter how hard ya tried to forget," said Ed, standing and approaching, too. "It was always there, that little voice, always accusing you. Of abandoning your people,"

"Of bein' a coward," said Floyd. "And even though you tried to forge a new life, it wouldn't leave you alone. You heard, even after you left, of what had happened, what they'd done. And you couldn't think of anything but you mighta been able to stop it all if you'd acted that night. If you'd at least tried."

"So, you tried to drown it, with booze, with drugs," said Rick, his tone soft and gentle for the first time. "Anything to dull the voices."

"But regret don't work that way. It's a rot from the inside out, and no amount of liquor or smack gonna tamp it down," said Silas, coming to join the group gathered around Bill's trembling form. "Eventually, you did the only thing you knew to silence the voices. You killed yaself.

"It's got to be dealt with, inside here or back out there, in the wild, so as to speak," Rick said. "We chose this, a long time spent here to rectify ourselves to ourselves."

"You, honey, chose back out there, a whole 'nother life to prove your worth, but to no one but yourself," said Bernie, stroking the back of Bill's neck softly to calm him. "It was the longer, rougher road, sending you back out there, to start from scratch. Do it all again. That's what you wanted, and that's what you done. But it's time, now."

"You heard the music, heard it a few times, callin' ya. Each time, you came, but left. This time, you come to stay," said Ed.

"I don't believe that," Bill said, rising. "Can't accept that. I'm William Tyler, not Hiram whoever."

"Step on over here and take a look," said Rick from behind the bar. He was the only one who wasn't gathered around Bill.

The group parted, and Bill walked to the bar.

Rick hooked a thumb over his back, at the mirror behind him, framing the bar.

Bill saw, over Rick's shoulder, the reflection of a huge man, well over six feet tall. Broad shouldered, with a thick, heavy torso, a big head with blunt features.

He looked ineffably sad but managed a small smile.

Hiram.

Hiram Washington, Bill knew instantly.

Me.

He slumped onto the bar and wept.

"You're messin' up my bar with your waterworks, Hi," Rick said, wiping the area around him with the cloth he seemingly always carried.

"But I'm Bill Tyler," Bill said to his granddad, who'd come to sit beside him. "Was that all a dream? Didn't it mean anything?"

"Course you are and course it did," said his granddad. "You's both, in and out. We all take that trip sooner or later, different lives, same soul. Time to put 'em both together and leave all this regret behind."

"You haven't," Bill sniffed. "Not really. If you have, why're you still here, in Midnight Land?"

The others stared back in silence, didn't respond.

"You're all just so caught up in it, the past and what happened, what we did, you can't see any way forward," Bill said. "It's not just me who has to make amends for what they did, it's all of you. All of us."

"Well, first *you* gotta deal with what actually happened, not what mighta been or what you mighta done," Ed offered.

"Exactly! And how are any of you dealing with that in here? What's it done to ease the regret you say you feel?"

Nothing.

"Even with me, how did living a whole other life do anything to address what he'd…what I'd done before?"

Still nothing.

"No, there's gotta be another way, something else. Gotta be some way to put this all back together, to get on the right road. To forgive ourselves and move on."

Bill stood again, walked away from the bar.

"Seems to me it's such an individual thing."

"What's that?" Bernie asked.

"Judgment. Seems everyone can accuse anyone, but only one person can remove that regret, forgive you. And that's yourself. Only I can name my pain. Only I can say what it means to me, what it takes from me. In the end, only I can say how it's best dealt with. And when it's over."

"Such a smart, smart boy," Joe Boussard said from the bar. The others nodded in agreement.

"And it's over…for me, at least."

Bill drifted toward the door.

"Where you goin?" asked Silas.

Bill turned, saw the flames were extinguished around his legs, the noose was gone and he was clothed. Every bit the handsome, debonair young man his granddad had described.

That, at the very least, seemed like something to Bill. A victory, of sorts.

"Don't know," he said. "Forward."

No one said anything as Bill drifted toward the door. He wanted them to, desperately. To say something, stop him, urge him on.

Something.

But no one did, and so Bill didn't waiver, didn't look back, didn't stop. He pushed the door of Midnight Land open onto the sunlit forest.

The sign was dark.

Even so, it didn't feel so oppressive out here anymore.

The light felt warm and comforting, and the sound of birds chirping and insects buzzing reached his ears. No longer the closed, uncomfortable feeling the Outside once had, that cloying, oily feel of the air, the eerie silence.

Perhaps he wasn't in the Outside any longer, but someplace else. Someplace new.

He kept walking, but not in the direction he'd left his cruiser, he was sure of that. He assumed Mike would have found the car by now. Who knew how much time had passed in the "real" world since he'd been here?

Not that it mattered. He knew that instinctively. The cruiser, his job, his life, Miller's Grove, none of it lay in any direction. He was elsewhere now, and the possibilities of that, the dangers excited him.

Just the same, he walked in the opposite direction of where he thought the cruiser was, deeper into the Outside that wasn't really even the Outside any longer.

As he crunched through the forest, the noise cycled up again, buzzing like bees in his brain, insistent. It seemed weak now, and he ignored it. Less a call or a warning than a wave goodbye. Eventually it faded, even its echo forgotten.

Time to leave it all behind. Bill Tyler. Hiram Washington. Miller›s Grove.

Midnight Land.

Everything. Everyone.

Time for a clean slate.

With no regrets, he moved on to whatever lay on the other side of the deep, dark forest.

THE END

ALL THE STARS DIE ONE BY ONE

I. Thoroughly Trained, No Public Awareness

The end comes and we aren't any more aware of it than we are of the beginning. Or even the middle. People just aren't that aware of their lives, passing through them like ghosts through a ruined manor.

Let's just stick with the end, okay?

When you think of it, how many people are aware their end is coming? Oh, I guess if you've got some terminal illness, perhaps. Maybe if you're already wearing the paper gown, tubes and needles stuck in your body, your breathing labored, pain ratcheting up every nerve that isn't already, as the poet says, etherized on a table.

Then again, maybe not. Even when you're stretched out, ready to French-kiss Death, maybe even then the end comes as a bit of a surprise.

Can we ever really see our end?

I'd always hoped not.

This began, as every mission does, with a bunch of gobbledygook.

Barnstable: I see *Artemis's* shadow out there.

Hoagland: Two seventy-five, down at two point five. Nineteen forward.

Barnstable: Three point five down. Two hundred twenty feet. Thirteen forward.

Barnstable: Eleven forward. Coming down nicely. Two hundred feet. Four point five down. Five point five down.

Barnstable: One hundred sixty feet. Six point five down. Five point five down. Nine forward. You're looking good. Hundred twenty feet.

Hoagland: One hundred feet. Three point five down. Nine forward. Five per cent. Quantity light.

Barnstable: OK, seventy-five feet and it's looking good. Down a half. Six forward.

Mission Control: Sixty seconds to bingo, *Artemis*.

Barnstable: Roger that. Lights on. Sixty feet. Down two point five. Forward. Forward.

Hoagland: Forty feet, down two point five. Picking up dust.

Barnstable: Thirty feet, down two point five… shadow.

Hoagland: Four forward. Drifting to the right a little. Twenty feet. Down a half.

Mission Control: Thirty to Bingo.

Hoagland: She's drifting forward a little. That's good.

Barnstable: Contact light.

Hoagland: Okay, engine stop. ACA out of detent. Mode control: both Auto. Descent Engine Command override: off. Engine arm: off. Four-thirteen is in.

Mission Control: We read you down, *Artemis*.

Hoagland: Houston, Aitken Base here. *Artemis* has touched down.

All to say it was 1975, and we'd just landed on the dark side of the moon, in the Aitken Basin. There to explore a supposed Soviet discovery of an ancient city

An *alien* city.

In 1972, I was in the astronaut training corps at NASA. Great gig, really. Trained on equipment all day. Flight tests. Dips in the Neutral Buoyancy Simulator—essentially a huge swimming pool—at Marshall. Took periodic trips into the southwestern deserts to practice survival skills. It was like being in summer camp and getting paid. Not to mention the drinks it bought me. And, let's be honest, the women.

In 1972, the politicians—who'd been so eager to beat the Russkies to the moon—now decided it was too expensive. We'd been there five times by then, so the stuffed shirts pulled the plug. NASA had enough hardware and cash to manage one more mission, Apollo 17, but that was it. Done. Out of the moon landing business for good, or so it seemed.

My training shifted. No more dreams of kangaroo-hopping over the surface of the moon for me. No, I shifted over to earth orbital stuff. There was this project called Skylab. I was actually training to be a back-up crew member, but after just three manned visits, it, too, was terminated. After that, the picture for my career as an astronaut started to look a little bleak. What exactly had I been training for anyway?

I was already forty-eight years old, and while there were plans for future spacecraft—something called a "space shuttle" was in the works—I was likely to be fifty-five or older when it came online.

Suddenly, I began to see a life that wasn't all summer camp, free drinks and free pussy. I saw a life spent driving to work every day, sitting behind a desk from nine to five, coming home to my wife and kids, falling asleep in front of Johnny Carson, then getting up and doing it all over and over until they tipped me into my Arlington grave.

Just as I was at my absolute nadir, I started to hear whispers of something going on, a project in the deepest, hush-hush places of NASA. Nothing too much, not really any *information* about it. But it was very off the books.

I think it was in mid-'74 when they finally dragged me in. A few nervous NASA reps, John Young, who was then the Chief of the Astronaut Office, three military men with serious faces, and three men in dark suits with impassive faces.

I'd done my stint in the military, so I was accustomed to humorless generals. And I'd been in NASA long enough to know its guys always looked nervous. Both were accustomed to sending men to their potential deaths, but it always struck me funny how different their responses to this were.

The other three men were of a type I'd never encountered before. Intelligence officers from the CIA. Poker-faced, bland-looking men accustomed to secrets—protecting ours, identifying others, and stealing them.

Young came and got me at my desk. I'd been daydreaming of all the missions I'd come close to being on, imaging myself finally making the grade, making that leap to an astronaut who finally *astro'd*, finally went up there, *out* there, floated, walked, moon-hopped, tooled across the bleak lunar maria in the rover they'd sent up in the later Apollo missions.

Even then, Young was a legend in NASA. He'd flown in the first Gemini mission, flew the command module in Apollo 10 and commanded the Apollo 16 mission to the moon. He'd also been tapped to head up the new space shuttle project.

He looked drawn, terse, and I instantly knew he was calling me in to tell me that some program or another was being cut. Shit, who knew? Maybe they were completely defunding NASA. Young certainly looked like something of that magnitude was happening.

Let's face it, America in 1975 had seen better days. We'd talked ourselves out of winning in Vietnam, Nixon had been run out of office for spying on the Democrats. There were economic crises, gas shortages, inflation, race problems, crime. Nothing was going our way. We made sure of that ourselves.

I followed Young down drab, bureaucratic hallways, took an elevator with him, then another series of hallways, these less populated, to a corridor that dead-ended at a non-descript door with two armed military guards standing on either side.

Young nodded at them, and they opened the door. A bunch of guys—the ones I already described—sat at a long table in a room with no windows. A projector screen was on one wall, and a small eight-millimeter projector was on a cart at the other side of the narrow room.

I began to think this wasn't about defunding NASA or even about letting me go.

Young went to sit at the end of the table nearest the door, leaving only one open seat between the two other NASA functionaries and two of the three men I was sure were intelligence officers.

I squeezed in beside them, saw a thick, closed file on the table before me. I went to open it, but the man to my right put his hand on mine, stayed me.

"Capt. Hoagland," said one of the military guys, an Air Force general whom I didn't recognize. "You've been at NASA since, when, 1968?"

"Sixty-nine, sir. Came in right after a stint in Vietnam. Operation Rolling Thunder," I said.

"You've flown in what? What aircraft?"

"I started off in '66 sitting in F-4s, then F-105s. Also got experience with the Tomcat, the F-15, and even a few hours on the 16. Various trainers, props, even a few hours in helicopters. But, no offense, general, you knew all that before you called me in," I said.

The general nodded and smiled. "Yes, captain, we most assuredly did."

The army general sitting next to him cut in. "We have a situation. We need a uniquely skilled pilot for a highly classified project. A man like you, an experienced pilot, but also an astronaut."

"And son," the air force general said. "We need an astronaut who's been thoroughly trained but who doesn't have the kind of public awareness that would make people wonder where he's gone or what he's doing. Understand?"

"A nobody," I said with a wink, warming up to this. "Check."

He smiled again.

One of the intelligence guys seated next to Young stood.

"Since we're pressed for time, let's fill Captain Hoagland in on the background. Let me remind everyone here the following briefing is Top Secret SCI. You understand, captain?"

"Of course, sir," I said, bristling a little at the thought I wouldn't know or understand what that meant.

He picked up on my irritation. "Not meaning to insult you, captain. It's just you don't have much exposure to secrets at this level, and we don't have time to bring you up slowly. You're about to get a crash course, if you'll excuse me."

I didn't reply, a little embarrassed he'd seen right through me. But then I realized it was what guys like him were trained to do.

"The film you're about to see was shot mainly by Cosmonaut Svetlana Zaitsev onboard the Soviet *Zvezda*, a lunar landing mission sent up in '74."

"Not the first time they've sent a woman into space. Remember Valentina Tereshkova? She went up in '63, did forty-eight orbits in seventy-one hours," said Young. "Right after Gordo set a record for us in *Faith* 7. Twenty-two orbits in thirty-four hours. We've got some training, secretly, if you remember,"

I did remember.

"Where was I?" the irritated intelligence officer began again. "Very top-secret project, both for us and for the Soviets, reasons for which will be made plain. At any rate, the mission was primarily to answer our Apollo program but also to start the process of building a lunar base for them. They chose an area on the far side, in the Aitken Basin, near the lunar south pole. This site was chosen first to keep what they were doing from prying eyes, mainly ours, and also because geologists think the crust there is thinner, which would be conducive to lunar mining, a key component of their building strategy."

He pointed to another guy sitting at the projector. He dimmed the lights, and the projector clacked to life. There was the usual film jumping, a countdown, then a warning about the top-secret nature of what was to come.

Black-and-white footage of cosmonauts being helped into a Zond capsule, though larger. Five men, all suited up, technicians got them situated, then bolted the capsule's door shut.

Was it wrong I wondered which one was the woman, Svetlana?

I couldn't tell.

Cut to the launch of a huge N1 rocket, nameless Soviet functionaries clapping in a control room. Then another cut to cosmonauts in orbit doing the exact same things American astronauts did—float around, mug to the camera, eat food squirted from toothpaste tubes. Nothing unusual here, though the thought they were going to land on the moon—a moon where no one but Americans had trod—set me aback.

I also knew it went wrong. It was why the Soviets hadn't crowed about this everywhere, why I was here in this room with these men.

Lots of different, shaky, poorly framed footage of activities, a spacewalk, routine stuff.

"The orbital command module, the LOK, was a larger Soyuz variant of the craft. It carried five men, one who would orbit, four who would touchdown. Their lander, LK, would descend, allow the cosmonauts exactly seven days on the lunar surface, then liftoff, dock with the LOK, then back to earth. Very much like our Apollo missions," Mr. Intelligence said.

"But something went wrong," I said.

He ignored me.

Suddenly, we were there, the four cosmonauts exiting their squat, greenish lander and hopping about on the moon. The images instantly caused a pang of regret.

"In most regards, the Soviet mission was like ours. Except they sent two unmanned missions ahead of the *Zvezda:*one carrying supplies and two Lunokhod rovers; the other carrying the first parts of an expandable habitat to house the cosmonauts on the surface and, they hoped, form the first part of a huge Soviet presence on the moon."

I watched as the footage showed the four figures bounding over to a cylindrical lander near their own. They opened hatches and winched down the two rovers, appearing to be meticulously copied from our own, which I supposed they had. A few more stretches of unloading gear and supplies, stowing it aboard the rovers, then setting out across the lunar terrain towards, I guessed, where the habitat module had landed.

Here's where things became a little hard to follow. I figured I wasn't seeing the entire film here, only the cut version some intelligence operative had spliced together from a much longer reel. Even that probably wasn't the complete one.

Jump cuts to the squat steel cylinders housing the habitat, gleaming silver in the harsh lunar light. Behind them, towering into the dark, star-strewn sky. Not the blunt, low-laying lunar hills. Not more Soviet habitats.

It looked, for all intents and purposes, like buildings, a cityscape lifted from the surface and thrust into the no-air.

"What's in the background?"

More jump cuts. Now they were coming quickly, jerky, hazy shots. Bouncing toward this lunar *fata morgana*, worryingly clearer with every cut.

The cameraman climbed from his rover, and there were hurried, clipped exchanges of Russian I couldn't follow, even though I knew a little, picked up here and there.

Then, a quiet, stunning pan of the camera across the horizon and up, up, up.

Great domed structures, spires and towers hundreds of feet tall, though scale was hard to tell. It was all like a child's playset, except these were all grey, as grey as the dust they sprang from.

The ruins of a great ghost city on the far side of the moon.

When the realization hit, I looked around the table. Several of the men weren't even paying attention anymore. The NASA guys, though, they paid *close* attention, even Young. It wasn't as much attention, though, as it was a sort of wide-eyed disbelief. I suspected they'd seen the film before, but only recently, perhaps right before I was brought into the room. They were still digesting it.

The intelligence guys? They watched *me*.

I cast my attention back to the screen. Closer, closer, the Soviets got to the city until they walked its streets, its wide, unpopulated streets layered with grey, lunar dust accumulated over who knew how many centuries. The structures towered above them, not the rectilinear shapes of earth buildings, but great, curved things, swoops and arcs and not one straight line or ninety-degree angle I could see anywhere.

It was so awesomely different, so *alien* in the truest sense of the word it left me speechless.

The rest of the film spooled through at bewildering speed.

A huge hole in the surface just inside the city. It didn't seem an accident, that hole. Not a surface collapse or a crater. No, it seemed part of the city, constructed, a central feature the city had been built around.

The hole sloped into darkness.

The Soviets rode their Lunokhod rovers down into it. Here the film became its jumpiest, its grainiest.

Faces, excited Russian chatter.

Bodies in beige capsules…

A cemetery?

A face swam into view, cloaked in cloth. Mummified perhaps. Humanoid, with dark, leathery skin, huge, closed eyes, nostril slits. A full head of long, dark hair.

The cosmonauts carrying this body to one of the rovers, still wrapped in whatever material it was swaddled in.

Back in what I guessed was the habitat module, all lit and functioning now. The creature or whatever it was laid upon a table, its weirdly serene, weirdly inhuman face artificial under the unforgiving lights.

The three cosmonauts had doffed their headgear and were shouting loudly at each other. I noted they were all men. Svetlana must be the one filming all this.

Jerky footage. The creature being wheeled into a lab or room, strapped tight to the gurney.

Alive?

It was *alive?*

Lots of Russian arguments between the cosmonauts, their faces drawn and haggard. Lots of notes taken by at least one of the cosmonauts, trying to communicate with the creature. A shot of his journal, with pages of Cyrillic the intelligence boys made no effort to translate for me.

How long? Hours? Days?

A decision is made, a hard-won decision evidently. To let the creature out. Maybe they thought it would tell them more if it were free.

All hell breaks loose, and I couldn't make heads or tails of it.

The thing they'd returned with was bounding about the room.

Was that blood, there…and there?

Then, the camera settles, we're with at least one cosmonaut back in the lunar lander. Breathing hard, shaking hands flipping controls, toggling switches, yelling into the communicator but getting no response.

He shoves the camera up to a window. The stark vista stretches right to the horizon. You can clearly see the footprints of the cosmonauts, a lone set of tire tracks leading to the lander.

As the footage shakes with the ignition of the lander's rockets, the lone cosmonaut takes one last shot through the window. Its ultra-grainy, probably enlarged and image enhanced.

The stiff Soviet flag with its red background and yellow hammer and sickle flaps in the lander's exhaust.

Lurching from the shadows nearby, a…

A what? A thing?

That thing?

Impossible.

The film ends, the last inch or so of the strip flapping wildly until the projectionist turns the machine off. The lights come on, and one of the intelligence guys stretches and yawns. Everyone looks around the table measuring reaction.

Most everyone, though, seems to be measuring mine.

I started to think this must be a joke to yank my chain in a fun little way before handing me my gold NASA watch and showing me to the door of early, forced retirement.

"Are you shitting me?" I asked. No one answered, chuckled, snorted or even batted an eye.

"Is any of that even real?" I asked, expecting ribald laughing would start, the cake and champagne would be wheeled in, maybe a few of the secretaries would join us.

There was no cake or champagne, no smiles and certainly no pliant secretaries.

"It's a joke, right? The Russkies are seeing just how gullible we are," I said. No one answered. "Oh, come on."

"Every last frame of it has been verified by DOD, NASA, the CIA and the NSA. It's real, all right," the intelligence guy said.

"Sure, the film is really Russian, but how do we know it's *real?"* I asked, idiot that I was. "I mean, we're suddenly taking the Russians at face value? How do we verify?"

The esteemed gentleman at the table all looked at each other now, not at me.

"Funny you should mention that, Rich," Young said from his end of the table. "It's why we invited you here today."

When he was done telling me what the mission was, what my role would be, it was as if a tremendous weight, a sodden, grey raincloud had lifted over my head and the sun shone down on me.

I'd finally be *astronauting*.

The *Artemis* was a helluva lot bigger than the Apollo lunar landers. About a three-fold increase in square footage, oversize to accommodate our three astronauts. Or should I say two astronauts and one cosmonaut. In addition to Fred Barnstable, another holdout from astronaut training, we went up with Cosmonaut Svetlana Zaitsev. Remember her? The cameraman aboard the *Zvezda*? The only survivor of that doomed expedition.

Not bad for a commie bastard, at least that's how Fred described her. And, yeah, she was a stand-up officer. Solid, reliable, well-trained there at the Baikonur Cosmodrome, the top-secret Soviet launch facility. She was an environmental engineer. Her main job in the *Zvezda* mission was setting up the habitat modules and getting them working.

Fred had elbowed me. "She's a Russian homemaker."

It wasn't the reason she was with us. There were two far simpler reasons.

First, the Soviets had cancelled any additional moon missions following the *Zvezda*, repurposing rockets for other orbital and unmanned projects. While they might have decided eventually to go back to the Aitken Basin, they couldn't get there in time to stop us from going after we found out. Yes, of course, we found out.

They played their hand to their American rivals. *Here's what happened. Here's what we found. Want to help us figure out what's going on up there and, in the process, potentially discover something about the universe and our place in it no one else has seen?*

We did, of course. We very much did. To get a peek at the cards the Soviets hadn't played up to that point, we agreed to take Svetlana with us. Not much of a concession since we were going to demand she come anyway. She'd been there, seen what had happened.

Let's be honest. We would have gone anyway, even had they not agreed to send Svetlana, even if they'd never told us about any of this. We were going there from the moment we got a hint of what occurred through our intelligence sources.

They knew that.

Better to at least have a representative from the U.S.S.R. than to allow the Americans to get there by themselves.

There were other ground rules imposed by the Soviets—we weren't to touch or take any of their equipment chief among them. Yeah, sure, we won't touch your toys. They surely knew we would be studying the hell out of them, though. What could they do about it?

Three of us aboard the *Artemis*—me, Fred and Svetlana. Above us, orbiting in a command module more than three times as big as its Apollo counterpart, our own woman astronaut, Vanessa Ramirez commanded the *Aegis*.

Why were our ships so much bigger than the Apollo?

Stowage. We needed ample room not only to bring back anything interesting we'd find, including strange, mummified bodies, but also Svetlana's three fallen comrades. The other Soviet demand was its cosmonauts be brought back for heroes' burials.

How could we refuse?

We'd landed about two klicks from where the *Zvezda* had, just a bit off from the central peak of the Von Kármán crater, Mons Tai. There was a huge debate between NASA and the military as to exactly where we'd land. Should we touchdown closer to the abandoned city than the Russians had, to have better logistical access to whatever was there? Or should we land a bit farther out, to give us a margin of safety should things start to slide?

You can tell, I'd guess, which argument was NASA's and which was the military's.

The military won. We decided to land closer, actually just a half click away from where the Soviets had dropped their habitat modules. Before we suited up, Svetlana took a pair of binoculars and scanned the area. She excitedly pointed out the modules, gleaming unnaturally in the harsh lunar light, handed the glasses over to Fred and me.

I looked through them, siting the steel cylinders of the habitats and observing them only briefly. For behind them, shimmering in the distance like the ghost of Christmases Past, the spindly, skeletal structure of that faint city hovered on the horizon, between us and the wall of the Leibnitz mountains, which seemed no more solid than this specter.

I held those binoculars to my eyes. The effect of seeing this here, now, not in a cramped secret conference room on a cheap, NASA eight-millimeter projector was overwhelming. This assemblage of alien structures, alien curlicues, alien non-linear architecture, even if it was just the *ruins* of an alien civilization, was almost enough to vapor-lock my human brain.

I knew from his look when he passed the binocs over to me, Fred had been affected in much the same way.

"See?" Svetlana said. "I didn't lie."

I stared at her, unable to process a response.

I thought to myself, over and over as we suited up to leave.

No. No, you didn't lie.

I took my time climbing out of the *Artemis*, onto the surface. I wanted to feel at least a little of what Neil had felt. Okay, maybe not the millions of eyes—*billions?*—as the cameras recorded his every move, his every word for posterity. But that awesome, indescribable feeling of stepping foot onto ground that was not earth.

The surface was soft and talc-like. The other guys described this effect of feeling your foot sink inches into the stuff, but it was weird. Not at all like walking in sand, the sinking, slightly purchaseless feeling you get there. It was like walking through fairy dust, soft and ephemeral, like ash or feathers. It stuck to you once touched, each gray grain clung like clothes fresh out of the dryer. Soon our boots and lower legs were flocked with the stuff.

We used hand tools to unbolt several sections along the lower skirt of the *Artemis* to gain access to the winch and lower the new version of the lunar rover the NASA techs had cobbled together especially for this mission. It could hold four riders and featured a short flatbed capable of hauling about 500 pounds of…well, whatever we wanted to haul out of there and back to earth.

It took us about an hour of winching, unfolding, tightening bolts and powering up the beast, telling the boys down at NASA to cut the chatter while we worked. Once it was fully deployed, it was a wonderful, beautiful contraption NASA had put together, the first pick-up truck on the moon.

Svetlana nodded in appreciation. "Very American," she said, and I couldn't argue with that assessment. I was almost surprised the engineers hadn't welded a gun rack behind the seats.

We unpacked a whole host of kit—cameras, ropes pitons and other climbing gear, auto winches, a bag of small hand tools, and a small surprise, probably from our friends in the intelligence service.

Guns.

A small cache of weapons, to be precise—four forty-five caliber Colt Combat Commander army pistols, four M16s and a shitload of accompanying ammo. Yes, if you're wondering, guns can fire on the moon.

Svetlana's eyes widened when she saw what was in the case.

Evidently her people hadn't provided her with anything, which I found curiously comforting in a way.

I nodded, passed her a gun and a couple clips of ammunition. She seemed surprised by this, but watched closely as we loaded ours, then followed suit, stowing the extra clips in her suit pockets, as did Fred. We took our seats aboard the rover—Fred driving, Svetlana riding shotgun to get a better look and offer directions.

I sat in back. As Fred set off, I made sure to stow my own handgun, then lifted an M16 from the stockpile, held it at the ready.

We approached the city in the dust.

II. Into the Well of Ancient Sorrows

Every year for vacation, my father drove us from the midwestern city where I grew up to Colorado. Every year. The old man loved the state, and it was and is a beautiful one, for sure. His reasons were his own, lost now with his death. My sister and I enjoyed the trips—at least the early ones before we grew into bored teenagers—for its roadside attractions and touristy trappings. We begged dad to stop at every strange offering, every roadside stand hawking apple cider or faux Indian souvenirs. We ate up tours of Cave of the Winds and the Seven Falls, thrilled at crossing the bridge over the Royal Gorge, the nights spent at chuckwagon dinners under the stars complete with goofy fifties-era cowboy musical shows.

My dad, he was in it for the natural beauty of the state. We'd grown up in Missouri, a beautiful state in its own way, but mostly gentle green hills and dense, dark forests. Colorado was mountains soaring up unbelievably into the crystal blue sky, tall, spindly pines and snowy crags.

I'll never forget my dad's face after that first all-nighter through Kansas, a state flat as a piece of plywood and just as featureless. He'd timed the drive to cross the Colorado-Kansas border very early in the morning, about three a.m. By the time the sun rose, the mountains had appeared on the horizon, growing and growing as we neared Colorado Springs.

His face became rapturous, hands so tight on the steering wheel of the old Chevy I thought his bones would pop through the skin. I felt something of the same each morning in our motel room, throwing open the curtains like a magic trick to see those same mountains outside the window, now looming spectacularly over everything.

It was revelatory in an almost religious way that moved me unexpectedly, even as a child.

In the back of this lunar rover, hauling ass over a landscape burnt out, built of ash, racing toward the ghostly mirage of a ruined alien city in a place where nothing of those three words should exist, I experienced that feeling again, this time so powerfully it thrummed through my body.

The nearer we approached, the ghostlier it seemed to get, paradoxically more real from a distance than close up. A movie set, a ViewMaster slide of a child's convoluted drawing blown up into exaggerated, three-dimensional life.

I tried to communicate this best I could back to Mission Control. The weird architecture of the thing made my skull throb, though, just as its phantom, opalescent outline made my soul soar. We humans, rigid as we are, build in right angles and straight lines so exclusively most modern architecture fades into the background of our lives.

Not here. Those who built this—*city? base?*—eschewed straight lines and right angles so thoroughly it seemed they'd never seen them. Everything was curved, rounded, ovoid, spherical. Wavy squiggles and spiraling curves and strange sweeping arcs, improbable puffs of a material that had fallen away from its underlying structure leaving what looked like dead dandelion heads.

No human hand had built these. No human brain had designed them. No human foot had ever trod there until now. Well, until the Soviets had undertaken their tragic exploration.

How old was this place? As we came into the outskirts of the city proper, it was apparent the structures were ancient, long abandoned. Like the dandelion building, things had begun to collapse, fall in on themselves.

Fred had found what looked to be a looping thoroughfare, twisting into the city. It was covered with lunar dust, but where its surface showed, it shone like glass.

Svetlana filmed it all with the bulky portable unit the boys from NASA had developed especially for this mission. Both our guys and the Soviets wanted as much visual information from this mission as we could get, trusting neither our eyes nor still cameras.

She spoke as she went, I'm sure thinking we figured she was narrating the footage.

I knew better.

When we were deep in the city, Fred stopped the rover, and we clambered out. The structures rose up on all sides around us now, lit starkly by the harsh sunlight against the lunar sky.

It was even more awe inspiring than the Colorado mountains outside the motel window. Unlike the mountains, though, these didn't reach up to the heavens but slumped and collapsed and spilled over the landscape, dust sloughed atop dust.

"So how do we do this? Split up or stick together?" Fred asked. The NASA boys had told us to stick together. I ignored them.

"You stay with the rover," I said. "Sveta and I will poke around a bit. Keep the motor running." That last was a joke. The rovers were electric vehicles, essentially golf carts. "Be ready."

"For what?" Fred laughed.

"Anything," Svetlana answered before I could.

She followed me as we hopped from Fred and the rover to the pile of rubble heaped against the nearest edifice.

"What do you make of this?" she asked, and I flinched, didn't expect her to speak. And her English was spot on. Gold star for all that Soviet training. I only spoke a few sentences of Russian, and even my best was nowhere near as good as anything Sveta said in English.

She was running her hand over the remains of what looked to be the balustrade of a spiral ramp that corkscrewed a hundred feet into the air before crumbling away, whatever it led to long gone.

"City of some kind, I expect," I said. "With these wide sorts of highways between structures. High rises where, I guess, they did business, lived their lives."

"Human?"

I shook my head as much as I could within my helmet, tried not to laugh. Were the Russians teaching pseudo-science in their astronaut schools?

"Nah. Moon's never had air to speak of. Look around. No signs of a dome or any structure to hold in an earthlike atmosphere. Not likely that any ancient human astronauts put down here."

"Ahh, I see, Von Däniken. Yes, but his writings could be right."

Shit, she even got my jokes.

"Could be, could be," I said, not believing any of those four words.

We moved down what I thought of as Main Street, toward that deep depression in the lunar soil. It became clear, the nearer we got, that it wasn't just a depression or a crater. It was the entrance to a cave or a subterranean structure.

Its entrance was wide and shallow, like a catfish's mouth. More than wide enough to accommodate the rover.

The rover moved slowly toward us, kicking up spumes of grey dust.

"What up, boss?"

"That," I said, gesturing toward the entrance. "Let's take a little drive inside, if we can, see what they were doing down there.

Sveta and I climbed back aboard, and Fred mashed the pedal. Soon we were shooting down Main Street toward whatever this was.

I watched the buildings slide past as we went. It became instantly apparent from this vantage that the entire city spread from this opening. It was like the dot to the city's exclamation point.

The opening was upon us, the ground sloping away so gradually that we were well under the top of its open maw before we realized we were inside and headed down. As we passed the terminus of the upper opening's shadow, two things happened.

Lights snapped on, small, low to the road, octagonal lights, bluish in color, seemingly set off by our passing. The cast a welcome light onto the road, which we saw was now spiraling around itself and headed down, farther into the recesses of the moon.

All comms cut off, too. The near constant chatter of Mission Control, as well as, I noticed, the Soviets, too.

"No com," I said, as much to myself as the others.

That the ceiling over the road was smooth, not like a cavern at all…at least not any I'd seen on Earth. No stalactites or other accretions, just smooth, as if the passage had been bored through the rock. No, smoother still than that.

As if had been melted through.

There was a lot of oohing and ahhing as we drove on, I gotta tell ya.

The passage corkscrewed down, blue lights clicking on as we passed. It seems we drove maybe two kilometers, and then yellow overhead lights came on in tandem with the blue, which gave everything a surreal green glow.

Except the yellow lights were flashing.

"Anything seem strange about this," Fred asked.

"Everything. Absolutely everything," I said.

"The flashing lights, they seem like a warning, don't they?" Sveta said.

Fred turned to me and shrugged as best he could in his bulky suit.

"They might," I replied. "They just might. Why don't we slow it down a bit—"

"Bozhe moi!"

The smooth-bore chamber opened suddenly into a space the size of a vast amphitheater on Earth, huge and oval, with the dome of its ceiling lost in the shadows. Around this was a series of looping tracks, must have been miles of the stuff, as flimsy and haphazard as my son's Hot Wheels setup.

The yellow lights circled the space, too, flashing on and off.

All agog about the huge room and its loopdy-loo tracks, we almost missed the enormous hole in the ground at its center. Almost drove right into it.

Fred slewed the rover hard to the left, and I grabbed hold as best I could. Sveta, though, had not been so lucky. She was thrown from the vehicle, rolled and bounced on the gritty surface.

"Sveta!" I yelled, and Fred, not missing a beat, came around without once even applying the brakes. He circled back as she came to rest, just a few feet from the lip of the pit.

Before the rover had completely stopped, I leapt out, careful not to push too hard and sail into the damn hole myself, and went to her. She was getting to her feet, and I offered a hand.

"Spasiba, spasiba," she breathed, her breath fogging what I was sure the look of terror on her face. "I'm good…fine. Spasiba."

We both stood there, gaping into the hole.

There was no way to tell how deep it went. There were no lights inside it or other features to give a perspective. It was simply a black pit at the center of this arena.

Its edges were smooth, almost glassine, like the passageway that had led us here. Its sides, too, at least as far down as we could see. "Jesus, Sveta, sorry," Fred said. "Should have given everyone more warning."

"No worry, Fred," she said. "Spasiba."

I heard Fred breathe a sigh of relief into his helmet. As we attempted to regain our wits, we looked around the chamber more closely.

There, on those loops and loops of Hot Wheels tracks, there were cars.

Capsules. Pale, lozenge-shaped items, stacked end to end, looking like a traffic jam on I-45. Each one was identical, a pale, ivory tone in the dim light.

"What…what are those?" Sveta asked, shouldering the camera again to ensure this discovery, too, was cataloged.

"I dunno," Fred said. "Looks like a Tic-Tac assembly line."

"Hard to tell from this distance, but they look big enough to hold something. Almost—"

"Human-size," Sveta said.

"The track seems to come around that side," I said, moving my hand left to right, then down there."

"Looks like it terminates on the other side of this hole," Fred said.

I was able to just make out what looked like a straightaway length of track, pointed in our direction.

"I'll bring the rover over," Fred said.

"I'll walk, get more of this on film," Sveta said.

"I'll go with her," I said. "We'll meet you on the other side," I said, then shuffled slowly away, Sveta following.

"There's a structure over there," Sveta said. Fred, driving the rover, came around us, then sped off. "A…looks like a mechanism."

I knew the camera offered Sveta a telescopic view, so she saw things better. "A mechanism for what?"

"I can't tell from here," she was breathing hard, loping behind me, trying to keep the camera as steady as possible for the poor image processors back home. "But something seems broken. No, wait. It looks clogged. Jammed."

I broke into the kangaroo hop—as close as one gets to running in lunar gravity. I heard Sveta's breathing even heavier as she fought to keep up.

Ahead in the distance, the rover came to a stop, Fred getting out.

I saw what Sveta had seen through her viewfinder.

The track indeed uncurled its loops about a hundred meters away, from the lowest circle of the amphitheater, to cross the flat plains of what on earth would be the playing field. It came straight to this weird structure, almost like an exposed elevator shaft on the lip of the hole.

It appeared this was designed to load a single capsule and…put it onto the track?

I kept hopping, joining Fred at the side of this contraption.

Now, I saw it was jammed. One of the capsules was stuck in its jaws, cock-eyed, preventing it from operating. The design of the thing was simple, just a few moving parts, but no sign of what actually powered it, kept it moving.

As Sveta huffed into place near us, I saw Fred was staring intently not at the mechanism, but at the capsule stuck in it.

"Is that a window in the capsule?" he said, almost whispering. "And is that a face?"

Sveta, not at all stymied by what he'd said, moved closer to the device.

"Da, Fred. Da, da. It *is* a window, and it *is* a face. Like the creature we saw in the *Zvezda* mission."

I put my hand on the holstered sidearm on my hip. "Fred keep an eye on our surroundings. I don't want anything sneaking up on us."

"Roger that."

I went to the mechanism, just a few twists of metallic material really, encaging the capsule that was lodged crookedly in its embrace.

There was a window, at approximately where a head might be. It was foggy, dusty maybe rather than anything inside clouding it.

Staring back from me was a face—Humanoid, with dark, leathery skin, huge, closed eyes, nostril slits. A full head of long, dark hair. Impossible to tell what sex it was…if that was even a thing with these creatures.

"Just as with the *Zvezda*," Sveta said, to her credit still filming.

"Except this one isn't running around killing folks," I said. "I wonder why that is."

"Looks like it was pulling these capsules out of the hole, lining them up around this entire arena," I said, peering into the hole, still seeing nothing. No track on which capsules might move up the hole, nothing to grab them and place them on the track.

Something seemed out of whack. Whatever this was, we weren't getting it. But at least this creature was…what? Dead? Asleep? Who knew?

"Fred?"

"Got nothing, boss. All quiet."

"What's it look like to you, Sveta?"

She shouldered up to me, lowered the camera, accessed the situation.

"I don't think they were loading capsules from the hole to the track," she said, in the matter-of-fact manner many Soviets use to communicate serious information.

"Then what?" Fred asked.

"They were dropping them in," she said, peering into the darkness. "Into the hole, not out."

"But…," Fred started.

"Alive?" I asked, but instantly knew she was right. Horrifyingly, terrifyingly right.

"Alive or in hibernation. Maybe their kind hibernates. Maybe it was induced."

She moved even closer, stepped onto a metal bar jutting from the mechanism to get a better look inside the capsule.

"Careful," I warned her.

"All these little cars, these capsules, all winding around, coiling around this arena, ultimately to be thrown one at a time into this abyss."

"Well, that's a fucked-up theory. What are you suggesting? Was it a sport, a game, like car racing? If it was, where did they all gather to watch?" Fred asked.

"Look around, Fred," I said, the partial realization of what this place was sinking in.

"Well, what else would you be doing in a space this big?"

There was a ratcheting *clank!,* and Sveta cried out.

The mechanism creaked to life. Sveta must have pushed the capsule aggressively enough to shift it. It thunked into what must have been its optimal position, waivered upright over the pit. After a brief pause, there was another sound—more felt than heard—and the capsule dropped into the pit, disturbingly slow motion in the moon's low gravity.

I grabbed at Sveta's ankle, afraid she would fall in after it, but she flailed with one hand until she caught the side of the structure, steadied herself.

The camera, though, spun in slow circles, followed the capsule into the pit.

"Yob tvoyu mat!" Sveta called after it, slamming her free hand against the support.

"Come on down, Sveta!" I yelled. "Now."

She saw the next capsule behind her slide into place, ready to be positioned over the pit. With no time to spare, she pushed away, launched herself backwards.

I broke her fall as best I could, and we both tumbled to the ash-grey floor, rolled.

"Spasiba. Again, spasiba," she said, our faceplates pressed together when we came to a halt.

"Seems like you're hellbent on going into that hole with 'em."

Laying atop me, out of breath and pumped full of adrenaline, she burst into laughing.

Later, at the lunar module. Radio silence all the way back.

Even though this module had been made with three crewmen in mind, it was still cramped quarters. The discussion that had incurred between the pit arena and here didn't stop or even slow down.

"…feels like we should go, boss," Fred said. "That's all I'm saying. We haven't heard from Houston in three hours."

"Baikonur, too," Sveta said.

"You think, you really think that capsule falling into the pit did… what? Set a millions-year-old mechanism in motion? For what? To do what?"

"I don't know, but nothing good, I'm sure."

"He might be correct," Sveta said, putting her helmet on the dashboard over the main controls. "Whatever I accidentally did, it set that chain back into motion. Even as we left, I watched it. One capsule after another. Plunk! Down the hole."

I rubbed my eyes with my ungloved hand. The interior of the craft smelled like fireplace ash and spent gunpowder.

"We need to get this all to Mission Control. They've gotta be freaking out over all this dead air. I'll handle that. Fred, take a few moments to rest, then go out and get the second rover ready to go. We'll let the other recharge for a while. Sveta, there's at least one spare camera in stowage. Why don't you unpack it, get it ready?"

Fred and Sveta both began re-suiting.

"I mean, after a rest. No need to rush."

They looked at each other, nodded slightly, resumed suiting up.

"Fine, at least make sure you're both strapped before you head out," I said.

"Strapped" asked Sveta, patting the sides of her suit as if something had come undone.

Fred laughed, patted at his holstered sidearm.

"Ahh," she said, patting her own. "Strapped."

Once they were out of the module, I went about flipping switches and turning dials.

I didn't tell them the com in my suit was directly wired to Mission Control in Houston, so they could get reports on-the-fly, before the official briefings with the Soviets. It, too, hadn't worked since we'd gone inside that cavern.

I was a bit worried that, even after returning to the surface, it still wasn't working.

After listening to static for a few minutes, I threw it over to Vanessa orbiting overhead in the Command Module *Aegis*.

"*Artemis* to *Aegis*, this is Hoagland. Do you copy? Repeat *Aegis* this is *Artemis*. Do you copy?"

"*Aegis* to *Artemis*. Rich, where the hell have you been? You guys have been blank for nearly three hours. Everyone all right?" Her voice sounded tight and concerned.

"We're fine, commander. Just a little…well, overwhelmed, I'd say." I leaned over the console to peer out the windows, like I would have at my own kitchen sink in Houston. Below me, Fred and Svetlana went about their business.

"Umm…are we private?" Ramirez asked.

"Actually, more than you'd think," I said. "But yeah."

"You guys find strange shit down there?"

"You can say that, yes," laughed. "Trying to figure out what it means, what to do. We're gonna regroup here, assess. I'll be in touch soon. By the way, are you having any com problems?"

"Yeah, cut out right after you did. I'm getting huge interference up and down the EM band, just waves of it rolling over everything—radio, ultraviolet, infrared. I've been kind of blind and deaf up here. Can't tell you how relieved I was to hear your voice, Rich. Anyone's voice."

"Copy that. We won't stay silent for that long again. And we'll brief you before we take any action, until we raise Houston. I'm guessing we're going to need our getaway car in position. So be ready."

"Roger that, commander."

"*Aegis* out."

I hung up the receiver.

A wave washed over me, one of terrible isolation. Not just being on the moon, a million miles from home, but also being cut off, unable to run any of this past anyone but Fred and Sveta.

There aren't many places a human can stand in this universe and know that they are truly, uniquely alone.

We were on the only one that mattered at the moment.

III. After Party at Sveta's

Fred came back into the module after about thirty minutes. I helped him off with his helmet and gloves. He seemed brittle, edgy, as if a slight nudge would send him into orbit with Vanessa.

"What's Mission Control have to say about all this?" he asked, putting his helmet in the cubby atop his gloves.

"Yeah, funny thing about that," I said, trying to keep the news easy, almost cheerful, though I felt neither. "Can't reach them. Neither can the *Aegis*."

"You reached Vanessa, though?"

"Yup."

"Instrument failure?" he asked, trying to sidle around me, to get to the access panels for the com cluster.

"No, nothing like that. Vanessa reports a giant electromagnetic wave that's just rolling off the moon," I said.

"From what?"

"We don't know, but she said it started right after she lost com with us, and that was when he went into the cavern entrance."

"The alien mechanism?"

"Yup."

Fred looked to see where Sveta was.

"So, what's going on here, boss? What's the plan?"

"I wish I knew, Fred. That contraption underneath the city might be ancient, but after a million years it snapped back on in a goddamn awful hurry. Whatever it's doing is shrugging off EM waves across the spectrum."

"Soviets?"

Now it was my turn to frown.

"Are you asking me if I think the Soviets have anything to do with either of those things? No, Fred, I don't. I think they're bound to be as flummoxed as we are, though they might not let on. By the way, where's Sveta?"

"I don't know," he said. "She wandered off a couple minutes before I came in. I just figured she was unpacking more stuff."

I looked at him with real anger, and he seemed to wither.

"Get your stuff back on. We're going out to check on her."

Grumbling, he pulled out everything he'd put away, started putting it back on. I did the same, all the while trying to raise Sveta on the channels reserved for the suits.

I wasn't sure if she didn't answer because of the EM interference or because she just didn't want to answer.

I had a pretty clear idea of where she was, though.

"Do we just knock?" Fred asked after we got out of the rover and walked to a *Zvezda* habitat module that was upright. There was a bright light outside the one main hatch and a bank of windows set too high for us to see into.

I knew she was in here. I just didn't know why.

I intended to ask her directly. If she let us in, that is. I waved Fred on, and he pounded on the metal hatch with all the vigor of a pissed-off landlord.

I also went through the suit channels, telling her that we were outside, to let us in.

"Sveta, pozhaluysta," I said. "Pozhaluysta."

There was nothing from within, and I dialed back to the first frequency, prepared to start our pleas over again, when I saw the hatch lock rotate and the door opened.

There was no one to greet as we went into the airlock, closed the door behind us, waited for the antechamber to pressurize.

I saw Fred had his gun unholstered, ready for action.

A brief rush of air as the pressures equalized.

The place was a disaster, a horror movie.

The lights were all on, clinical and too bright, too white. Papers and crates and all sorts of debris littered the place. Wires hung from the ceiling, as did a few important looking conduits.

And the blood.

Dried to splotches and splashes and streamers of rust. On the floor, dried lakes of it, spatters across the walls, the ceiling.

Weirdly enough, though, no bodies.

A table was turned over, and I recognized it from the briefing film as the table the cosmonauts had hefted the alien body onto. The alien body they'd thought was dead but had proved to be quiet lively.

Sveta came around the corner from another chamber, unhelmeted, frowning.

"What the hell is going on, Sveta? You come here without telling any of us, without saying a word? With everything we've got going on? With everything that's already happened, particularly right here?"

I wasn't happy yelling through my helmet at her, but she took what I said in the usual, stereotypical stoic Soviet way. Her face was unmoving. She didn't raise as much as an eyebrow.

"I think, Captain, that we all have our secrets, da? You have that secret frequency to your commanders at Mission Control, and I have a secret frequency myself to the Kremlin. Secrets, secrets, secrets. They will destroy us all, I think."

Fred looked confused. "What's she talking about, Rich?"

"She's right," I sighed. "A discrete line directly to the White House to report on our situation and take direct orders. Didn't know you had one to your handlers, too, Sveta, though I'm not surprised. Mine's not working, is yours?"

She shook her head.

No one said anything, but I could feel the recriminations as loudly as if they were shouted. The most aggrieved was Fred, and as the only other American here with boots on the ground, I could understand.

"Look, okay, we're both reporting offline to our people. Fine. It's what they expect, but we've got to decide on how to proceed now that—"

"Where are the bodies, Sveta?" Fred asked.

There were no body bags. It didn't appear that Sveta came here to look after her fallen comrades.

"I mean, all this blood and mess…" he said.

"They're not here," Sveta said tersely.

"For that matter, where's the body of the alien that caused all this?" I said, gesturing around as if she required visual explanation of what I meant.

"Not here, either."

"Then where?"

"I don't know," she shrugged. "But I have a theory."

I noticed then that she was holding a sheaf of papers, crumpled, bloodstained.

"One of my…the cosmonauts lived long enough to take notes over the course of a few days."

"A few days?" I asked. "I thought this all happened over a few hours

"No days. They needed time to communicate with the alien, learn a few things."

"And?"

"Just a few scribbles really, barely legible. Communication was difficult. I think they got sense of what it was so upset about," she said.

"Being woken up a million years after being put to sleep would be enough for me," Fred said.

"Almost, but more so the creature was upset about being here in this habitat and not in the Arena," she said. "Mostly though about being in the habitat with us…with *humans.*"

That stopped me. Why would it be upset about being with one of us particularly? I mean a million years ago, humans were pretty primitive. We're talking about *homo habilis* and *homo erectus.*

Why would they be concerned about us at all.

Unless…

"What were they doing here on the moon, Sveta? Any indication of that?"

"The creature seemed aghast at our presence, as if it couldn't believe that we'd originated on earth. There was something very peculiar, the cosmonaut noted, about how it refused to believe when they tried to communicate that we were from Earth. As if there was nothing of any value there.

"All that was superseded by the fact that it wanted to get back to the Arena. *Needed* to get back there. You asked, Fred, where the creature went. I believe it went back to the Arena. I think it took my crew with it, dead or alive. I believe that in trying to jump the line and send everyone into that pit, the creature was the one that caused the jam, brought the entire mechanism down."

"But why? What was the point?" I asked.

Sveta thrust out the wad of papers, shook them at me.

"Sergei's last written words were kormit," she said. "To feed."

Fred watched this last back and forth, confusion then horror on his face.

"To feed what? To what?"

"Drevniy," she said. "Ancient One."

"Sacrifices," I said.

Fred appeared aghast. "What?"

"They were sacrificing themselves. Think of pre-Columbian civilizations. The Inca sacrificing children on mountaintops or the ritual sacrifices of the Aztecs," I said.

"But on this scale? There must be hundreds, maybe thousands of these capsules lining the walls of this amphitheater. It appears the entire city was here just to support this."

"Maybe they were," Sveta said. "Maybe this whole system here on the moon was nothing more than a sacrificial city they designed to placate a god-figure. Maybe this was just a satellite of their greater community doing the more important work."

"And where would that be? Venus? Vulcan."

"Earth," I said. "Earth."

Sveta turned to me and smiled. "Von Däniken?"

I nodded, letting the implications of what I'd said, what it meant to believe the thing I'd just said.

Sveta and I looked at each, each unwilling to utter what we were thinking.

"That system in the Arena," I said. "I guess it's not there to just sacrifice the creatures in the capsule, at least not in the way we were thinking."

"Da. They weren't sacrifices. They were *food*. It was feeding them to something down in that pit," Sveta said. "In trying to get back to that, to take its place back in the mechanism, it jammed the system."

"I'm not following all this," Fred said. "A system for what?"

"I don't know, but from the number of capsules in that arena, it was nearly finished with whatever it was doing," I said.

"We started it again," Sveta said, with Soviet finality.

"You two sound like that's a big deal," Fred said, almost pleading. "How is that a problem?"

"Again, I don't know, but they were here for a reason. They were sacrificing themselves—the entire fucking city, from appearances—for a reason. Look around, there are no other alien bodies anywhere we've seen, except in the cavern, in the Arena. There are no apparent signs, no statues or monuments or anything hinting that there was a belief structure associated with all this."

"That a helluva leap there, Rich," Fred said. "A lot of assumptions."

"What else do we have to go on? Hard to see back a million years into an alien mind," I said.

"This entire city, on the dark side of the moon where the crust is thinnest. A cavern that accesses a deep, deep hole. Then this," she said, waving the papers again.

"It all seems very deliberate," I agreed. "They were doing this to feed something.

"Something alive."

"We started it again," Fred said, his tone hinting that he'd finally caught on.

"Its timer is almost done," Sveta said. "Then what?"

"Who wants to make sure we never find out?" I said.

Sveta snapped her helmet on, and we went outside.

The ride back to the arena was silent.

We all hit the ground armed. In a sort of duly agreed upon, silent pact, we'd each loaded with as much firepower as we could carry.

Whatever it took to fuck that mechanism up as much as we could.

Around the arena, the number of capsules circling around on the track was significantly less than when we'd left. Every minute or so, another capsule was loaded, moved over the lip, and dropped into oblivion.

"There aren't a lot of capsules left, so we'd better figure out a way to stop this thing before it runs out," I said.

Sveta was much more direct. She unshouldered an M-16, took aim at the swingarm of the mechanism, let loose a spray of bullets, most of which went harmlessly across the arena. The ones that struck, though, spanged off in a shower of sparks and nothing more.

The arm kept grasping and dropping. The capsules kept moving forward.

"We need to find the controls for this," Fred said. "Shut it off there."

"I don't think there are enough capsules left for the amount of time needed for a search. We need to jam up the mechanism, shut it down like before."

"Right," Sveta said, and she hopped over to the thing, ducked beneath the swinging arm, knelt to examine the track underneath. I came up beside her, to make sure she wasn't either crushed by a capsule or plucked and dropped like one.

There was a cog system inside the track that had a single tooth on it. This tooth grabbed the bottom of the capsule via an indentation on its underside, pulled the entire thing along.

It wasn't very complicated, taking into account the importance these aliens placed on it, but then I suppose it didn't have to be. Why would they think anyone from Earth would be along to disrupt it?

Then it dawned on me. This entire facility, the mechanism? *All for a job that was supposed to be completed a million years ago.*

Sveta found that the length of her M-16 fit perfectly between the tracks, and the carrying handle wedged up into the depression on the capsule.

The track tried to move against the stricture of the rifle but couldn't. The pressure it exerted had to burst somewhere, and it did.

"Sveta, get away from there!"

She fell backward off the track, away from the overstrained system. As she bounced across the landscape, the capsule bucked off the track, more capsules piling up behind it, spilled like beans across the grey dirt.

I moved to help Sveta, heard Fred through my helmet.

"Some of them have broken open," he said. "Oh my god..."

I didn't look up. I was too focused on making sure Sveta was okay, that she hadn't broken her faceplate or punctured her suit.

Gunfire started.

"Get down!" I shouted, which obviously confused her as I was simultaneously trying to pull her up. She opted to disregard the "get down," so we both jumped to our feet, bounced around like circus clowns until we saw what it was Fred was dealing with.

The situation at the track was way more dire. More of a multi-car pileup on I-45, where additional cars kept coming and coming, crashing into each other, flipping over. The only thing missing was sound and explosions.

There, Fred firing his M-16 into the wreckage.

Also, beings crawling from the smashed capsules, standing on wobblily legs, looking from Fred to us, trying to figure out what was going on.

As Sveta pulled our her sidearm and I unshouldered my own rifle, a curious thing happened.

The three or four aliens who stood there in confusion, started running.

But not toward Fred.

Rather, toward the pit.

"Nyet, nyet, nyet!" Sveta shouted, but they couldn't hear her. They ignored us completely, racing across the dusty lunar surface on large, spatulate feet, clad in little but breechclouts, wavy black hair spilling behind them. They took no notice of the lack of air, of the lesser gravity as they ran.

Within seconds, the first of them was at the edge of the pit, then over, seemingly not panicked, not fearful at all as they arced into that nothingness. Each closed their eyes, sailed into that void as if they were made for it.

I thought of those last seven words as Sveta and struggled to get to Fred, to stop him from shooting at them. It wasn't doing any noticeable damage, and the aliens took no notice of it.

However, when we were just a hop or two away, one of the aliens snapped its attention to Fred as it ran by. It didn't lose a step or miss a beat, just grabbed Fred, ran with him several steps before flinging him into the pit, following behind.

"Fred!" I shouted "Fred!"

"Rich," I heard him over the suit com. "Can't see anything, though I know I'm falling. Twisting, spinning. Gonna be hard to maintain…consciousness."

"Fred…I…," I said, coming to the edge of the pit and staring down into all that depthless black. I felt Sveta's gloved hand on my arm, a guarantee in case I tried to follow.

"Don't worry, Captain," he said, static beginning to lick around the edges of his transmission. "Been an honor and all that. Tell my family that I l—"

A *sqwork!*, then nothing.

"Fred!"

No response. I was about to yell again, pointless as it seemed, when there was one more burst of static.

"…lights…moving…"

I stayed there a long time waiting, as more and more aliens sailed into the pit around us, paying us no heed.

Eventually, Sveta's hand pulled me around to face her.

"We still need to stop this if we can!" she said, holding my faceplate in both hands, putting her face right in mine.

I nodded. I didn't know what she meant, didn't know how we were supposed to do that or why on earth it made any difference now. All I was thinking of was standing at a doorstep I was very familiar with, all in my dress blues, a flag and a sealed envelope in one hand. Having to tell Maryanne that Fred didn't come back with me, didn't make if off the moon.

I pushed that to the side. I'd have the entire trip home to think about that, the de-orbit, the splashdown, the debriefing. All the time. Too much time.

I thought, anyway.

There were capsules piling up behind the mechanism, the occasional alien hurtling itself into the pit. I didn't see how many were left to go, but suddenly it seemed not to matter.

Under our feet, the ground began rumbling. Hard to tell from my padded boots, but it seemed to come from deep within the moon.

Whatever the aliens were feeding, it was waking up.

"Sveta, we gotta get out of here," I yelled. "I don't think there's any way to stop it now. Whatever is happening is happening."

She flashed me a look, at first seeming to not agree with my assessment. Then she nodded resolutely.

I shouldered my rifle, hopped for the rover, Sveta following.

We clattered into the rover. I took the driver seat, felt a pang for Fred. But we peeled out, as fast as our electric motor could generate. We made a tight loop, kicking up dust all the way, and shot into the passage leading to the surface.

I toggled the com system for the *Aegis*.

"Hoagland to Ramirez, come in, come in!"

"Aeg...sqwankzzzzz...transmission garzzzssssss. Detecting... massive seismic activity in your area. Better pack..."

"I think she wants us out of here," Sveta said.

"I think *we* want us out of here," I shouted, veering tightly right to start the spiral ascending to the surface. I looked in the rearview mirror, saw nothing following.

Once, twice, the ground humped underneath, like a dog shaking fleas, and the rover's four treads all left the surface at one, send us flying forward.

I fought for control each time we landed. Luckily, the engineers at NASA had built the thing to be nimble. Not that they had any of this in mind.

As we crested the final spiral, I noticed the blue runner lights were now flashing yellow. I didn't know what that color meant to the aliens, but it wasn't the calming blue they had been.

We sailed out from the mouth of the cavern, and now the ground shook constantly. We straightened out onto the main road, the shaking ground levelling the remains of the city. Half-fallen buildings and spans collapsed into dust, rained across the lunar surface. Soon, our entire field of vision was choked with dead, grey fog. The rover's headlights couldn't cut through it, and I had to slow a bit to ensure we stayed on level ground.

We couldn't afford to lose our way now. I just wished we had a sort of remote start for the lander. Even with an emergency lift-off, it'd take ten minutes or to cross check everything and light the engines.

The dust began to clear, but the ground hadn't stopped rumbling.

Up ahead, I saw the Soviet habitat modules rolling across the plain like children's toys. I steered between them, and the LEM appeared. It bounced lightly on its four landing struts, a balloon without enough air to fly.

I slowed the rover to a stop.

"Go!" I yelled to Svetla. "Get inside!"

I stood by the foot of the ladder, helped her up. She cycled the airlock, climbed inside. I followed quick on her heels, feeling the lander jump and shake around us.

She'd taken off her helmet, had begun to start the lift-off sequence. I dumped mine, too, joined her at the console.

"*Aegis* this is *Artemis*. We are go for liftoff, repeat for liftoff."

"Roger that, *Artemis*," Vanessa said. "Meet you up here, and we'll get home. What went on down there?"

"Tell you when we dock. We gotta get out of here now," I said, toggling switches in tandem with Sveta.

"We'll skip the checks and balances here," I said. "No time. Ready to get out of here?"

She nodded, and I toggled the engines. There was a rumbling beneath us, deeper and closer than the moonquakes, then we felt weight again as the rockets kicked in and lifted the top half of the lunar module away.

As we ascended, smoke and raining debris covered the area where the ancient alien city had stood. We could also see boulders falling from cliffs, great cracks appearing in the brittle surface.

"Got out of there just in time," I said.

Sveta gave me a thin Soviet smile, said nothing.

IV. Diapers and Pins

The beginning comes and we aren't any more aware of it than we are of the end.

Something like that.

Anyway, our little lunar module ascended quickly, lighter one astronaut.

Our portholes faced out into space, away from the moon, so we were surprised when Vanessa's voice scratched from the intercom.

"Are you seeing this, Rich? I mean *Artemis*. I bet you can't. Your attitude isn't right. There are cracks appearing on the surface, branching out in all directions from where the alien city was. The entire Aitkin Basis is coming apart. Seismic activity is off the chart."

"*Artemis* to *Aegis*," I said, holding the receiver. "What's Mission Control say about any of this? I haven't been able to reach them since we went into the caverns."

"Radio silence from Mission Control, *Artemis*. I'm just feeding reports as I do. I hope they're still getting telemetry from both crafts, but nothing. No orders or comments. Nothing."

"What are we supposed to—" I said, then something hit the lunar module. It sent our little craft careening, spinning. Sveta and I were thrown against the hull, pinned there by the centrifugal force of the rotation.

"Moon's coming apart!" I heard Vanessa scream. "It's blowing apart."

I was able to fire a couple bursts of the reaction control thrusters, and our spin was slowed, then stabilized. Now the ports faced the moon.

What was left of it.

Its entire surface, the entire structure of the satellite was fractured, broken as thoroughly as the shell of a dropped egg. Massive flumes of it were shooting into space, chunks as big as Everest hurtling off. We'd been hit by one big enough to send us tumbling, though not puncture the hull.

It was apparent we'd be hit by more, by bigger, fully capable of punching a hole right through us.

The moon was exploding, and we were still in orbit.

"Coming to get ya *Artemis*," I heard Vanessa shout. "Hang in there!"

"*Aegis*, stay away, break orbit and head home immediately. That's an order!" I shouted back.

"Bullshit!" Vanessa replied. I looked over to Sveta, and she seemed relieved by that defiance. I know I was.

Out the portal, near the one still mostly intact limb of the moon's horizon, I saw the flash of the *Aegis* in the sun, getting larger. The darkness between us was filled with huge boulders and chunks of the moon whose size defied imagination.

I took the attitude controllers in my hands, but quickly realized that it was an impossible task to try to avoid all the debris. Getting out of the way of one would likely just put us in the way of another. Even if we could, we'd quickly run out of fuel for the reaction control thrusters. They hadn't been designed for this.

The front hull of the *Aegis* grew larger and larger, to get into position to dock. I nudged the ascent module over headfirst, to line up with the nose cone of *Aegis*.

You could hear the rocks and dust peppering our hull, but there was nothing we could do. I made myself not scan our immediate surroundings for any large stuff that might hit us. Instead, I laser-focused on the job at hand, just as I'd been trained. I heard Vanessa counting down the approach distance, kept a hand on the controllers to compensate from impacts big and small.

There was a larger bump, momentarily terrifying, then Vanessa announced we had a secure dock. Sveta wasted no time in grabbing her helmet, floating up to the hatch that led to the small crawlway over to the *Aegis*.

So close to home. I heard the hiss of the seal as the hatch was opened.

"Come on," Vanessa yelled, this time plainly heard and not over the com. "Haul ass!"

Sveta gave me a look back, then smiled.

The Soviet smiled back at me.

She disappeared into the *Aegis*. I like to imagine her climbing into her couch, plugging into the *Aegis'* oxygen, its systems. Confident of a return trip to Earth that might be difficult, but a return nonetheless.

As I grabbed my helmet, prepared to launch myself into the crawlway, something struck us. *Hard.*

The impact sent us spinning again. I looked to the hatch and saw black, spinning space, stars, rocks.

Whatever it was had disconnected the *Artemis* from the *Aegis*. I needed to get back to the controls to stabilize my ship, assess what had happened.

That hatch needed closing first, as it was doing nothing but venting atmosphere.

I got it shut, locked it tight, tried Vanessa on the com.

Nothing.

I pulled myself down, grabbed the controllers, eventually stabilized the *Artemis* again.

There was no *Aegis*, not even any wreckage. What mountain-sized chunk of the moon hit it had completely obliterated it.

I was alone.

I tried for several minutes to get Mission Control over the line, but nothing. As I looked back out the porthole to the moon, I began to realize that down there, they had their own concerns that dwarfed the safety of four astronauts, now down to one.

At least a third of the moon was gone at this point, and much of that debris was headed straight for Earth. What was there for me to do but sit and watch it all happen? I had mental images of those mountain chunks slamming into the atmosphere, edges glowing red, piece of it slagging behind, sheering off.

The horrific explosion it would set off when it hit the surface. Or the ocean.

Explosions.

I had the best seat in the house to watch the destruction of my home world. Soon to be the only seat.

When I'd settled in, let the knowledge of what was going to happen wash over me, seep in, it got worse.

So much worse.

From the left port, I could just make out the disintegrating moon, pieces of it ejected into the void. I saw the dust swirl, saw the tongues of lightning or whatever EM force leap through the dust field.

Something else curled from out of the hollow of the remaining moon.

Hundreds, thousands of cilia swayed out, difficult to tell from this distance how thick they were or how long. Just that they weren't grey like the rest of the debris, but green and distinctly organic.

Alive. Sentient. They reached out, grasped fragments, considered them, played with them, then let them go, reached farther.

As I watched, wide-eyed and unbelieving, it shouldered itself out from the broken shell, massive and dark green, covered in hot, laval eyes that were as big as houses back on Earth, neighborhoods. They swirled independently, watching the careening trajectories of its former egg, the collisions, the hot sparks of power and flashes of sunlight.

Tentatively, with the trepidation of a newborn, it moved away, still nearly as big as the moon. A huge, bulbous body bristling with eyeballs and cilia, palping away at its new world, trying to make sense of it just as I was.

Its head, if it could be called that, ended in a beak enshrouded by cilia, pushing debris into its mouth.

It cried, cried out as any newborn might for comfort.

I turned to the right port, saw the illuminated face of Earth shine in the darkness of it all, pieces of this creature's former home falling across that face, leaving burning weals in their track.

I've got about ten percent of my oxygen left. I should be able to see my end just because of that, even though I'm the only one left. Might buy me a couple of hours more, though.

I looked out onto a fractured night, the space between filled with dust and rocks and ice, strange, flickering fires and bolts of violet lightning leaping between them.

There's that shriek again. I can feel it ripple through the metal skin of the craft, vibrating on the cabin air.

Doesn't matter how utterly alien it is, I had a kid of my own.

I know a cry of hunger when I hear one.

THE END

AFTERWORD

I am not a Lovecraft scholar, let's be clear about that straightaway, if you held that view of me.

Far from it. I'm not a scholar of anyone's writing. I am not even, strictly speaking, a huge fan of old Howard Phillips. I have enjoyed *some* of his work, to be sure. "The Colour from Out of Space" or *The Shadow Over Innsmouth*. I liked *At the Mountains of Madness*, though I think Poe did it better in *The Narrative of Arthur Gordon Pym of Nantucket*.

Gasp. The horror community clutches its pearls and takes to its fainting couch.

Let's set aside any discussion of Lovecraft as a person, shall we? I didn't know him, no one I know knew him. However, his writing—not just fiction but personal letters and essays—make it clear that he was, as is so clinically put these days, *difficult*. He was difficult beyond any discussion of his legacy, but in day-to-day dealings with those in his life. In his attitudes about things, people, culture.

Was he an influential writer? Absolutely. He created the bones of a great mythos that even today resonates through three genres—science fiction, fantasy, and horror. His influence is keenly felt in horror particularly, with what is called *cosmic horror*. That he continues to hold sway, some hundred years from his birth, says something…right?

But is he a good or even great writer?

I will go on a ledge here and say, in my opinion, meh. His stuff seems, again to me, to be stulted and stiff, dry as a bleached bone and minus any sort of spirit or levity. Perhaps a sign of the times he wrote in. Perhaps a sign of the rigid New England life he grew up in. Poe, on one hand, seems mad at times, with a kind of lunatic's energy and a droll, macabre sense of humor. Lovecraft, on the other, seems like a pompous, lecturing university don, secure in his knowledge of the story and caring hardly at all if you, the reader, do.

Today, Lovecraft is spoken of with the same veneration horror writers reserve for other, greater horror authors—Poe, of course, but Matheson, Bloch, Bradbury, Barker, King, Rice, Straub. I don't consider myself a member of this current Church of Horror. Like I said, I enjoy some of his stuff, but I believe the greater part of Lovecraft's current fame is due more to writers who followed him and expanded his mythos—August Derleth chief amongst them.

Many horror writers wouldn't agree with my assessment, though. In fact, some get quite hot when they believe proper respect isn't given to old H.P. Oh well, I was an English major and I really, really didn't care for Hemingway, either. You can imagine the reaction of my college professors, akin to a divinity student asking "Just who is this Jesus guy, anyway?"

Still, Lovecraft has a pull, doesn't he? The world he dabbles in is dark and wet, squamous as it were. If you're into man being insignificant, Lovecraft is the author for you. His is a universe littered with dead and dying gods and their many acolytes, both human and not quite.

Now, I've been writing horror for thirty years or so, reading it since I could read. Nursed on Poe and Lovecraft, King and Straub and Rice and Barker. You can bet that I've expressed my opinion about Lovecraft for almost as long. Sometimes it gets a quiet nod, sometimes there is agreement and discussion. Often, though, my low opinion is taken in and rejected.

"Taff's a nice guy, for sure, but his opinion on Lovecraft is just *wrong*."

I have to say, these days, anyway, I find myself agreeing with you.

Huh?

Despite my strenuous objections, I find that my work steers more and more into the cosmic horror area. Not necessarily Lovecraft but *Lovecraftian*. In stories such as "The Melting Point of Meat" and "Shug," I explore themes that are very much similar to those explored by Lovecraft—isolation, insignificance, a mechanical universe filled with little meaning.

To the point where we find ourselves here, at the end of a novella collection of my Lovecraftian horror stories.

Oh well.

Times change. Authors do, too.

I'm not quite prepared to say Lovecraft is equal to Poe. I don't know I will ever be able to say that. But I can say I look on old Howard Phillips with a new sense of acceptance. If not for who he was as a person, then for who he was as a writer and the legacy he helped set into motion.

You can't have the influence that he's had over three huge literary genres if there's really nothing there in the writing. Personally, I don't think I would be coming back again and again to the themes he addressed if something wasn't there.

It's with this humble acceptance of his influence I offer you these six stories. I hope you enjoyed them.

If you didn't, well, I can understand that, too.

John F.D. Taff
Southern Illinois
January 2023

NOTES

Some people like what authors have to say about the writing of their stories. Some people don't care at all. So, here are notes for those who care. Those who don't? Skip 'em.

"After the Cut, the Blood"

I have professed my liking for the band Guster before. Love them, seen them live several times. I often get inspired by music—the actual tune or lyrics or even a song title. I paraphrased this title from a Guster song, "That's No Way to Get to Heaven," from the band's album *Easy Wonderful*, which is both a) easy and b) wonderful. It seemed to fit. When I got the idea to do *All the Stars Die*, this is the story that came through the strongest. Again, for a very musical reason.

My wife Deb and I had been watching the Ken Burns documentary *Country Music*, and though I'd never been a particular fan of the genre (detecting a theme in this book yet?), the documentary *really* resonated with me. I found myself getting into the music and what it said and what it did for the country at that time. Up until around the 1970s…then it lost me.

Still all that old-time country stuff sparked the idea for this. The power and the pain of music. Plus having a calling but not having the talent for it, being isolated. What you give up in your life to be an artist. All that is in there, I suppose. Plus, a longing to make things right.

"Fin de Siècle"

This one is the close of a cycle of stories that began back with the anthology I did with four fantastic writers—Joe Schwartz, Erik T. Johnson, J. Daniel Stone, and Josh Malerman. It was from Grey Matter Press, and it was called *I Can Taste the Blood*, a phrase I saw scrawled—I kid you not—on a bathroom stall. My story appeared as "Vision V," but was originally titled "Toothsome." I did a follow up to that story in Doug Murano and D. Alexander Ward's *Shadows Over Main Street 2*. It was titled "Shug." "Shug" is really the middle story between the other two, forming the connective tissue, as it were. Though "Fin de Siècle" was the story that came to me first, it was actually the third story I wrote for this collection. I was able to layer in my love for astronomy and telescopes, which is always a cool thing.

"Her Mouth Was Filled with Secret Soup"

This title was one of those AI experiments I read about where a computer program was tasked with watching years of commercials for the Olive Garden chain of restaurants. Torturing AI is a thing, evidently. Sounds about the best use for it. Anyway, afterward the AI was instructed to write one of its own. This was one of the lines of script it wrote, and I ran with it. Seemed whacky enough to be fertile ground, and this is what grew.

I was still digesting the aforementioned *Country Music* documentary, and the traditional traveling medicine show motif. But it was what this show in this story was doing that proved the ultimate pull. This story and "After the Cut, The Blood" are two of a kind, each dealing with a similar historical period in America, each with its roots deeply in that era's music, each cosmically disturbing in its own way.

"In the Dim Meadows, Desolate"

This one is a reprint, having been brought to market originally a few years back by the late Patrick Beltran's Cutting Block Books. Patrick was a great guy and a great editor. I worked with him on a few projects, *Horror Library V, The Seven Deadliest* and this. The novella's title was changed to "The Desolate Orchard," which I saw the practicality of yet never really liked. Here it is with its original title. I really enjoyed writing this, and was dissapointed the piece never really reached a large audience. It touches on similar cosmic themes, just a little differently than the others. And of course, the time period is spot on. So, here it is…again.

"Tell Me What It Means to Me"

I added this story at the last minute because…well it seems to organically fit. It was originally written for something else that ended up falling apart. But it always seemed, to me at least, to be one of the weightier things I've written. So, it needed a home, and it clicked with this project. The tale is of an uglier time in America, and how bad things happened to good people. But it's really about shame and grief and all of those emotions that are carried in the wake of horrible events. Where do they go?

Midnight Land, of course.

"All the Stars Die One by One"

The last story and the eponymous one to boot. I felt like a cosmic horror collection needed to be sent off in a cosmic way, so we have this story. I grew up with a huge love of NASA and what America was doing in space. I wrote constantly to NASA and its many facilities, to the point where I was granted a GSA account to access other materials from other government agencies.

At the age of ten or so. And I got to the point with my pestering—asking for materials and pictures on just about every NASA mission ever, from Apollo to Voyager—that I was routinely asked to *stop* writing. Politely. Firmly. Which, of course, I did, but only many years later. I figured, after thirty years of writing fiction, it was probably time to put all that knowledge to good use. When I crammed it into some conspiracy theories of a post-Apollo 17 mission, it generated its own story.

ACKNOWLEDGMENTS

This one took a while to come together. But it wouldn't have happened without a lot of help. To that end, let me first thank my wife, Deborah, who is behind everything I do. I couldn't do this without her. Second, I want to thank the person I'm proud to have as both a friend and a publisher, Doug Murano. He's revitalized my career not only by the publication of this book, but also by re-publishing my earlier collection *The End in All Beginnings* and, next year, *The Fearing*. He's a great guy, a great editor, and he's got his fingers on the pulse of horror.

I'd also like to thank some of my colleagues—first and foremost among them the inestimable John Langan, for his wonderful introduction. Then, to Alma Katsu, Josh Malerman, and Brian Evenson for their kind words about this book. Also I'd like to thank my sounding boards—Joe Schwartz, Brian Kirk, John Foster, and Mark Matthews. Wonderful authors all.

Finally, let me thank Sam Araya, the fantastic artist who created the cover art, and Todd Keisling, for his work on the interior design. Both of which helped to make this book what it is.

And finally, thank you for allowing me to do this, more or less successfully for 30 years!

John F.D. Taff is a Bram Stoker Award® and World Fantasy Award short-listed horror and dark fiction author with more than 35 years experience, and more than 125 short stories and seven novels in print. He has appeared in *Cemetery Dance, Eldritch Tales, Unnerving, Deathrealm, Big Pulp* and *One Buck Horror*. Recent anthology contributions include *Human Monsters, Long Division,* and *The Hideous Book of Hidden Horrors.* Taff's novella collection, *The End in All Beginnings*, was called one of the best novella collections by Jack Ketchum and was a Stoker Award® Finalist.